F
DAI   Dailey, Janet

          Calder storm

LP F DAI
Calder storm /

Dailey, Janet.
39088001813617   BKS

9780006745103

CALDER STORM

JANET DAILEY

LARGE PRINT PRESS
An imprint of Thomson Gale, a part of The Thomson Corporation

THOMSON
GALE

Detroit • New York • San Francisco • New Haven, Conn. • Waterville, Maine • London

LIBRARY OF CONGRESS CATALOGING-IN-PUBLICATION DATA

Dailey, Janet.
    Calder storm / by Janet Dailey.
        p. cm.
    ISBN 0-7862-8703-9 (lg. print : hc : alk. paper)
    1. Calder family (Fictitious characters) — Fiction. 2. Ranch life — Fiction.
3. Montana — Fiction. 4. Large type books. I. Title. II. Series: Thorndike
Press large print core series.
PS3554.A29C35 2006
813'.54—dc22   2006011435

ISBN 13: 978-1-59413-224-7 (lg. print : sc : alk. paper)
ISBN 10: 1-59413-224-0 (lg. print : sc : alk. paper)
Published in 2007 by arrangement with Kensington Books,
an imprint of Kensington Publishing Corp.

Printed in the United States on permanent paper.
10 9 8 7 6 5 4 3 2 1

Calder Storm

Prologue

The headquarters for the Fort Worth–based conglomerate known as Maresco, sleekly modern in its glass and granite architecture, stood a modest four stories tall. But, as owner and chairman Max Rutledge, was fond of saying, Dallas could have the soaring skyscrapers; Fort Worth had the money. And the digits of his total net worth numbered in the billions.

On the building's top floor, his suite of executive offices occupied one entire side of the structure. Few pieces of furniture could be found in his personal office. The minimalist approach was in keeping with the suite's contemporary decor, but its purpose was to limit the number of obstacles that the wheelchair-bound occupant had to face.

Power, wealth, prestige — Rutledge had it all.

No one was more aware of that than his valet and personal nurse, Harold Bennett, as he entered his employer's office without being summoned. He paused just inside the door, waiting to be noticed. But Rutledge had his back to the door, his wheelchair facing the glass-walled exterior, as he sat hunched forward in it.

Bennett cleared his throat rather loudly. When that failed to draw a response, he spoke. "Excuse me, sir."

A faint whirr came from the motorized chair as it pivoted to face him. "What is it?" Rutledge glowered at him.

"You didn't respond when your secretary buzzed you on the intercom. Your ten-thirty appointment is waiting."

"Reschedule it. I'm busy."

Without a word, Bennett crossed to the desk and relayed the instruction, then paused to cast a worried glance at his employer. More silver grizzled the old man's hair and the gauntness in that age-lined face had become more pronounced these last few months. But it was these dark and brooding moods that troubled Bennett the most.

Briefly he wondered what had triggered the black mood this time. Then he noticed the newspaper lying open on the desk. Near the bottom of the right-hand page was a short article. Bennett read the first few lines of it.

The findings of an inquest into the stabbing death of Boone Rutledge, son of prominent Texan Max Rutledge, were released today. It was ruled to be a case of self-defense on the part of Quint Echohawk, grandson of Chase Calder, owner of the famed Triple C Ranch in Montana . . .

There was more, but Bennett had seen enough. He glanced at the page number. "They buried it on page seven," he murmured with some surprise.

"And it cost me a helluva lot to get that done," Rutledge snapped, then gestured to the newspaper. "Throw it away. Then track Donovan down and get me a number where I can reach him."

"Donovan." Bennett knew what that meant. "You're going after the Calders. Why?" he blurted without thinking. "You saw what the inquest ruled. Boone was the one who went after Echohawk with the knife. The Calders aren't responsible for his death."

"Not responsible!" Rutledge boomed in outrage. "My son is dead! He was a fool and a hothead, but he was my son! And, by God, they're going to pay for it!"

PART ONE

*It hit like a bolt
from out of the blue.
It was the hottest storm
this Calder ever knew.*

Chapter One

The afternoon sun was on its downward drift toward the western horizon, throwing its bright light across a vast Montana sky ribboned with wispy mare's-tail clouds. Springtime cloaked the wide plains with its fresh green hues and scented the air with the raw vigor of new life, all sharp and clean.

Jessy Calder breathed in its wild fragrance as she stepped out of the pickup's passenger side. Emblazoned on the truck's door panel was an enlarged version of the Triple C brand. Below it, block letters spelled out the name *Calder Cattle Company.*

There was little about Jessy Calder that would suggest to an outsider that she was the current head of a ranch that numbered over a million acres within its boundary fences. As usual, the widow of Chase Calder's only son was dressed in cowboy boots, blue jeans, and a brown Stetson hat. A smoothly tailored white blouse was the only exception to typical working attire.

A feathering of lines around her eyes and mouth revealed that she had passed the fifty mark a few years ago, but she had yet to lose her lean, boyish figure. And the silvering of gray in her hair had only the effect of lightening its once dark-honey color.

Without a doubt, Jessy Calder was a handsome woman, indelibly stamped with an aura of calm competence. Much more subtle was the air of authority that emanated from her as well.

Turning, Jessy reached into the truck's cab and collected the western-cut suede jacket lying on the front seat, then closed the passenger door. The freewheeling whine of a semi on the interstate drew her eye to the divided highway. Almost automatically her glance leaped beyond it to the sweep of far-reaching plains that stretched north.

It was a big land, spreading beneath an even bigger sky. Strangers saw monotony in its seeming flatness without discerning its rippling muscles. But Jessy had been born and raised on these lonely, rugged plains. She knew the riches they possessed, and she also knew how harsh and unforgiving they could be.

This was a land that bent to no man's will for long. But for those who chose to live with it, there was a bounty to be had. The continued existence of the Triple C Ranch was proof of that.

Almost with regret, she pulled her gaze away from the wide land and scanned the collection of vehicles parked in the motel's paved lot. The absence of a particular one cut a puzzled crease in her forehead as she joined the tall, lanky cowboy waiting for her at the curb.

He went by the name of Laredo Smith, although Jessy had long known that wasn't his real name, just as she knew he was a man with a past that wouldn't bear scrutiny. Yet she had never attempted to learn his true identity. On the Triple C, people still lived by the codes of the Old West. Foremost among them was the unwritten rule that a man was judged by what he did, not what he had done. And Laredo Smith had proved his loyalty and worth years ago. More than that, she loved the man, something that still slightly amazed her, especially when she recalled how certain she had been that her late husband was the only man she would ever love.

"I don't see Trey's pickup," she said to Laredo, referring to her twenty-four-year-old son and the Triple C heir. "He left the ranch before we did. I thought for sure he'd be here by now."

A smile lit Laredo's blue eyes, the twinkle in them softly chiding. "Tank Willis and Johnny Taylor rode with him. Judging from the tent and sleeping bags I saw piled in the back of Trey's truck, I'm guessing they plan on setting up camp at the fairgrounds. I don't imagine either Johnny or Tank favor the idea of wasting money on a place to sleep when they don't plan on doing much of that this weekend."

"That doesn't exactly surprise me," Jessy said with a wry smile.

"I didn't think it would," Laredo replied easily. "After all, can you think of a better time or place for a bunch of young studs to roar and paw the ground than at the famous Cowboy's Mardi Gras?" Tucking a hand under her arm, he leaned close and whispered near her ear, "Maybe an old stud, too."

Jessy laughed as she was meant to do, but not without a little curl of anticipation at the veiled suggestion in his voice.

A Cowboy's Mardi Gras was the nickname the locals had attached to the annual Miles City Bucking Horse Sale, traditionally held on the third weekend in May. The three-day event was part auction and part rodeo. Owners from across the country brought their rough stock, both broncs and bulls, to Miles City; riders, many of them area cowboys, bucked them out of the chute. Afterward, the animal was auctioned off; those that were rank — cowboy vernacular for bucking hard — were usually sold to rodeo stock contractors for high dollar. The rest went for a considerably cheaper price.

The chance for local cowboys to win prize money in the rodeo arena was a definite draw, and the other festivities held in conjunction with the sale, a parade and street dances among them, doubled its allure. With spring in the air and a long, cold winter behind them, people came from far and wide to cut loose and party, swelling the population of Miles City to twice its size or more.

A couple in their mid-fifties was at the registration desk when Jessy and Laredo entered the hotel lobby. With a trace of impatience the man demanded, "Can't you at least check with some of the other motels and find out if they have a room available?"

"Don't need to," the clerk replied. "There isn't a single room to be had in

Miles City. In fact, you'll probably have to go a good ways down the road before you'll find a vacancy." The telephone rang, harshly punctuating his statement. The clerk reached for it, dismissing the pair with a rueful but definite, "Sorry." His glance skipped past them to Jessy. "Be right with you, Ms. Calder."

When the frustrated and travel-weary couple moved away from the counter, Jessy took their place while Laredo shifted to one side, propping an elbow on the counter and half-turning to keep an eye on the lobby entrance. With the phone call handled, the clerk laid a registration form and pen in front of Jessy.

"By any chance has my son checked in yet?" she asked.

"Not yet."

"I'll register for him, then." Jessy proceeded to fill out the form, pausing only to nod in Laredo's direction. "Laredo will be sharing the room with him, so he'll need a key," she said, then reminded the clerk, "Our reservations called for adjoining rooms."

"That's what you've got," he assured her after checking the computer, then busying himself with programming the electronic key cards. "Did you hear that the weather forecast calls for clear skies all weekend? Those old-timers who claim it always rains on the Bucking Horse Sale are going to be wrong this year."

A crooked smile lifted one corner of Jessy's wide lips. "You're talking to a rancher. As dry as it's been this spring, I wish it was pouring buckets."

"Next year it probably will be." The man shrugged with a touch of resignation.

By the time the check-in process was complete, the lobby was aswirl with new arrivals waiting to register and clutches of guests waiting to be joined by a missing member of their party prior to leaving the hotel. A dark-eyed blonde with mascara-thickened lashes separated herself from one of the latter groups and sailed across the lobby to intercept Jessy and Laredo. Jessy recognized the eighteen-year-old girl instantly as Kelly Ramsey, the daughter of a veteran Triple C ranch hand and a direct descendent of one of the original cowboys to work for the brand.

"Hi, Jessy. Hi, Laredo." Her greeting was breezy and familiar. "No rain. Can you believe it? Although heaven knows we need some," she added hurriedly, as if belatedly remembering whom she was addressing.

"That's true," Jessy murmured, casting a

glance over the girl's attire. A short tank top bared her middle, and a pair of low-riding jeans with frayed hems hugged her hips and thighs like a drumskin. And the faded jeans jacket she wore did a poor job of providing any show of modesty. But Jessy withheld any comment on Kelly's attire, remembering too well the many arguments over clothes she'd had with her daughter, Laura, Trey's twin sister, during her teen years.

Laredo showed no such restraint, grinning his admonishment. "You're liable to catch cold in that getup tonight."

Kelly laughed, unconcerned. "That's what Daddy said." Her glance quickly darted around and behind them in a searching manner. "Isn't Trey with you?"

"No. He left the ranch before we did," Jessy replied.

"Oh." Disappointment gave the curve of her mouth a downward turn, but only momentarily. Forcing a brightness into her expression, she said, "I'm sure I'll see him at the fairgrounds. We're headed that way now. Catch you later."

She flashed them a parting wave and scooted back to her family. Jessy raised an acknowledging hand to the Ramseys, a gesture they returned before moving en masse toward the door. But Jessy's attention remained on Kelly.

"She has her sights set on Trey, doesn't she," she murmured to Laredo.

"Are you just discovering that?" His smile was rich with amusement.

"You aren't surprised at all." She shook her head in mild dismay at this realization. "Sometimes I think you know more about what's happening on the Triple C than I do."

"That's because you're too busy running it to listen to all the gossip that comes through the range telegraph. Besides, there isn't a single woman in five hundred miles who wouldn't like to throw her loop around your son."

"I just hope he makes the right choice when the time comes." And she hoped it wouldn't be soon. But Jessy knew those decisions weren't hers to make.

"You aren't worried that he'll get fooled into marrying some gold-digger, are you?" Laredo chided. "Don't forget, Trey learned all about feminine wiles from his sister. At one time or another he saw Laura use every trick in her arsenal on some poor, unsuspecting male. When it comes to women, that boy is much wiser than his years."

"True," Jessy agreed. "Did I tell you Laura called last night?"

"No. But you better tell me about it outside," Laredo suggested as more people entered the hotel, familiar faces among them. "This place is getting busier than a bar on Saturday night. We'd better get our bags out of the pickup and up to our rooms before we get trapped in the lobby."

"It isn't that bad." But Jessy didn't object when he steered her through the stream and out the door, giving her only enough time to exchange nods and brief hellos with those she knew.

Moving to her right shoulder, Laredo asked, "So how's the new bride doing?"

"Laura's doing well, and still sounding very much like a bride. Nearly every other sentence started with 'Sebastian said' or 'Sebastian suggested.' "

"I think it's called love," he teased as they crossed to the ranch pickup.

Jessy ignored the playful gibe. "I'm just glad she's happy. I only wish that she lived closer. England is half a continent and an ocean away."

"You and Cat both are dealing with an empty nest, aren't you?" Laredo remarked astutely. Cat was Jessy's sister-in-law, Catherine Calder Echohawk. Widowed almost a year ago, Cat had moved back to the Triple C to look after her aging father, Chase Calder. "First your Laura gets married in November. Then her Quint ties the knot in April. Now you're wondering if Trey will be next." As he reached into the truck bed for his duffel bag, he looked up and paused, sliding a dry glance at Jessy. "Speak of the devil."

With a nod of his head, Laredo directed her attention to the pickup just pulling into the motel lot. Three cowboys sat shoulder to shoulder in the cab, their faces shadowed by the hats they wore and the dim interior. But Jessy easily picked out her son from the others even before they piled out of the pickup after it pulled up at the motel entrance.

Standing six feet, three inches, he was easily taller than the average man, wide in the shoulders and chest, yet youthfully lean and supple, with a rider's looseness about him. One look at his deep-set eyes and rawboned face and there was no doubt he was a Calder. That hard vitality was like a tribal stamp.

At his birth, Jessy had proudly named him Chase Benteen Calder after his grandfather and the family patriarch. His great-great-grandfather had carried the same name, the Calder who had formed the Triple C Ranch more than a century and a quarter ago. Within weeks of his namesake's birth, the baby was dubbed "Trey Spot," which was soon shortened. He'd been called Trey ever since.

As Trey swung his long frame toward Jessy, he was hailed by Kelly Ramsey. "Mind if I ride with you to the fairgrounds, Trey?"

Laredo was quick to detect the wary tensing of Trey's body, but the smile was easy, without the coolness of rejection. "Sorry. There's no room. I've got Tank and Johnny with me."

His response was clearly not the one she wanted to hear. She wavered for an instant, as if assessing the odds of changing his mind, then showed some wisdom and accepted his answer with good grace.

"No problem," she said, already taking the first retreating steps back to the Ramseys' double-cab pickup. "I'll see you later."

Trey was quick to turn away and shoot a glance at Laredo. It was one of those man-to-man looks that conveyed his utter lack of interest in the girl and his relief at avoiding her company. Laredo dipped his head down, hiding a smile, as Trey loped over to them.

"Did you two just drive in?" he asked when he joined them.

"We've been here long enough to check in." Jessy eyed her tall, strapping son with a mixture of affection and quiet pride.

"I guess that means all I have to do is pick up a key." His grin had a reckless and carefree quality to it that spoke of his youth.

When Trey reached over and took the suitcase from Jessy, she surrendered it without objection — this from a woman who staunchly believed everyone should pull his or her own weight, making no exceptions for either status or sex. But here was a son helping his mother, not an ordinary ranch hand carrying his boss's luggage.

Trey made a quick visual check of the truck bed, verifying that there were no more bags to be retrieved. "Gramps decided to stay home, did he?"

"Like he said," Laredo answered, "someone needed to stay behind and keep an eye on things at the ranch." He made no mention of the comment Chase Calder had added, saying matter-of-factly, "There's not much point in me going, anyway. All my contemporaries are either in rest homes or the cemetery."

"As crowded and noisy as it's likely to be, I couldn't imagine Gramps coming, but I don't put anything past him." Mixed in with the easy affection in Trey's voice was a deep note of respect for his grandfather.

It was hardly surprising. Following his father's death when, Trey was barely more than a toddler, Chase had stepped in to fill the role. At an early age, Trey had learned from his grandfather that as a Calder, he would be held to a higher standard. Like it or not, he would be expected to work longer, be smarter, and fight rougher than anyone else. No favor would be shown to him, no concessions made, and no special privileges granted because he was the son and heir. On the contrary, the reverse would be true. During his growing-up years, Trey was often assigned the dirtiest and hardest jobs, the rankest horses in the string, and the longest hours. Any problems he encountered along the way were his to solve. If he found himself in trouble, he was expected to fight his way out of it with his fists or his wits.

Trey had never really known the fine line his mother and grandfather had walked to push him as hard as they dared without pushing too far and breaking his spirit. It was all preparation for the day when he would take control of the Triple C.

It had been no easy job to carve out a ranch the size of some eastern states back in the days of the Old West, and in these modern times, it would be no easy job to keep it. Some in Trey's place might have shrunk from the pressure of that job, but he had always viewed it as a challenge he was eager to tackle. Maybe that was due to the way Chase had put it to him, or the belief he sensed that his mother and grandfather had in him that he could do it.

At the age of twenty-four, Trey shouldered responsibility with the ease of one accustomed to its weight. It hadn't dulled the gleam in his dark eyes, the gleam that said there still lived in him the boy he had once been, reckless and a little wild. For the most part, Trey kept that side of himself reined in, but it was still there.

"You should have heard Gramps carrying on last night, reminiscing about some of the crazy shenanigans that went on during past bucking-horse sales." That gleam in Trey's dark eyes now became an impish twinkle as he addressed his mother. "He even told me about the time you took Uncle Mike's place in the chutes and rode the bronc he'd drawn. Gramps said the gasp that came from the crowd nearly sucked up all the arena dust when your hat flew off and all that blond hair tumbled loose."

Laredo turned a laughing look at her, both amused and curious. "Is that true?"

"I did it on a dare," Jessy admitted with neither regret nor pride, regarding it as simply a foolish escapade of youth. "My brothers goaded me into it."

"According to Gramps, you stayed on for the full eight seconds and probably would have scored the highest ride of the day if the judges hadn't disqualified you."

"That was a long time ago," Jessy said, dismissing the incident. To ensure that it stayed that way, she asked, "What took you so long getting to the hotel?"

"Johnny and Tank wanted to scope out where they're pitching their tents," Trey said, then explained with a grin, "You know Johnny — he isn't about to spend a dime for something if he can figure out a way to get it for nothing." A pair of short, sharp honks of the pickup's horn drew Trey's glance to his compatriots parked a few spaces away. "Do you get the feeling they want me to hurry up?" Despite the careless toss of the question, he obligingly swung toward the motel entrance, striking out with long strides to take the lead while adding over his shoulder, "They're anxious to get out to the fairgrounds and find out what their draw is for tonight."

"Tank doesn't usually ride the bulls," Jessy said with some surprise.

Trey stopped to explain. "Johnny talked him into it. The riders get paid a few bucks just for climbing on board, and Johnny convinced Tank he had a fifty-fifty chance of drawing a bull that couldn't buck worth a damn. 'Course, ever since Tank found out that a contractor is unloading his rodeo stock at this year's sale, including two bulls selected for the National Rodeo Finals a couple years ago, he's been sweating his draw."

"With cause, I'd say," Laredo remarked dryly.

"Damn right." Trey flashed the older man a look of grinning agreement as he reached for the door and gave it an outward pull. He came to a dead stop one second before he walked into a brunette on her way out. Having shifted to one side to allow Jessy to precede him, Laredo had a clear view of the near collision. He saw the startled looks that were exchanged, one male and one female, and sensed a primitive current of something more that shimmered between them like a living thing.

Recovering, the brunette murmured a faintly apologetic, "Excuse me," and Trey pivoted out of her path. His gaze tracked her as she slipped past him and headed for the parking lot. The dazed and rather avid look in his eyes was that of a man whose hunger was fully aroused.

"You look like you were just struck by a thunderbolt," Laredo observed after the girl had disappeared among the parked vehicles.

"Something like that," Trey murmured in admission, then turned back to them. "Who is she? Do you know?" He looked straight at Jessy.

"No one I've ever seen before," she replied without hesitation.

"Me either." Trey tossed a last thoughtful glance toward the parking lot, then flashed Laredo and Jessy a grin. "She was sweet, though."

In the process Trey almost convinced himself he had identified the force of the attraction that had struck him so hard. Yet it didn't explain the sudden surge of restlessness that flowed through him, leaving him with a vague feeling of discontent and unsatisfied needs, a sense of something missing. All of which he had experienced before, but this time the feelings seemed a lot stronger.

Like always, Trey used physical action to sweep the uncomfortable thoughts away, his quick, long strides carrying him into the relative dimness of the motel lobby after he told Jessy, "I'll bring your suitcase as soon as I get my key." He slowed only long enough to allow his vision to adjust from the sun's bright glare to the interior's fluorescent glow.

The owners of a neighboring ranch were just collecting their keys when Trey arrived. That old edgy impatience surfaced again, even though his wait for the clerk's attention was a short one.

"Trey Calder," he said to the clerk after a brief nod of greeting to his ranch neighbors. "My mother already signed in for me."

"Sure thing, Trey. I've got your key right here." The man pushed it across the counter to him.

Trey laid a hand on it, then paused, something prompting him to ask, "That brunette who just left when I came in, can you tell me who she is?"

The clerk shook his head. "Sorry, I must have been busy. I don't remember seeing her."

"Blue eyes, five-seven or thereabouts." Trey struggled to call up more specific details, only to realize that he had focused only on the deep blue of her eyes and the ripeness of her parted lips. "Her hair was long, I think," he added, recalling the vague impression of its darkness framing her face.

"Good-looking, was she?" The clerk smiled in understanding.

Irritation rippled, but Trey wasn't sure whether it was directed at himself or the clerk. Again he deliberately made light of his interest in the brunette. "You know she was."

He scooped up the key card and moved away from the desk toward the hall, again seeking to push the encounter from his mind.

Chapter Two

The rodeo grounds were a hive of activity. Few seats in the open-air grandstand were vacant, and unseated spectators — garbed in the almost-requisite boots, blue jeans, and cowboy hats — milled about the grandstand's front apron, either doing a bit of socializing or standing in line at the concession stands. For the time being the bulk of their attention wasn't focused on the arena. The collective sound of their voices created a steady thrum of background noise.

Over the loudspeakers the auctioneer maintained his steady singsong chant while a big gray bull trotted loose in the arena, having dispatched the rider from its back. The bull's breeding was mostly Brahman, as evidenced by its size, the distinctive hump on its back, and the pendulous dewlap that hung from its neck. After half-heartedly hooking a horn at a rodeo clown safely ensconced in his barrel, the bull trotted for the open gates and the holding pens beyond. As if on cue, the auctioneer brought his gavel down.

"Sold!" The emphatic announcement swept through the crowd. Once again eyes swung toward the arena with the expectation for action even as the announcer declared, "You've bought yourself a good one, Fred."

A fresh flurry of movement broke out around the chutes, most of it centering on the number two chute, its side rails clotted with cowboys. Teamwork was required to get the rigging looped under an animal, and a number of fellow riders were always on hand, ready to lend a hand with the task. There were the usual snortings and clash and clatter of hoof and horn slamming against the chute as the bull protested both the cowboys' efforts and the tight quarters that trapped him.

In the crowded alleyway behind the chutes Trey listened to the commotion from chute two with only half an ear. The air had an electric feel to it. The familiar smells of dust and animal excrement were in his nostrils.

There was also the faint scent of fear, most of it coming from the fresh-faced cowboy standing before him, double-checking the fit of the padded flak jacket he wore.

"I kinda wish I had one of those helmets some of the pro riders are wearing," Tank Willis murmured on a wistful note. Although given the name Marvin at birth, his penchant as a boy for swimming in stock tanks had long ago saddled him with the nickname of Tank.

"You don't need it," Johnny Taylor scoffed, a wad of chewing tobacco tucked inside his left cheek.

"Oh no? Well, get a load of the horns on that bull," Tank countered with heat.

Unconcerned, Johnny responded with a mild shake of his head. "The weight of the helmet can throw you off if you're not used to it. 'Sides, that bull shakes out to be an easy ride. He'll take a couple hops out of the chute and start spinnin' to the left. All you gotta do is stay on your hand and don't slip into the well."

"I don't know why I let you talk me into this," Tank grumbled, not for the first time. "I should'a stuck with the broncs."

"In that case," Trey said with a grin, "all you have to do is tell yourself that you're straddling a bronc with horns."

Tank found nothing remotely humorous in Trey's remark.

The gate was opened on chute two, releasing the bull and rider it contained.

With Tank due to ride next, the time for further advice — well-meaning or otherwise — was over. Spurs jangling, he climbed onto the chute rail.

"You can do it, Tank." Trey gave him an encouraging slap on the back.

Out of the corner of his mouth, Tank muttered to Johnny, "You're buying the beer tonight, by God."

Trey found a vacant perch along the arena-side rail next to the chute and hauled himself onto it. He had a glimpse of the rider from chute two getting flung to the dirt.

A scattering of applause from the crowd accompanied the announcer's call of "No time."

Meanwhile Tank had lowered himself into the chute within inches of the white-faced bull's back. Its horn spread was nearly as wide as the chute. As the auctioneer broke into his rhythmic call for bids, Tank took up some of the slack in the buck strap. The bull snorted and swung its big head, cracking a horn against a side rail.

"Easy. Easy," Tank murmured uselessly and waited a beat for the animal to settle down before inching the strap tighter.

The bull lunged upward, front hooves

reaching for the top of the chute. A half dozen hands, Johnny's among them, hauled Tank out of harm's way while a skinny photographer in a billed cap and multi-pocketed vest snapped a couple of quick shots of the action before abandoning his perch at the head of the chute.

Once all four feet were back on the ground, Tank again inched his way closer to the bull's back, his features set in a look of grim determination. By the time the auctioneer finished the bidding on the previous bull, Tank was pounding his leather-gloved fingers over the rope to ensure a tight grip. The bull shifted, muscles bunching when it felt the rider's weight settle on its back.

With his free hand in the air, Tank didn't give the bull a chance to throw another fit in the chute. He gave the gateman a short, sharp nod, and the gate was thrown open.

The big Brahman cross exploded out of the chute. "Stay with him, Tank!" Trey shouted as Johnny climbed onto the rail beside him.

His gaze fastened on the bull and rider, Johnny said, "Do you reckon I should've told him that bull can be hell for a cowboy on foot?"

"He's going to find that out himself right

about . . . now," Trey said, grinning.

After two hard-jarring jumps out of the chute, the bull made a snaking twist to the left in midair that whipped Tank to the right. The successive clicks of a camera registering the action came from somewhere behind Trey's left shoulder as Tank was slung sideways through the air.

When the white-faced bull swung back to look for him, a rodeo clown quickly put himself between the bull and the downed rider. Momentarily distracted from its original target, the bull gave chase while a second clown pulled Tank to his feet and gave him a directional push toward the fence without letting his attention stray from the bull.

Tank tossed a glance in the animal's direction to verify its lack of interest in him before he limped toward the fence. His slower pace was a contrast to the darting swiftness of the clowns, and one that the bull was quick to spot.

"Look out, Tank!" Johnny shouted the warning at almost the same instant that Tank heard the approaching pounding of hooves.

The limp forgotten, Tank scrambled to reach the fence with the bull hot on his heels. Certain that his buddy wouldn't be able to scale it in time on his own, Trey leaned down, grabbed Tank by the back of his belt, and hauled him across the toprail, dislodging the photographer who had occupied the spot. The fence shook when the bull sideswiped it before swinging back to the arena.

Immediately Tank started swearing a blue streak, proof in itself that he was no worse for the ride. In the edges of his vision, Trey registered the image of the photographer lying flat on the ground, the camera protectively raised. Something wasn't the same, though, and it drew the fullness of his glance.

The billed cap had fallen off, exposing a tumble of sun-streaked brown hair. The skinny photographer was a female. Trey swung off the fence and moved to her side as she sat up, a sleek curtain of hair falling forward to conceal her face from him.

He caught hold of her arm, helping her roll to her feet. Not until she was fully upright did she allow the strap around her neck to take the full weight of the camera. Immediately she started brushing the dust from the back of her pants.

"Are you all right, ma'am?" The question was prompted by an inexplicable need to see her face.

With a screening lift of her hand, she flipped her long hair aside and glanced up. Crazily, Trey wasn't at all surprised to find himself face to face with the girl from the motel. The sight of those blue eyes looking back at him was like a clean wind sweeping through him, all heady and fine.

"I'm okay," she said. Then recognition set in, and her lips curved slightly at the corners. "We meet again."

"That's my good luck." And Trey knew he had never uttered a truer statement as he drank in the details that had escaped his notice before, like the thickly stroked arch of dark eyebrows, the soft jut of cheekbone, and the cleanly angled line of jaw. But he kept coming back to the frank boldness of her returning gaze. "I didn't catch your name the first time."

"I don't recall throwing it at you." Her laughing smile took any sting from her mocking rejoinder. "But it happens to be Sloan."

"Just Sloan?" he questioned.

Her blue glance made a rapid and assessing sweep of his face, a note of caution surfacing in her eyes. "I think that's enough," she said and quickly began scanning the ground around her feet.

"Mine's Trey," he volunteered, then

reached down and scooped up her ball cap. "Looking for this?"

"Thanks." She took it from him, dusted it off against her leg, then slipped the bill between her teeth, and set about winding her hair atop her head to once more confine its length under the cap.

Although he'd been raised not to trespass on another man's territory, it was her hesitancy to share more information about herself that prompted Trey to ask, "Do you belong to someone?"

"Yes," she said, even though her fingers were bare of any rings. As she slipped the cap over the knot of hair, she slanted him a curious look. "Aren't you going to ask who that might be?"

"Whatever you'd say, I wouldn't like the answer." His reply was a little curt — a reaction to the sudden twisting in his gut at the news she already had a man in her life.

"I never said it was a man," she chided dryly.

A puzzled frown cut a thin crease in his forehead. "Then who?"

There was more than a little pride in the sudden lift of her chin. "I belong to myself."

All the knots suddenly smoothed, and Trey was quick to take advantage of the green light she had just given him. "Are you going to the street dance when you leave here tonight?"

"Is that an invitation?" She tipped her head to one side, all the while making another careful study of him in an attempt to determine the degree of danger he might be to a woman alone.

"It is," Trey confirmed.

After a slight pause, she made her decision about him. "Where should I meet you?"

"How about by the stage where the band will be playing?" he suggested.

"That's fine with me." She lifted her camera, tipping the lens up and blowing softly to remove any dust particles on it, then flicked him a quick glance. "I need to get back to work. I'll see you there, Trey."

"I'll be waiting," he replied, as she crossed to the arena fence and began scanning the action inside. Softly, for his hearing alone, Trey murmured the name she'd given him. "Sloan."

It was an unusual name. But nothing about her seemed ordinary to him, certainly not his own hungry reaction to her. This time Trey made a point of noticing the black turtleneck she wore beneath the bulky vest, the slim khaki slacks, and the thick-soled hiking boots on her feet.

Someone jostled his shoulder. All the noise and activity that had receded into the background now asserted itself. Belatedly Trey looked around for Johnny and Tank. He spotted them on the opposite side of the open alleyway and waited for a gap in the intermittent flow of cowboys moving behind the chutes, then crossed the space to join them.

When he noticed Tank hunched over, rubbing his right kneecap, Trey recalled the way he'd limped in the arena. "How's your knee?"

"Aw, he just twisted it a little." Johnny dismissed the injury.

"How would you know?" Tank threw him a challenging glare. "It ain't your damned knee." He shot a look at Trey. "That's the last damned bull I'll ever throw my leg over. Whatever you do, don't ever believe anything Johnny tells you."

"Come on," Johnny protested. "It was just the luck of the draw."

The phrase reminded Trey of his own luck in running into that blue-eyed brunette again. Sloan. The mere thought of her name brought a quicksilver rush of feeling. He looked over his shoulder, his glance running arrow-straight to her. Head bent, she was busy switching a new roll of film for an exposed one, accomplishing it with practiced ease. Anticipation flowed through him, keen and sweet, for the evening to come.

Johnny said something to him, dragging Trey's attention away from Sloan. The next time he looked, she was gone from the spot. A few minutes later, he caught a glimpse of her farther down the line.

Johnny was among the last group of bull riders. To Tank's never-ending delight, he was thrown a quarter of a second short of making the eight-second buzzer. Tank was happier yet when the bull stepped on Johnny. Thanks to the padded jacket, his friend escaped with only a bruised rib.

Tank needled him as they made their way to the pickup parked in the infield. "Hurt to breathe, does it, John-boy?" he observed on a note of feigned sympathy. "Not to worry. It's nothin' but a little bruise."

"Shut up, Tank." Johnny pushed the words through gritted teeth.

"Best thing is to keep movin'. That way the stiffness won't set in," Tank declared, echoing the advice Johnny had spouted to him.

Most times Trey would have joined in,

offering some good-natured ribbing of his own, but his thoughts were all for the blue-eyed girl called Sloan. The smooth lilt of her voice played in his mind, unique, to him, in its absence of any discernible western accent. The image of the way she'd looked at him was there, too, the gleam in her eyes that had been so bright and alive to him, yet wisely just a little guarded. He recalled as well the silky appearance of her hair that seemed to invite his fingers to run through it.

As the trio continued its drift toward the collection of vehicles and stock trailers parked in the infield, night's shadows deepened and lengthened. Trey cast a look back at the lighted arena and grandstand area and scanned the mix of spectators, contestants, and workers exiting the grounds, hoping for another glimpse of Sloan. The vast majority sported cowboy hats; the rest were bare-headed; and he saw no one in a billed cap.

As near as he could recall, he hadn't seen her after the top riders started their competition for the night's prize. It could be she hadn't stayed around to watch it.

"You looking for somebody, Trey?" Johnny asked, all curious.

"Not really." The question served to bring his attention to the front.

"He was probably checking to see if Kelly was on his back trail," Tank suggested slyly.

Johnny was quick to voice his opinion. "I told you that you should have turned her down when she asked you to that school dance this spring. Now she's got her loop set for you."

That was a road Trey didn't want to go down, not after all the ribbing he'd already taken about it. Trey had long ago learned the best way to deflect was to attack. And he did.

"You know why she's doing it, don't you?" he said in light challenge, spotting the pickup and angling toward it.

" 'Cause she's got her sights set on being the next Mrs. Calder, that's why," Tank declared.

"You're wrong," Trey replied calmly, a touch of devilry shining in his own eyes. "She's just using me to make Johnny jealous."

"Me?" Johnny looked at him in pure shock.

"It's one of the oldest strategies in a woman's bag of tricks," Trey told him. "I saw my sister use it plenty of times."

"Kelly isn't interested in me." But there was a faint note of uncertainty in his voice.

Trey hid a smile. "Don't kid yourself. She's got her eye on you. Why don't you ask her out and see what happens?"

"Johnny ask a girl out? That'll be the day," Tank declared. "You know he's too cheap to do that. Right, John-boy?"

"Shut up, Tank," Johnny muttered as he climbed into the cab.

Trey slid behind the wheel and inserted the key in the ignition. "By the way," he said after Tank had crawled into the cab next to Johnny and closed the door, "you two might have to find your own way back tonight."

"How come?" Johnny frowned.

"Because I'm going to be tied up." Headlights on, Trey swung the steering wheel and took aim at the infield gate.

"Since when?" Tank added with surprise. "You never said anything about having a hot date earlier."

"That's because I didn't."

"Who's the girl?" Tank asked, his curiosity doubling.

"It isn't Kelly, is it?" Johnny eyed him with suspicion, the faintest hint of possessiveness in his voice.

"No, it isn't Kelly," Trey said, smiling in reassurance.

"Then who — ?" Tank began, then

snapped his fingers. "That female photographer you were talking to — it's her, isn't it?"

"Yup."

Tank chortled softly. "You sure didn't let any grass grow under your feet."

"Who is she, anyway?" Johnny wondered. "Has she got a name?"

"Sloan." Trey pulled onto the main road, joining the line of vehicles heading into town.

"Is that her front name or back name?" Johnny said with a frown.

"Don't know yet, but I plan on finding out." The anticipation of seeing Sloan again was back, all heady and strong.

The traffic and congestion in the downtown area were thick, complicated by the three-block-long section of Main Street that had been cordoned off, forming a people corral of sorts. Luckily, Trey found a place to park a few blocks away.

The dancing, drinking, and carousing were in full swing when the trio arrived on the scene. After the quiet of the side streets, the collective hammer of voices, rollicking laughter, and amplified music all blended together to form a wall of noise.

Intent on slaking their suddenly dry throats, Tank and Johnny split off to get a beer, leaving Trey to make his own way to the makeshift stage, where a local country band performed. Couples swarmed the dance area in front of it, creating a veritable sea of hats and twirling partners. Onlookers stood around the edges, two and three deep.

Trey shouldered his way to the inner circle near the stage and scanned the faces close by with a rising eagerness. But Sloan wasn't among them.

He waited and watched. One song gave way to another, then another, with still no sign of Sloan. Restlessness pushed him to widen his scope of vision. He drifted around the stage and skirted the dance area, his gaze constantly moving, checking, looking for any new arrival. He saw a dozen people he knew and exchanged brief greetings with a few of them, but none held his attention.

A hand clamped itself on his shoulder with manly familiarity. He turned to find Johnny and Tank, each with a cup of beer in his hand.

"Still waiting for her to show, are you?" Tank surmised.

"She'll be here," he insisted, although privately he had started wondering.

" 'Course she will," Johnny agreed. "No

female in her right mind would stand up a Calder."

Ordinarily Trey would have agreed with him; however, in this case, Sloan didn't know he was a Calder unless someone else had told her. He certainly hadn't volunteered that piece of information.

"Tell you what," Tank began, and paused to take a quick gulp of beer, "we're gonna head down the way. If we happen to see her, we'll drive her in your direction."

"Do you know what she looks like?" Johnny stared at Tank in surprise.

" 'Course I do. Come on." He took Johnny by the arm and turned him around, cursing roundly when some of the beer sloshed out of his cup.

Trey hesitated, then headed in the opposite direction. Away from the dance area people tended to gather in clusters or travel in twos and threes, making it easy for him to spot a solitary figure. There were a few of those, but all male.

Then he spotted her coming his way, the neon light of a bar sign flashing over the sheen of her hair, and everything lifted inside him, his blood coursing hot and fast through his veins. His long, striding walk lengthened even more, carrying him to her.

A smile broke across her lips. "You

forgot to say which stage. There happens to be three of them."

The glistening curve of her lips and the sparkle of pleasure in her eyes acted like the pull of a magnet. When mixed with the pressures of waiting, wondering, and wanting, the combination pushed Trey into action.

His hands caught her by the waist and drew her to him even as he bent his head and covered her lips in a long, hard kiss, staking his claim to her. There was an instant of startled surprise that held her stiff and unresponsive, but it didn't last. It was the taste of her giving warmth that lingered when Trey lifted his head.

Through eyes half-lidded to conceal the blatant desire he felt, he studied her upturned face and the heightened interest in her returning gaze. He allowed a wedge of space between them but didn't let go of her waist, his thumb registering the rapid beat of the pulse in her stomach. Its swiftness signaled that she had been equally stirred by the kiss.

"I was just about convinced that I'd have to turn the town upside down to find you," he told her in a voice that had gone husky.

"It wouldn't have been a difficult task," Sloan murmured. "After all, you know where I'm staying."

"I forgot," Trey admitted with a crooked smile. "Which shows how thoroughly you've gotten to me."

She laughed softly, paused, then reached up, fingertips lightly brushing along a corner of his mouth. "You're all smeared with gloss."

He pressed his lips together and felt the slick coating, but it had no taste to it. "You use the unflavored kind, too." He wiped it off on the back of his hand. "My sister claims that a man should taste her and not some fruit."

"You have a sister," Sloan said, absorbing this personal bit of information about him. "Younger or older?"

"Younger." By less than two minutes, but Trey didn't bother to divulge that and have the conversation diverted into a discussion of the twin thing. Instead he took note of the change in her attire — the bulky, multi-pocketed vest and tan pants replaced by a femininely cut tweed jacket and navy slacks. "You ditched the camera and changed clothes."

"The others were a bit grimy from all the arena dust." Her matter-of-fact answer made Trey wish that he had taken the extra time to swing by the motel, shower, and change his own clothes, but he'd been too anxious to get here. A quick smile curved her lips, rife with self-mockery. "This is my first street dance," she said. "So I had to ask the desk clerk what to wear. He assured me it would be very casual."

"Your first street dance, is it? In that case it's time I showed you what it's all about." Grinning, Trey shifted to the side and hooked an arm behind her waist, drawing her with him as he set out for the dance area.

"I should warn you," she said, with a sideways glance, "I'm not much of a dancer."

His gaze regarded her in frank appraisal. "I'm surprised. You have the grace of one." He guided her through a gap in the row of onlookers, then turned her into his arms, easily catching her off hand. The band was playing a slow song, which suited Trey just fine. "Don't worry about the steps," he told her with a lazy smile. "Dancing was invented solely to provide a man with a good excuse to hold a woman in his arms."

A laugh came from low in her throat, soft and rich with amusement. "Something tells me it was a woman who came up with the original idea. How else would she ever coax a man onto the dance floor?" she teased.

"And something tells me you're probably right." Despite the lightness of his talk, the subject was of no interest to him, not with her nearness stimulating all his senses.

There was an awareness of how naturally she fitted herself to his length. Even the light weight of her hand on his shoulder felt right, as if it had always belonged there. The idea wasn't something Trey questioned — he simply enjoyed it.

Every step, every rocking sway brought them into closer alignment, an unconscious seeking and adjusting to the contours of the other. Trey found it impossible to ignore the round shape of her breasts pressed against him or the evocative stir of her breath along his cheek and neck. Giving in to the building ache in his loins, he released his grip on her fingers and splayed both hands over the hollow of her back. With a slight turn of his head, he explored the silken texture of the sun-streaked strands along her right temple. Some subtle fragrance wafted up, embedding itself in his mind.

All too soon the song ended, and Trey was obliged to loosen his hold, allowing space to come between them.

"Didn't I tell you dancing was easy?" he murmured.

There was a knowing gleam in her eyes when she met his gaze. "I'm not exactly sure that was dancing."

"Is that an objection?" An eyebrow arched in question even as he matched the teasing banter in her voice, yet her answer mattered to him — and not in the way it usually did when he was making a move on a girl. This time, Trey realized, he was much more serious than he had ever been before.

"Not really." And the wide smile Sloan gave him was completely without reservation.

"Good," he said as the band struck up another tune, much quicker in tempo. "We're moving on to the advanced version. Are you game to whirl around the floor?"

"Why not," she agreed with a careless shrug.

He caught her up and twirled her into the mix of dancing couples, each pair choosing its own combination of steps to match the music. As Sloan had warned him, she was far from adept, but neither cared as they spun and laughed and spun some more, endlessly jostled and bumped by others.

When the cymbal clashed on the final note, Sloan collapsed against him with a breathless laugh. "That was too advanced for me."

Trey grinned at her. "You sure showed plenty of try."

"That's rodeo talk for a rider making an all-out effort. I heard it used at the arena and asked." Sloan studied him with a curious and considering look. "I never asked how you fared with your bull tonight."

"I didn't ride." His arm loosely circled her shoulders, keeping her close to his side.

"Really?" Her eyes widened in surprise.

"I'm too tall to be competitive on the rough stock," Trey explained.

"Why? What has that got to do with it?"

"It gives me a high center of gravity, and that means it's a lot harder to keep your seat on an animal that's determined to buck you off." His mouth crooked in an amused but confident smile. "Now when it comes to the roping events, I can hold my own with the next cowboy."

"Now that I think about it, nearly every rider I've seen has been under six feet. I guess when I saw you behind the chutes I just assumed you were competing."

"A couple of my friends were."

"And you were lending moral support," Sloan guessed.

"Something like that." Fiddle music filled the air, its notes slow and plaintively sweet. "Sounds like that song is about your speed. Shall we?"

Smiling her answer, she turned into his arms. This time she lifted both hands around his neck, linking her fingers behind it. His own hands settled on the rise of her hipbones as they shifted in place to the dreamy rhythm, bodies brushing with an ease that already felt familiar.

A hand tapped his shoulder. Half irritated by the interruption, Trey threw an impatient glance to his left as Tank waltzed into view with a town girl in his arms.

"I see you found her," Tank said, tipping his head in Sloan's direction.

Trey responded with a curt nod and a tight smile.

As usual, Tank wasn't the least bit put off by his obvious reticence. An impish glee entered his expression. "Get a load of who Johnny's squiring around the floor." A jerk of the thumb directed Trey's attention to the couple ahead of them along the outer circle.

Lifting his glance, Trey was quick to spot Johnny, rocking from side to side like a metronome gone awry. And the blonde bobbing with him was none other than Kelly Ramsey.

"Kinda looks like you started something." Tank exchanged an amused look with Trey before he swung his partner away.

"Those are your friends, aren't they," Sloan guessed.

"They are," he confirmed, regarding the pair as hardly a subject worth discussing, especially not with Sloan.

But she clearly didn't share his opinion. "Sounds like you've been doing a little matchmaking."

"Believe me, it was just a joke that took an unexpected turn."

To Trey's regret, Sloan continued to watch the other couple. "I'm surprised she isn't seasick," she murmured on a note of utter marvel. Trey threw his head back and laughed. "Well, it's true," Sloan said in defense of her comment, then laughed along with him, a little self-consciously at first, then with open mirth.

It became a private joke between them the rest of the evening whether circling the dance floor or strolling on the crowded street to check the other action. A dozen times or more Trey was hailed by someone he knew. Most times he got by with an answering wave; with others he was obliged to exchange a few words before moving on.

By midnight the crowd had been thinned of its families with adolescents, leaving the hard-core revelers behind to party away the balance of the night. Rather than abating, the noise had lifted to a more raucous level.

Trey steered Sloan clear of a couple of cowboys who already showed signs of having a few too many beers. The altered course carried them onto the sidewalk as a group of Triple C riders, some with their wives or girlfriends in tow, approached. He was instantly recognized.

"Hey, Trey," one of them yelled. "We're all goin' in and grab a beer. Come on and join us."

Before Trey had a chance to decline, Sloan spoke up, "Not me. I'll pass, thanks."

"Later," Trey called and waved the group on their way, then redirected his attention to Sloan. "The invitation didn't appeal to me, either."

"It wasn't that so much," she said. "It's just that if I want to be bright-eyed for tomorrow, it's time I called it a night."

The instant the words came out of her mouth, Trey knew there was nothing he wanted more than to go somewhere quiet, away from the blaring music, the laughter and loudness of half-drunk voices, with no one else around but the two of them.

"I'd better walk you to your car — just to play it safe," he told her.

Offering no objection, she gestured in a southerly direction. "My car's parked that way."

Chapter Three

Someone called to Trey as they approached the corner of a barricaded side street. He acknowledged the greeting with a lift of his head and continued.

"A lot of people here know you," Sloan observed, studying him with a sidelong glance.

"Most of them are friends or neighbors," Trey replied in easy dismissal, then explained. "My family owns a ranch north of here."

"For some reason I keep forgetting that you're not a stranger to the area like me," she admitted with a touch of chagrin.

The subject was dropped as they came under the scrutiny of two uniformed officers checking to make sure they weren't leaving the cordoned area with any open containers. The delay was a brief one.

Passing the barricades, they entered the side street, the bright lights and noise fading behind them. But the privacy that Trey had hoped to find wasn't there, as he spotted the shadowy figures of a half dozen others, traveling singly or in pairs along the street in search of their vehicles.

His eyes took in the clean lines of Sloan's profile and the faint impression of a smile that edged her mouth. "So what did you think of your first street dance?" he asked idly.

Her smile widened into a definite curve. "It was a little crazy and a lot loud. Quite honestly, I've never seen so many people intent on having fun and not caring one bit how ridiculous they looked to others in the process." After a slight pause, she added, "I am a little disappointed that I didn't see any fights. According to the desk clerk, brawls aren't uncommon."

"They used to be," Trey agreed, recalling a few of the ones his sister had caused in her teen years, not to mention the black eyes and split lips he'd suffered coming to her rescue. "But there are a lot more cops on duty now. As soon as they see a quarrel start, they step in and break it up before it can escalate into a fight."

Just ahead a couple stood next to a pickup parked at the curb, arguing over who would drive it. The woman insisted her companion was too drunk to be at the wheel, and the man naturally took exception to that. The issue wasn't revolved by the time Trey and Sloan passed them.

"If I was a betting man, I'd put my money on the woman," Trey remarked in a low voice as they crossed an intersection.

"She sounded determined, didn't she?" Sloan agreed.

"That's one way of putting it."

"My car's parked over there." She pointed across the street to a compact sedan sandwiched between two pickups.

With no traffic moving in either direction, Trey guided her across the street, cutting an angle to her car. Keys jangled from the ring Sloan pulled out of her jacket pocket. A jaw muscle tightened in irritation when Trey noticed two cowboys strolling none too steadily toward them.

Sloan unlocked the driver's door and turned to face him, but Trey never gave her a chance to utter any parting words. Instead he spoke first.

"My truck's parked around the corner. Give me a minute to walk to it, and I'll follow you to the motel." He reached around her and opened the car door, then advised, "Be sure you lock it after you get in."

"I always do." The easy assurance in her voice let him know that she was accustomed to taking such precautions, suggesting it was far from the first time she had traveled alone.

After she was settled behind the wheel, Trey pushed the door shut and waited those few extra seconds to hear the click of the door lock. He saw the look of amusement she gave him over the fact that he had lingered. At the same time, he realized how thoroughly she had aroused all of his protective instincts.

Trey had time to think about a lot of things during the drive to the motel. And every one of them revolved around Sloan. There was an awareness of the scant amount of personal information they had exchanged, most strikingly their last names.

For Trey, there had been a natural reluctance to bring up the Calder name and encounter that sudden avid gleam that inevitably followed. As for Sloan, he could only suppose the reason was the hesitance of a woman alone to share too many personal details with a man who was virtually a stranger.

He had an intense desire to know every single thing about her. No detail seemed too trivial. Yet, at the same time, he had a feeling that the minute she turned those dark blue eyes on him, he wouldn't care about any of them. That knowledge rattled him a little — that, and the realization that no other woman he'd met had ever affected him this way.

When they arrived at the motel, Trey wasted no time moving to her side. He caught a glimpse of the sharp-eyed night clerk taking note of their passage as they crossed the lobby. The minute they turned into the softly lit corridor, a hot tension gripped him, knotting everything inside him.

"Have you made any plans for tomorrow?" He heard the ring of demand in his voice and shot a quick look at Sloan, but she didn't appear to have noticed.

"Me and my camera will be checking out the parade," she answered lightly, then eyed him curiously. "Will you be riding in it?"

"No." His answer was more abrupt than he meant it to be, but it didn't seem to be something he could control and still keep a tight rein on all the lusting needs ripping through him.

"This is it." She angled toward a door, then faced him with a natural grace, idly letting a shoulder rest against the frame. "I guess I'll see you tomorrow at the arena."

Her casual tone was almost indifferent. It acted like a verbal stiff-arm to keep him at a distance. Trey halted, muscles tensing in resistance, knowing that he felt anything but indifference toward her. And he had no intention of hiding his feelings on that score.

"Tomorrow can't come soon enough as far as I'm concerned," he stated. "And that isn't a line. It's the truth."

"Thanks." She smiled, a deep pleasure lighting her eyes. Then it faded to something wistful and tinged with regret. "I'm looking forward to it, too."

But the response seemed to be the polite kind dictated by good manners — and that was far from satisfactory to Trey.

"I hope you mean that, because I'd like to end this evening the same way we started it." His gaze never left her face, alert for those subtle signals from a woman that every man recognized.

Instead of averting her eyes or lowering her chin, both indications of a reluctance to repeat the earlier kiss, her glance slid to his mouth, then flashed to his eyes, her head tilting fractionally in an age-old invitation.

Trey didn't wait for the words. Bracing one hand against the wall near her head, he cupped the other to the side of her neck, tipping her head the rest of the way while he brought his mouth down to the soft line of her lips. He tasted their yielding warmth, but it was the responding pressure of them, seeking and exploring in return, that inflamed him.

Still, he made no move to gather her into his arms, pride insisting that any further contact would be instigated by Sloan. With senses honed razor-fine, he felt that first small sway of her body toward him. Her hands glided onto his rib cage as if to steady her balance.

Their touch broke through the restraint Trey had placed on himself, and he gathered her in, fitting her round shape to his hard contours. He fed on her lips, eating them with a hunger that forced them apart. Inside was her tongue, waiting to eagerly mate with his.

Heat swirled and needs rose. His hands moved over her, alternately caressing and molding her more firmly to him in a vain attempt to absorb her into him. Frustration only increased the demand.

Her hands flattened themselves against his chest in mute resistance. Their pressure had no more than registered when she twisted her head away to break off the kiss.

The glance she lifted to his face was sharp with challenge. "It's late." It was no innocent phrase, but a demand to be released, couched to appeal to his nobler side.

At the moment, Trey wasn't sure he had one. Part of him knew he could change her mind. Yet instinct warned him against pushing Sloan into a decision she wasn't ready to make.

Stone-hard with need, he had to force his arms to his side. "See you tomorrow."

"Tomorrow," she echoed quickly and turned to slide the key card in its slot.

Not trusting himself, Trey walked away before he gave in to the urge to push his way through the door after her. Behind him, he heard the soft snick of the door unlatching and blindly lengthened his stride.

Heavy drapes blocked any outside light from invading the motel room, creating an unnatural darkness. Yet Laredo awakened a split second before light spilled into the room from the corridor. A light sleeper from long habit, he had detected the faint scrape made by the releasing door latch.

A quick glance identified the tall, wide-shouldered and narrow-hipped figure as

Trey. Never one to pretend to be asleep when he wasn't, Laredo said, "Better flip on the light. It's black as pitch in here."

Trey's only response was the snap of a light switch. A lamp came on, illuminating a table in the room's far corner. Without a word, Trey closed the door and turned the dead bolt. Laredo rolled away from the lamplight and slid an idle glance at the digital clock radio on the bedstand. Surprise had him taking a second look at the green glowing numbers.

"It isn't even one o'clock yet." There was nothing sleepy about the assessing look Laredo swept over Trey. "You usually don't stagger in until around three. What's going on?"

"Just made an early night of it." Trey swept off his hat and tossed it onto the long, low chest that faced the pair of double beds. Immediately he swung away. "I think I'll take a shower before I turn in."

It wasn't so much his words as the flattened pitch of his voice and the closed-up look to his expression that made Laredo suspect Trey had something heavy on his mind. The younger man disappeared into the bathroom and closed the door behind him. Within seconds Laredo heard the gush of the shower spray turned on full force.

As the minutes stretched and the water continued to flow, Laredo smiled to himself, certain that there was a woman behind whatever was ailing Trey. A shower was often the only remedy for that kind of trouble.

The water was still running when Laredo finally dozed off.

Laredo woke to the same sound, but with a difference. This time the volume was lower, suggesting it came from the sink faucets, and the bed next to his was a tangle of blanket and sheets, indicating it had been restlessly slept in. Again Laredo glanced at the bedside clock and saw that it was a few minutes before six in the morning.

Tossing aside the covers, he swung his legs out of bed. In the bathroom, a faucet squeaked under the turn of a hand, shutting off the water flow. The door opened, and Trey stepped out, his hands busy fastening the buttons on his white shirt.

"You're up and about with the sun this morning," Laredo observed, catching the sharp tang of the aftershave Trey had used.

"Thought I'd catch an early breakfast." Trey tucked his shirttails inside his jeans as he walked over to retrieve his hat.

There was a degree of haste in Trey's movements. Coupled with the memory of the previous night's extra-long shower, this observation made Laredo suspect Trey had awakened with a hunger of another kind.

"Is she anyone I know?" he asked. "Like maybe that brunette you nearly ran over when we arrived yesterday?"

Trey flashed him a quick grin. "Maybe."

"Maybe, hell," Laredo scoffed at the evasion.

Trey pushed the hat onto his head and started for the door. "See you later."

Laredo called after him, "Don't forget. That meeting with the investigators is set for eleven-thirty. Jessy wants you there for it."

Pausing halfway out the door, Trey turned back, frowning. "That's today?"

"Eleven-thirty."

"Right." He gave the door a tap and stepped into the hall, pulling it shut behind him.

There was a determined glint in his eyes and a lift to his stride when Trey retraced last night's route to the room Sloan occupied. He rapped sharply on the door, waited, and knocked again.

Finally a muffled and sleepy voice called out, "Who's there?"

"It's Trey," he replied in a clear, strong voice.

There was a delay, accompanied by a few odd thuds. Then the door swung open about a foot, and Sloan showed herself while still absently tugging at a thin cotton robe she had pulled on over a sleeper tee. Her dark hair was all mussed and tousled, and she gazed at him with a kind of sleepy-eyed confusion.

"What are you doing here?" she asked with a slight frown.

Leaning a hand against the doorjamb, Trey smiled. "I wondered what you'd look like first thing in the morning." He ran his glance over her face, taking note of the relaxed line of her lips, bare of any gloss.

Her frown deepened a little. "You're crazy."

"You could be right," Trey conceded. "I only know you were the last thing I thought about before I fell asleep and the first thing on my mind when I woke. Care to join me for breakfast?"

"It isn't even six o'clock yet."

"I know. But since we're both up, we might as well get something to eat." Only the twinkle in his eyes gave lie to the perfectly reasonable tone of his voice.

Her lips parted on a silent laugh as

Sloan shook her head and leaned a shoulder against the frame. "I give up. Breakfast it is. But I'll need a few minutes to get ready."

"Not a problem," Trey replied, satisfaction running strong through him. "Just one question — what's your morning beverage of choice?"

Amused by the question, she paused a beat before answering. "I usually have a double latte. Since I already know Miles City doesn't have a Starbucks, coffee with cream will do."

"I'll have one waiting for you." He pushed off the jamb to stand erect. "Twenty minutes from now — in the lobby. Will that give you enough time?"

"Better make it thirty so I can have time to shower."

"Thirty minutes," Trey agreed and backed up a step. "Make sure to bring a jacket with you. It's liable to be a bit nippy at this hour."

"I will," Sloan promised.

Turning away, Trey struck out for the lobby. He had an incredible urge to whistle but resisted it, his smile widening instead. There was definitely a fresh flavor to the morning.

Sloan entered the lobby a scant three

minutes later than the appointed time. Trey pushed the plastic lid back on his coffee container, scooped up a twin to it, and rose to meet her.

There wasn't a trace of the rumpled, drowsy-eyed woman who had opened her door some thirty minutes ago. Sloan looked fully put together, casual yet vaguely professional thanks to the tailored jacket she had paired with jeans and a buttery soft top.

Her hair was pulled back from her face and secured at the nape with a large gold clasp that echoed the gleam of the stud earrings she wore. Her lashes were subtly darker, intensifying the blue of her eyes, but it was the pink sheen to her lips that drew Trey's glance. They lay softly to-gether, warm and inviting.

If his hands hadn't been full, he would have done something about that. As it was, he settled for moving toward her and lessening the space between them.

"Sorry." Her apology came out in an easy rush. "I had trouble getting my hair to dry."

"No problem." He extended the hand with the container of milk-diluted coffee. "Your coffee as promised, Ms. —" He checked the movement. "You never did tell me your full name."

"It's Davis," she replied without hesitation, her eyes sparkling. "Sloan Davis."

"Trey Calder," he volunteered and once more offered the cup to her.

Her head lifted, a flicker of surprise mixing with the look of recognition. "Of the Montana Calders?"

Her reaction to his family name was one Trey had seen too many times to be surprised by it. "Fifth generation," he confirmed. "I guess I don't have to ask whether you've heard of the Calder ranch."

"Who hasn't," she chided wryly.

"Nearly everyone in Montana has, that's for sure." Making a half turn, he gestured to the exit. "Ready to go?"

"All set."

Together they crossed to the door. Sloan didn't wait for Trey to open it but pushed it herself and stepped into the crisp, bracing air, as yet unwarmed by the newly risen sun. Its very coolness seemed to invigorate all five senses.

Trey gestured to the pickup that he had recently parked in front of the entrance. This time he held the passenger door and gave her a hand into the cab, then circled around to the driver's side and slid behind the wheel.

As he drove out of the parking lot onto

the main road, he stole a glance at Sloan, watching while she took a careful sip of the hot coffee. He felt a high contentment, seeing her sitting there, sharing the seat with him. It was something rare and new, like the day.

One-handed, he flipped off the lid to his own coffee container and downed a swallow of it. At this early hour there was little traffic on the streets to slow them.

When they passed the third restaurant, Sloan darted a curious look at him. "Where are we going for breakfast?"

"A quiet, out-of-the way spot I know." Trey deliberately refrained from being more forthcoming than that and changed the subject. "Where's home for you?"

"Louisiana, originally. At least that's where I was born."

"For someone from Louisiana, you don't have much of a southern accent." He ran an idle glance over her, conscious that last night he hadn't been the least bit interested in hearing her life story, and this morning he wanted to know everything about her.

"That's because I've lived all over the place since then. Right now I have a beach house on Maui that I use as my home base."

"You live in Hawaii?" Shock flattened his voice as a kind of alarm tingled through him.

"I do." There was a trace of laughter in her voice. "You seem surprised."

"I am." Trey saw no point in hiding it. "I just assumed you worked for one of the area newspapers."

"I'm a free-lance photographer." An amused smile curved her mouth.

"So what's a free-lance photographer from Hawaii doing covering the Miles City Bucking Horse Sale?" His curiosity was aroused, but it wasn't nearly as strong as the certainty he felt that he didn't want Sloan to leave when the auction came to an end.

"I'm wrapping up work on a coffee-table book that deals with rodeo traditions like the Calgary Stampede and the Cheyenne Frontier Days — as well as the Bucking Horse Sale at Miles City. It's my job to supply the photos, and somebody else writes the copy that goes along with them."

She made it sound routine. And Trey suspected it had likely become that for her. But he was wise enough to realize that such things didn't just happen without cause.

"You must be good at your work," he concluded.

"I am," she said simply.

"I figured you must be, or you wouldn't be able to make a living at it. It's bound to be a highly competitive field. Is it something you've always been interested in?"

The question caught Sloan in the midst of another sip of coffee. She swallowed and nodded. "Since I was nine years old. I got a camera for my birthday, and it's been my passion from that day on." She sat a little sideways on the seat, a shoulder brushing the passenger window, her body angled toward him and both hands curled around the hot cup. When he turned onto another street, her attention shifted to the front. Immediately she straightened in sudden alertness. "This is the way to the art center. What are we doing here?"

"It has a great little park area overlooking the Yellowstone River. It's an ideal place for a picnic," Trey replied, with a sidelong watch for her reaction.

She laughed softly in surprise. "A picnic breakfast. That's a first." An instant later, Sloan made a quick visual search of the floorboard area by her feet and the empty section of seat between them. "Where's the food?"

"I stowed it behind the seat."

Head tipped to one side, she gave him a

long look. "You must have been very busy after you left my room."

Trey laughed low in his throat. "Let's just say that if you had gotten to the lobby on time, you would have been waiting for me."

"Next time I won't bother to get my hair all the way dry." She settled back in the seat, a glow of anticipation in her eyes.

No phrase had ever sounded sweeter to Trey than the one Sloan had used. It told him that she expected there to be a "next time."

Chapter Four

Sunlight glistened on the dew-damp grass, intensifying its young green color. A few yards away, at the foot of the bluff, the Yellowstone River followed its snaking course eastward. A wide sweep of prairie flowed from the opposite bank, stretching the eye with its bigness.

A vagrant breeze flipped up a corner of the blanket that served as both a table and protection from the damp grasses underneath. Sloan sat cross-legged on it, a half-eaten flaky croissant in one hand and a plastic glass filled with a mixture of champagne and orange juice in the other.

More croissants were piled atop the paper sack that had contained them. Next to it sat a plastic box of California strawberries. Their luscious red color was a contrast to the bunch of shiny black grapes lying atop a paper napkin.

A cardboard box that had seen duty as a picnic hamper sat off to the side. Even now it held the opened champagne bottle, the orange juice carton, a thermos of coffee, a pint of milk, plus more napkins, extra glasses, and a collection of plastic flatware.

Trey sat at right angles to Sloan, propped upright by a bracing arm. He had one leg stretched out its full length while the other was bent to act as a support for the arm casually hooked over the knee. Every inch of him was male, from the raw-boned strength in his features to the muscled leanness of his body. He certainly did not appear the kind to have croissants and mimosas for breakfast.

"I have to admit," Sloan began, "when you pulled out that paper sack, I thought for sure there would be sausage-and-egg biscuits inside it. This isn't what you usually have for breakfast, is it?" she asked in open doubt.

His lazy smile, combined with the gleam in his eyes, seemed somehow sexily reckless and challenging. "My choice tends more to the steak-and-eggs side of the menu. But I figured that a woman who starts her morning with a double latte probably favors something lighter and a little more European."

"You certainly accomplished that," Sloan declared. "About the only thing missing is some yogurt and granola. Don't get me wrong," she added hastily, holding up a cautioning finger. "As far as I'm concerned, this is more than enough."

"I'm glad you approve."

"Wholeheartedly," she assured him.

The steady regard of his gaze grew slightly serious. "So what happens when you finish up here? Will you be flying back to Hawaii?"

"Probably." She took another bite of the pastry and used the little finger of that hand to brush the flaky crumbs from her lips.

"I figured that." He nodded. "Although there was the off chance you might be stopping off somewhere to visit family."

Sloan shook her head and quickly finished the bite in her mouth. "I don't have any family. Both my parents are gone, and I was the only child of parents who were only children themselves. It's been just me for so long that I've gotten used to it." She sent him a quick glance. "That probably sounds strange to you."

"Not really. My father died when I was just a little tyke. I don't remember him at all."

His words touched a chord in Sloan. Since she lost her parents when she was six, her memories of them were sketchy at best.

"It couldn't have been easy for you, growing up," she said, thinking of her own childhood.

"I always had Gramps." The corners of his mouth lifted in a smile of affection, but it was the brightening light in his eyes that spoke of his deep regard for the man. "I was named after him — the same as he was named after his grandfather. Chase Benteen Calder. Gramps is the one who started calling me Trey so there wouldn't be the confusion of two people being called by the same name. Which is the way it should be," he said with a shrugging lift of his head. "There's only one Chase Calder."

Always a stickler for details, Sloan frowned. "Aren't you forgetting about your great-great grandfather? His name was Chase Calder, too."

"According to Gramps, he never used it. He went by Benteen."

"I wonder why?" she murmured.

"Who knows?" Trey said, unconcerned, and downed the rest of his champagne drink in a series of manly gulps.

He examined the empty plastic glass for a moment. Then a restlessness seemed to sweep through him, and he rolled to his knees, shooting her a look as he shifted toward the picnic box.

"I'm ready for some coffee. How about you?" he asked.

"Not right now," Sloan told him.

But she took advantage of the chance to study him unobserved. She thought back on the previous day's encounters with him, first at the motel, then later at the rodeo arena. Initially she had regarded him as a rugged-jaw cowboy hunk with a smile that could make any woman's pulse race. She certainly hadn't been immune to it. But now she saw something more in him.

When he had suggested meeting at the street dance, she had agreed on a whim — partly to escape the monotony of another night in a motel room, partly out of curiosity about the event, and partly because of that potent smile. Any personal risk had seemed small, since it was a public event and she was furnishing her own transportation to and from it.

Just the same, Sloan had assumed she would be spending much of the evening fending off the advances of her lusty rodeo Romeo. However, except for that initial kiss that had relied more on raw heat than finesse, the evening hadn't turned out that way.

The noisy crowd and loud music had kept any conversation to a minimum, which had suited Sloan just fine at the time. Then later, outside her motel room, when Trey had kissed her that second time — the mere memory of its slow, drugging force was enough to make her toes curl all over again with a remnant of that delicious ache she'd felt.

Studying him while he poured steaming coffee out of the thermos, Sloan was struck again by the fact that he looked every inch a cowboy. He had the physique of a rider, wide at the shoulders and narrow at the hip, with all lean, sinewy muscle in between. And he had a horseman's way of walking as well, one that suggested he was more at home in the saddle than on foot.

In looks he was a throwback to something from the past, all steely strength and iron resolve. Handsome was too tame a word for the compelling quality of his features, features that were formed out of hard angles and smooth planes, without a trace of softness to them until he smiled and took a woman's breath away.

Yet an ordinary cowboy he wasn't. This breakfast selection showed Trey had a worldly side. More than that, it revealed he could be thoughtful and caring. And that discovery made Sloan wonder all the more about the kind of lover he'd be.

After tightening the thermos lid, Trey set the bottle back in the box and made his way across the blanket to rejoin her. His nearness coupled with the direction her own thoughts had taken started her pulse drumming a little erratically. To cover it, Sloan popped the last of the croissant in her mouth and reached for a napkin.

Trey helped himself to a handful of strawberries, then offered Sloan her choice. "Have one?"

Using hand signals and an exaggerated chewing motion, she indicated she already had a mouthful of food. His mouth quirking, he nodded in understanding and proceeded to stem the fruit in his hand and, one by one, eat the berries whole.

As Sloan washed down the last of the croissant with a drink of her champagne cocktail, Trey remarked, "It's a beautiful morning."

"It certainly is." She let her gaze wander to the prairie-scape on the opposite side of the Yellowstone. "I wish I'd brought my camera."

"Is this your first trip to Montana?"

"No, but all the other times I was here, I was always in the mountains or Glacier Park. The mountains are always big and beautiful, but here . . . there's a different kind of bigness."

"A big land and a big sky," Trey agreed.

But he wasn't looking at either. She could almost feel the touch of his gaze moving over her face, as in a caress. She felt self-conscious, wondering what he saw. As always, the attack of nerves prompted Sloan to keep her hands busy. She selected a big, ripe berry and made slow work of removing its stem.

"Where did you come by an unusual name like Sloan?" Trey asked. "There's bound to be a story behind it."

The question came almost as a relief. Mostly because the answer was easy. "Not a story exactly, but a reason. But before I tell you, I need to explain that my full name is Sloan Taylor Davis. Sloan is my mother's maiden name, and Taylor is my dad's mother's maiden name. Which makes my name also my lineage. That's become something of a custom in certain southern circles. Therefore, when you meet someone, you already know everything about their background. So it really isn't unusual to meet a southern-born woman with a given name of Campbell or Fallon or Sloan."

"That's bound to make you think twice

about the name of the person you marry," Trey suggested, his voice dry with humor, "Can you imagine saddling a girl with a name like Lipshitz or Bumgartner?"

Sloan laughed. "I never thought of that, but you're right. It's for sure I'm never going to name any daughter of mine Davis."

"That's good." He broke off one of the larger branches from the grape cluster.

"I thought so." Sloan bit into the strawberry. Juice gushed onto her chin and she immediately tried to catch it in her hand. "Why didn't you tell me how juicy these are?" she complained and hurriedly set her drink aside, freeing her hand to grab a napkin.

"You never asked." Using his teeth, Trey calmly pulled a grape off its stem and rolled it into his mouth.

Sloan absently watched him devour the grapes while she wiped the stickiness from her hand. For a man who usually breakfasted on steak and eggs, she knew croissants and fruit could hardly satisfy his morning appetite.

"You must be starving," she said with feeling.

He aimed his steady gaze at her. "Only for you."

His look was too blatantly sensual for Sloan to misconstrue his meaning. For a split second she was totally robbed of speech even as her heart began thudding madly against her ribs.

She made a shaky attempt to laugh it off. "You're very direct, aren't you?"

"You aren't giving me enough time to court you the right way."

Oddly flustered by his answer, Sloan wasn't sure how seriously she should take it. So she strove for a response that would fall somewhere in between.

"What an old-fashioned choice of words."

"It surprises me, too," Trey admitted. "But since I met you, I realize that I want it all — strolling hand in hand across a meadow of flowers, sitting on a front-porch swing on a moonlit night, stealing kisses, and hoping nobody turns on the porch light."

The images pulled her as much as his presence. "No one has swings on their front porches anymore." Sloan found herself regretting that fact.

"I know." Trey leaned toward her. "That's why a guy has to steal a kiss when and wherever he can."

He cupped a hand behind her neck, exerting light pressure to eliminate the space between them. The kiss was sweet and warm, heady in its strength and incredibly easy to return. His mouth tasted of grapes and coffee and — most stimulating of all — desire.

Sloan was never sure how it happened. One minute they were straining closer to each other, and the next, Trey was on his back and she was lying half across him.

With the coolness of morning all around, she found warmth in his arms, an all-pervading heat that came from the delving hunger of his kiss, the molding caress of his hands, and the muscled solidness of the body beneath hers. It was something to bask in and explore.

There was no camera separating her from the experience. It wasn't enough simply to record it; she had to participate to feel for herself the springy thickness of his hair, taste the sharp tang of aftershave on his skin, and glory in the half-strangled moan that slipped from him when she nibbled at his ear.

In the next breath, the tables were turned and Trey was the one administering the love nibbles, igniting a series of thrilling shivers radiating from them and eliciting a groaning sigh of her own. Then his mouth was there to swallow the sigh and claim her lips.

When she felt the first invading touch of his hands sliding under her top, she drew in a quick breath that was all pleasure. It wasn't something she had known she wanted until she felt the splaying of his hands over her skin. The stretchy fabric of her sports bra acted like a second skin when he molded his hand to the underswell of her breast, his thumb making a stroking search to find the hard nubbin of her nipple. Sensation spiraled through her, and the ache grew.

Confusion reigned when he ripped his mouth from hers and started swearing bitterly, his hands gripping her ribs and pushing her off him even as he rolled after her.

"What's wrong? Why — ?" she began, half in anger.

"I spilled my damned coffee," Trey muttered tightly.

Recalling the hot steam that had swirled above the cup, Sloan asked quickly, "Did you get any of it on you?"

"It's all over the back of my shirt." He sat up, giving the side seam a tug to survey the damage.

"I'll get some napkins." But it was her turn to swear when she scrambled to her feet and accidentally stepped on the remaining croissants. She pulled her foot away from them too quickly and knocked over the strawberry container. Letting them lie, Sloan gathered up the extra napkins from the cardboard box and returned to Trey's side. "Did it burn you?" She blotted at the coffee-sodden shirt.

"No. It was just the shock of something hot and wet against my skin."

"I can imagine." Reassured that no harm had been done, she continued to use the napkins to absorb as much of the excess moisture as possible. "I hope you didn't want anything more to eat. I pretty well demolished what was left of our breakfast."

"Food is about the last thing on my mind." His eyes were twinkling with amusement when he said it.

Sloan smiled in answer, letting him know she understood perfectly. After a moment more of working on the wet stain, she sat back on her heels. "That's about the best I can do."

"It's fine," he said and rolled to his feet, scooping up his hat along the way. "What d'ya say we go for a walk? We can clean up this mess later."

"Sounds good to me." Sloan pushed to her feet.

When she stepped off the blanket to join

him, he reached out and took her hand, linking fingers. Side by side, they started off paralleling the bluff's edge.

After they had traveled a ways, he studied her with a sidelong look.

"I admit there are no flowers, only grass, but this still feels good and right." His elbow bent, raising their clasped hands.

"Are you always this romantic?" Sloan teased, mostly to contain the swirl of emotion within.

His reply was quick and firm. "Not by a long shot."

She waited, a kind of flatness setting in. When he failed to say more, Sloan prompted, "Aren't you going to say that it's different with me?"

"It's an old line, isn't it?" His mouth crooked in a knowing smile.

"Very old." The variations on it were endless. Only a few times had she wanted to believe them. In the end, it hadn't mattered that it hadn't turned out to be true.

"I imagine you've heard your share of them," Trey guessed.

"Let's just say that in my line of work I travel a lot, and I've learned to be very selective about where I sleep."

"I already figured that out," he told her.

"It's all an old story. Only one thing can make it new."

He left it at that, offering no further explanation and letting Sloan come to her own conclusion. Only one came to mind, and that was love.

Upon entering the hotel's private meeting room, Jessy quickly inspected her surroundings, the line of her mouth tightening when she noticed Trey's absence. An opened briefcase lay atop the table. Its owner sat behind it, only a jacketed shoulder and sleeve visible. A side serving table against the wall held a tray of assorted cold cuts and cheese, a basket of sandwich rolls, and another of chips along with the usual condiments. A second man poured coffee from an insulated carafe into a cup, but he was angled away from the door, preventing Jessy from getting a look at his face.

When she closed the door behind her, a head popped out from behind the raised briefcase lid. The wire-rimmed glasses and short-cropped hair seemed to suit his accountant looks. But, as Ed Walters, head of the investigative agency, had often pointed out to her, spreadsheets and financial records usually provided more information than could be gained from interviewing a hundred people.

"Hi, Jessy." Ed Walters rose to greet her, extending a hand to shake hers when she approached. "I don't think you've met Doug Avery. He's been heading up the Texas side of this for me."

"Good to meet you, Mr. Avery." Jessy turned to the second man, who could have passed for Joe Average, neither too tall or too short, too heavy or too thin, yet attractive in a nondescript way.

"My pleasure, ma'am." He gripped her hand briefly, then gestured to the drink selection. "Can I get you something?"

"Just coffee for now," she replied. "I hope you don't mind, but to avoid the interruptions of waiters coming in and out, I had the hotel prepare the sandwich trays so we could make our own."

"To tell you the truth, we've already sampled them." Ed grinned. "We thought it would be easier for you to eat and listen than it would be for us to eat and talk. So, how's Chase doing these days?"

"He's still going strong," Jessy replied truthfully.

"I always picture him sitting in the den behind that big desk of his, and that old map of the Triple C on the wall behind him." An absentminded smile curved his mouth at the image in his mind. The digression didn't last long, and he quickly centered his thoughts on the present. "Where's your son? I thought he was to be here, too."

"Unfortunately, Trey's been held up." Just why or how, Jessy didn't know, but she intended to find out before the day was over.

"It's probably all that traffic from the parade," Avery concluded. "I thought we were never going to get here from the airport. The town's jammed with people."

"It always is, on the third weekend in May," Jessy said as the door opened behind her and Trey walked in.

"Sorry I'm late." He crossed directly to an empty chair and slipped off his hat. "I hope you haven't been waiting long."

"Not at all," Walters assured him and introduced him to his associate.

"Got caught in that traffic, did you?" Avery guessed as they shook hands.

"Actually, I spilled coffee all over my shirt so I had to go back to the motel at the last minute and change into something dry."

Which was the truth, as far as it went. Trey simply omitted the part that dealt with Sloan and how easy it had been to lose track of time when he was with her. Indeed, it was where he wanted to be that very moment — with Sloan. The knowledge that she would be leaving when the weekend was over only made that feeling more urgent.

"I suppose you'll be riding some of those broncs this afternoon," Walters guessed.

"No sir." Trey helped himself to some coffee. "The ranch has put together a team to compete in the wild horse race, and I'm one of the members of that. Ropin' is more my line than rough stock."

"Quint mentioned the two of you used to do a lot of team roping events," Avery remarked.

"We were a hard pair to beat." There was no boast in his words, just a statement of fact. "But with Quint heading up the Cee Bar Ranch down in Texas for us, that's past history."

The reference to Quint served to redirect all their thoughts to the matter at hand. It was at Quint's suggestion that the investigation had been started some five months ago after Rutledge's efforts to force a sale of the Cee Bar Ranch had extended to infecting the Cee Bar cattle with anthrax.

At the time, all the evidence against Rutledge was circumstantial. As a former

ATF agent for the Treasury Department, Quint hoped an investigation would uncover something more concrete. He had also recommended that all of Rutledge's past and present activities be scrutinized for other evidence of wrongdoing.

"Shall we get started?" Avery suggested, pulling a folder from his briefcase.

At a nod from Jessy, he started his report with a summary of all the information obtained. When there was documentation, such as laboratory tests that identified the anthrax as a manufactured strain, he produced it.

Most of it Trey had heard before. His thoughts soon strayed to Sloan, wondering where she was and what she was doing. He had asked her to have a late lunch with him, but she had vetoed the idea, reminding him that she needed to be at the rodeo grounds as soon as the parade was over and that she'd probably grab a quick bite there.

"We're ninety-nine percent sure," Walters was saying, "that we know which laboratory was the source of the anthrax spores that infected your cattle. We can link Rutledge's son, Boone, with one of the technicians working there, but we can't find any tie to Rutledge himself. The few people in the area who were willing to talk to us about it all pointed fingers at Boone as the one giving the orders. In my opinion, Rutledge got to all of them and turned his dead son into a scapegoat. As much as I hate to admit, Jessy," he said with a wry grimace, "when it comes to the trouble you had at the Cee Bar, we've come to a dead end."

"What about his other activities?" A thoughtful frown creased her forehead.

"It isn't much better. You can fill her in, Doug." Walters leaned back in his chair to let his associate take over.

"We can document hundreds of incidents where his tactics have been heavy-handed, and all of it right on the borderline of being illegal. When we dug deeper into his past business activities, I thought we had found something. Remember when all those savings-and-loan scandals erupted in Texas a few years back? Well, Rutledge was implicated in a number of them, but the Feds hit a stone wall when it came to proving it, which is why he was never indicted. It was a cold trail, but we followed it anyway. Unfortunately, it soon became obvious that those who might have been able to implicate Rutledge were all dead. Some died in prison and others of natural causes."

"I know Chase isn't going to like hearing this, Jessy, but we've pretty well run out of leads to follow," Walters concluded.

"You're right. He won't like it." Jessy agreed. "He's convinced Rutledge represents a potential threat to the family. Like Quint, Chase was hoping you would find something that we could hold over his head."

"So far we've struck out. But we'll keep digging if that's what you want."

"It's what Chase wants," she replied, leaving little doubt that while she ran the Triple C operation, Chase Calder still ruled it.

"Any particular avenue you want us to pursue?" Walters asked, then turned toward Trey. "You haven't said much during this, Trey. Have you got any thoughts?"

Conscious of being the cynosure of all eyes at the table, Trey had to scramble for an answer. Personally, he didn't share his grandfather's concern about Rutledge. But that wasn't the Calder line.

"I'd concentrate on the anthrax angle," he said. "If Rutledge has paid somebody to keep his mouth shut, then that person came into some cash, a new job, college tuition for his kids, or an operation for the wife. Something changed hands somewhere."

"You're right. We looked for the obvious cash trails, but there are always others." Walters glanced at the other investigator, a gleam of new possibilities in his look.

A discussion followed, going over the options. But with little of substance that could be added, the meeting began to break up.

Trey made his exit at the first opportunity, a fact Jessy was quick to note. She stayed to the last, shaking hands with both men as they left.

Seconds after the door closed behind them, Laredo slipped into the room. His eyes made a quick skim of the room, verifying she was alone, then made a thorough examination of her expression. He cocked his head to one side. "How'd it go?"

"After five months, basically they have nothing." Jessy scratched her name across the credit card chit and slipped a copy of it in her pocket before turning to him. "Somehow Rutledge has succeeded in shifting all the blame to Boone. Convenient, isn't it?"

"Very." Seeing the frustration in her face, he decided a change of subject was in order. "I noticed Trey left early."

Jessy pulled in a quick, cleansing breath and nodded. "He said he had to get to the fairgrounds. Why, I don't know. The team race isn't until later."

"I have a feeling a certain blue-eyed brunette might be the reason." When Jessy looked at him in surprise, Laredo added, "He saw her last night at the street dance, and I suspect he had breakfast with her this morning."

The significance of that wasn't lost on Jessy. Having grown up in a man's world, working cattle side by side with men her entire life, she had few romantic illusions about them. In her experience, rare was the man who cared to see the same woman in the morning that he'd been with the night before. Her own son was no different. Obviously, this woman was.

"Who is she? What's her name?" She was immediately curious.

With a shake of his head, Laredo signaled his ignorance. "That's something you'll have to ask Trey."

Common sense overruled her maternal curiosity, and she said, "If it's serious, I'll find out soon enough. And if it isn't, it doesn't matter who she is."

Laredo couldn't argue with that logic. And since Jessy hadn't asked his opinion, he kept it to himself.

Chapter Five

The breeze channeled itself through the alleyway behind the chutes, kicking up little eddies of dust and swirling them along it. Trey took little notice of that as he dawdled at the entrance, one shoulder propped negligently against a post. The whole of his attention was focused on Sloan, some twenty feet away.

Again she was wearing that bulky vest, its many pockets bulging with assorted rolls of film, a light meter, and camera attachments. To anyone passing by, it appeared that she was chatting with one of the save men, still in his clown makeup, and every now and then idly snapping a picture of him.

But Trey had been watching her all afternoon, long enough to realize there was nothing idle or casual about anything she did. Even now, while she was engaging in idle chitchat to keep her subject relaxed, she kept constant track of the sun's angle and adjusted her position to compensate for any change in it.

She was all business, to the exclusion of everything else, including Trey. And it had been that way ever since he'd arrived at the rodeo grounds. After scouring the arena fence and chutes, he had finally located her in the rear area, busy taking pictures of a pen of bucking horses.

His greeting had barely gained him a glance before she was once again studying the scene through the camera's viewfinder. "Sorry. This light isn't going to last," she had told him in a distracted murmur.

Personally, Trey hadn't seen anything particularly unusual about the light or the pen of horses, but he had waited until she finished. Yet, almost the moment she moved away from the pen, her eyes had begun a search for her next subject. They had quickly fastened on an injured cowboy being helped to the first-aid station. She had immediately set off in the same direction, talking and smiling at Trey, yet he had sensed that her mind was elsewhere.

After the injured cowboy, she had focused on another cowboy, this one making a careful inspection of his saddle cinch. Then she had gravitated to the action in the arena.

And Trey had followed — until he started feeling like a damned puppy dog, panting at her heels, waiting for her to remember he was there. Pride wouldn't let him dog her any more, but he continued to keep her within sight.

Logic told him that Sloan was here to do a job. Yet he found her single-minded devotion to it frustrating and irksome. There was little solace in remembering that Sloan had told him that photography was her passion. At the time Trey hadn't thought she meant it literally. Now he was beginning to wonder.

Watching her, his anger and impatience growing by the minute, Trey struggled to accept the notion that he was jealous of a camera. Yet it was true. The time she spent with it, the care she took of it, and the undivided energy she gave to it — he wanted all that for himself. It shook him how much he wanted it.

"Hey, Trey!" A bright, happy voice called to him, female in pitch. It pulled him out of the swirl of black thoughts and dragged his gaze in its directions as Kelly Ramsey approached him, all smiles. "Hi. How's it going?"

The impulse was there to brush aside this unwanted intrusion, but out of the corner of his eye, Trey had seen Sloan throw a glance in his direction.

Instead of cutting Kelly short, he smiled. "Hi, Kelly. What are you doing behind the chutes?"

She tucked her fingers in the hip pockets of her jeans, an action that thrust her young breasts forward to enhance the rounded shape they made beneath her T-shirt. She tipped her head at a flirtatious angle.

"Looking for Johnny," she said. "I wanted to wish him luck in the race. And you, too, of course," she added, having planned that to sound like an afterthought, before darting a look around and asking, "You wouldn't happen to know where I can find Johnny, would you?"

"Not really, but he's around here some-where." Trey used the excuse of locating Johnny to let his gaze return to Sloan. His mouth tightened slightly when he saw her shake hands with the rodeo clown and drift off in another direction.

Kelly had noticed her as well. "Isn't that the girl you were with last night?" she asked.

"Yeah."

Undeterred by his single-word response, Kelly observed, "She's pretty. With a tan like that, though, she can't be from around here. Where's she from? Do you know?"

"Hawaii."

"Really?" Kelly stared at him with a surprise she didn't have to feign. She was secretly pleased by the news. "Hawaii is a heck of a long way from here."

Trey didn't bother to comment on that. Instead he turned. "Let's go find Johnny. He's usually somewhere behind the chutes."

He escorted Kelly into the alleyway, convinced that Sloan was too wrapped up in her work to remember he even existed. That knowledge didn't set well, not when he couldn't get her out of his mind.

The cheers of the crowd, the announcer's voice over the loudspeakers, the pounding of hooves, and the assorted snorts and whinnies were background noises that Sloan had long ago tuned out. With one knee on the ground and the other serving as support for her elbow, she steadied the camera and examined the framed shot in the viewfinder, then adjusted the focus on the sea of equine legs and shaggy fetlocks. Satisfied, she snapped the picture.

Instantly the camera whirred, signaling the end of the roll. Out of habit Sloan pulled a new roll out of her vest pocket and stood up, ready to make the switch once the rewinding process was complete.

No longer focused on her subject, she idly looked around, letting her surroundings make their impression on her. The rodeo announcer was in the midst of some lengthy introductions. Sloan didn't pay much attention to them until she heard the words, ". . . Chase Calder's grandson, Trey Calder, along with . . ."

She lifted her head in shock as the realization struck that the wild-horse race was about to start. She set out for the arena fence at a running walk, hurriedly switching the camera film as she went.

By the time she found an opening along the arena fence, a half dozen horses were running loose, pursued by an equal number of cowboys on foot, swinging ropes. Her heart lifted the instant she located Trey among them. Before she could raise her camera and snap a picture of the action, he let his rope sail out, and the noose settled around the neck of a wiry bay horse still wearing its heavy winter coat.

The bay unleashed an angry squeal, a protest echoed by other roped horses, Sloan temporarily lost sight of Trey as plunging and rearing horses blocked her view and more cowboys raced onto the scene, hauling saddles. She snapped a few quick shots of the chaos.

When she finally caught sight of Trey again, he had crowded the bay horse close to the opposite fence while a teammate attempted to sling a saddle onto the animal's back. But the bay was having none of it, first plunging forward, then letting his hind feet fly.

It was a scene of flailing hooves and brute strength pitted against brute strength, shouted words of encouragement and warning. Sloan gasped in alarm more than once when it appeared that Trey was in danger of being run over and trampled or struck down by a pawing hoof.

A big chestnut broke free and bucked across the arena, its saddle hanging off one side and threatening to slide under its belly. It was an image that clearly illustrated the wild and woolly scene, but Sloan never lifted her camera to capture it. She couldn't, when the whole of her attention was trained on Trey.

Unconsciously she held her breath when Trey took a snug hold on the horse's head and used his body to wedge the bay against the fence. When the saddle cinch was pulled tight around its belly, it reared, hauling Trey into the air with it. Both came down safely, and that long-held breath quivered from her.

A teammate grabbed hold of the saddle horn and swung into the seat. The wiry bay leaped forward in a plunging rear. This time Trey made no attempt to check the horse. Instead he stepped away, letting the pair go.

He would have been in the clear if the bay hadn't doubled back. A warning cry rose in Sloan's throat, but she never had a chance to utter it as a back hoof clipped his forehead, and Trey went down on all fours.

"Oh my God," she murmured.

Sloan stayed long enough to see Trey's dazed stagger when another cowboy helped him to his feet. Then she scrambled off the fence and raced along the alleyway, worry curdling her stomach.

When she finally reached him, all of her worst fears seemed to be realized. One whole side of his face and neck was covered in blood. More stained the wadded-up kerchief he held against his forehead. A shoulder was propped against an inner fence rail.

She climbed over the fence, shouting to anyone who would listen, "Get the paramedics. Quick!" Then she was on the ground beside him, moving to slip a supporting arm around him. "I'll —"

"Sloan." He focused an eye on her in surprise. "Where did you come from?"

"It doesn't matter," she said, relieved that he appeared to be lucid. "Come on. Let me help you out of here."

"Not yet," he said, then shouted, "Stick with him, Johnny!"

"Just lean on me," Sloan instructed and shifted to hook his arm behind her neck.

"Gladly." The amusement in his voice drew her glance upward. "But I promise you this isn't as bad as it looks."

Sloan saw only the coagulating blood on his face. "I don't think a doctor would agree with you."

"Head wounds always bleed a lot," he told her.

"Yours certainly is." Unable to get him to move, Sloan changed tactics and commandeered the blood-soaked cloth he held against his forehead. The instant she lifted it, a fresh flow of blood streamed from the nasty crescent-shaped gash above his eye. "And it's still bleeding."

She pressed it hard against the cut. Pain stabbed through his head. Trey flinched and sucked in air through his teeth.

"It'll quit in a minute," he insisted in a tight mutter.

"You hope."

Catching the hint of anger in her voice, Trey made a closer study of the strained tension in her expression. "You're really worried about me, aren't you?"

"Of course I am." She glared at him, but there was a telltale glisten of tears in her eyes that made Trey forget all about the throbbing in his head. "I saw his hoof when it struck your head."

His glance slid to the camera, hanging from the strap around her neck, totally forgotten; all of her attention was on him — just the way he had wanted it. Suddenly he no longer cared whether Johnny stayed in the saddle for a full circuit of the racetrack.

"If it'll make you feel better, you can take me over to the first-aid station and let the nurse slap a bandage on," Trey suggested and straightened away from the fence, turning toward the gate. "Come on."

He had to hide a smile when her arm tightened around his middle to offer needless support.

"Where are you going, Trey?" Tank called from his vantage point on the top rail.

"The lady thinks I need a bandage," Trey replied.

Tank snorted. "You need a washcloth."

"That too," Trey agreed.

A little late, Sloan noticed that nobody else seemed to be overly concerned about Trey's injury. It made her wonder if she had overreacted. But she couldn't so easily dismiss the sight of all that blood.

"You don't really think this is necessary, do you?" she said, half in accusation when they went through the gate opening. "You're just going to humor me."

"You're wrong about that." There was something warm and intimate in the look he gave her. "Because I happen to be glad you care enough to worry about me."

"Who wouldn't worry, with all that blood on your face?" Sloan countered, unable to get past the sight of it. "You should have enough sense to go yourself without waiting for someone to make you."

"It's natural that you might think that way. But where I live, we don't have a doctor around the corner. In fact, the closest one is fifty miles away, and he's only there two days a week. You learn quick to make your own assessment of the potential seriousness of your injury. The ones you can take care of yourself, you do." His mouth quirked. "You'd be surprised at how handy I am with a needle."

"I'll take your word for it." Oddly, she was relieved by his explanation and the logic behind it. Initially she'd thought that his resistance to medical attention was part of some macho cowboy thing.

By the time they arrived at the first-aid area, the flow of blood from the cut was down to a slight ooze. The paramedic on duty made short work of cleaning the worst of the blood from Trey's face and neck, checked to make sure there was no sign of a concussion, then opened an antiseptic bottle.

As he was about to swab the crescent-shaped cut with it, Kelly Ramsey came sauntering up. She leaned close to inspect his injury and grimaced in empathy when Trey winced at the solution's sharp sting.

"That's a nasty gash, Trey," Kelly stated, then sighed. "Too bad it isn't on your cheek. It would have left a sexy scar."

The casual and slightly cavalier dismissal of his injury was an echo of Trey's own unconcern for it, a fact that Sloan duly noted. It made her even more self-conscious about her own reaction to it.

"Next time I'll try to be sure I'm struck on the cheek," Trey replied in a similar tone. "So, who won the race? Did Johnny make it all the way around the track?"

"He made it all right," the girl confirmed. "When he came around the turn, he was so far ahead of the others, it looked like Johnny was going to be an easy winner. About twenty yards from the finish, the horse spooked — who knows at what — turned end for end and went into a bucking frenzy. Johnny stuck tight as a burr on that saddle, but he couldn't get that crazy bronc to turn around in time. The casino team won." Her shoulders lifted in a fatalistic shrug. "Now Johnny's spittin' mad, stomping around, cursing his luck."

"He'll get over it," Trey said without sympathy.

"He'd better. Right now he isn't fit to be around."

Finished with the antiseptic, the paramedic put it away and took out a prepackaged bandage. Sloan threw him a sharply questioning look.

"Aren't you going to put stitches in it first?" she challenged, darting another glance at the gaping cut.

"I probably could," the man conceded. "But these butterfly bandages work just about as well at holding the flesh together as stitches do. And they're a lot less painful."

"You know best," Sloan admitted, then found herself the subject of the blonde's openly curious stare.

Trey took notice of it as well and made the introductions. "Sloan Davis, meet Kelly Ramsey. Her dad works at the Triple C."

The young blonde was quick to stretch out her hand. "Hi. I remember seeing you with Trey last night in town."

"That's right." Sloan clasped the girl's hand in brief greeting.

"Say," Kelly began, dividing a bright glance between them, "a bunch of us are going to the street dance tonight. You two are welcome to join us."

Sloan didn't hesitate in her answer. "Don't count on me. I'm going to pass on the street dance tonight."

"Too bad. They're a blast," Kelly declared and took a preparatory step back. "I guess I'll go see if Johnny's cooled off any. Catch you later, Trey."

Trey responded with an acknowledging lift of his hand, then sat silently while the paramedic applied the bandage to the cut. When the man finished, he turned away and began tidying up the area as he said, "You know the drill, Calder — keep the wound clean and dry, change the dressing in a day or two, so on and so forth."

"No problem." Trey rose from the chair. "And thanks."

"Don't thank me," the man countered. "Just be glad you Calders are a hard-headed lot."

"Always." Trey grinned and eased his hat back on, taking care to keep the band away from the bandage's adhesive ends. There was a twinkle in his eyes when he moved to Sloan's side. "Satisfied?"

Amusement tugged at the corners of her mouth, but she was serious when she said, "At least now you don't look like something out of a Halloween movie."

"That bad, was it?" As one, they drifted in the direction of the arena.

"It was."

His interest in small talk faded the closer they got to the chutes and the mix of contestants and onlookers. And Trey was reminded of the shortness of time they had.

"Did you mean that about not going to the street dance tonight?" He let his gaze travel over her face, certain he would never tire of looking at it.

She nodded and slid him a quick look. "Last night was fun, but once is enough," she said, then admitted, "I've never been much of a party-hearty type."

"After a while it gets to be all the same, doesn't it? A lot of drinking, loud talking, and equally loud laughter." That hadn't always been his attitude. Yet lately Trey had noticed that rowdy nights spent carousing had lost much of their excitement and fun. "So what are your plans instead?"

"I haven't really made any. But after two days of the crowds and noise, a quiet dinner somewhere sounds good."

The prospect appealed to him, too. But he knew the unlikelihood of that happening. "I don't think there's a place in town where you can have a quiet dinner this weekend. But I do know a good place to eat."

"Not another picnic," she teased.

His answering smile was wide. "No. I had in mind a sit-down dinner with someone else doing the serving. Are you game?"

"What time?"

"Whenever you say."

Halting, she checked her watch, made some quick mental calculations, then cast a thoughtful look over the chute area. "I'm losing the natural light. From now on it's going to be a battle to get a good shot with the sun at this angle. Since the rodeo will still be going on tomorrow, there isn't any reason why I can't wrap it up for today and head back to the motel. Say, an hour to shower and change, and I could meet you for dinner sometime between six-thirty and seven. Is that all right?"

"That will give me time to clean up, too."

"You need it. There's blood on your shirt and a few crusty bits of it near your temple." Without thinking, Sloan reached up and touched the places, then felt a modicum of surprise at the sense of freedom she felt to do it. It was rare for her to be the one to initiate contact. "But don't get the bandage wet," she added in quick admonishment.

"Yes ma'am." The laughing glint in his eyes was at direct odds to his polite answer. "Do you want to meet in the lobby, or shall I come by your room?"

"Let's make it my room." The answer was given in an off-hand delivery, but she felt anything but off-hand the instant the words were uttered. Her choice suggested a familiarity and intimacy between them that they hadn't yet reached. With a sudden, heady rush of certainty, Sloan realized it was something she wanted.

"I'll be there with bells on," Trey told her, his voice a little husky with promise.

"With bells on," she repeated and released a short, soft laugh. "What a strange expression. I've never understood what it means."

"It's not so strange," Trey stated. "It goes back to the old days out West. Back then, when a cowboy got dressed up to go to town, he attached jingle-bobs to his spurs."

"Really?" She injected the single word with both doubt and hope.

"Really."

"I'm glad. I like the story." Again her gaze strayed to the chutes. "I wonder if anybody is wearing jingle-bobs on their spurs. That would be a great shot." Sloan caught herself and laughed. "That better wait until tomorrow or I won't be ready when you knock at my door tonight." With an odd reluctance, she moved away from him. "See you in a bit."

As far as Trey was concerned, the time couldn't pass soon enough. Turning, he headed in the direction of the pickup parked in the infield.

Six-thirty on the dot Trey arrived at the door to Sloan's motel room. There was a dark sheen to his hair, still damp from his recent shower, and his face was shaved smooth of any end-of-the-day stubble. Blood ran hot and strong through his veins, part of the heady anticipation that put the dark and eager sparkle in his eyes.

A rap of his knuckles on the door drew an immediate and muffled response. "Be right there."

The seconds' wait seemed interminable. At last there came the rattle and click of the security chain and dead bolt. Then the door swung inward.

"Come in." Sloan backed away from the opening in further invitation, a bath towel in her hand and a white terry-cloth robe swaddled around her slight frame. Her hair was a tousle of slick, wet strands that framed a face absent of any makeup, revealing a beauty that was absolutely natural. "I'm running a little late, I'm afraid," she said and turned away, reaching up to briskly towel her wet hair as she retreated into the room. "When I checked with my answering service, there were some calls I had to return, and they took longer than I planned."

"No problem," Trey told her and stepped into the room, closing the door behind him.

"Have a seat." Sloan waved a hand at the room's lone chair. "I promise I won't be long."

"You don't have to hurry on my account." But Trey made no move toward the chair, not with a king-sized bed dominating his view.

For a moment he stared at its smoothly made surface, the sight of it conjuring up images of the way he wanted the night to end. The rawness of all those desires made him restless and edgy. He took off his hat and turned it absently in his hand, while his glance scoured the rest of the room. Except for a black carry-on bag on the luggage rack and a smaller leather bag on the floor next to it, there was little evidence of the room's occupant.

"Are you always this neat?" he asked, thinking of his sister, who would have had her stuff strewn all over.

Sloan moved back into his line of vision, flipping open the carry-on and retrieving a cosmetic bag from it. "It isn't so much a matter of neatness as it is organization. Keeping things put away eliminates the risk of leaving something behind and makes the packing process go much faster."

"Makes sense." It also made sense that

she could leave at a moment's notice. It was a knowledge that reached down into his guts and churned them up.

"It does to me." Sloan disappeared into the bathroom.

But she didn't close the door. Trey gravitated to the opening, arriving as the loud hum of the hair dryer started up. Sloan stood facing the mirror, holding the dryer in one hand while she finger-combed and fluffed with the other. She turned her head to aim the dryer at the other side and caught sight of him in the doorway.

"This really won't take long," she told him, her voice lifting to make itself heard above the dryer's noisy hum. "I just want to get it damp-dry."

"No hurry. We've got all night," Trey replied, but his mind locked on the night thing.

Remnants of the shower's steam edged the bathroom mirror, beading into moist droplets. Its presence prompted Trey to notice the bathroom's excessive warmth and heavy humidity. His glance strayed to the combination tub and shower and the wet sheen of its sides.

With no effort at all, he visualized Sloan standing beneath the spray, water sluicing down her shoulders onto her breasts and stomach. It was an easy leap to imagine himself showering with her, his hands gliding over her slick skin in an exploration of its rounded curves.

The blood started hammering so loudly in his head that he never heard the hair dryer click off. But the clear sound of Sloan's voice penetrated to shatter the images in his mind.

"Why don't you go watch some television while I finish getting ready?" The tone of suggestion was in her voice, but her hand was reaching for the bathroom door as if to close it on him when Trey jerked his gaze back to her. "The remote should be on the stand by the bed."

Not trusting his voice, Trey nodded and turned from the opening. He was conscious of the bathroom door swinging shut as he took his first steps away from it. That forward impetus carried him partway into the room. Then he halted at the foot of the bed.

Television held no appeal to him, not with all these fevered longings coursing through him. They left him raw and hungry for the feel of Sloan in his arms. With all his senses sharpened by it, he turned the instant he heard the releasing click of the bathroom door latch.

Chapter Six

Sloan stepped out of the bathroom clad in a simple tan dress that intensified the golden hue of her skin. A smile curved her lips, the warmth of it matching the glow in her eyes.

"I told you I'd be quick. Unfortunately" — she turned, presenting her back to him — "I think the material's caught in the zipper. Would you get it for me?"

It was a task Trey had performed countless times for his sister. But this wasn't his sister. This was Sloan.

Rather stiffly, Trey crossed the intervening space to stand behind her, conscious of the roiling needs within. His hands shook when he fumbled with the zipper, finding it hard to concentrate on anything but the nearness of her skin over the ribbon of her spine.

"Your hands are trembling," Sloan murmured on a marveling note.

"Damned right they are," Trey admitted with some force. "That's because they'd much rather be figuring out how to get this zipper down than up."

With a turn of her shoulders, she gave him an over-the-shoulder look that held amusement and something else. "Most men wouldn't admit that to a girl."

"I'm not most men." The curtness of his reply was a reflection of the tight control he was exercising over his baser instincts.

"I'm beginning to realize that." There was a new light in her eyes, a darkening and deepening of interest that seemed to mirror his own.

His own desires were too close to the surface for Trey to care whether he had imagined it or not. He gave up any pretense of interest in the zipper and took her by the shoulders, turning her to face him.

"Do you have any idea how many times I've made love to you in my mind?" His voice was thick and husky.

But it was the possessive darkness in his gaze, so stark and hungry, that stole her breath and charged her senses. Her hands rested lightly on his chest, yet she could feel the heat of his body through his shirt. And it was a barrier she didn't want. The certainty of that made her bold.

"Did I enjoy it?" she asked, her lips

parting on the last word, and her head lifting in invitation.

"Let's find out." It was a challenge and a statement, issued an instant before his mouth covered her lips.

The kiss was rough with need, filled with pent-up longings that awakened her own. Eagerly she returned its hot urgency, ready to be swept up in its seductive force and a little stunned that she hadn't realized she could want this much.

Delicious shudders quivered through her when she felt the zipper slide apart and the air touched her bare skin, but not for long. His big hand took its place, the hint of callus on it creating a pleasant rasp to go with its searing warmth. She swayed against him, her body arching under the slow stroke of his hand.

It seemed the kiss had barely begun when he dragged his mouth away from her lips and onto her cheek, yet her lungs were starved for air. But the breath she took ended in a gasp and a moan when he nuzzled that sensitive hollow near her ear, igniting a dance of erotic shivers over her skin. They only increased when his tongue traced the inner shell of her ear.

For a moment she was lost to the delights of his nips and nibbles and the moist heat of his breath on her skin. When his hands first pushed the dress off her shoulders, she resented the subsequent pinning of her arms to her sides and initially resisted until she realized his intention. In an eager and liquid move, she lowered her arms and quickly pulled them free of the garment's sleeves. The dress slid to the floor, puddling around her feet.

The lacy slip she wore beneath it was like a second skin, blocking none of his body heat or the sensation of his caressing hands. When his attention shifted to the long cord in her neck and the pulsing vein that ran alongside it, Sloan tipped her head, giving him greater access and thrilling to the fresh wave of shivers that swept over her.

She felt a great welling up of need within her, rising and expanding until she thought she would burst with it. She was slow to realize that part of the sensation was caused by Trey's hands, traveling up from her hips to her rib cage and drawing her slip's silken length along with them.

This time she knew instantly that his intention was to rid her of it. It was what she wanted, and yet a sliver of panic raced through her as Sloan realized that if she didn't take control, she would soon lose it.

Self-protection came into play, born of a need to keep from becoming too emotionally involved.

"Let me," she whispered, as she stilled his hands. Her voice breathy with the disturbances he'd created within.

His fingers released the folds of her slip. She imagined that he expected her to remove it. Instead she went to work unfastening the buttons of his shirt. He was quick to help her by tugging the tails loose from his jeans. With the release of the last button, he shrugged out of it and gave it a toss behind him, leaving Sloan free to feast her gaze on the breadth of his shoulders and all his tanned, hard flesh.

She studied the complex roping of muscle, lean, and sharply defined, as if by a sculptor's hand. From the ridged flatness of his stomach to the broadening sweep of his chest and shoulders, there wasn't an ounce of fat to be found. He was the image of youthful manhood, virile and strong.

"I wish I had my camera," Sloan murmured even as she smoothed her hands onto the center of his ribs.

"Oh no you don't. You aren't hiding behind any lens tonight." His voice had an edge to it that held its own warning.

"Not tonight," Sloan agreed and let her

hands glide up to invade the wiry nest of chest hairs, then traveled on to the masculine flatness of his breasts and their pebble-like nipples.

Curiosity had her lipping one, an action that drew a half curse from Trey. She smiled, pleased that her touch disturbed him, and let her hands slide down to his waist.

Moving against him, she used her hands and her body to nudge him backward toward the bed. "I'll help you off with your boots," she told him, tipping her head to smile at him.

He responded with a small, negative shake of his head. "Nope. Your slip, then my boots."

The smoldering darkness of his gaze had her heart tripping over itself, but she managed a soft laugh. "A negotiation, is it?"

"Or a fair trade." His quick hands had already caught hold of the slip and gave it an upward pull.

Acquiescing, Sloan raised her arms. Like liquid, the slip slid up and over her head, then went sailing after his shirt. When she focused on his face again, her breath was taken by the caressing way his gaze moved over the lacy cups of her underwire brassiere, then down to her matching lace briefs.

There was so much desire in his face that it took her a moment to find her voice. "Your boots." In another attempt to seize the initiative, she gave him a quick, firm shove, overbalancing him and sending him backward onto the bed.

He sat down heavily, the springs creaking under his weight. Not giving him a chance to recover, Sloan quickly picked up his left foot and swung around to straddle it facing the boot, cupping a hand under its heel.

"You push. I pull," she instructed.

Just as she tightened her grip on his boot, he clamped his hands on her waist and pulled her sideways and down, onto the bed beside him. The suddenness of it drew an outcry of surprise from her, then a laugh when she bounced on the mattress.

"That's not fair," she protested.

"It wasn't fair that there was no place for me to do any pushing, not as dirty as the soles of these boots are." He leaned forward and proceeded to tug off his own boots. "As attractive as the view was, it would have taken too long."

"I could have managed," she murmured idly, taking advantage of the chance to study, unobserved, the rippling movements of his arm and shoulder muscles.

"But I couldn't." One boot after the other thudded to the floor, followed by his socks. Swiveling around, he leaned back on an elbow beside her. "The trouble is — a man has no graceful way to get out of his clothes — not like a woman does."

She marveled that he would think that. Honesty made her say, "It feels just as awkward for a woman."

"That's reassuring." The slow spread of his smile was incredibly sexy and warm. Sloan couldn't help being moved by it. Like him, she found herself wishing there was a way to take the mundane and make it rare — as rare as the feelings within.

The instant that thought crossed her mind, she banished it as foolish, as the kind of thought that invariably ended in disappointment. Even though the number of lovers in her life had been few, it was a lesson she had learned well not to let her expectations get too high.

"What is it?" His hand touched her cheek, his gaze narrowing on her in sharpened study.

"Nothing." Her smile of assurance was quick, a little too quick. She saw at once that he didn't believe her.

"Sloan . . ." he began.

Instinctively she silenced him with a kiss

that was as hungry for love as her heart was. But her heart's hunger wasn't something a kiss alone could satisfy.

She rolled her mouth over and around his lips, murmuring against them, "We've already talked too much. Let's not spoil it with more."

With her lips moving hotly all over his, talking was the last thing on Trey's mind. Earlier he had been willing to indulge her essentially playful antics, but this was what he wanted, what he needed.

Using the weight and length of his body, he pressed her backward onto the mattress, not caring that the spread still covered it. He made short work of stripping away her lacy bra and panties and shedding his own clothes.

As he rejoined her, he was glad of the room's light that allowed him to see every feminine inch of her. There was high satisfaction in knowing she was his to explore. And there was much to discover, from the rounded shape of her small, firm breasts and the rosy brown nubs of her nipples to the sexy little bulge of her stomach and the silky matt of her pubic hair.

The pressure grew with every touch and every taste, the heat mounting like a wildfire about to rage out of control. He didn't need the urging of her hands and hips or the little mewling sounds that came from her throat. The instincts that drove him, shifting him onto her, were much more primitive.

Some sane part of him registered the wondrous cry of pleasure that slipped from her when he filled her. Then it all blurred together, bodies straining in rhythm, blood pounding, hands digging, the ache intensifying, coiling into an ever tightening circle. The release, when it came, was like an explosion of sensation that shook and shattered even as it melted away all the tension, leaving them both limp and trembling.

Body slick with sweat, Trey drew her along with him when he rolled off her and onto his back, lying in a loose, spent sprawl, yet keeping one arm securely hooked around her. His heart had yet to slow its rapid beat, and his chest continued its rise and fall with the quick, deep breaths he took.

But nothing registered as strongly as the feel of Sloan curled against him, the feathering of her hair on his arm, and the warmth of her breath on his skin. She stirred, and he automatically tightened his hold to keep her close.

His own action surprised him. With other women, this was usually when he tried to figure out some tactful way to slip free and get dressed. But this time was different. Everything was different, Trey realized, and it had been from the first moment he met her. He had felt that it was different then, and the feeling was even stronger now.

In a slow, catlike movement, Sloan lightly rubbed her cheek against his chest. "I suppose we should get dressed and go eat, but I don't feel like moving."

"Me either," Trey agreed, his voice a low, lazy rumble. "Too bad we can't call room service."

There was amusement in the dismissing breath she released. "You can forget that."

"I know." He rolled onto his side, shifting her from his body onto the bed, giving him his first look at the contented glow in her eyes. "I'm in no big hurry, anyway. Are you?"

"No." Her hand came up and traced the line of his jaw with her fingertips, then lingered near his mouth, touching the heads of perspiration along his upper lip. "You're all sweaty."

"I wonder how that happened," Trey

mocked lightly, his eyes agleam with amusement and satisfaction.

"I wonder," Sloan murmured in return, a smile deepening the corners of her mouth.

"It couldn't be that you had something to do with it, could it?" he challenged, unable to remember a time when he had enjoyed this intimate kind of banter.

"Maybe a little," Sloan conceded with a touch of smugness.

"Little, hell," he growled and claimed her lips in a quick, punishing kiss. One taste only made him hungry for more. He nuzzled a corner of her mouth. "That shower of yours looked big enough for two. Care to join me?"

"Only if you promise to scrub my back," she whispered in answer.

"That's a deal."

Just as he had imagined, Trey washed much more than her back. Wrapped in a cloud of steam and pummeled by the shower's pulsating jets, they made love again, this time with slow and infinite pleasure.

The bathroom mirror was completely misted over when they finally emerged from the shower and toweled dry. Finishing, Trey wrapped the damp towel around his hips tucking in a corner to hold it in place.

His gaze slid to Sloan, watching as she squeezed the excess water from her hair. Her kiss-swollen lips lay softly together, and there was a kind of inner beauty to her face that gave it a new radiance. A possessiveness rushed through him with a potency that shook him.

"Must be nice to have short hair," she observed idly.

"It has its advantages," he admitted absently. "This is just about where I came in — here you are, fresh out of the shower, your hair all wet."

"But this time I'm not even going to try to dry it." She ran a comb through it, slicking it away from her face. "It will be a lot quicker just to braid it."

"While you do that, I'll go round up our clothes."

The minute he left the bathroom, Sloan felt his absence. But it was eased by the small sounds she heard coming from the outer room. A heady contentment hummed through her, making her feel all tingly and warm.

When Trey returned a few minutes later, fully dressed, to deliver her clothes, Sloan was struck by how natural it seemed, as if it had always been that way. It wasn't a feeling she examined too closely; experience had taught her to live in the moment. And she was determined to do that.

The restaurant was crowded when they arrived, but Trey managed to find a booth tucked in an out-of-the-way corner. They sat on the same side, without an ounce of space between them. A lot more snuggling and kissing went on than talking. But words seemed unnecessary when there was a much more satisfactory and elemental form of communication to be enjoyed.

It was nearly ten o'clock by the time they finished and headed back to the motel. Nothing was said; it was simply understood that on this night Trey wouldn't be leaving Sloan at the door.

Trey followed her into the room and paused to shut it behind him, flipping the dead bolt into its locked position. When he turned away from it, Sloan was nowhere in sight. Three steps into the room, he spotted her perched on the edge of the bed by the nightstand, her back to him. He dropped his hat on the low bureau and turned toward her.

Curiosity made him ask, "What are you doing?"

"Setting the alarm." The task accomplished, she rose from bed, an easy smile curving her lips when she turned to him. "It's back to work for me tomorrow."

Some of his earlier resentment flared at the thought of the camera claiming her time the next day instead of him. "Haven't you taken enough pictures?" He managed to keep the challenge light, but just barely.

Her smile widened. "Don't you know that's one of a photographer's secrets to success? We play the numbers game. You take a couple hundred shots in hopes of getting one that's really good."

"That's the key, is it?" There was a touch of grimness around his mouth, but it faded as she wandered toward him while reaching behind her head to pull free the elastic band securing her braid. The action drew the dress's tan material across her breasts, outlining their perfectly round shape and drawing his attention to them. "What time are you planning to get up?"

"Six." She swept the loosened braid onto a shoulder and finger-combed her hair free of its plait.

"Why so early?" Displeasure put a hard edge on his voice, but Sloan didn't appear to notice it. "Nothing's going on at that hour. Competition doesn't resume until the afternoon."

"I know, but I want to get some early-morning shots when it's all deserted and it's only the horses in the pens. I have my fingers crossed that it will be chilly enough to see their breath." Her attention was turned inward, picturing the ideal shot in her mind. Belatedly she focused on him. "Actually, that was how I planned to spend my morning today, but somebody took me out for a picnic breakfast instead."

She halted in front of him, her head tipped up to meet his gaze. Her nearness unraveled all the little knots of anger, and his hands moved to settle on the points of her shoulders.

"Do you think that same guy could per-suade you to have breakfast with him in the morning?" Trey murmured.

" 'Fraid not." Sloan smiled in easy refusal. "But he is welcome to come along with me in the morning and act as a sort of helper."

It wasn't the sort of offer that appealed to Trey, considering he had already tagged behind her earlier in the day, and it wasn't an experience he cared to repeat.

As a result, he opted for a somewhat dry non-answer. "That's kind of you."

"I thought so."

Idly he fingered the wavy strands of hair that curled over one of her shoulders. "Your hair is still damp."

"I know. Maybe I should cut it short like yours," she suggested, strictly in jest.

"Don't. I like it this way." Even damp, he could feel the silken fineness of its texture as he brushed it off her shoulder, then left his hand along the side of her neck while his thumb traced its long curve. Desire stirred through him, hot and disturbing. "Do you have any idea how beautiful you are?" he asked in a voice that had grown husky with want.

There was a small, denying shake of her head. "I only know how beautiful I feel when you touch me." Reaching up, she curved a hand behind his head, applying pressure to draw it down.

The kiss was gentle and deep, more satisfying and seductive than hard passion. The wonder of it was in her blue eyes when she drew back from him. It made it easier for Trey to let her go.

"I'll only be a moment," she murmured, her voice just above a whisper, then she moved past him and slipped into the bathroom.

Trey stood there a minute, listening to the sound of water running in the sink.

Then his gaze slid to the king-sized bed that dominated the room. Something half the size would have suited him better to-night. This was one night when he wanted to know he wasn't sleeping alone.

Wasting no more time, he crossed to the head of the bed and peeled back the covers, exposing the bottom sheet. Then he stripped out of his clothes and laid them in a neat pile on the low bureau near his hat.

When Sloan came out of the bathroom, once again wrapped in the terry robe, all the lights were out except for the lamp on the bedstand. Trey was already in bed waiting for her, the top sheet drawn up around his middle, pillows propping him in a reclining position. She ran an openly admiring gaze over his naked torso and those broad pectoral muscles that formed his flat breasts. The ache was there to feel them under her hands.

With slow fingers, Sloan began unknotting the sash around her waist and walked to the bed and the empty space that he'd left on the outside, the sheet folded back in silent invitation.

"I didn't expect to see you there. I thought men preferred sleeping on the out-side." It was amazing how careless and carefree she felt with him. But the intimacy felt easy and natural.

"Not in this bed, I don't." His response was quick and definite.

"What's different about this bed?" she wondered.

"It's so big I could lose you in it. That isn't a risk I want to take." There was so much written in his eyes that she almost grew dizzy reading all the sensual messages.

A little breathless, Sloan turned and slipped out of the robe, letting it fall to the floor in a pile within easy reach of the bed. She sat down on the edge of it and leaned over to switch off the lamp.

The darkness was total and instant, freezing her in place if only momentarily. Yet before Sloan could swing her legs into bed, a large pair of hands slid onto her waist, simultaneously lifting, twisting, and drawing her onto him.

Her outstretched hands encountered the solid wall of his chest. His flesh was hard and vital beneath her hands, making her conscious of the raw energy rippling through his muscles. Then his mouth sought and found her lips, covering them in a hungry kiss, but not for long.

Abandoning her lips, his mouth took a

slow track to the curve of her neck and followed it to the hollow of her shoulder. The grip of his hands tightened, lifting her higher while his mouth continued its downward journey. One hand slipped forward to cup a breast and guide it to his mouth. Sharp pleasure spiraled through Sloan as his tongue and teeth licked and played with its rosy crest.

She curled her fingers into the springy thickness of his hair, cupping the back of his head and pressing him more tightly to her breast. Then he was moving, the moist inside of his mouth transferring its attention to her other breast.

Desire intensified, weakening her limbs. She tried to brace her knees against the mattress while leaning more of her weight on Trey. But that helped only for a short time; then she began sinking.

His arm steadied her a moment. Then he was rolling, flipping her onto her back. In the darkness, she felt the fan of his rough breathing before his mouth nuzzled her cheek. Then it lifted, and she sensed him looking at her.

"It's hell being apart from you," he muttered thickly, "even for a few minutes."

Her breath caught on the stark need in his voice. Then his mouth lowered onto hers and kissed her with drugging insistence. In the next moment, he was levering himself onto her. Sloan felt the stiffening muscle rising from his loins, hard and virile. She had an instant to marvel at the physical differences between a man and a woman — and how perfectly they fit together.

After that, there was no time for reasonable thought as she was caught up in a rush of sensation that engulfed them both. As in the previous times when they made love, she glimpsed this closeness, this raw demand, this wondrous urgency, without ever guessing it could always be that way.

Yet, there was no end to it. Because they could never get enough of it — just as they could never get enough of each other.

Chapter Seven

Early morning sunlight streamed through the motel room window, the heavy drapes being drawn back to let it fill the room. The long angle of its light reached all the way to the first double bed, the covers of which were undisturbed. Only the second bed had been slept in, and it had recently been vacated.

Laredo stood in front of the bathroom mirror, naked from the waist up save for a hand towel slung over his shoulder. Focusing his attention on the reflection in the mirror, he skewed his mouth to one side and watched while the razor stroked a path through the lather on his face.

Stroke after stroke, he scraped away his night's beard, pausing now and again to rinse the blade under the faucet, then returning to the task of exposing more of his face. The cheeks, the upper lip, the chin were shaved in order. He had only a few more strokes along his neck to finish when he heard a sharp, insistent rapping.

"Be right there!" he called and turned off the faucet. Using a corner of the towel, he wiped the stray bits of lather from his upper face and mouth as he exited the bathroom. Ignoring the door to the hallway, he walked to the connecting door to the adjoining bedroom.

A smile played across his mouth as he opened the door and leaned an arm against it while his gaze wandered warmly over Jessy's strongly attractive face.

"This is a welcome change," he declared. "It isn't often a beautiful woman pays me a visit so early in the morning."

She looked momentarily flustered and pleased by his remark. And he liked knowing that he could still unsettle that calm composure of hers even after all these years. He liked it even better when her glance darted past him into the room.

"Is Trey up already?" she asked.

"Couldn't say," Laredo said blandly.

Jessy gave him a puzzled, uncertain look. "What do you mean?"

"Just what I said. For all I know he could be awake, but not here." He swung the door open wider. "His bed hasn't been slept in."

"You mean — He never came back last night?" she said as her gaze made its own confirmation with a quick sweep of the un-rumpled bed.

Wise to the smallest nuance in her tone and expression, Laredo detected the note of concern. "I wouldn't worry too much about it," he told her. "If Trey's in any trouble at all, it's probably the female kind."

"The photographer he was with yesterday," Jessy guessed, an acceptance settling into her expression, the kind that came from being a woman in an essentially male world, with all its occasional crudities. If she personally found it offensive that a man took a woman purely for his own sexual gratification, she had learned to keep it to herself.

"That would be my guess," Laredo agreed. "Looks like you're ready to head out for breakfast."

"You're not." She touched a finger to the patch of lather on his neck.

"It'll only take me a couple minutes to finish up."

"In that case, I'll make a quick call to the ranch and see how things are there." Her glance again strayed to the unmade bed. "I imagine Trey will show up sometime — to shower and change clothes."

"He always does." Laredo's tone was dry with amusement.

A reluctant smile tugged at her mouth. "I sound like a mother, don't I?"

"I kind'a like it," Laredo said. "You don't often let yourself be female."

Rising on her toes, she pressed a warm kiss on his mouth, all tender and loving, then drew back before Laredo could turn it into something more. "Go finish shaving," she ordered. "I'm hungry."

Uncowboy-like, Trey put his hat on last and snugged it down, then cast a glance about the motel room. Sloan had rolled out of bed the minute the alarm went off and headed straight into the bathroom, emerging a few minutes later fully dressed. With a couple of pillows propping him up, Trey had watched while she knelt beside the camera case and loaded her vest pockets with film and gear.

"Aren't you coming?" she had asked, managing to spare him an over-the-shoulder glance.

"I'll catch up with you later in the morning," he told her rather than admit that pride wouldn't let him compete with a camera for her attention.

Satisfied that she had everything she might need, Sloan had crossed to the bed and leaned across to give him a warm, lingering kiss, then eluded his attempt to pull her onto the bed with him.

"I'd bring you some coffee, but I don't want to lose the light." Then she had gone, leaving him alone.

Trey wasn't really sure how long he had lain there before he finally got up. He only knew he wasn't in the best of moods, and he wasn't sure who or what to blame for that.

In a weary gesture, he rubbed a hand over his mouth and cheek and felt the scrape of his beard growth. A shower, shave, and change of clothes were in order. Then he could figure out the next step.

Though he was aware that time was passing, there was no hurry in his stride when he crossed to the door and opened it. As he stepped into the hall and paused to pull the door firmly shut, footsteps sounded behind him. Casting an idle glance in their direction, he saw a sleepy-eyed Kelly Ramsey. With her face strangely bare of all makeup and her blond hair straggling loose from her ponytail, it took a second for Trey to recognize her.

Kelly had no such difficulty as her expression took on a stricken look. "Trey." His name slipped out, and her hand lifted to smooth her hair. Her mouth twitched with a self-conscious smile. "I guess you can tell I just got up," she said, then went still for a split second before darting a sharp, quick look at the door to Sloan's room. A swirl of questions and suspicions was in her eyes when she shifted her gaze back to him. "Did you just get up, too?"

Her question was anything but innocent, and Trey knew it. "A little while ago," he replied and let her think what she liked.

"We missed you at the street dance last night. I guess you were otherwise occupied." Her smile was taunting.

He ignored her latter comment. "Had a good time last night, did you?"

"Of course."

"Glad to hear it." Trey nodded a little curtly. "See you around."

He struck out down the hall, his strides lengthening to put distance between them. He figured that Kelly knew it wasn't his room, considering that the range telegraph usually worked as well in town as it did on the ranch, and most Triple C ranch hands knew which rooms the Calders occupied.

His pace never slowed until he reached the room he shared with Laredo. He unlocked the door and walked in. Laredo stood near the foot of his bed, buckling his belt. Sharp blue eyes skimmed Trey. "I guess I don't have to ask where you were last night," he remarked idly.

"I guess you don't." A raw and restless energy carried Trey past Laredo.

"Did you take her to breakfast already?" Laredo eyed him curiously.

"No. She headed off to the arena first thing to get some early morning pictures." Trey swept off his hat and dropped it on the bed, then turned to the opened suitcase on the luggage rack.

"And you couldn't change her mind," Laredo guessed. "That explains why you're here earlier than I thought you'd be."

Trey tossed a clean pair of jeans on the bed, added a shirt, then paused in sudden decision. "I'm going to marry her."

A soft, barely audible whistle came from Laredo. "Does she know that?"

"Not yet." Trey rummaged around for a pair of socks and shorts.

After a short run of silence, Laredo asked, "Do you mind a piece of advice?"

It was rare that Laredo ever offered any, once claiming that Trey got enough of it from others and didn't need it from him. It was part of the reason Trey always felt easy in his company. It was like having an older brother or an uncle, someone who would listen without making judgments.

Still, Trey felt he should warn him. "You aren't going to talk me out of it."

"I wouldn't try," Laredo replied calmly. "But I would suggest that before you go rushing her off to the preacher, you take her to the Triple C. It's a big and empty stretch of land. Not at all the sort of place that appeals to women. Most have a hard time handling the loneliness and isolation of it. It seems to take a special breed of women to thrive on it."

"You're thinking of Laura," Trey said, remembering that his twin sister had grown up on the Triple C. It was her home and she loved it. But it also bored her.

"Actually, I was thinking of the stories I've heard about your father's marriage to Tara and how much she loathed living on the ranch. I got the impression life was pretty miserable for both of them. And you can be sure neither of them thought when they got married it would end in a divorce." After a small hesitation, Laredo moved his shoulders in a careless shrug. "Like I said, I'm not trying to talk you out of marrying your lady — just making sure you look at any problems square in the eye first."

"I will," Trey replied as a thread of unease ran through him.

★ ★ ★

A drifting of clouds marred the sharp blue of the midmorning sky while below a breeze rolled an empty paper cup across the infield. Most of its grass was flattened, trampled by the constant traffic of vehicles and pedestrians.

The high-pitched shouts and laughter of children at play caught Sloan's attention. Turning, she spotted a family next to a pickup camper. The parents, both in cowboy gear, were seated in lawn chairs, having coffee, while a pigtailed girl in a cowboy hat and boots chased her little brother, swinging a loop over her head with the clear intention of roping him.

Sloan snapped a picture of the action even though she knew it wasn't one she would ever use. Mostly she took it because it resembled nothing she had ever known.

Turning away from the scene, she snapped on the lens cap and switched off the camera. The sun was too far up in the sky to provide the kind of angled light she wanted, signaling an end to her morning's work.

It was moments like this, when she was at loose ends, with nothing to do and no particular place to go, that Sloan disliked the most. *Keep busy,* she thought. The phrase had become her mantra.

Not for the first time, she found herself wishing that Trey had come along this morning. The early quiet of the grounds, the sparkling dew on the grass, the whisper of the breeze in the trees — she would have liked to share it all with him. Yet there was always a chance that he wouldn't have been impressed by any of it and his lack of interest would have spoiled her own enjoyment. So she told herself that it was just as well he hadn't come with her.

Although Trey had said he would join her, she debated whether she should wait for him or head back to the motel on the off chance he might still be there. A second later the decision was taken out of her hands when she saw his tall, familiar shape coming toward her. Joy, all heady and light, swept through her with a kind of beauty that she had never experienced before.

"Perfect timing," Sloan called and quickened her own steps to shorten the distance between them. "I just finished up a few minutes ago."

Not a single word of greeting was offered. Trey let the moist heat of his kiss do all the talking, the driving insistence of it bending her backward over his circling arm. Her heartbeat lifted and quickened, stimulated by the earthy contact. Only the camera, hanging from the strap looped around her neck, kept her from being molded to his length.

Almost reluctantly he ended the kiss and lightly rubbed his mouth on her forehead, a disturbed heaviness to his breathing. "I never realized I could miss you so much in just a couple hours."

"I missed you, too," Sloan admitted, although until that moment she hadn't realized how true it was.

A horn honked somewhere nearby, and the sound acted as a reminder that they were in a public place. His encircling arms loosened their hold on her as he drew back, his hands settling on the points of her hips.

"Did you get the shots you wanted?" His velvety dark gaze made a slow journey over her face.

For a moment Sloan couldn't think what he was talking about. Then she remembered. "Maybe. Although I didn't have the conditions I hoped I might."

"I guess Mother Nature doesn't always cooperate." His mouth curved in understanding.

Her soft, answering laugh was dry with resignation. "Rarely. But that's what makes it so challenging and rewarding."

"I'll have to take your word for it." His smile became more pronounced; his gaze never left her face. She felt absorbed by it, as if nothing and no one else existed. It made her feel incredibly unique and special.

He tipped his head to one side. "So what's next on your agenda?"

"Nothing, really."

"Good, because there's something I want to talk to you about," he stated, something serious creeping into his tone.

"What's that?" She tensed up a little, not at all sure what to anticipate.

"When are you scheduled to fly out of here?"

"I have an early morning flight. Eight or nine, I think. I'd have to check my reservations."

"Is it mandatory that you have to leave tomorrow? Could you push your departure back a few days?"

"I don't suppose a day or two delay would mess up my schedule very much. Why?"

"It just seemed to me that since you were this close, it would be a shame not to spend a few days at the Triple C." He seemed to choose his words carefully, giving them a casual sound, yet there was an intensity to his gaze that was far from casual. "I'll be driving back right after everything winds down here. You can ride with me."

Her first impulse was to agree, but her practical side surfaced. "What about my rental car?"

"We can turn it in now, then swing by the motel so you can pack and check out, and still make it back here in time for the first events."

"I suppose we could," Sloan murmured while making her own mental calculations.

Trey misread her hesitation. "Look," he began, a gravity in his features and a stark need in his eyes. "It feels like I've been waiting for you my whole life. I'm not going to let you get away from me now."

"I want this to be real, too — something that can last," she admitted. "But nothing ever has for me."

"That's because it was never right until now." The shine in his eyes and the certainty in his expression were dazzling.

"I want to believe that, Trey." But experience made her wary.

"Believe it," he stated with a warm firmness and cupped a hand under her chin, framing and tilting it up.

A deep tenderness ran through his kiss,

creating an intimacy beyond mere passion. Life, in all its vitality, seemed to fill her with its heady glow. He was solid and strong. The smell, feel, and touch of him livened all her senses.

They were slow to separate. A breath feathered from her that was not a sigh but a reaction to the glory she had glimpsed.

"You still haven't given me an answer." Trey stood close, close enough that her body tingled with its awareness of him. "Are we going to turn your car in?"

"We are." The decision made, Sloan was determined not to look back.

"Then let's get it done." Trey wasn't about to give her any chance to change her mind.

Roughly an hour later Trey loaded her bags in the pickup and headed back into the motel. Sloan turned away from the registration desk, creasing the receipt in precise folds, when he entered the lobby. But the sound of a familiar voice coming from the hall drew his attention away from Sloan's approach.

"All set," she told him and slipped the receipt into one of the vest's pockets.

"Just a minute." He lightly took her arm and turned her back toward the desk.

"There's someone I want you to meet."

He felt the touch of her curious glance, but his own gaze focused on the hall entrance as his mother walked into view, followed by Laredo.

"It'll be good to get home," Jessy said to Laredo, then noticed Trey in the lobby. The beaming look on his face and the proprietary way he tucked a hand under the arm of the woman beside him immediately shifted her attention to the brunette.

Tawny streaks lightened the dark color of her hair. She was slimly built and tall — almost as tall as Jessy herself. The clean line of her features and the flawless quality of her skin gave her an impression of beauty, but it wasn't the breathtaking kind that so often blinded men. Jessy took some comfort from that.

Automatically she altered her course away from the desk to approach her son. "I was about to check out. Did you drop off your room key?"

"I took care of that earlier," Trey confirmed, then turned a soft, warm glance on the woman beside him. "Mom, I'd like you to meet Sloan Davis. I invited her to spend a few days at the ranch with us. Sloan, this is my mother, Jessy Calder. And that's Laredo Smith behind her."

"It's a pleasure to meet you, Mrs. Calder." Sloan was quick to extend a hand in greeting, yet there was just a trace of self-consciousness in her demeanor that betrayed an otherwise undetectable vulnerability. "I hope it won't be too inconvenient for me to come on short notice."

"Not at all. Company is always welcome on the Triple C — on short notice or no notice at all. Trey knows that." She spoke the absolute truth. "And please call me Jessy. Everyone does."

"Thank you."

Laredo stepped forward, touching his hat in greeting. "It's good to meet you at last, Ms. Davis. I guess you know Trey hasn't had anything else on his mind since he met you."

The man's wide smile made it impossible for Sloan to take any offense at his comment, yet the reference to her relationship with Trey made her a little uncomfortable, mostly because she wasn't used to total strangers making personal remarks.

Trey, on the other hand, was completely unfazed by it as he curved his arm around her shoulders and smiled down at her. "I know a good thing when I see it."

"I'll take that as a compliment," Sloan

replied and exchanged a quick glance with Trey.

"You should," Laredo replied. "I meant it as one."

"Thank you."

"I'll call Cat and make sure she has a guest room ready when you arrive," Jessy said to Trey, then clarified, "You are driving back tonight, aren't you?"

He nodded. "As soon as the last rider touches the ground."

"Laredo and I will be leaving before that," she told him and smiled at Sloan. "I'll see you later tonight at The Homestead."

"I'm looking forward to it," Sloan echoed.

Trey touched her arm. "We'd better go if you want to grab something to eat before the action starts."

"Of course." Sloan let Trey draw her away.

"Be careful on the road," his mother offered in parting.

"Always," Trey responded with his usual answer to the admonishment.

It wasn't until they were outside in the pickup that Sloan's curiosity got the better of her. "What did your mother mean when she said she would see us later at The Homestead? I thought the ranch was called the Triple C. Or is The Homestead just your name for it?"

"It's the name for the house where we live." Trey turned the ignition key and started the engine. "It was built on the site of my great-great-grandfather's original homestead claim, and it's gone by that name ever since."

"Really?"

"You sound surprised."

"I suppose I am," Sloan admitted. "I guess I never thought of ranchers as homesteaders. And I certainly would never have suspected that the Triple C Ranch started as a one-hundred-and-sixty-acre claim."

"The ranch has a long history behind it. You'll have to get Gramps to tell you about it. He knows all the old stories." Trey pulled out of the motel parking lot. "Did you want to go to a restaurant or grab something to eat at the fairgrounds?"

"The fairgrounds," she answered without hesitation and absently touched the camera that hung from her neck.

He saw the movement in his side vision and knew without being told that she wanted to be on hand when the first chute opened so she and her camera could capture the action. It was a pairing that always left him the odd man out.

It was her work. A dozen times that afternoon Trey told himself that he respected that. The pride she took in it and the satisfaction she got from it were obvious. But that didn't make it any easier for Trey to stand on the sidelines and watch while she moved from one vantage point to another, always intent on getting the next shot.

Horse after horse went out of the chutes, some bucking respectably, a few bolting into a dead run, others crow-hopping half-heartedly, and a small number successful in dumping their riders. None of it held Trey's attention.

Impatient and restless, he gravitated to the alleyway behind the chutes. He spotted Tank standing off to one side, buckling on his chaps. Johnny was there as well, an Ace wrap girdling his right knee.

Joining them, Trey nodded at the wrapped knee. "What happened to you?"

"Caught it on the chute when I went out on that last damned horse," Johnny muttered. "Twisted the hell out of it."

Tank grinned. "He's worried about losing the ride money if his knee isn't strong enough to make his last horse. 'Course, I said I'd take his ride for him."

"And the money for it, too," Johnny added sourly.

"You aren't going to let a sprained knee keep you from riding, are you, Johnny?" Trey taunted, the bite in his voice coming from his pent-up frustrations.

"Damned right I'm not," he retorted. "And you can put money on that."

"I wouldn't get any takers," Trey replied, already losing interest in the exchange.

"Where you been keeping yourself, Trey? It's the first time I've seen you around the chutes all afternoon," Tank remarked.

"That's a danged fool question to ask." Johnny snorted in disgust.

"Why?" Tank gave him an innocent look, then glanced at Trey. "You're still trailing after that Hawaiian girl, are you? I thought you'd already scored with her last night?"

Mouth thinning, Trey made an educated guess as to the source of Tank's information. He could too easily imagine the kind of talk Kelly had spread after seeing him come out of Sloan's room this morning.

"Lay off, Tank." His voice was low with warning.

But it was a cowboy's nature to keep poking when he found a sensitive spot. And Johnny and Tank were both dyed-in-the-wool cowboys.

"Did she teach you the hula?" Johnny asked with an almost gleeful grin.

Tank snickered. "If she did, I bet her hips were doing the talking, not her hands."

Anger that had simmered below the surface exploded with a rush. Trey whirled on Tank, lashing out with a fist that Tank didn't quite manage to duck. It clipped his jaw and propelled him sideways into a pen.

Johnny limped to his assistance. "What the hell's the matter with you, Trey? He was just giving you a hard time. He didn't mean any harm."

"Just keep your mouth off of her." The harshness of his temper still vibrated in his voice.

"You could've said so." Tank held on to his jaw and worked it from side to side.

"I did, but you didn't listen." Already regretting his loss of temper, Trey offered his hand in apology. "Sorry. No hard feelings."

After a slight hesitation, Tank took hold of it. "That was a helluva quick way to get a man's attention."

"It was," Trey admitted, then added. "You might as well know that she's coming back to the ranch with me for a few days. The Crawfords said you could ride with them."

Johnny gave him a surprised look, eyebrows raised. "So that's the way the rope flies."

"That's the way of it." The steady regard of his gaze never wavered. Johnny was the first to look away, with a slight downward tuck of his chin.

"Hell, we didn't know, Trey," Tank began. "I mean, a girl from Hawaii —"

Johnny cut in, "You talk too much, Tank. Why don't you shut up and think about that horse you've got comin' up."

"Guess you're right," Tank murmured, throwing another glance at Trey before the two of them moved off toward the chutes.

Trey didn't follow. Instead he located Sloan atop one of the chutes trying to get a picture of the activity in the next one.

He didn't have to be told that talk would fly now. By the time they arrived at the ranch, news of Sloan would have flashed to its farthest corners — and likely beyond. In some ways, that suited Trey just fine since it would eliminate the need to explain who she was and why she was there. Everyone would know he had staked claim to her.

Chapter Eight

The setting sun slipped below the western horizon, leaving the sky awash with swirling streamers of crimson and salmon. Its colors tinted the wide-open plains while evening shadows crept into the hollows, accenting their rolling pitch.

Reaching forward, Trey flipped on the pickup's headlights, throwing new illumination on the two-lane highway that tracked across the emptiness. The road looked deserted except for a pair of red taillights far ahead of him. Now and again, he caught the reflection of headlights in the rearview mirror, but that had been the extent of the traffic so far.

Sloan sat next to him, their hips and legs touching, her shoulder tucked against his side. The contact made him aware of her every movement. As a consequence, his glance slid to her when she shifted forward to peer around him at the western sky.

"What a gorgeous sunset," she murmured. "Just look at all that color."

"It's caused from too much dust in the air. We haven't had the kind of spring rains we needed, so it's dry everywhere around here." In the fading twilight, he spotted a cross fence a few hundred yards ahead and pointed to it. "That's the Triple C's south-boundary fence coming up."

"Already?" she said in surprise.

Trey chuckled at her anticipation of their imminent arrival. "Don't get excited. We've still got a long ways to go yet. It's another fifty miles to the east gate, and forty miles after that to The Homestead."

"That far!" she marveled and settled back in the seat, automatically nestling against him. "I've always heard the Triple C was a big ranch. That's a hard concept to grasp, but I'm beginning to."

"Gramps would tell you it takes a big chunk of land to fit under a Calder sky." Trey smiled, remembering all the times he'd heard the comment.

Sloan made a sidelong study of his profile. Its ruggedness was purely masculine and roughly handsome. "Tell me about the people I'll meet when we get to The Homestead."

"Let's see," he said, gathering his thoughts. "You've already met my mother. She'll be there, of course. She runs the ranch now that Gramps has stepped down. And I've already told you about Gramps. You'll like him. The ones who don't are those who've had the misfortune of tangling with him."

"Your mother mentioned someone named Cat," Sloan prompted.

"That's my aunt, Cathleen Calder Echohawk, but everyone calls her Cat. She moved back to The Homestead this past winter when Gramps had pneumonia, and she's stayed on to look after him."

"Isn't she married?"

"Widowed." His expression sobered. "Logan was the local sheriff. He was killed last year."

"I'm sorry," she murmured, sensing from Trey's tone that his death had been a shock.

"Logan was one of a kind — sheriff, ex-Treasury agent, and a rancher. He had a small spread on the Triple C's north boundary."

"Did they have any children?"

The corners of his mouth lifted. "A son. Quint is five years older than I am. Growing up, I wanted to do everything he did, go everywhere he went. We've always been as close as brothers."

"Does he work at the Triple C, too?"

"He runs our operation down in Texas." He slanted her a twinkling look, his smile deepening. "He just got married this spring, which means there have been two weddings at The Homestead in the last year."

"Who was the first?" Sloan asked, slowly acquiring a picture of his life and the people in it.

"My sister, Laura."

"Will I meet her tonight?"

"No, she lives in England." He paused a moment, then concluded, "That's just about everybody, except for Rachel Niles. She's married to one of my mom's brothers and gives Aunt Cat a hand with the cooking and housework."

An indigo color bathed the sky ahead of him, darkening it with the beginning of night's mystery. "It's your turn now. Other than you were born in Louisiana and lost both of your parents, you've hardly talked about yourself."

"You left out that I'm a photographer and I live in Hawaii," she teased lightly.

"Besides that," he said in a chiding tone.

"Believe it or not, that just about sums it up."

He responded with a doubting shake of his head. "I don't buy it. Come on. Where did you grow up? How old were you when you lost your parents?"

A tension ran through her, born of a reluctance to talk about her childhood. Yet she sensed Trey would insist on getting answers.

"Six."

An instant of stillness followed her response. "You were six years old, or you lost them six years ago?"

"I was six years old." Stiff with pride, she stared straight ahead, avoiding the sharp, stunned look he gave her. "But don't worry. I wasn't shuttled off to a bunch of foster homes or anything like that. As their sole beneficiary, I ended up with a very sizable trust that more than took care of my every need. I was old enough to go to a boarding school and summer camps. Actually, I preferred it, because nobody else had parents there, either — except sometimes on the weekends."

"What about the holidays?" The question was quietly worded, without any demand in it.

Darkness invaded the pickup's cab, and Sloan welcomed its cover even though her expression never lost its dispassionate quality. "Those first years I usually spent with my father's business partner and his family. He was the administrator of my trust, and his wife had always wanted a little girl. But after Aunt Barbara died — she wasn't any relation to me; I just called her that. Anyway, after she died, I didn't go there much. Sometimes I'd stay at a friend's house or with one of the teachers." She paused a beat. "That's the whole story. And it wasn't nearly as bad as it sounds. In fact, I've had a very good life, regardless of how it looks to anyone else."

"Life knocks all of us in the teeth, sometimes more than once." His voice had a smile in it. "My grandfather always says that the strong ones get up afterwards, and the weak lie there and whine."

Sloan looked at him in amazement. In the past, people had responded to her story with either clucks of sympathy or encouraging platitudes. But never admiration and approval.

"Thank you," she said in utter sincerity.

"For what?" His head turned, the dashboard lights playing over his questioning look.

"Understanding."

"You mean, that life can be rough at times, and all you can do is ride it out?"

Sloan laughed softly. "Is that more of

your grandfather's cowboy philosophy?"

"Probably."

"I'm definitely going to like him." She rested her head on his shoulder, using it as a pillow.

"I know you will."

Silence settled between them, the companionable kind that felt no need for words. Just being together was enough. Sloan couldn't recall ever being that comfortable with anyone before.

Night was on the land when they turned into the ranch's east entrance. Other than the twinkling of a few stars, the pickup's twin beams were the only light to be seen, and they were trained on the straight road before them, giving Sloan few glimpses of the terrain that flanked it.

She wasn't sure when she noticed a faint lightening of the horizon directly in front of them. As the miles went by, the impression of light grew stronger. It reminded Sloan of a city-glow visible at a distance.

Finally she gave in to her curiosity. "It looks like lights up ahead, but I know we aren't coming to any town. What is it?"

"Triple C headquarters." An amused smile tugged at his mouth. "Just about everybody who comes here the first time makes some remark about it resembling a small town. In a way, I guess it is. We have our own commissary that doubles as a kind of general store, complete with movie rentals, a gas station, first-aid dispensary, and a central mail area. We even have our own fire station. When you add to that the usual assortment of ranch buildings, housing for the hired men and their families, a cook shack, and a bunkhouse, it is just about the equivalent of a small town. But it's all there out of necessity. Blue Moon is the closest thing that passes for a town, and it's roughly fifty miles away. It's not a drive you want to make every day, so we try to be as self-sufficient as we can."

"You don't have any other choice," she said in realization. This new grasp of the ranch's isolation raised more questions about such things as education, utilities, and maintenance, and Trey patiently answered all of them, explaining that most families home-schooled their young children, identifying the tradesmen they kept on staff, and telling her about the wells and disposal systems in use. None of which were things she would have normally associated with a cattle ranch, but they spoke to the size and scale of the Triple C.

As the lights ahead grew brighter, Sloan sat forward, eager for her first sight of the ranch's headquarters. But the moment it came into view, her eyes were drawn to the towering white house that stood apart from the rest of the buildings. Lights blazed from the porch that ran the length of it, illuminating the series of massive columns that marched across its front.

"Is that what you call The Homestead?" she asked Trey.

"It is." He pointed the pickup at it.

"The name's a misnomer," she declared.

He flashed her a grin. "Expecting something a bit more rustic, were you?"

"To be honest, yes. I thought it would be something big and sprawling — an over-sized ranch house. I certainly never expected to see something that resembles a southern plantation here in Montana."

"Don't forget, the Calders originally came from Texas." Trey parked the truck near the wide sweep of steps leading to the porch and switched off the engine. "There were plenty of cotton kings there in its early days."

"True," Sloan admitted and climbed down from the cab.

By the time she walked around to the driver's side, Trey had retrieved their luggage. Automatically Sloan took charge of the oversized leather case with her camera and gear.

"I've got the rest of it." He motioned for her to precede him. As she started up the steps, she noticed a pair of old-fashioned wooden rockers off to her left. Seeing her interest in them, Trey explained, "Gramps likes to sit out here on warm days."

Before Sloan could respond, the front door opened and a petite woman stood on the threshold, the porch light shining on her midnight-dark hair, styled in a youthful short cut.

"You must be Sloan. We've been expecting you." Her smile was warm with welcome as she thrust out a hand in greeting. "Welcome to the Triple C. I'm Trey's Aunt Cat."

"Yes. He told me all about you." But Sloan thought Trey had failed to mention what a vibrant and beautiful woman she was.

Amusement sparkled in the woman's green eyes. "But not that I favor my mother in looks instead of the Calders, right?" she guessed.

Sloan laughed softly in admission. "He did leave out that detail."

"Calder men don't think of such things,"

Cat replied as if in friendly warning. "Come in."

When the older woman stepped back, Sloan walked through the doorway, followed by Trey. The wide entryway opened to a sprawling living room with a hall leading off it.

"Is Gramps still up?" Trey asked as his aunt closed the door behind him.

"He's in the den with your mother, going over ranch business. They shouldn't be much longer." Cat's voice betrayed the faintest trace of exasperation. "I'll hurry them along and let them know you're here. In the meantime why don't you take Sloan to her room so she can have a chance to freshen up after that long drive. I thought she could have Laura's."

"It's this way," Trey said to Sloan, nodding in the direction of the big oak staircase that emptied into the living room.

Sloan looked about with interest as she crossed to the stairs. The living room had a masculine sparseness about it, with heavy old furniture and lots of leather — missing were the usual decorator's touches. The sturdy pieces of furniture showed their age, just as the blackened rock around the fireplace's maw did, yet everything had a comfortable lived-in quality that appealed to her, mostly by its lack of pretension.

"Tired?" Trey asked when they started up the stairs.

"Not really," she denied with a dismissing shake of her head, then raised a curious face to him. "Why?"

"I just wondered. You haven't said much." A rueful smile immediately quirked his mouth. "Although I admit, Aunt Cat never gives anybody much of a chance to get a word in."

"When you told me about her, I think I imagined someone quiet and matronly," Sloan admitted.

"That's definitely not my aunt."

"She mentioned that she takes after your grandmother."

"When you put photographs of them side by side, it's hard to tell they are two different women. Sometimes Gramps even slips and calls her Maggie." He pointed to a door near the top of the steps. "Your room is right there."

A lamp on the bedside table was already on when Sloan opened the door. She took note of the shiny satin spread on the bed, the plushly cushioned armchair in the corner, and the door to an adjoining bathroom, then turned, watching as Trey set her black carry-on bag on the floor and straightened to face her. Suddenly she was acutely aware of everything about him. The room that had seemed so big and spacious now felt small.

"I never asked which room was yours." She recalled the number of doors that opened into the second-floor corridor.

"Down the hall — unfortunately." His big hands cupped her shoulders. "Right now I'm wishing that we'd stayed at the hotel tonight."

The note of longing in his voice kindled her own. "I guess we should have thought of this before."

"Actually, I did, but I didn't want to run the risk that you might change your mind about coming to the ranch."

Smiling, Sloan swayed into him, her hand sliding onto the muscled wall of his stomach. "Now I'm here — with no way to leave."

"That was the general idea." The line of his mouth softened, and his eyes crinkled at the corners, their dark gleam holding no trace of remorse.

"That's called kidnapping," Sloan declared in mock reproval.

"No." He shook his head, his smile fading as his gaze darkened on her with need. "It's called love."

To prove it, his head dipped toward her, his mouth settling on her lips, kissing them with a building hunger. Before he could give in to the urges pushing him, he pulled away, drawing in a long, steadying breath.

"You're addictive," he murmured and stepped back, breaking contact. "I'll be downstairs. You can join me whenever you're ready."

"I won't be long," she told him.

Exiting the room, Trey headed for the staircase and ran lightly down it. When he reached the bottom, he swung toward the den.

One of the double doors stood partially ajar. He gave it a push and walked through. His mother stood in front of the massive stone fireplace, one booted foot resting on its raised hearth.

As usual, his grandfather sat behind the long desk. His thick hair was shot with silver, and his craggy face looked as creased and weathered as the old hand-drawn map on the wall behind him. Chase Calder had once been a tall, robust man with a muscular physique that rivaled Trey's, but age had shrunk him, making his clothes hang loose on him.

Yet his mind was still as sharp as the dark eyes he turned on Trey. A smile softened his hard, bony features. He rocked forward in the big leather chair, dislodging the walking cane hooked on its armrest and sending it clattering to the floor. The cane offered mute evidence that he wasn't as steady on his feet as he once had been.

"Cat said you were back." His voice still possessed that familiar rumbling strength. "Where are you hiding that young lady I understand you brought with you?"

"Upstairs freshening up. She'll be down shortly." Automatically Trey walked around the desk and retrieved the cane, returning it to its hook over the armrest.

Thick, heavy brows came together, hooding his grandfather's dark eyes as his gaze narrowed on Trey. "What'd you do to your head?"

Trey touched the bandage on his forehead. He had forgotten it was there. "I got kicked by a bronc." He hooked a leg over a corner of the desk and rested a hip on it to face his grandfather. "So, how'd things go while we were gone?"

"No problems. But I didn't expect there would be." With barely a pause, he added, "Quint called earlier today and said to tell you hello."

"Sorry I missed his call," Trey said with

true regret. "How are things going at the Cee Bar?"

"Other than some minor storm damage, everything is going well."

Trey nodded. "That's good. For a minute I thought Rutledge might be giving him problems again."

"Rutledge isn't going to cause Quint any trouble."

His grandfather's flat statement should have reassured Trey, but he caught the emphasis that had been placed on his cousin's name.

"So you don't think Rutledge will try to get his hands on the Cee Bar. Then why worry about the man at all?" Trey frowned his confusion.

"He doesn't care about the Cee Bar anymore. I'm convinced of that," Chase stated, a weariness stealing over his face. "If there's anything he wants, it's to get even for his son's death. To do that, he'll come after us."

Trey listened, as he always did to his grandfather, but this time the older man's reasoning struck him as faulty. "We aren't responsible for Boone's death. He came at Quint with a knife. It was self-defense — even the inquest ruled that."

"Don't count on Rutledge to look at it

that way," Chase warned. "Grief doesn't listen to reason. His only child is dead. That leaves Rutledge with his pride and his money."

"I can't imagine him coming after us." Trey shook his head in doubt. "Leastways, not here in Montana. I know he swings a wide loop in Texas, but that won't count for much around here."

"Don't be too sure of that." There was patience in the steady regard of his grandfather's gaze. "There will always be someone around with nothing more against the Triple C than a resentment of its size. And Rutledge won't come at us in the open. That isn't his way. His tactics will be subtle — and as deadly as he can make them. I doubt he'll make a move any time soon, figuring that we'll forget about him if he waits." He pointed a gnarled finger in emphasis. "You remember that. And if anything starts to go wrong, look behind the source and make sure Rutledge isn't standing somewhere in the shadows."

Lately when his grandfather got on a topic, he tended to preach on it. Trey sensed a sermon coming and resisted the urge to sigh. It was with relief that his ears caught the tread of light footsteps on the stairs. "That sounds like Sloan." He swung to his feet and headed for the double doors. "I'll bring her in so you can meet her, Gramps."

As long, eager strides carried Trey from the room, Chase watched with a touch of envy, recalling the lost days when he had moved with the same ease. But he didn't choose to comment on that.

"That boy has the ears of a wolf. I didn't hear a thing." His attention swung to Jessy, probing in its study of her. "This is the first time Trey's ever brought a girl home, isn't it?"

"Yes," she confirmed, partially distracted by the mixed murmur of voices coming from the living room.

"What's your impression of the girl? You've met her?"

Her expression softened, a slight curve to her wide lips. "I don't think we have to worry. I didn't get any sense at all that she was like Tara."

"That's good." If Chase noticed the careful way she referred to her late husband's first marriage and avoided any direct mention of Ty himself, he never showed it. It was rare that he ever mentioned his son by name or voiced any of the grief that lingered even these many years since his death. Chase had been raised in the Western tradition that dictated such feelings were not for public display, but to be kept to oneself.

Catching the sound of two sets of footsteps approaching the den, Chase picked up his cane and levered himself out of the chair. Ignoring the protest of his arthritic joints, he hobbled around to the side of the desk just as the couple entered the den.

After the introductions were made, Chase listened with only half an ear while Jessy asked about the drive and whether the room was satisfactory. He was too busy observing the pair, especially the way Trey kept a possessive hand on the girl's waist, the special glow in his eyes, and the big smile he wore, the width of it rivaling the ranch boundaries. A reflection of it could be seen in the girl as well, but a bit reserved. Yet, that was to be expected given her situation of being thrust among strangers and new environs.

For a moment Chase envied the two of them for that exultant rush of young love with all its heady flavors and sweet sounds. He remembered the excitement of that feeling and the way his fancies had wanted to shout it to the stars.

Once all the usual pleasantries were exchanged, Sloan remarked on the wide sweep of horns mounted above the fire-place mantel. "Those almost make me think I'm in Texas."

"It's right that you should think that way," Chase told her, "considering they belonged to a true Texas longhorn — a big brindle steer called Captain. He led the first cattle drive my grandfather made, traveling from Texas all the way to the spot where I'm standing."

He went on to tell her about the subsequent drives that were made to stock the ever expanding ranch with cattle — with Captain leading the way in all of them. Then he directed her attention to the framed map on the wall, the one his grandfather had drawn, delineating the ranch's boundaries and the location of various landmarks, watercourses, and out-camps. The paper itself had long been yellowed with age, but the markings on it had been made by a strong, bold hand more than a century and a quarter ago; as a consequence, they were still clear and sharp.

Cat arrived with coffee and a platter of sandwiches. Everyone insisted they weren't hungry, but the sandwiches managed to disappear. The talk continued nonstop, most of it generated by Cat. Chase participated in less and less of it as a weariness settled over him. He caught himself nodding off and darted a quick look around to see if anyone else had noticed. Giving in to the tiredness, he reached for his cane.

Cat's sharp eyes observed the action. "Going to call it a night, Dad?"

"You young people have a lot more energy and stamina than I have," Chase said by way of an answer. "But when you get to be my age, you'll need your rest, too."

Amidst the chorus of "good nights" that followed his announcement, Cat rose from her chair, gathering up the empty coffee pot. "I'll walk out with you. I need to refill the pot anyway."

Chase grunted a response to that and waited until they were outside the den before he spoke. "I can get my own self into bed, so don't be thinking I'll need your help."

"The thought never crossed my mind," Cat denied, but he didn't believe a word of it. "She seems like a nice girl, doesn't she?"

"Who?" Out of orneriness, Chase pretended he didn't know who his daughter was talking about.

"Sloan, of course. As if you didn't know." She threw him a chiding look, then looked toward the den. "I do hope she's as bright and level-headed as she seems. It's so obvious Trey is head-over-heels in love with her."

On that score, Chase couldn't disagree.

Chapter Nine

The following morning, right after breakfast, Trey took Sloan on a shopping trip to the commissary and outfitted her in appropriate ranch attire, from the straw Resistol hat on her head to the tough Justin boots on her feet. In the days that followed, she had plenty of occasions to wear them as she accompanied Trey just about everywhere he went, lending a hand to whatever task he was about. What she lacked in skill, she made up for with effort.

On a ranch the size of the Triple C, Sloan soon learned that the work was never-ending. There were colts to be halter-broken, fences to be mended, stalls to be cleaned, daily chores to be done, cattle to be checked, parts to be delivered, sick or injured animals to be doctored, water supplies and range conditions to be monitored — all of which was just a small sampling.

Twice she rode along with Trey when he drove to one of the half-dozen outlying camps that formed a circle around the ranch headquarters, dividing its vastness into manageable districts. The trips gave Sloan a glimpse of the private road system that linked all the various parts of the ranch.

Always there was the land, stretching from horizon to horizon. The dominating expanse of sky overhead gave it a flat look, but it was riddled with benchlands and breaks, cut-banks and coulees, as Sloan discovered when she rode over it with Trey.

And Trey seemed to know every inch of it and the things that lived on or under it. When Sloan made some passing comment about the curly, matted grass beneath their horses' hooves, Trey identified it as buffalo grass. Like the taller blue joint, it was native to the area and more nutritious for the animals than any other kind of grass. Renowned for its hardiness, it was resistant to heat and drought. There was no brag in his voice when he explained that the grass was the source of the ranch's wealth; it was a simple statement of fact.

Except for the huge irrigated hayfields along its south boundary, most of the land within the Triple C fences had never been touched by a plow. It was much the way it had been when the first Calder rode over it.

Day's end always brought them back to The Homestead, where the family gathered for the nightly meal. The dinner conversation invariably centered on ranch business, though Sloan was never made to feel left out. Afterward nearly everyone lent a hand clearing the table, but Cat always shooed Sloan out of the kitchen, refusing any further help and insisting she go off somewhere with Trey.

Sometimes they cuddled on the couch to watch a movie or went for a long walk. One night they made love on a blanket beneath a cottonwood tree with only the stars to witness their union. Another evening, Cat dragged out the family album with its pages of photographs and regaled Sloan with stories of the rowdy and rambunctious boy Trey had been.

For a while, time seemed to stand still. Then, suddenly, there was little of it left. As they made the long walk from the old barn to the front steps of The Homestead, the knowledge rested heavily on Trey that this time tomorrow Sloan would be on a plane flying to Hawaii. Tension coiled through him.

Beside him, Sloan swept off her hat and

shook her hair free of its confining band. "What a day," she said with a sigh. "I was beginning to think you were never going to get that calf out of the mud. It was lucky you heard that cow bellowing. The calf might have died if you hadn't found him. But," she added, "I guess that's why you make regular checks of the pasture." She flashed him a smile.

"Yup." The one-word answer was all he could manage. Too many important things needed to be said for more time to be wasted on small talk. "Are you glad you came? You never have said."

"Are you kidding? I wouldn't have missed it." Sloan was emphatic about that.

Still not satisfied, Trey asked, "Then you weren't bored?"

Laughter came from low in her throat. "When did I have time to be bored?"

"Not much, I guess," he admitted. "Just the same, some people find all this open space a bit monotonous."

"I suppose," she agreed on a thoughtful note. Then her expression lifted and a soft marveling light entered her eyes. "But there's something about the lonely grandeur of this land that grips your heart."

A new ease flowed through him, unraveling the previous tension. There was a buoyancy to his stride as they reached the front steps. "I guess you'll be heading straight upstairs to take a shower before supper."

"A long, hot one," Sloan confirmed. "At least I'm not as stiff and sore as I was after the first time you took me riding."

He grinned. "We'll make a horsewoman out of you yet."

A teasing smile deepened the corners of her mouth. "Your grandfather warned me that this land has a tendency to make people dream big. He was right."

"Speaking of Gramps," he said, his thoughts already turning to look ahead as they climbed the steps in unison, "I need to talk to him before I clean up."

Just as he expected, he found Chase in the den, ensconced in the big leather chair behind the desk. Trey closed both double doors behind him, ensuring their privacy. The significance of his action wasn't lost on Chase.

He lifted his head, his eyes narrowing with sharpened interest. "This must be important."

"It is," Trey replied and then said his piece in plain words.

When he finished, Chase cocked his

head to one side. "Are you asking my opinion?"

"No sir."

Chase studied the quiet resolve etched in his grandson's expression and nodded. "That tells me you're sure of your decision."

"I've never been more sure of anything in my life." It was a simple statement, made with no attempt to impress Chase with its certainty. But then Trey hesitated, regret showing. "I know I'm asking a lot, but —"

Chase cut him off in mid-sentence. "It's yours."

"Thanks." Gratitude and affection mixed together in the look Trey gave his grandfather.

Knowing glances were exchanged when Trey suggested to Sloan that they go for a walk at supper's conclusion. Everyone knew it was Sloan's last night. It was understandable that the couple would want to spend it alone together.

Hands tucked in the pockets of his denim jacket, Trey stood at the top of the front steps, but he made no move to descend them. Sloan paused beside him, slipping a hand through the crook of his arm and drawing close. The gesture was a natural one that spoke of the ease she felt in his company. Like him, she faced the night scene before them.

A rising moon silvered the ranch yard with its light while overhead the black sky was alive with stars. Along the river, the trees made intricate dark shapes against the silvered grassland beyond them. A flurry of snorts and hoofbeats came from the corral by the barn. Then all was quiet again.

"It's a bit chilly tonight. I'm surprised we can't see our breath." Sloan blew one out in a testing fashion to see if she could.

"The wind's out of the north." But Trey was more conscious of the warmth of her body pressed along his side than with the coolness of the air.

"So," she said in a subtly prompting fashion, "are we going for that walk?"

"Not yet." His gaze shifted to her, his head turning slightly. He sensed that he would never tire of looking at this incredible woman with her sun-streaked hair and midnight blue eyes. In many ways, she was a contradiction — strong and self-contained, yet vibrant and alive without artifice.

"That's fine with me." Supreme contentment was in her expression.

The moment of waiting was passed. Trey turned, angling his body toward her and touching the flawless skin on her cheek to draw the fullness of her attention. "There's something I want to ask you, Sloan," he said. "And 'no' isn't going to be an acceptable answer."

"Don't." There was a pained look in her eyes as she placed her fingers to his mouth. "As much as I don't want to, I have to leave tomorrow. I can't stay any longer. Try to understand that."

In answer, he caught hold of her hand and pressed a kiss in its palm, then lifted his head to claim her gaze. "I do understand, and that isn't what I was going to ask you."

"You weren't?" she said in surprise. "Then what?"

"Marry me." It was more of a statement than a question, yet Trey waited for her answer, watching the chase of emotions across her face — disbelief, delight, and, ultimately, doubt.

"It's so soon, Trey," she began.

"For you, maybe. But not for me. I want you to be my wife. A week from now, a month from now, a year from now isn't going to change that." With no hesitation, he reached into his jacket pocket and pulled out a diamond ring. "This belonged to my grandmother, Maggie O'Rourke Calder. I think it's right that my wife wear it."

The ring was a snug fit; he had to work a little to slip it on her finger. Not a sound came from Sloan the whole time. But the moonlight showed him the tears that shimmered in her eyes. Love was like a tight ache in his chest.

"Those better be happy tears." There was a huskiness in his voice that hadn't been there before as he experienced the first flicker of uncertainty about her answer.

With a sound that fell somewhere between a laugh and sob, she flung her slim arms around his neck. In the next breath, her lips were all over his, breathing their sweetness into his mouth while she murmured over and over again, "Yes, yes, yes."

He crushed her to him, driven by the need to bind her close and claim what she had given him. Blood hammered hot and fast through him. When he finally lifted his head, he was trembling with the powerful force of his feelings.

"I love you so damned much." There was a disturbed heaviness to his breathing and a thick-lidded passion in his dark eyes.

Sloan thrilled to both of them. "And I love you. I never thought I could feel this happy, but I do," she murmured, then mused idly, "Sloan Calder. I like the sound of that."

"So do I." He stole another kiss. "I hope you aren't planning on a long engagement."

"Until two minutes ago, an engagement wasn't anywhere in my plans." Her eyes sparkled as brightly as the diamond in her ring.

Trey studied her upturned face. "And now that it is?"

"No longer than necessary, I suppose," Sloan said with a vague shrug, then fired a sharp glance at him, a touch of worry showing. "The wedding. We don't have to have a big one, do we?"

"Not as far as I'm concerned." He bent his head and nibbled her neck, breathing in the fresh scent of her skin. "In fact," Trey murmured near her ear, "it's become something of a tradition that the ceremony takes place here at The Homestead in the den. It's where all the Calders have been married since the Triple C came into existence."

The single exception was his father's first marriage to Tara that eventually ended in divorce, but Trey didn't bother to mention that.

Sloan agreed readily. "It sounds simple, and that suits me just fine."

"Are you sure?" At the moment he would have roped the moon and hauled it out of the sky if that was what she wanted.

"Positive." She nodded once in emphasis. "After all, what would be the point of having a big, lavish affair? I don't have any family, and there is only a handful of friends that I would even invite." She paused, her gaze straying toward the house. "What will your family think when we tell them? We've barely known each other a week."

"Why don't we find out?" Trey suggested.

"Now?" Sloan questioned in surprise.

"Can you think of a better time?" Trey smiled in challenge and steered her toward the front door.

Nerves. Her stomach fluttered with them the instant she set foot inside the house. Until that moment Sloan hadn't realized how very much she wanted the approval and acceptance of Trey's family. Yet, even if they were withheld, she didn't regret the decision she had made.

The minute they walked into the living room where everyone had gathered, they were the center of attention. Laredo was the first to acknowledge their presence.

"That has to be the shortest walk on record," he remarked dryly.

Chase looked straight at Sloan's left hand, then lifted his gaze to Trey, a warm smile creasing his leathery face. "I see you talked her into it. Congratulations."

"What are you talking about, Dad?" Cat frowned. But Jessy didn't have to ask. She saw the proud, possessive way her son looked at the girl. An emotion as old as time made a brilliant light in his dark eyes. And she remembered when his father had once gazed at her in that same way.

"Sloan has agreed to marry me," Trey announced without taking his eyes off her.

Laredo rolled to his feet and thrust out his hand. "I can't say I'm surprised, considering you told me last Sunday you were going to marry her. Congratulations." He gripped Trey's hand in a firm shake and slapped him on the shoulder with the other, then shifted his attention to Sloan and winked. "I have the feeling he's the lucky one in this match."

His warm and ready approval had a steadying effect on Sloan. Although Laredo Smith claimed to be nothing more than an ordinary ranch hand, it was obvious to Sloan that the Calder family considered him to be much more than that. On various occasions, she'd sensed that there was no one the family trusted and respected more than this man.

"Thank you, but I'm the one who feels lucky," she told him, then noticed Trey's mother waiting to take his place.

As always, Jessy Calder conveyed a quiet strength and calm composure. The effect was softened now by the warm light in her eyes and the faint curve to her wide lips. Sloan searched, but she could detect no sign of falseness. Still the tension remained.

"Mrs. Calder," she murmured awkwardly, unconsciously reverting to a more formal address, mostly as a kind of self-defense, "I know this probably seems very sudden to you."

Jessy shook her head in silent denial. "Trey has always known exactly what he wanted ever since he was a little boy. I learned very quickly that he knew his own mind — and his own heart. Others have sometimes thought he acts rashly, but I've always known better. Welcome to the family, Sloan." She brushed a kiss on her cheek.

Sloan never had a chance to hear what

Jessy said to Trey as Cat came up and gave her a hug. "I'm so happy for you both," she declared with her usual exuberance. "Let me see your ring. What kind did he get you?" Obligingly, Sloan raised her hand to show Cat. "A solitaire. How perfect. It looks almost exactly like the one my mother wore."

"It is your mother's," Sloan admitted.

Surprise rounded her green eyes. "How — ? When — ?" Cat abandoned both questions and turned to look at Chase. "When did you give mother's ring to Trey?"

"Sometime before supper," he replied.

"You mean you knew Trey was going to propose to her tonight, and you never said a word to any of us about it?" Cat accused.

"That's right." He waved a finger in Sloan's direction. "I thought the young lady had the right to give him her answer before I said anything. It would please your mother to know another Calder bride is wearing it."

"You're right, of course." Cat sighed and smiled wryly at Sloan. "You'll discover for yourself that he usually is."

"You don't mind, then?" Sloan uneasily fingered the ring.

"Of course not," Cat assured her. "It was just the surprise of seeing it."

"This calls for a drink, doesn't it?" Chase challenged and waved to Laredo. "Roll that liquor cart in here so we can have a toast to this couple."

Drinks were poured, glasses were raised, and toasts were offered with the usual mix of teasing and laughter. But it wasn't long before Trey stole Sloan away again to go for that walk they'd never gotten around to taking.

After their departure, Chase called it a night and headed to his ground-floor bedroom in The Homestead's west wing. Laredo trailed after Jessy and Cat when they carried the drink glasses to the kitchen.

"Another wedding." Cat shook her head in amazement. "Do you realize that this will make three at The Homestead in less than a year? It has to be a record."

"At least you've had plenty of experience planning them." Laredo leaned sideways against the counter, watching the two women at the sink.

"That's true." Cat slipped the stopper in the drain and turned on the faucets while Jessy emptied the glasses of their ice and liquid in the companion sink. "I do hope some of Sloan's friends can come. She doesn't have any relatives. It would be awful for her if we were the only ones at the ceremony."

"I imagine that's why she wants to keep it small and simple," Jessy inserted.

"I suppose so." Cat then added thoughtfully, "She's a very private person, isn't she? I don't think I've ever met anyone who talked less about herself. Oh, she talks about her work and the places she's traveled, but little about her personal life."

"Maybe that's it," Laredo suggested.

"What is?" Cat frowned, not following his meaning.

"Work takes up the bulk of her life," he replied and slid a pointed look at Jessy. "Like someone else I know."

Grinning, Cat eyed her sister-in-law with amusement, but Jessy took no notice of either of them. "Do you get the feeling she's not listening to us?"

"I do." Laredo nodded, then reached out and gave Jessy a light poke in the arm. "Hey, where'd you go?"

"What?" She looked up with a slight start, before slipping the last dirty glass into the dishwater. "Sorry. I was thinking."

"We noticed," Laredo said in dry amusement. "Care to share it with us? You looked like you were miles away."

"I suppose I was, in a sense," Jessy admitted. "I was remembering Trey telling us about that calf that was stuck in the mud at the Broken Butte range. I thought I'd better head over there tomorrow and check it out for myself. If the water in the creek has gotten low enough to create mud bogs, we probably need to move those cattle to another range."

With eyebrows raised, Cat sighed and looked at Laredo. "Cattle. We should have known it had something to do with the ranch."

"Tell you what," Laredo straightened away from the counter and took Jessy's arm, drawing her away from the sink, "why don't you let Cat wash these few glasses and walk me to my pickup?"

"You don't have to leave right now, do you?" Jessy said in mild protest.

"It's a long drive to the Boar's Nest," he reminded her referring to the old line shack that he had converted to a snug cabin years ago.

"Go on, Jessy," Cat urged. "You two rarely have the chance to spend any time together. Don't waste it when you do."

Advice from a woman who had recently lost her own husband was too wise to ignore. Jessy smiled her thanks and walked with Laredo out the back door.

Night and its shadows enveloped them as they descended the steps, arms brushing. There was an invigorating coolness to the air that sharpened the senses. When Laredo hooked an arm around her shoulders at the bottom of the steps, Jessy automatically slid hers around the back of his waist.

"How does it feel knowing that soon both your children will be married?" His eyes were warm and curious in their study of her.

"It's the way of things." A small shrugging motion accompanied her statement. "Children grow up, get married, and make a life for themselves. I'm just glad Trey won't be moving away."

"Something tells me it won't be long before there'll be little ones running around here calling you Grandma." The chrome bumper on his truck gleamed silver in the moonlight.

"Probably." She smiled at the thought. "I think Sloan will make a good mother. She seems to be a caring person, intelligent and level-headed."

"Want'a bet Trey isn't counting up her good qualities? He probably couldn't even name them without giving it some thought first. He just knows he loves her. And when you get right down to it, that's all that matters."

"I know." Jessy noticed with regret that they had arrived at the pickup's door. "You know there's really no reason you have to live at the Boar's Nest. The Atkins' house has been sitting empty since Ruth died. You could move there."

"I suppose I could." Laredo made a lazy turn to face her, his arms forming a loose circle around her. "It's for sure it would be within walking distance of The Homestead. But there's too many neighbors living too close, whereas the Boar's Nest gives me privacy, and I like that, especially when a certain someone pays me a call," he added with a wink.

Tipping her head back, she laughed softly in her throat. "Everyone on this ranch knows we're seeing each other. They have for years."

"I don't care that they know. I just don't want their imagination working overtime just because they live next door. Me loving you might not be a secret, but I'm damned sure going to see that it stays private."

"You have a point there," Jessy conceded. "Right now they spend most of their time trying to figure out why you haven't made an honest woman out of me. I understand there's been some wild speculation about that."

"Let them wonder all they want — just as long as you don't." This time there was no smile, just an earnest need to know that she understood.

"I don't." Long ago Jessy had learned to embrace the good things life gave her and never cry because there wasn't more.

From the very beginning, she had known Laredo would never marry her. His reason lay somewhere in his past. What it was, she had never asked, although she suspected Chase knew, and possibly Cat's husband, Logan, had learned of it, too. Whatever it was, it hadn't mattered to them, and it didn't matter to her.

"So what are the chances of you spending Saturday night at my little hideaway in the hills?" Laredo wanted to know. "It would do you good to get away from the phones and the pressure, and just be a woman."

"Sounds good." But Jessy knew it would depend on whether she decided to move the cattle off the Broken Butte range. But she didn't say that. She was too busy enjoying the very thorough and satisfying kiss Laredo gave her with a promise of more to come.

Chapter Ten

Palm trees towered over the beach house, their fronds dipping and swaying with the strong breeze that came off the ocean. The taxi followed the curving driveway to the front door and stopped there. The driver, of Polynesian descent and dressed in a colorful Hawaiian shirt, immediately hopped out of the cab and opened the rear passenger door for Sloan.

Smiling her thanks, Sloan hooked the strap of the leather case over her shoulder and stepped out of the vehicle, too weary from the long flight and time change to notice the tropical warmth and the air's fresh tang. The strap slipped slightly when she stood up. As she reached to adjust it, the single-carat diamond on her ring finger flashed in the sunlight. There was a newness to the weight of it — and to the heady joy she felt. Some of the tiredness fell away at the remembrance of them.

The driver retrieved her bag from the trunk of the taxi and carried it to the front door. Sloan followed and handed him the fare along with a sizable tip.

"Mahalo," he said, using the Hawaiian word for thank you.

"Mahalo," Sloan echoed.

Stepping to the door, she took out her house key and inserted it in the lock. As she pushed the door open, she was greeted by the ring of the telephone. She ignored it long enough to set her bag inside and lock the door behind her, then hurried to pick up the living room extension.

Using both hands, she carried the receiver to her ear, the anticipation of hearing Trey's voice bringing a smile to her lips. "Hello."

But the male voice on the other end of the line didn't belong to Trey. "Sloan. This is a surprise. I expected to talk to that answering machine of yours."

The hint of a drawl mixed with the gruffness was instantly familiar to Sloan. "Uncle Max. You are lucky. I just this minute walked in."

"I figured it was something like that."

"What do you need?" Sloan asked, unable to remember a time when her former guardian had ever phoned merely to chat.

"It's time to update the proxy you gave me for your stock. A new form's in the mail. You just need to sign it and send it back, but remember to have a notary witness your signature. That's assuming, of course, that you still want me to vote your shares?"

"You know I do. I don't know why you bother to ask."

The stuffiness of a house that had been closed up for days made its impression on her. Taking the cordless phone with her, Sloan walked over to the double set of French doors that opened onto the lanai and cradled the phone against her neck while she unlocked them and swung them wide. A breeze swept in, bringing with it the soothing rush of the surf as it tumbled onto the rock-and-sand beach beyond the house.

"Did you send that regular mail?" she asked, but never gave him a chance to answer. "What am I saying? You always express everything you send me."

"You're damned right. I'm not about to risk it ending up on some freighter. For the life of me, I'll never understand why you didn't settle somewhere here in the States instead of out there in middle of the Pacific Ocean."

"I am living in the States, it just happens to be the state of Hawaii," she countered smoothly.

"You know damned well what I meant, but that's old ground," he said, dismissing the subject. "So, how soon are you leaving again?"

"Probably in a week or two. It depends on how long it takes me to wrap up a few things here." Sloan wandered onto the lanai and gazed at the blue ocean, amused to find it reminded her of the rolling grassland of the Triple C.

"Where are you off to this time?" he wondered.

"To the wilds of Montana." Absently, she rubbed her thumb over the underside of her diamond ring. "By the way, congratulations are in order, Uncle Max. I've gotten myself engaged."

"Since when?" came the quick demand.

"Since yesterday." She could almost see the scowl on his face.

"To whom? One of your photographer friends? Really, Sloan," he began, disapproval thick in his voice.

Sloan never gave him a chance to finish. "I'm going to marry Trey Calder. In fact, I just got back from spending a week at his family's ranch in Montana. So I don't think you have to worry that I picked someone who's only interested in getting his hands on my inheritance." For a long run of seconds there was dead silence on the other end of the line. "Uncle Max, are you still there?" Sloan frowned in uncertainty.

"I'm here — just speechless." There was a flatness to his tone, as if all emotion had been pressed out of it. "I guess I wasn't aware you even knew the Calders."

"I didn't. At least, not before this past weekend." Aware that nothing less than a full explanation would satisfy him, Sloan supplied the details. "I had to go to Miles City to photograph their rodeo for the Berringer book. That's where I met Trey. After that, it was one of those proverbial whirlwind courtships. And here I am, engaged to be married."

"You sound happy," he observed.

"I am." She was definite about that.

"Then I'm happy for you. Have you set a wedding date?"

"Not yet. It will be soon, though, probably the end of next month. But it won't be anything big and lavish, just a quiet ceremony there at the ranch with a few family and friends. Naturally you're invited."

"Unfortunately, I doubt that I can make it. I have a trip scheduled out of the country that I can't postpone, but I'll be there in spirit."

"I understand." Sloan was neither surprised nor disappointed. Since his wife Barbara had died, Max hadn't attended a single one of her functions. She hadn't expected her wedding to be an exception, yet courtesy dictated that she invite him.

"How much have you told him about yourself?"

She smiled in amusement. "You make it sound like there's something to tell."

"I was thinking in terms of your inheritance."

"There wasn't any reason to discuss it. I think I mentioned that a trust had been established after my parents died, but that was about it. We certainly never sat around comparing portfolios, if that's what you're wondering." Which, Sloan suspected, he was. With Max, everything was always about business and making money. Those were the only two subjects that interested him.

"I don't suppose you would," he admitted, but in a distracted way. "This probably isn't the time to bring this up, but in your father's stead, I feel duty bound to insist that there be a prenuptial agreement signed, one that would protect your separate properties. I'm sure the Calders would be in favor of that. I understand it's become very common these days to have one. After all, no one ever enters into a marriage thinking it will end in divorce, but statistics tell you otherwise. That's why it's important for you to make sure your inheritance never gets tied up in some bitter property dispute."

In her heart, Sloan resented the idea of a prenuptial agreement, but her mind argued that it was unquestionably the sensible thing to do. "Is that something Cal Hensley can handle?" she asked.

"If not, there'll be someone in his firm who can."

"I'll call him first thing in the morning," she promised.

"Do that. Because if you truly intend to get married within a month, this isn't something you want to leave to the last minute."

"I recognize that."

"But you don't like it. I can hear it in your voice. I suppose I sound like a heartless old bastard to you. Here you are all excited about getting married, and I'm talking about protecting your money. But your father left you a lot of it. You've always tried to ignore that, but the fact remains that you're a very wealthy woman in your own right."

"You never let me forget it, Uncle Max," Sloan replied without rancor. "And I promise I'll phone in the morning."

"You're telling me to shut up, aren't you?"

She laughed, low and throaty. "Yes."

"Let me just add that you've made a good match. Congratulations."

"Thanks."

"Just the same, I'll be calling you every week until I hear that you've got that prenup signed."

"I'll tell Cal to run it past you before he sends it to me."

"Good idea." With that, Max said his good-byes and hung up the phone.

Night's shadows pressed against the windows of the Slash R ranch house, turning their glass panes into mirrors that cast dark reflections of the room's Texas-chic furnishings. But Max took no notice of them, his back to the windows, his brow furrowed in hard thought.

He never glanced up when Harold Bennett, his valet and personal nurse, paused beside the desk and placed a glass of bourbon and water in front of him. "Did I hear correctly, sir?" Harold asked, as always careful to keep the appropriate degree of respect in his voice. "Is Sloan getting married?"

Hard eyes shot him a brief look. "She's engaged. It remains to be seen whether she actually marries."

The statement rang of portent, too much for Harold to ignore. Hesitating, he frowned in question. "Sir?"

For a moment he thought no explanation would be forthcoming as Max picked up the drink and swirled the ice in the glass. "She's engaged to Trey Calder. Ironic, isn't it?" His mouth twisted with black humor.

"Very," Harold said, too stunned to do anything but agree. "What are you going to do, sir?"

"Let things play themselves out, of course." Amusement gleamed coldly in his eyes. "See whether it becomes necessary to send an expensive wedding present."

"Of course," the valet murmured, confused by his employer's apparent acceptance of the idea.

"That'll be all for now, Bennett." Max dismissed him with a waving flick of his fingers. "I'll call you when I'm ready to retire."

Harold nodded an acknowledgment and withdrew from the room. But this was one time when he wished he could crawl into his employer's mind and see how that crafty intellect worked. He knew it would be a thing to behold.

Thunderheads made a dark blotch against the southern horizon. Observing them, Laredo noted that if anything, their line was narrowing. It was raining somewhere, though not on Calder land.

His attention shifted back to the short, thick branch in his hand, already partially stripped of its bark. With another stroke of the knife, Laredo sliced away more of it as he sat on the veranda's edge, his feet dangling over it and one shoulder negligently propped against a pillar.

When the front door opened, he glanced around, expecting to see Trey, but it was Chase who emerged from The Homestead, his cane thumping on the veranda's wooden deck. As usual, Cat was not far behind him, carrying a tray with two mugs and an insulated coffeepot on it.

Chase halted at the sight of Laredo. "What are you doing out here?"

"Waiting for Trey." Another stroke of the knife blade sent a sliver of bark and wood arcing to the ground.

"Where is he?" Chase directed the demand at Cat.

"In the den, talking to Sloan." She carried the tray to the wooden table that sat between the pair of tall ladder-backed rocking chairs.

"He's still on the phone with her?" Chase frowned. "It's been a good hour since she called. Don't those two know it's long-distance."

"They have a lot to talk about, Dad."

Chase harrumphed at that statement. "They should talk faster, then." He shuffled over to the nearest rocker, the cane striking the floor slightly ahead of him with each swing. The moment he settled himself into the rocker, Cat moved toward the door. "Where are you going? You said you were going to sit and have a cup of coffee with me."

"I'm coming back," she assured him. "I'm just going to get an extra cup for Laredo and get that list I was working on."

"What list?"

"The invitation list for Trey's wedding," Cat answered patiently. "He asked me to make one for him."

"Invitations? What do you need those for?" Chase demanded. "I thought they were having a small wedding, just family and some of her friends."

"The actual ceremony itself will be

small, but there will be a reception after-wards. Everyone on the ranch will expect to come. And there's all our friends and neighbors," she reasoned. "Wedding announcements have to be sent, or people will feel slighted."

"I'll tell you one thing, we never went to all this fuss and bother back in my day," Chase declared with a decisive nod of his head. "People got married and that was the end of it."

"That's not true, and you know it," Cat corrected him. "Weddings have always been social occasions — a time when family and friends gather to wish the new couple well. Heaven knows, we have few enough reasons for everyone to get together out here. And I can't think of a better excuse for a party than your grandson's wedding."

"She's got you there, Chase." Laredo grinned, then flicked a glance at the front door when it opened and Trey walked out. "You can forget about bringing me that cup, Cat. Looks like I won't be needing it." He snapped the jackknife closed and rolled to his feet.

"It's about time you got off the phone." Chase ran a critical eye over his tall grandson, quick to note the hint of gravity in his expression. "I'll never understand what you young people find to talk about. Or is she getting cold feet about the wedding?"

"No, it's nothing like that," Trey easily dismissed the suggestion, a quick smile lifting the corners of his mouth, but that sober light never left his eyes. "We just had some things to discuss, that's all."

"How much longer is she going to be over there, anyway?" Chase wanted to know, sensing something was amiss. "I thought she wasn't going to stay much more than a week."

"It's going to take her a couple more days to wrap up her work. She had planned to stay another week to pack up all her stuff and arrange to have it shipped here, but I talked her into leaving it for now. We can go there on our honeymoon and take care of it all then."

"That's a great idea," Cat declared with enthusiasm. "One that's both romantic and practical."

"I thought so," Trey said with a curt nod and turned away, cutting a look at Laredo. "You ready to shove off?"

"I've been ready for the last twenty minutes or more." But there was an indulgent amusement in the light gibe rather than the sting of reproof.

"Sorry." Trey headed for the steps and the ranch pickup parked a short distance away.

Only Laredo offered any parting words to Chase and Cat, flicking a hand in their direction. "See you later tonight."

That fact was not lost on Chase as his gaze tracked the two men all the way to the pickup, with most of his attention centering on Trey. "That boy has something heavy on his mind." Not until he heard the rumble of his own voice did he realize he had spoken the thought. He jerked a quick glance at Cat. She stood motionless, but her expression was alive with the beginnings of some new, exciting idea. "I thought you were going to fetch that list from the house," he prodded.

"What?" There was a vagueness in the look she gave. "I'm afraid I didn't hear what you said. I was thinking about something else."

"That was obvious," he countered dryly.

Laredo had also noticed the far-off look in Trey's eyes that indicated his thoughts were elsewhere. And the ridged set of his jaw suggested they weren't exactly pleasing ones. Withholding comment, Laredo climbed into the cab's passenger side.

Trey never said a word as he slid behind the wheel and started the truck. In silence he drove out of the ranch yard and turned onto the inner road that led to the South Branch camp.

Dust boiled behind them in a thick cloud. For a long run of minutes, there was only the hum of the pickup's engine to break the stillness.

"So, what's the problem?" Laredo finally asked.

"There's no problem." The touch of curtness in Trey's voice suggested otherwise.

"That's good to hear. I had the impression there was something wrong. Naturally I thought you and Sloan might have disagreed about something." Laredo maintained a tone of idle interest, careful not to press.

"We didn't." Another long stretch of silence followed his statement. Laredo had just about decided that Trey wasn't going to share his thoughts when Trey spoke, "I guess Sloan inherited a sizable amount of money from her parents."

"Is that right? So, you're about to marry an heiress, are you?" He studied Trey with a sidelong glance, not at all sure how this could be a problem.

"I guess you could say that," Trey admitted, his expression still wearing that troubled and distracted look. "She has a bunch of financial advisors who, more or less, handle it for her. They want her to get a prenuptial agreement drawn up."

There was a telltale tightening around the corners of Trey's mouth that had Laredo lifting his head fractionally in new alertness. "Like Laura did, you mean?" It wasn't so much a question as it was a probe.

"That's the hell of it, Laredo." The words came from Trey in a hot rush. "I never thought a thing about it when my sister wanted one signed before she married Sebastian."

"But it bothers you that Sloan wants one," Laredo guessed.

"Yes!" Force lent emphasis to the single-word response. An instant later, a sigh gusted from him as his gaze made an agitated search of the empty dirt road in front of them. "To be fair, it wasn't really her idea. It came from those guys in suits."

"They're just doing their job, trying to protect her interests."

"I know." Trey shifted both hands to the top of the steering wheel. Tension remained in every line of his body. "I don't fault them for it. But that doesn't mean I like it. I guess I'm more old-fashioned than I realized. To me, marriage is a forever thing. This agreement is like planning the divorce before you ever have a wedding. The whole thing smacks of distrust."

"Did you tell Sloan that?" Laredo suspected he already knew the answer.

"How could I? She talked like it was the natural thing to do. Maybe in some circles it is, but not here in Montana."

"So, how'd you leave it with her?" Laredo cocked his head at a curious angle.

There was grim resignation in the shrugging lift of Trey's wide shoulders. "I told her to have her lawyers draw one up so I could have ours review it. What else could I do? I couldn't very well argue against it when I don't have anything more than a bad feeling about it. What kind of reason is that?"

"I don't know of any lawyer who would buy it."

"That's what I mean," Trey acknowledged.

"It could be that you're looking at the whole thing wrong," Laredo suggested.

"Look, I know an agreement would protect the ranch," Trey began, impatient and half-irritated.

But Laredo never let him finish the thought. "That isn't what I'm talking about."

"Then what?" For the first time, Trey gave the other man his full attention.

"It doesn't matter what document you sign, whether it's a marriage certificate or a prenuptial agreement. The only thing that will keep you together — or push you apart — is what's in your hearts, not a couple of signatures on paper."

The troubled light went out of Trey's eyes, and an easy smile broke across his face. "You're right. That's the only way to look at it."

"I think so." Laredo tipped his head back and deliberately changed the subject. "So you're going to honeymoon in Hawaii, are you? That should be fun. Beaches and bikinis, palm trees and hula girls."

"Good God, now you sound like Tank and Johnny." There was an undertone of laughter in Trey's voice.

News of the engagement spread across the Triple C with its usual speed. Those who had observed the couple together had seen the engagement coming, but none had expected it to be this soon. The men just smiled and shook their heads, declaring that Trey had never been the kind to sit on his hands.

The reaction from the women was a bit more mixed. The older ones thought Trey had acted much too rashly and regarded Sloan's immediate acceptance of the marriage proposal with raised eyebrows, while the very young found the swiftness of the courtship thrilling, like something out of a romance novel. However, the handful of single girls of marriageable age reacted with regret, mourning the loss of the Triple C's most eligible bachelor. Although most wouldn't have admitted it, every one of them at one time or another had fantasized about catching his eye. Trey's engagement — to an outsider, no less — had shattered that dream.

This was true of no one more than Kelly Ramsey. She paused outside The Homestead's front door and wished for the thousandth time that her mother hadn't volunteered her services to help with the laundry and house-cleaning. Two weeks ago her stomach would have been fluttering with excitement at the prospect of changing the sheets on Trey's bed, gathering up his dirty clothes, maybe even having lunch with him. The only thing she felt now was a kind of quiet dread.

A part of her wanted to turn and run, but pride wouldn't let her act the coward. Squaring her shoulders, she assumed a pleasant expression and opened the front door. The instant she stepped into the entryway, she was greeted by a steady run of conversation coming from the dining room.

Mentally bracing herself for the coming moment in which she would have to meet Trey, Kelly turned in the direction of the conversation. Through the archway, she could see the entire family gathered around the table, empty breakfast plates before them. Without hesitation, she walked directly into the dining room. Her naturally outgoing personality immediately took over. "Good morning. Looks like I arrived just in time to help with the breakfast dishes." Careful not to give anyone a chance to respond, she looked straight at Trey as she continued smoothly, "Hey, I hear you got yourself engaged. Congratulations."

"Thanks." His smile was quick and warm, but it was the way his face lit up, all the hard edges softening at her reference, however indirect, to Sloan that hurt.

Unwilling to let the pair take root and grow into something more, Kelly kept talking. "Did Tank tell you the news?" She addressed the question to Trey, then included everyone at the table with a sweeping glance.

"What news is that?" Trey voiced the question that the others were thinking.

"About Harry's," Kelly replied.

Jessy frowned. "You mean the bar in Blue Moon? Sally's old place?"

"Yup." Again Kelly addressed Trey. "While you were gone, chauffeuring your fiancée to the airport, a bunch of us went to town Saturday. You aren't going to believe this, but it looks like Jack has actually found a buyer for the place."

Chase reared his head back in shock. "You're kidding. What fool would want to buy that place?"

"Some guy from Wyoming, according to Jack. He didn't give his name," she added with a shrug. "I don't have to tell you the news was a bigger shock to everybody than Trey's sudden engagement."

"I should think so," Cat agreed, a slightly stunned look lingering in her expression. "He's had that place on the market for what? Two years now?"

"More than that," Jessy inserted. "It was right after the coal mine closed down."

The staccato beat of a helicopter's blades

invaded the dining room, its loudness only partially muffled by The Homestead's thick walls. All eyes shifted their attention to the room's windows as if expecting to see the craft.

"That sounds like a helicopter. I wonder who that could be," Cat mused aloud.

Chase released a contemptuous snort. "Why would you even wonder? It's bound to be Tara. Who else uses a helicopter to get around the way most people use cars?"

Jessy pushed her chair back from the table. "It's time I got to work, considering we all know Tara hasn't come to see me."

Trey rose to his feet as well and slid an amused glance at Cat. "She's all yours."

He collected his hat from the seat of the adjacent chair and headed out of the room, nodding to Kelly as he passed her. She found a measure of satisfaction in the knowledge that Trey had no idea how difficult this meeting had been for her.

It mattered little that Kelly had seen it coming. That night at the street dance in Miles City when she had observed him with Sloan, she had sensed right away that he was lost to her. That was why she had partnered up so quickly with Johnny as a means of saving face and preventing others from guessing how much it hurt.

She didn't pretend to herself that she was heartbroken, aware that her romance with Trey had been one-sided. But Kelly was haunted by the what-might-have-beens.

Cat's voice broke into her thoughts. "Would you give me a hand clearing away these dishes, Kelly?"

"Sure." She moved quickly to help.

By the time Tara arrived at The Homestead, Jessy and Trey were long gone, Chase had hobbled off to take refuge in the den, Cat was in the kitchen stowing the last few perishables in the refrigerator, and Kelly was gathering up the tablecloth so it could be laundered.

Tara's arrival was announced by the sound of brisk, purposeful strides crossing the entryway hall and halting near the dining room's entrance. Turning, Kelly glanced at the woman standing in the archway's center. The black slacks and crimson silk blouse she wore could have been casual attire, but Tara had taken them a step beyond that with the addition of a gold necklace and earrings. She scanned the room, as always looking through anyone she deemed not worthy of her notice. And Kelly knew she fit into that category.

"Good morning, Mrs. Calder," Kelly

said and returned to her task, fully aware that the family barely tolerated the woman. Judging from the stories she'd heard, Tara had made considerably more enemies than friends on the ranch during her brief marriage to Trey's father. Kelly marveled that Tara continued to force her presence on the family. Trey's twin sister, Laura, had been the only one who actually enjoyed Tara's company.

"Where is everyone?" Tara demanded.

"Cat just went into the kitchen. She should be out directly. The rest have gone to work." Kelly bundled the tablecloth into her arms, then paused to catch up a loose corner.

As if on cue, Cat returned to the dining room. "Hi, Tara. I heard the helicopter and assumed it was you. I was surprised, though. I heard you had a houseful of company at Wolf Meadow. I thought you'd be entertaining them."

"They flew out yesterday," Tara replied. "I intended to leave later today myself, but then I heard the most amazing rumor that Trey is engaged. Is it true?"

"It is," Cat confirmed and laughed at the startled look on Tara's face. "Don't look so surprised."

"I can't help it. I talked to Laura on Saturday, and she never said a word about it."

"That's because she didn't know yet. I don't think Trey called her with the news until Sunday morning. There's coffee in the kitchen. Would you like a cup?"

As an answer, Tara moved in that direction. "This engagement is a bit sudden, isn't it? I wasn't aware that Trey was even seeing anyone on a regular basis."

"I suppose you could call it sudden, but you only have to see them together to know they are madly in love." Cat led the way to the kitchen while Kelly trailed behind both.

"Who is she? A local girl?"

"She isn't from around here. Her name's Sloan Davis —"

Tara instantly seized on the name. "Don't tell me she's part of the Davis family from Phoenix."

Cat laughed softly. "I don't think so. In fact you probably won't find her in any of your social registrars. She's a professional photographer from Hawaii."

"A photographer," Tara repeated with just a trace of disdain.

Cat was quick to challenge it. "Is there something wrong with that?"

"Of course not." With an elegant shrug of her shoulders, Tara dismissed the suggestion. "It's simply that I had hoped Trey would marry someone who could further the interests of the Triple C. But as long as Trey is happy with her, that's all that really matters."

"I'm glad you see that." The firmness in Cat's voice was almost a warning. "Because he's definitely happy. I swear, Trey has been walking on air ever since Sloan said 'yes.'"

"Have they set a wedding date yet?"

"No, but it will be soon." Cat crossed to the kitchen cabinets and removed two cups from the shelf.

"That doesn't surprise me." Tara pulled out a chair, inspecting its seat before sitting down. "I've never known a Calder yet who believed in long engagements. Certainly if Ty had had his way, we would have eloped." She sighed rather dramatically. "Now I have to start thinking about what I can get them for a wedding present. Any ideas?"

"Truthfully, I haven't given it any thought." Cat placed a steaming cup of coffee on the table in front of Tara and carried her own to another chair, taking a seat.

"Wait a minute." Tara lifted a hand in sudden thought, an innate liquid grace in the gesture. "By any chance will they be occupying the master suite?"

"Probably. Why?"

"Because, knowing Jessy, nothing in those rooms has been changed for years. What could be a better present for them than to bring in a designer to redo the entire suite? At my expense, of course," she added. "And I know just who to get."

"That's very generous of you," Cat offered cautiously. "But that might be something Sloan would rather handle herself."

"Don't be silly. No woman in her right mind would refuse the chance to have a professional in charge. And naturally I'll see that Trey and his fiancée have total approval over everything."

"Still . . ." Cat began.

There was a bell-like quality to Tara's soft laugh. "Don't bother to say it. You simply aren't going to talk me out of it, not when I know it is absolutely the ideal gift."

"And I'm sure they will appreciate it," Cat said dryly, deciding there were worse things Tara might choose to meddle in, like the wedding plans, as she had done with Laura.

Chapter Eleven

A long, hard day spent in the hay field showed on Trey as he climbed the oak staircase to The Homestead's second floor. His work shirt was streaked with drying sweat, and his skin was gritty with a day's accumulation of chaff and dust. Each time his boot hit a stair tread, more bits of hay were dislodged from his clothes, leaving a trail behind him.

As he neared the top, his gaze lifted and his steps quickened in anticipation. It mattered little that his marriage to Sloan was less than a month old, time hadn't lessened his desire for her. It ran as strong and hot as ever. The only difference was the new comfort he felt, knowing that Sloan would be here waiting for him at the end of the day. Her presence had given "home" a fresh meaning for him, one that was full of all the deep, good things.

Trey was smiling long before he reached the door to the master suite. Pushing it open, he walked in, then stopped short when he saw the jumble of boxes stacked about the sitting room, some ripped open, their contents partially disgorged, while others remained taped shut.

Out of habit, Trey swept off his hat and looked for a place to put it. In the end he set it on top of an unopened box. After his initial scan of the room failed to locate Sloan, he started to pick his way through the cardboard maze, finally spotting her half-hidden behind some boxes. She sat cross-legged on the floor with her back to him, studying something with rapt interest. His eyes took in the blue tank top and white shorts she wore before shifting to all the tanned flesh the summery attire exposed.

She seemed completely oblivious to his presence. Trey was briefly curious about the item that held her attention to the exclusion of all else. Then he caught a glimpse of a photo's glossy surface and realized, with a flash of annoyance, that he should have guessed the cause.

"What have you got there? I thought you looked at all your pictures before we packed them."

Sloan jerked her head around when she heard his voice, her blue eyes wide with dismay at the sight of him. "Trey. What are you doing here?" She scrambled to her feet. "It can't be that late, can it?"

Now that he was, at last, the subject of her undivided attention, he smiled. "That isn't how a wife is supposed to greet her husband," he teased. "The right way is to throw your arms around his neck and tell him how glad you are to see him."

She grinned back at him. "You just keep dreaming, sweetheart." She slipped sideways between two boxes that separated them to stand before him. "Maybe someday it will come true."

Even as his hands reached out to settle onto the soft points of her hips, she was sliding her hands behind his neck and linking her fingers together. She rose on tiptoes, meeting his kiss halfway. The heat and the need were instant, on both sides. The impulse was there to take it to the next level, but the fresh, clean scent of her skin reminded Trey of the sweat and grime on his own, and he pulled back.

"*Aloha,* my *paniolo,*" Sloan murmured, a warm hunger in her adoring look.

Trey dragged in a deep breath to resist the temptation of her upturned lips, still moist from his kiss. "*Aloha,* yourself. Unfortunately, your cowboy is a little rank from sweating all day in the hay field."

"Is that where you picked up all these yellow flecks?" She brushed some off his shirtfront.

"It's hay chaff. And I've gotten it all over you, too."

"It's okay. It brushes right off." She stepped back to demonstrate.

But Trey didn't want to be distracted by the movement of her hand across her breasts. Instead he shifted his attention to the jumble of boxes.

"I see all your stuff arrived. I thought it would take longer to ship things from Hawaii," he remarked idly.

"It would have if I hadn't sent it by air." A sudden sparkle of excitement came into her eyes. "Guess what else came today?"

"What?" To his knowledge, nothing else was expected.

"Our wedding pictures. I was just looking at them when you came. She took his hand, eager to show them to him.

"So that's what you were so engrossed in when I arrived," he said, secretly pleased by this bit of news, and attempted to follow when she slipped between the two boxes.

But the space wasn't quite wide enough for him to pass through. He paused to shove the pair farther apart, then joined

Sloan on the other side of them. She was once again crouched on the floor, busily spreading out the photos for his review.

"There isn't a bad one in the bunch," Sloan declared. "I swear Wyley has an absolutely uncanny knack for capturing the essence of someone. Just look at this one of your grandfather. Old, and a little worse for the wear, he might be, but you can tell he still has the heart and soul of a lion."

But the picture that spoke to Trey was one of the two of them, facing each other. All he could see was the look on his face, full of raw hunger and a kind of reverential love. It bothered him that he had bared his feelings like that, especially ones as private and intimate as these, considering that he had been taught his whole life to conceal them.

"That's a favorite of mine, too," Sloan remarked when she identified which photograph held his interest. "It just shines with love, doesn't it?"

"That's an understatement," he murmured.

"Does that bother you?" There was a twining of curiosity and surprise in the questioning look she gave him.

"Why should it?" he countered, this time guarding his true feelings behind a teasing smile. "Isn't that the way newlyweds are supposed to look at each other? A little sappy and love-struck?"

She slapped his shoulder in playful reproval. " 'Sappy and love-struck,' that sounds like something Tank or Johnny would say," she declared and instantly dismissed it from her mind as she placed another photograph in front of him. "I love this one of you with Quint and Laura. It's like a reunion shot of the three musketeers."

"We were nearly inseparable growing up," Trey acknowledged.

"You know, Laura is nothing at all like you, is she? And I don't mean just in looks. Or your mother, either, for that matter, although she does favor her."

"Laura has always danced to her own music. Mom used to think it was Tara's influence, but it's just the way she is." His attention shifted to a grouping of photographs taken at the reception. A grin split his face when he saw one that showed Tank with a floral lei around his neck. "These are good."

"Everyone really seemed to enjoy our updated version of a luau, didn't they?" Sloan sat back on her heels and marveled over the fact. "To be honest, I was worried that they might take it wrong and think I was saying something against the life here."

"Are you kidding?" Trey looked at her in surprise. Until that moment he hadn't realized how anxious she was to be accepted by his extended ranch family. "Everybody got a real kick out of it. Since we got back, I swear, somebody asks me every day when we're going to have another one. One of the guys even referred to it as a Hawaiian pig roast."

"Really?" A laugh of delight bubbled from her.

"Really." He nodded in emphasis, then tapped a forefinger on the photographs. "But you don't have to take my word for it. These pictures show how much fun everyone's having."

"They do, don't they?" She moved a few around, then paused. "Do you know what I just noticed? Laredo isn't in any of these shots — except this one, and it just shows the back of his head."

"That doesn't surprise me. Laredo's always been camera-shy." He placed his hands on his thighs and levered himself out of his crouching position. "I'll look at the rest of the pictures later, after I've had a shower. Care to join me?"

"I might, considering I need to change before dinner anyway." Her upward glance was both suggestive and challenging. "Although something tells me you have more than just a shower in mind."

"It's that getup you're wearing." His eyes once again traveled over all that bare, suntanned flesh. "It reminds me of Hawaii, the two of us all alone on the beach, your skin glistening with oil, the waves lapping around our feet, and the salty taste of you." He caught hold of her hand and pulled her upright to stand beside him, the memory and her nearness heating his blood. But desire seemed to be an ever-present thing whenever he was with her, and sometimes even when he wasn't. "We went skinny-dipping afterwards. Remember?"

"Very well." She swayed against him, fingers slipping inside the waistband of his jeans. "Your skin was gritty that afternoon, too. Only this time you're wearing a lot more clothes."

"I can fix that!"

"Not here. Let's keep all this hay stuff in the bathroom, where it'll be easier to clean up."

"Now you sound like a practical little wife," he mocked and looked pointedly at the cardboard boxes that littered the sitting room. "Although I don't why you're worried. The room's already a mess."

"And you aren't going to get it any messier." Sloan gave a tug on his waistband, pulling him in the direction of the adjoining bedroom and the private bath beyond it. "Come on."

"Lead the way," he said, adding a playful taunt. "If you can find one."

"It isn't that bad, and you know it," she countered in mild protest.

Trey traveled about three steps and halted to stare at a free-form sculpture in bronze that stood about three feet tall. "What in the world is that thing? I don't remember seeing it at the beach house."

"For a good reason. It didn't come from there," Sloan replied easily as she paused to study the abstract piece with a kind of resignation rather than pleasure. "It's a wedding present from Uncle Max. It was delivered along with the rest of my things. It's probably horribly expensive."

"What's it supposed to be?" Trey frowned at the piece.

"Your guess is as good as mine," she admitted. "I'm hoping the designer will find some out-of-the-way place to display it. Tara called to let me know she'll be bringing him over in the morning."

Trey didn't exactly welcome that bit of news. "It isn't too late to change your mind. I mean, we can thank her kindly for the offer and suggest she buy us something else instead. She couldn't come up with anything worse than that." He indicated the sculpture with a wave of his hand.

"We've been through this before," Sloan reminded him.

"I know we have." And he regretted that he'd ever agreed to accept Tara's offer. "But there isn't much that needs to be done in here — new tile in the bathroom, a fresh coat of paint on the walls, maybe some different drapes."

"I think you've overlooked the sofa that's on its last leg, and the new big chair you wanted," Sloan countered. "I've worked with a decorator before. And, believe me, it's easier when you have a professional who's experienced at coordinating fabrics, paint colors, and tiles."

Trey had no argument for that. "Just make sure Tara stays out of it. Given a chance, she'd turn this place into a pink-and-gold satin nightmare."

Sloan laughed. "I can promise you that won't happen."

"I know it won't," Trey conceded. "But I don't think you realize what you're getting yourself into." He moved past her into the bedroom, shedding his shirt as he went.

★ ★ ★

Tara arrived at The Homestead promptly at nine-thirty the following morning, accompanied by the designer, Garson St. Clair. Somewhere in his late thirties, he had the trimly muscled build of a man who frequented a health club. Yet a mane of dark, curly hair worn shoulder length gave him the look of an artist.

When Tara introduced him to Sloan, the decorater reluctantly broke off his assessment of the surroundings and greeted Sloan with an air that managed to be both deferential and aloof. "I'm looking forward to working with you, Ms. Calder."

"Thank you, Mr. St. Clair. But I think it will save a great deal of confusion if you call me Sloan."

Tara all but purred the words. "It will eliminate any question whether Garson is addressing you or me."

"Or Jessy," Sloan inserted.

"And her, too, of course," Tara agreed coolly and turned immediately to the designer. "I know how anxious you are to see the suite of rooms, Gar. Let me show you where they are."

She instantly took the lead, ushering him from the entry hall through the living room to the oak staircase, leaving Sloan with no choice except to follow. She climbed the steps after them, her features set in a look of firm resolve.

At the top of the steps, Tara walked straight to the master suite, pushed the door open, and swept into the sitting room with an air of ownership. St. Clair sauntered in after her, his head on a swivel as he took in the height of the ceilings and the room's dimensions.

Sloan was right on his heels. "You'll have to overlook the boxes," she stated, although only a few remained in the room. The rest she had managed to unpack the night before with Trey's help.

"You did warn me that your belongings had arrived from Hawaii." Tara cast a dismissive glance at the heavy cardboard boxes. "Is this all you shipped?"

Inwardly bristling a little, Sloan managed a cool smile. "No. But there isn't anything in these particular boxes that I need right away."

"Then you need to have one of the hands carry them up to the attic for you," Tara stated with a disdainful look at the room's furnishings, "along with everything else in here. It's just as I told you, Gar — the room needs to be totally redone."

"Not necessarily totally," Sloan corrected quickly.

"Even if there is a piece or two you can use, why should you?" Tara reasoned. "After all, this is my gift. So don't you listen to her, Gar," she admonished, a coy smile curving her red lips. "Money is absolutely no object, not where my late husband's son is concerned."

An absent sound of acknowledgment came from his throat as he paused next to the free-form sculpture, lightly touching it with his fingertips. "This is an unusual piece."

"Yes, it is." On that, Sloan could agree.

"Do you collect modern art?" His questioning glance made a probing study of her.

"No. It's a wedding gift."

"A generous one," he said and immediately lost interest in it as he wandered over to one of the windows and looked out. "Quite a view."

"It is," Tara agreed. "But the room is absolutely flooded with light during the daytime. You'll need to install heavily lined drapery to block the glare."

"No," Sloan spoke up quickly and firmly. "I like the light."

Tara turned, an eyebrow briefly

arching, then lowering. "I forgot. You're a photographer by profession, aren't you? It's all about light for you."

Mixed in with the words of understanding was a note of condescension. Sloan stiffened, instantly taking exception to it. But before she could fire back a retort, Mr. St. Clair showed his diplomatic side.

"And harsh light is always screened," he inserted smoothly.

"But never blocked." Sloan wanted that clear.

Undeterred that her suggestion had been rejected, Tara eyed the windows in a reassessing fashion. "Plants would certainly thrive with all this natural light in the room — and provide you with a hint of the tropics you left, Sloan," she said, then explained to the designer, "She moved here from Hawaii."

"That doesn't mean I'm interested in turning this into a tropical retreat filled with rattan and wicker covered in the colors of the sea," Sloan challenged to quickly dispel that notion.

"Naturally you wouldn't," Tara agreed smoothly. "But you could focus on the Oriental aspect with a lot of dark woods and rich reds and gold. Or choose something with a Hemingwayesque flair to it. I can just see that gorgeous four-poster bed that Ty and I used, draped with gauzy fabric to simulate mosquito netting —"

"No, absolutely not," Sloan broke in. "Trey would hate that."

"My dear child," Tara murmured with great indulgence and a pitying smile. "Of course we have to consider Trey's likes and dislikes, but ultimately the decor needs to be what you want. After all, you're the one who'll be living in it day in and day out, not Trey. Other than spending an hour or two here in the evening, he won't be here at all, just you and these walls. Believe me, I speak from experience."

"In my case, it's different," Sloan replied, not the least bit concerned. "My work keeps me busy."

"Then you plan to continue your career, do you?" The possibility seemed to amuse Tara.

"Naturally."

"Is Trey aware of that?"

"Of course." But Sloan was forced to admit, if only to herself, that the subject hadn't been discussed; it was something she had simply taken for granted.

"Interesting," Tara murmured with a touch of drollness.

"What is that supposed to mean?" Sloan found it increasingly difficult to keep her temper in check.

"Nothing really," Tara replied with feigned innocence. "It's just that the Calders have always been very old-fashioned in their thinking when it comes to women."

Sloan smiled with considerable pleasure. "I think you've forgotten that Jessy runs the Triple C."

One shoulder lifted in a dismissive and graceful motion. "She's little more than a figurehead. Chase still calls the shots around here."

As much as Sloan wanted to refute that claim, she knew she was far from knowledgeable on the subject. A claim of ignorance could no longer be made when it came to Tara, however; Sloan knew exactly why no one in the family could stand her. The woman was absolutely maddening and insufferable.

Seeking to break off the exchange with Tara, Sloan turned to the designer. "Would you like to see the bedroom now?"

"In a minute." He was crouched next to a baseboard, using his fingers to push back the carpet pile at its edge. "Am I wrong to assume that, like the rest of the house, there is hardwood flooring underneath the carpet?"

"It seems likely, but I don't personally know that," Sloan admitted.

Not to be ignored, Tara interposed, "Carpeting is completely out of style. Even if this one wasn't so old and tacky, I would urge you to get rid of it. Everyone these days wants wood or stone floors.

"I'll keep that in mind." Her own preference was for hardwood flooring, but Sloan wasn't about to admit that to Tara, convinced it would only encourage the woman to offer more suggestions.

The designer straightened to his feet and turned a direct look on Sloan. "There was a mention earlier that you are a photographer. Will you be wanting a desk or small office area here in the sitting room?"

"No. I want our living quarters to be a comfortable place where both of us can relax and forget about work. Comfort is the key word," Sloan added, as much for Tara's benefit as the designer's. "Not style or elegance."

He responded with a distracted nod and motioned to the connecting door. "The bedroom's through here, right?"

"Yes." Sloan immediately walked over and opened the door to show him into the room.

Whether out of common courtesy or a

recognition of the money source, St. Clair allowed Tara to precede him. With one all-encompassing glance she took in the entire room. "I wonder what ever became of that grand king-sized bed Ty and I slept in," she murmured to no one in particular. "This room just cries for it."

Wisely, Sloan made no comment. Silence seemed to be the best tactic to use in dealing with the woman.

More time was spent exploring the master bedroom and its adjacent bath, assessing the available storage currently provided, and discussing lighting issues. After his initial inspection of the premises was complete, the designer stated his need to take precise measurements of each room, the size and location of its windows and doorway, as well as the location of all electrical outlets and light sources. Sloan offered to assist him, but he assured her he was used to managing on his own.

"You would just be in the way," Tara insisted before Sloan could form a protest. "Besides, this will give you and me a chance to get better acquainted. There was little opportunity at all for us to chat before the wedding."

As far as Sloan was concerned, a tête-a-tête with Tara held no appeal. Seeking to avoid it, she suggested, "Let's go downstairs and leave Mr. St. Clair to work in peace. I know Cat wanted to see you."

Any hope of pawning Tara off on Trey's aunt was dashed when Sloan found the note Cat had left stating that she had taken Chase to visit an aging and ailing ranch hand. As a result, Sloan found herself in the living room with Tara, pouring coffee for two.

Seeking to steer the conversation to safe topics, she plied Tara with questions, mostly about Trey's childhood. It worked for a while.

Then Tara settled back against the sofa cushions, a little finger raised as she stirred her coffee and studied Sloan with a kind of feline contemplation. "It's probably very wise of you to continue with your photography work. Heaven knows, this ranch provides few diversions unless you're a cow. But you do realize that the day will come when that won't be possible."

"You mean when Trey and I start our family," Sloan guessed. "Naturally I'll have to cut back on my work while our children are small."

"That's not quite what I meant," Tara corrected. "I was thinking more in terms of the time when Trey takes over the ranch. As his wife, you'll need to take on greater responsibilities. I know this ranch seems very insular, but its success is affected by decisions made outside its boundaries, whether by the government in Helena or Washington. You will soon discover that this ranch has a steady stream of politicians, lobbyists, and other powerful people stopping by each year. As the wife of a Calder, you will be expected to play a vital role, one that goes far beyond a mere hostess. And of course, there is always the private livestock auction held here at the ranch. The place is absolutely swarmed by the rich and famous. At times, it is no easy task keeping all those egos stroked, as I'm sure you can imagine."

"I can see that." Deliberately non-committal, Sloan took a sip of her coffee while using those few seconds to absorb this image of her future Tara had painted.

"I feel it's important that you know these things — and the role you'll be obliged to play," Tara continued. "After all, it's virtually the equivalent of a full-time job, certainly more than Trey could possibly handle. It's one thing to be his wife, but it's essential that you be his partner. I'm sure you can see that."

"Of course," Sloan replied, careful to say no more.

"Now don't be daunted by the thought of all the entertaining you'll be required to do," Tara admonished lightly. "I've had tons of experience at it. Teaching you the ins and outs of it all will be a simple matter."

"Thank you. I promise I'll remember that when the time comes," Sloan replied with as much good grace as she could muster, then looked up with gratitude when she heard the front door open and the familiar tap of Chase's cane in the entryway.

When Chase thumped into view, he nodded briefly at Tara and went directly into the den. But Cat, thankfully, joined them, the vibrant force of her personality having an immediate impact.

"What are you two doing down here?" she asked in surprise. "I thought you'd still be upstairs."

"Garson shooed us out so he could take his measurements," Tara explained, then smiled at Sloan. "Sloan and I have just been sitting here, having an old-fashioned feminine gabfest."

"I'm sorry I wasn't here. It sounds like fun." Cat sat on the sofa, angling herself toward Tara. "You are staying for lunch, aren't you? You'd better say yes, because I fixed a lobster salad, and I know it's your favorite."

"I wouldn't want to impose —"

"Nonsense. You do it all the time," Cat teased. "Besides, you know we always fix more food than we can eat on the off chance we have unexpected guests. So how long will you be staying up here this time?"

As easily as that, Cat steered the conversation to Tara and a discussion of her schedule and mutual friends. Sloan was relegated to the role of a listener, which she much preferred.

Both Trey and Jessy were absent from the table at noon. Sloan strongly suspected that they had correctly assumed Tara would be on hand and chose to avoid her company. She couldn't honestly blame them. Sloan still was finding it difficult to relax in Tara's company. She was too unsettled by their conversation in the living room and their sparring exchange upstairs.

The feeling didn't go away even after Tara and the designer left. After seeing them out, Sloan went to the kitchen to help Cat with the lunch dishes. Cat had the dishwasher half loaded. She sent Sloan a bright glance. "So, how did it go?"

"He said he'd be back the end of next week with design suggestions and samples," Sloan replied, barely containing a sigh.

"That's good — and definitely sooner than I thought it would be. But I was actually referring to Tara. You looked like you were doing your best to bite your tongue when I walked into the living room earlier."

"Truthfully?" Sloan challenged.

Cat reacted with a full-throated laugh and waved a hand. "Say no more. Tara can be a royal pain at times."

"I'm just surprised she didn't go through my closet and point out all the clothes I have that don't carry the right labels," Sloan half-muttered.

"I take it she shared her opinions on how she thought your rooms should be done."

"Trey had warned me she would, so I was ready for that." Sloan turned on the faucets and rinsed some of the serving dishes. "Now we'll just have to wait and see what Garson St. Clair suggests."

"Don't tell me that's what your little 'gabfest' was all about? Lessons in room decor?"

"Actually, it wasn't. Tara was lecturing me about my role as the wife of a Calder, and all the entertaining I'll be expected to do."

An eyebrow rose in a high arch. "I can just imagine how she made that sound," Cat remarked dryly, then eyed Sloan curiously. "Does that worry you?"

"It doesn't worry me. It's just not something I particularly like."

"You like people, don't you?"

"Of course —"

"That's all that's necessary," Cat said with a shrug. "The rest is easy."

"Tara certainly didn't make it sound that way," Sloan recalled.

"She wouldn't." Cat closed up the dishwasher and checked to make sure the door was tightly latched. "But, remember, things are casual here on the Triple C. I can count on my hands the number of times we've hosted anything that resembles one of Tara's black-tie affairs."

Sloan wasn't convinced that it was as easy as Cat made it sound. She'd had time to consider the myriad of details involved. "But there's the menus — like the lobster salad today —"

Cat immediately broke in. "Remind me to show you my secret. My mother was an amazing woman. Totally organized. She created all these menus — there must be three hundred or more of them — complete with recipes. All you have to do is pick and choose, change a dish here or there, depending on the season or the guest."

"The guest? What do you mean?"

"She kept a card file of just about every visitor. On them, she'd note whether they were married or single, the names and ages of their children, if any, their drink preferences, food allergies, or anything else that might be of use to her. When I was a teenager, I always wondered how she remembered the name of some man's child or that he only drank Johnny Walker Red when she hadn't seen him in a year or more. Then I discovered her secret. Now I have a file of my own. It's only a matter of jotting down a few pertinent details, and it lets you make a lasting impression on them. It's also why Calder hospitality is so renowned."

"You make it sound simple."

"It is," Cat assured her. "And it isn't like you'll be plunged into the role overnight. You have plenty of time to ease your way into it. Before you know it, it'll be second nature to you."

Listening to Cat, for the first time since Tara had left, Sloan felt at ease in her mind. She even found herself looking forward to next week when the designer returned to present his recommendations — even if it meant Tara would be with him.

Chapter Twelve

Tense and eager, Sloan sat on the edge of the chair, watching while Trey studied the sketches of the room designs and the sample board with its fabric swatches, paint chips, and pictures of assorted furniture pieces. She waited for some change in his expression, something that might reveal his reaction. Then her patience wore out.

"So, what do you think?" She struggled to contain her own enthusiasm for it. "It's everything we talked about, isn't it?"

"Exactly." He sounded a little stunned.

"I know. I couldn't believe he got it right on the first try, either, especially with Tara talking in his ear all the time." Sloan let her smile grow. "But there it is. The earth tones we wanted with enough punch of color to keep it from being boring. Good, substantial furniture, nothing too ornate, yet a little eclectic. The overall look is warm, comfortable, and uncluttered, just like the rest of the house."

"There's a lot of work here," Trey warned. "More than just some fresh paint on the walls, different curtains at the windows, and a new sofa."

"True, it is more extensive than we had planned," she admitted. "But, according to Cat, this carpet is at least twenty years old, maybe more. And we've already checked — there are hardwood floors both in here and the bedroom. I'd much rather refinish them than replace the carpet. It's obvious, though, it will be easier if we move out while all the work's being done."

"We've barely moved in," he reminded her as he laid the sample board and sketches atop the coffee table.

Aware that he still needed a bit of convincing, Sloan shifted onto the sofa, linking an arm through his. "I admit it will be inconvenient for a while, but it'll be worth it once the work's all done. And don't forget, Tara's paying for it."

"As long as we don't pay for it."

She jerked her head around. "Tara wouldn't back out at the last minute and stick us with the bills, would she?"

"No. She'd much rather brag about how much she paid to have it done. And I wasn't referring to money, anyway."

"Then what?"

A small smile showed. "Johnny informed me today that I was asking for trouble if we went through with this. He claims that more couples break up over the trials and tribulations of home remodeling than almost anything else. According to him, if we can survive this, our marriage can survive anything."

"I'm not worried," Sloan replied with serene confidence. "After all, we've already survived the ordeal of packing and moving me here. And it isn't like we actually have to live in the mess. We'll be a couple doors down the hall."

"Is that right?" Amusement deepened the corners of his mouth as he freed his arm from hers and draped it around her shoulders, drawing her with him when he settled against the sofa's back cushions.

"It is." Turning sideways, she spread a hand across his shirt front, conscious of the solid muscle beneath it. "So what do you say? I'm game if you are."

There was a subtle change in the darkness of his gaze, a heat building in it. "I suppose I could be persuaded."

It gave her a sense of power to know that she had aroused that glint of desire in his eyes. At the same time, his look of need ignited her own senses, quickening her pulse and stealing some of her breath. She suddenly felt sexy and eager to turn him on.

"That's encouraging." Pressing closer, she let her hand slide down onto the flat of his stomach, slipping her fingers inside his jeans and feeling the involuntary contraction of his muscles. Chin tilting upward, her lips parting, she invited his hungry kiss, anticipating the hot, delicious things it would do to her.

Sloan knew as well as Trey did that this wouldn't end with one kiss. It never did with them. They were both too greedy, and the primitive fires blazed too hot for that.

The instant his mouth claimed hers, Trey took the initiative away from her and drove her backward onto the seat cushions, his tongue mating with hers while his hand cupped the thrusting point of her breast. The rangy length of his body was pressed onto hers, making his hardness felt. It only made her body more aware of her own tingling ache.

From there it was a natural progression of events as the barrier of their clothes was dispensed with. They stroked, caressed, demanded, and coupled with a wondrous urgency, a sexual brilliance radiating between them. This closeness, this insistence, this raw need — it had always been this way between them. Neither could imagine that it would ever change.

A sun-drenched sky stretched its canopy over the Triple C headquarters while the heat of the day held the land in its grip. It looked to be one of those lazy summer afternoons with little stirring, a time of quiet contemplation.

But peace and quiet had become rare commodities at The Homestead now that work on the master suite had gone into full swing. There always seemed to be a steady stream of tradesmen and laborers tromping through the house, either on their way in or out. When one wasn't hammering, another was drilling, sawing, sanding, or ripping out something.

As usual, Chase took refuge outside on the front veranda, away from all the noise, dust, and chaos going on inside. He sat in his rocker, half-glowering at the collection of vans and trucks parked in front of the house, spoiling his view. When the front door opened, he threw an impatient glance at the fresh blast of noise, then tempered it as Cat emerged, balancing a pitcher of tea and two glasses on a tray.

"How about some iced tea? It's freshly made." She had a cheerful smile fixed on her face, but he detected a bit of tightness in it that suggested her nerves were as frayed by the constant racket as his own.

"Sounds good, as long as it isn't gritty from all the dust and who-knows-what in the air," he grumbled in ill humor.

"Now, Dad, it isn't that bad." She set the tray on the side table and poured them each a glass.

"Then how come my soup crunched at lunch today?"

"I told you that was probably a pepper chunk. For whatever reason, my pepper mill isn't grinding it as fine as it usually does," Cat replied with tested patience.

He grunted his skepticism and took a sampling sip of the cold tea. "It seems to be all right," he admitted grudgingly.

"Of course it is." She took a seat in the other rocking chair and picked up the cardboard fan lying on the side table. Idly, she waved it in front of her face. "It's really gotten hot today."

"Hot and dry." A rancher at heart, Chase never could overlook the lack of rain.

"It usually is in July."

The front door opened again, and a laborer muscled an oversized trash can through the opening. Without a glance in their direction, he lugged it across the deck and down the front steps, then dragged it to a Dumpster.

"What the hell are they hauling out now?" Chase frowned, his gaze narrowing as he tried to determine its contents.

"Probably wallpaper."

"Wallpaper? Where in God's name did they get that?"

Cat barely managed to suppress a sigh. "Don't you remember? Sloan told us — I think, it was either yesterday or the day before — that when they took out the wall sconces in the bedroom, they discovered that under the paint there were at least three layers of wallpaper. So they're stripping all of it off."

"Good Lord, how long is that going to take?" His big hands gripped the armrest in rigid anger. "At this rate, it'll be time for roundup before they finally get done."

"Keep your voice down," Cat said in a sharp hiss, her glance shooting past him to the front door.

"Why should I shush when they're banging away without a thought of all the noise they're making?" He caught a movement in his side vision and turned his head to see Sloan standing motionless a few feet away.

Regret clouded Sloan's expression, and the sight of it pulled at Cat. "Don't pay any attention to him, Sloan. He's just being his usual grumpy self."

"No, he's right. I'm the one who needs to apologize," she stated. "I just never dreamt fixing up two rooms could take this long. I'm sorry that I'm putting you through all this."

"We all live and learn, child," Chase stated, his irritation giving way to a sternness. "Next time Tara offers you a gift, you'll know to back up and take another look."

At the mention of Tara, Sloan darted an anxious glance at the collection of vehicles. "She isn't here, is she?"

"No. She said yesterday that she was flying back to Texas this morning," Cat replied.

"Good." Sloan's shoulders sagged in visible relief.

"Why? Is something wrong?" Cat wondered.

"No, nothing," The denial was accompanied by a quick shake of the head in emphasis. "The electrician's running the wires for the new ceiling fixtures in the bathroom, and they almost have all the wallpaper stripped. So I thought I might slip away for a little bit, maybe wander down to the commissary and pick out a video to watch tonight."

"You go right ahead," Chase told her, "and see if you can't find a good western."

"That means something with John Wayne in it," Cat interjected.

"Who else?" Chase retorted.

Sloan turned to the steps, then paused to glance at Cat. "By some wild chance, if Tara should show up, whatever you do, don't let her set foot in the house until I get back."

A soft, understanding laugh preceded Cat's answer. "Don't worry. I won't — not after the last time."

"The last time?" Chase repeated, then remembered. "You mean that day when Sloan went off with Trey, and Tara arbitrarily ordered the workers to gut the bathroom." He winked at Sloan. "Like I said, girl, we live and learn."

"And I learned that lesson well," she agreed, then waved to both of them and crossed to the steps.

Fifty yards from The Homestead, the attendant noise of the renovation receded to a faint murmur. But Sloan's tension wasn't so quick to fade. It remained, like a heavy anchor weighing her down. For the first time in her life, she looked around and failed to appreciate whatever view was before her, the warmth of the sun on her skin, or the mingling of scents in the air.

Her plan was to take an aimless stroll, but she traveled in a nearly straight line to the commissary. Stepping into the air-cooled building, she ran a disinterested glance over the merchandise.

As expected, she spotted a ranch hand on the hardware side and a woman browsing in the section with the boys' jeans. More voices came from the back. She had never been to the commissary when someone wasn't there.

Making small talk was the last thing Sloan felt like doing. So she chose a circuitous route to the video racks that would allow her to avoid the other shoppers. A step away from her destination, she was stopped by the sound of Trey's voice.

"Hey, Sloan. What are you doing in here?" He came striding up, his dark eyes agleam with the pleasure of seeing her.

She struggled to match his easy smile. "I could ask you the same question."

"I had to bring Hank Tobin to the dispensary. An old cow we're doctoring let fly with a hoof and sliced open his leg. While he was getting it stitched, I decided to check on a part we ordered last week." Trey swung an arm over the top of the video rack, his stance all loose and easy. "So, what's your story?"

"I came to pick out a movie to watch tonight. Your grandpa wants something with John Wayne in it." She drifted to the extensive selection of westerns available.

"Figures." Trey grinned. "How's the work going?"

"At a snail's pace — as usual." She tried to make a joke of it, but her tone of voice was much too grim.

His gaze sharpened on her. "Is there a problem?"

"Only one," Sloan replied on a disgruntled note. "That we ever decided to do this in the first place." She quickly held up a hand to stave off his expected response. "I know. You tried to warn me, but I wouldn't listen. Well, now I wish I had."

He cocked his head to one side, trying to get a better read on her expression. "What brought this on?"

Irritated and half-angry, mostly at herself, Sloan responded with biting mockery. "It couldn't be that we've started the third week of work, and the rooms are still a mess. Not a single thing is finished." She focused on the display, hot tears burning the back of her eyes, and added tightly, "I can just imagine what your family thinks of me."

His expression went cool. "Has somebody said something to you about it?"

"No, they wouldn't. But look at what I've done — the way I've disrupted their home and their lives. It isn't likely to endear me to them."

"It's not that bad." An amused tolerance was in the chiding look he gave her.

"Like you would know," she taunted. "You aren't there every day, all day long, with the dust and the noise, people coming in and out, up and down the stairs."

"Sounds to me like you've got a case of cabin fever." Trey smiled in sympathy. "You need to get away for a day and have a change of scenery."

"Wouldn't that look great?" Sloan countered. "I take off and leave your grandfather and aunt to cope with the chaos I caused. Thank you, but I don't think so."

"It isn't going to last forever, you know." Trey was gentle in his reminder.

"Sometimes it feels like it," she declared, then sighed. "Sorry. I guess I'm having my own little pity party. It's just that" — she turned to him, earnest and intent — "I really wanted them to like me, and I've gotten off on the wrong foot."

"Last I heard, there wasn't a deadline," Trey reasoned. "It seems to me you have plenty of time to switch to the other one. And a rip-roaring, shoot-'em-up movie with John Wayne would be a good start. Between you and me" — he darted a quick look around them, then leaned close, as if sharing a secret — "*The Searchers* is his favorite."

"Then that's the one I'll get." She located it on the rack, paused, and glanced questioningly at Trey. "There isn't a DVD version here?"

"Probably not," he admitted and waited while Sloan removed the cassette case from the rack, then followed her to the rear counter.

An apple-cheeked woman looked up at their approach. Sandy-haired and in her forties, she wasn't the clerk that Sloan was used to seeing, but her face was familiar. Sloan knew she had met her before.

"Hi, Sloan," the woman greeted her with familiar ease. "Now I know why Trey took off like an arrow a minute ago. Obviously he caught sight of you."

"I didn't know he was here, either, until he walked up," Sloan replied, stalling while she discreetly scanned the front of the woman's blouse, searching for a name tag. But they didn't bother with such things on the Triple C, where everybody knew everybody else.

Trey came to her rescue, slouching against the counter and resting an elbow on it. "Mark us down for a movie, Nancy."

"Will do. By the way, that part should be here no later than Tuesday." She retrieved a clipboard from under the counter and glanced at the title on the case. "*The Searchers.* Chase will like that."

"That's the plan," Trey confirmed.

"So how have you been, Sloan?" The woman asked as she jotted down the particulars on the clipboard's sheet. "I don't think I've seen you out and about for a while."

"No, I've been sticking close to The Homestead," Sloan admitted.

"How's the redecorating going? I swear the whole ranch is buzzing about it."

"The progress has been slow but steady," Sloan lied.

"I'll bet you're at the point where you're ready to tear your hair out," the woman guessed. "We remodeled the kitchen at our place a few years back, put in new cupboards and everything. After two weeks of living in that mess, I was in tears. Of course, it was too late to have my old kitchen back, no matter how happy I would have been to have it."

"I think I'm at that stage right now," Sloan admitted.

"Believe me, I understand," the woman assured her, and Sloan suspected she really did. Strangely, she felt better knowing that. Finishing her notations, the woman announced, "You're all set."

"Thanks." Sloan picked up the cassette case and started to leave.

"Sloan —" the woman began, then hesitated when Sloan turned back. She seemed to gather her courage. "Could I ask you a favor?"

"Sure." Not sure what was coming, Sloan darted a quick glance at Trey, but he didn't seem to have any more idea than she did.

"I know I shouldn't ask, but — Mike will be leaving for college this fall, and Donna will be a senior in high school. Roger thinks I'm silly, but I really want to have a family picture taken while we're still all together. And Roger absolutely refuses to drive all the way to Miles City to have one done." Worried and uncertain, she hesitated again. "I really hate to impose on you, but — you're a professional photographer. I thought, maybe, you might be willing to take one of us. I'll be happy to pay you for it," she added with a rush, as if sensing Sloan's withdrawal.

Trey had also observed the way Sloan had tensed up in an instinctive resistance to the suggestion. Unwilling to have Nancy Taylor get the wrong idea, he came to Sloan's defense.

"Ordinarily that would be the perfect solution, Nancy," he began. "Unfortunately, Sloan isn't a portrait photographer —"

Sloan immediately broke in, "What he means is, I don't have the lights and the different backdrops that they have in portrait studios. But if all you really want is a family photo, I know I could take a really good one of all of you outside. We can make it informal, so your husband won't have to wear a suit and tie."

"You'll really do it?" The woman's gaze clung to her.

"Of course." Sloan smiled with confidence. "How about Sunday afternoon? Will that work for you?"

"I think so. I'll have to check. The kids might have some plans. If they do, they can change them." Another flicker of uncertainty crossed her expression. "Are you sure it's all right if we don't dress up?"

"Since we're taking the picture outside, I think it will look more natural if you're in casual clothes. Everyone will be more comfortable and relaxed in them, too," Sloan assured her, then realized that wasn't the woman's major concern. "Don't worry. I'll stage everything so it will have that professional look."

"With you doing it, I'm sure it will." But the woman reddened a little, then smiled tremulously. "I can't thank you enough for this, Sloan. You just don't know what this means to me."

"It'll be my pleasure," Sloan insisted. "Unless I hear from you otherwise, I'll meet you at three-thirty on Sunday by the old barn."

Trey searched, but couldn't detect a note of falseness in Sloan's voice or expression. Puzzled by her ready agreement, he said, as they walked out of the commissary, "I thought you never took portraits." There was a subtle demand for an explanation within his comment.

"You saw her face, Trey," Sloan countered. "She didn't understand. To her, a photographer is a photographer. How could I turn her down without coming across like some prima donna who considered such a request beneath her? She wouldn't have said anything, but she would have been hurt, and I'd have had a black eye. Besides," she added, "it isn't that I can't take portraits, they just haven't been my focus."

Trey sensed there were two forces at work in her decision: her own caring nature and the need for acceptance. Not mentioning either, he simply smiled. "You made her very happy."

"That makes me feel good," Sloan admitted. "But you know what's even more amazing? I'm actually looking forward to Sunday. Do you know it's been weeks since I had my hands on a camera?" She cocked her head to one side, eying him with a teasingly flirtatious look. "Is there any chance I can talk you into acting as my assistant on Sunday?"

"I might let you twist my arm," he agreed, knowing it was what she wanted.

On the one hand, Trey was glad to see her looking so happy and excited, considering how low her spirits had been. Yet, on the other hand, he couldn't forget that he'd had no part in her switch of moods; it was that damned camera again.

"Wonderful," she declared as her thoughts shifted to something else. "I'll need to talk to Cat, though."

"Are you going to need her help on Sunday, too?" Trey frowned.

"Not Sunday." She absently chewed on her lower lip. "But I will need to figure out where I can set up a darkroom — at least temporarily — so I can develop the film."

Everything inside him bristled at the thought. "Can't you send it out to be developed like everyone else does?"

"For this, I probably could, but I prefer to control the process. Which means, sooner or later, I'll need to set up a permanent darkroom, but I planned to wait until all the redecorating was done. We're in enough chaos now." Her attention shifted to the big white house on the high knoll. "I'd better go talk to Cat. See you later."

The words of parting seemed to be offered almost as an afterthought. Trey stood there for a moment, watching as Sloan struck out for The Homestead, an energy in her stride that couldn't be ignored. His lips thinned a little at the sight of it.

In the next instant, he pivoted on his heel and headed for the first-aid dispensary, a hard impatience pushing him. In a twist of irony, he was now the one in a sour mood, but with no justifiable cause.

Inside the dispensary, Kelly Ramsey ran a dust cloth over the front windowsill, supplying herself with a ready excuse for standing there in case the ranch nurse Liz Carlsen came out of the treatment room and saw her at the window. But the whole of her attention was on Trey, just as it had been ever since he came out of the commissary with Sloan at his side.

Kelly had been watching for him ever since he left — for reasons she couldn't explain even to herself other than it had become a habit these last few years, and habits were hard to break. Yet that long habit had given her an insight into his body language. She could tell that the careless ease that had marked him earlier was gone. The long strides and hard strike of his boots suggested impatience and annoyance — or a kind of new tension at the very least.

Right away Kelly wondered what he and Sloan had been talking about. He certainly didn't give the impression he was any too pleased with the outcome. Considering all the talk about how extensive the redecoration of the master suite had become, Kelly suspected it was the source of their disagreement. It crossed her mind that Sloan might have made some new change without consulting him. Nothing would get a man's dander up quicker than that, and definitely a Calder's.

As Trey drew closer, Kelly turned away from the window and stuffed the dust cloth in the pocket of her white lab coat. There was no way she was going to let Trey walk in and find her cleaning. Instead she crossed to the counter, picked up a folder, and carried it to the filing cabinet. She had the metal drawer pulled out and the folder partially inserted when Trey walked in.

"Back already?" she said, throwing him an over-the-shoulder glance while removing the folder from the drawer. "That was quick."

"Isn't Hank done yet?" An edge of impatient demand was in his voice. It seemed to match the dark glitter in his eyes.

"I think he's arguing with Liz about the need to come back and have the bandages changed. You know Hank — he always likes to give Liz a hard time about something. He should be out any second." Kelly returned the folder to its place atop the counter, then swung back to face him, self-consciously slipping a hand in her pocket to disguise the bulge made by the dust cloth. "So, did you find out when that part will be in?"

Trey flicked an absent glance in her direction. "Next Tuesday," he replied and darted another look at the closed door to the treatment room. "Johnny tells me you're going to nursing school this fall."

Normally she would have been happy that he was showing an interest in her future plans, but it was too obvious that he was making conversation to kill time. "I might even go on to become a nurse practitioner like Liz. When I mentioned it to Liz, she said that since I was going help out here this summer, I might as well get a taste of all the paperwork that comes with the job." But her only response from Trey was an absent nod. "How's the redecorating going?" she asked. "I've heard everything is really torn up."

"They're making progress." His brief response was far from informative.

"After a while, it's bound to get on the nerves, though," Kelly suggested, hoping he might be more forthcoming.

"It's harder for Sloan. She's there with it all day. I'm not." The flat statement and disinterest in his voice seemed to dismiss the ongoing work as any source of contention between them.

"Sounds like she could use a break from it," Kelly ventured, unable to think of anything else to say. "I'd suggest that you take her out to dinner, but I don't know where you'd go, now that Harry's is closed for re-modeling."

His eyes met hers in surprise. "Since when?"

"I don't know," she admitted with a shrug. "Johnny stopped at noon and told me. He went into Blue Moon this morning and saw a sign on the door that said 'closed for remodeling.' When he asked Marsha over at Fedderson's about it, she said the new owner doesn't plan to open up for a couple weeks. Can you imagine anything worse? I mean — what's going to happen come Saturday night? Everybody always hung out there. After all, where else is there to go?"

"You'll think of something." His attention immediately shifted away from her, drawn by the releasing click of a door latch.

Hank Tobin hobbled out of the treatment room, a wide elastic bandage wrapped around his right thigh. "Sorry it took so long, Trey. I had to convince this female sawbones that there was no way in hell she was cutting off my pant leg. Why, these jeans aren't no more than a year old. Ellie'd have my hide if I let her ruin 'em like that. She'll be mad enough as it is 'cause of the mending they'll need. Say, did you hear Harry's is closed?"

"Kelly just told me."

"You'd better warn Pete over at the cook shack that he's liable to have a crowd come Saturday night," Hank advised. "Sure be nice to pick up a couple kegs before then, though. I bet that new owner doesn't know how much money he's losing by shutting down. And for what? There was nothing wrong with that place just as it was."

"He probably wants to spruce it up a bit, make a good first impression with everybody," Trey replied and turned to leave.

Hank grumbled behind him, "Closing the doors ain't the way to go about it."

PART TWO

The thunder rumbles.
The storm's drawing near.
Now this Calder will see
He has something to fear.

Chapter Thirteen

Miles from anywhere, the town of Blue Moon hugged the sides of the two-lane highway that sliced through it. Born in the early days, when cattle was king, it had boomed with the invasion of homesteaders to the area and withered, like their crops, when the region's drought cycle came. The grain elevator that had once stood as a testament to those days had been torn down some years ago when it became apparent it was no longer structurally safe.

For years Blue Moon had clung to existence by catering to the local ranchers and the odd traveler. Few had much hope for its future. Yet it boomed again when Dy-Corp arrived and established an open-pit mining operation to extract the coal that lay beneath the grasslands. The population mushroomed seemingly overnight; old structures were bulldozed, and new buildings sprang up in their place. The influx of new blood once again turned the town into a bustling, thriving community.

But the coal supply was finite. When it ran out, Dy-Corp locked the gates, leaving its workers without jobs and with no prospects for new ones. A mass exodus ensued, once again making the streets and buildings of Blue Moon mostly deserted.

And, again, the town was little more than a wide spot in the highway, anchored on one side by a combination gas station, grocery store, and post office called Fedderson's. On the other side stood a two-story structure that had gone by various names: Jake's Roadhouse, Sally's Café, and most recently, Harry's Hideaway.

Already the building had been stripped of the sign that had spelled out its former name in gaudy green neon. Workers crawled around on its roof, laying new shingles, while more scraped at the chipped and cracked paint on its siding.

Another crew was busy inside. Only one man stood idle, but his sharp eyes were alert for any hint of slacking by the others. Standing an inch under six feet, he wore a white T-shirt that revealed his bulging biceps and the insignia of the Marine Corps tattooed on the left one. His brown hair sported a butch cut that allowed its few strands of gray to merge with the white of his scalp. With his military-correct posture and stern-jawed features, Gordon Donovan looked every inch exactly what he was — a former Marine Corps sergeant who knew how to follow orders as well as give them.

This was the new owner of the restaurant and bar.

The door to the rear office opened, and a bleached blonde in high heels and shorts lolled against its frame, jaw working as she cracked the gum in her mouth. "Hey, Donovan," she called in a loud and bored voice. "You're wanted on the phone. It's long-distance."

Jaw ridged in anger, he crossed the intervening space with long strides. When she turned sideways to let him pass, he seized her wrist and gave it a savage twist, indifferent to the fear that leaped into her eyes.

"You stupid slut," he growled the words, his voice pitched low, intended for her hearing only. "I never told you to answer the damned phone. I said to call me if it rang."

"I'm sorry." The apology was barely more than a scared whimper.

He pushed his face close. "Don't ever touch my private line again, or your ass is grass. You got that, sweetie." Lips curling, he gave her wrist an extra twist, drawing a tiny outcry from her and a quick nod. "I can't hear you." Threat was in his low taunt.

"Yes sir." Pain trembled through her voice. "I'll never do it again. I swear."

"Damn right you won't. Now get." He jerked her out of the doorway and sent her stumbling into the now-vacant bar area. "And don't go strutting around the workers. Not till payday."

Staring after her, Donovan waited until he saw her start for the stairwell door that led to the rooms on the second floor. After a quick visual check of the workers, he stepped inside the small office, closed the door, and locked it. Only then did he cross to the desk and pick up the receiver lying atop its precisely organized surface.

"This is Donovan," he said, crisp-voiced, and lowered his muscled frame into the desk's companion chair.

"Who was that woman who answered?" Rutledge's familiar voice was on the other end of the line, just as he had anticipated.

"Sorry, sir. It was one of the girls. I've already made sure it won't happen again." He offered no excuse, aware that none were acceptable.

"See that it doesn't," came the terse reply. "What progress have you made?"

"About all I can, until I get this place open and have some traffic through here. There isn't much to learn from the people here in Blue Moon. Like I told you, it's one step away from being a ghost town."

"How soon before you open?" There was an underlying tone of irritation at the delay.

"It'll be another week at least." Donovan ran a disparaging glance over the dingy office. "You bought yourself a pigsty."

"I didn't buy anything. You did."

"Right." Donovan nodded and muttered under his breath, "Lucky me." Louder, he said, "The last of the new kitchen equipment is being installed as we speak, and the electrician is finishing up all the wiring for the machines. They're due here on Monday. The new menus are all set, and the food's scheduled to be delivered next week. I'm pushing to have a big blowout of a grand opening the weekend after next, complete with invitations sent to everyone within a hundred miles. I think I can count on the Calders being here."

"Good. I need all the information you can get me. No matter how meaningless it sounds to you, pass it on. I'll judge what's worthless and what isn't."

"You'll know everything I do," Donovan

assured him. "Which reminds me — I don't know if you're in the market for a ranch, but according to the gal that runs the gas station across the road, the Kaufman spread might be coming on the market."

"I don't think I am, but send me the information on it anyway. What else have you heard?"

"Nothing about the Calders, except that the lack of rain is hurting them just like it is all the ranchers in the area. For the most part, all the locals want to talk about is the good ole days when the pit mine was up and running, and the town was really hopping. If you want stories about that, I've got plenty of them."

"That was Dyson's operation," Rutledge mused, giving Donovan the impression he was talking to himself.

"That's right. His daughter Tara was once married to old man Calder's son. There are all kinds of stories about her and how extravagant she is. Nobody around here likes anything about her, other than her money. According to them, she treats it like sand in a desert. Right now she's footing the bill to redecorate some rooms at the main house as a wedding present for the Calder newlyweds. The price is going to be steep, I hear. But it sure made it easy for me to import all my workers without offending the locals."

"Has there been any talk about the mine reopening?"

"Just some wishful thinking. But it isn't something people around here would know, with the exception of Dyson's daughter."

"I doubt even she would know. Not that it matters. That coal operation won't be of any use to me anyway."

"It's your call," Donovan agreed readily. "My job is to get you information."

"Then get that place open and get me some. The Calders aren't invulnerable; nobody is. There's a way to get to them. Find it."

"Yes sir." But the line had already gone dead.

Spurs and cowboy hat in hand, Jessy closed the bedroom door behind her and headed to the staircase. The only sound to be heard was the hollow echo of her own footsteps. Silence had become so alien these last few weeks that Jessy couldn't fail to notice it. Automatically she glanced at the open door to the master suite.

A mix of curiosity and memories pulled

her to the opening. She paused in the doorway, a hand on the jamb, and looked around the sitting room, not so much noting its new wall color or its sparcity of furniture, as remembering her own time in it.

Before the past could take hold on Jessy, Sloan came out of the adjoining bedroom, armed with rags and glass cleaner, her hair pulled back in a ponytail. She came to an abrupt halt.

"Jessy," she said in surprise. "I thought you left over an hour ago."

"I forgot my hat, which shows I haven't spent much time outside lately." Again Jessy let her glance drift over the room. "It's close to being done."

"Finally." The ghost of remembered frustrations was in the sigh that followed Sloan's emphatic statement. "Now we're just waiting for the rugs and the rest of the furniture to arrive. Then it will be just a matter of dressing the rooms with pictures and things, and we can move back in."

Currently an overstuffed sofa with a side table and an old walnut rocker were the only articles of furniture in the room. But it was the old rocker that caught Jessy's eye.

"I see you still have that old chair in here," she remarked.

Sloan nodded. "It has good lines, and it's much more comfortable than it looks."

"I know." Jessy wandered over to it and absently touched the back of it to start its rocking motion. "After the twins were born, we turned the sitting room into a nursery. I spent many an hour rocking one or the other of them in this chair."

"I didn't know that," Sloan admitted with some surprise. Yet she couldn't help noticing that far-off look in Jessy's eyes that suggested she was remembering when she had occupied the master suite with her late husband. A little uneasy, she asked, "Does it bother you? All the changes we've made in here, I mean."

"No. It was time." The statement was made with a calm certainty that showed Jessy was completely comfortable with the situation. An easy smile curved her wide lips. "By the way, Nancy Taylor showed me the pictures you took of her family. She couldn't stop talking about what a great job you did. Deservedly so."

"Thank you. I thought they turned out well." Sloan was always more critical of her work than others were, but she did think the pictures had turned out well. "They may have opened the floodgates, though. Nancy must have shown them to nearly everyone on the ranch. Now they all want me to take pictures of their families. I guess it's a good thing Laredo set up that temporary darkroom in the basement for me."

Jessy laughed softly in understanding. "You'd better cross your fingers that Nancy doesn't take them into Blue Moon on Saturday night, or you'll be getting phone calls from everyone in the area. From what I hear, they're all going to the grand opening of Harry's old place."

"Yes. Trey told me we were invited." Sloan wasn't exactly enthused about the idea, aware that it was likely to be crowded and noisy, neither of which conditions appealed to her.

"A night out will do us all good." The words were barely out of Jessy's mouth when a horn honked outside. "That must be Laredo. He said he'd pick me up. See you later."

In place of the tall neon letters that had once identified the place as Harry's Hideaway, lights shone on a painted sign that proclaimed the new name, THE OASIS. In smaller letters were the words "Bar and Grill." Brightly colored pennants were strung along the covered porch, and the parking lot was packed with cars and pickups of every shape and size.

Chase leaned on his cane and surveyed the changes to the building. "Looks like this new owner spent his money where it matters — on a new roof and a fresh coat of paint." He arched a questioning glance at Cat. "What did you say this fellow's name was again?"

"Gordon Donovan," she repeated patiently.

"Donovan," he murmured to himself, then asked, "Do we know where he's from?"

It was Laredo who answered him. "From somewhere in Wyoming, I heard."

Chase was too wise to accept rumor. "I guess we'll find out soon enough. At least it doesn't look like he has any ideas in his head that this place is more than a local watering hole."

Behind him, Trey leaned close to Sloan to add quietly, "From the sounds of it, there are a lot of thirsty people in there tonight." The steady hum of voices and muffled music that emanated from the building offered its own brand of proof.

"I just hope there's a place for us to sit," Sloan offered in response.

"Don't worry about that," Cat assured

her. "I called to have a table reserved for us."

"Then let's don't be standing around out here," Laredo declared and gave Chase a joshing prod. "Get the lead out of that cane and let's get going."

Chase cut him a look. "We'll see how fast you move when you're my age," he declared and started forward.

With Chase leading the way, they trooped inside and were immediately surrounded by the seemingly nonstop chatter of voices interspersed with laughter and the distinctive dinging of slot machines.

The interior lights had been turned low, creating an abundance of shadowy spaces, not only in the bar but in the eating area as well. It was the first change that Chase noticed on the inside.

Bells went off somewhere to his right, and a cowboy hooted at his luck. The sudden flurry of excitement drew Chase's glance to the slot machines that lined one whole wall.

"Looks like he got rid of the pool table," he remarked to Laredo, then used his cane to gesture at the long bar, its dark wood polished to a high shine. "But he kept the old bar. There's been many a cowboy who rested his boot on that brass foot rail."

"I imagine so." But Laredo never bothered to glance at the old bar. He was too busy studying the trimly muscled man who approached them, clutching a sheaf of menus. "I think the boss is coming," he murmured to Chase and faded back a step to observe.

The man came to a halt in front of Chase, his feet coming together in military precision. "Welcome to The Oasis, Mr. Calder." His mouth curved in a polite smile. "The name's Donovan. Glad you could come tonight."

Slightly startled, Chase frowned in suspicion. "How did you know who I am? Have we met before?"

"No sir. But your picture has been in the newspapers. That made it easy for me to recognize you."

"I guess it would," Chase mumbled, annoyed that he hadn't considered that. To cover what he regarded as a slip, he reached out to Cat. "This is my daughter, Cat Echohawk."

Cat extended a hand in greeting. "Welcome to Blue Moon, Mr. Donovan."

His gaze sharpened on her as he briefly gripped her hand. "You're the one who called to make reservations. I recognize your voice."

"That was me," she confirmed with an easy smile. "I knew you would be packed tonight, and I wanted to be sure we'd have a table."

"I have one waiting for you," he assured her.

But Chase hadn't finished the introductions. "This is my daughter-in-law, Jessy Calder. She heads up the Triple C for me."

"Ma'am." Donovan acknowledged her with a respectful nod that Jessy returned.

"My grandson, Trey Calder, and his bride, Sloan."

Donovan's smile widened a bit. "You must be the newlyweds I've heard about. Congratulations, a little after the fact."

Trey shook the man's hand and left it at that while Sloan smiled and offered a warm, "Thank you."

Only Laredo remained, and Donovan's attention shifted expectantly to him. But it was the searching probe of the man's gaze, trying to size him up, that prompted Laredo to step forward without waiting for Chase.

"The name's Laredo Smith. I work for the Calders." He stuck out a hand, his smile all friendly and lazy.

Donovan briefly gripped his hand. "From Texas, are you?"

"Nope. That's just what they call me. But people always figure the same thing you did." Laredo never lost his smile. "How about you? Where do you hail from?"

"You name it and I've probably been there, though I grew up in Wyoming."

"Then you enlisted. Am I right?" Laredo grinned with certainty while maintaining a nosy, folksy air.

"Yes sir. U.S. Marine Corps, and proud of it," Donovan stated. "What gave me away?"

Laredo could have named any number of things, from the buzz haircut to his ramrod-straight posture. "Those knife-sharp creases in your pants. We don't see much of that around here except when one of our boys is home on leave."

"Old habits are hard to break, I guess," Donovan admitted without apology.

"So, how'd an ex-Marine end up in Blue Moon?" Laredo asked, and added quickly, "Don't get me wrong, now. We're glad to have you here. It's just that we're miles from anywhere."

Donovan never blinked an eye at the question. "For me, that was a selling point. I liked the elbow room and lack of competition. Naturally, the price was right, too."

"You sure have spruced the place up,"

Laredo declared. "Even added a little excitement with the slot machines."

As before, the new owner had an answer at the ready. "I don't want people to have a reason to drive somewhere else."

"Makes sense," Laredo acknowledged.

Chase spoke up. "I see you took out the pool table. The boys are going to miss it."

"It's only temporary," Donovan assured him. "I plan on turning that back-office area into a separate pool room." The door opened and another couple walked in. Seeing the new arrivals, Donovan made a ninety-degree pivot. "Your table is right over here, Mr. Calder."

With his square-shouldered shape leading the way, Jessy no longer had to contain her curiosity at Laredo's strange behavior. She couldn't recall a single time in the past when he had drawn attention to himself that way or been so chatty with someone he didn't know. He had always kept in the background, content to watch and listen — until tonight.

"What was that all about?" She kept her voice low and slid him a puzzled look.

"He was trying to put a label on me, so I tried to make sure he tagged me with the wrong one."

His reply raised more questions than it

answered, but they had arrived at the table, and Jessy had to put her curiosity on hold while they took a seat. She was quick to use the brief confusion to make a visual reassessment of the new owner, trying to figure out why Laredo hadn't taken the man at face value.

Donovan distributed the menus. "We don't have a large selection, but you'll find everything on the menu is good. If you have any questions, Mary Ann will be your server. Enjoy," he said with an all-inclusive nod and moved away.

Chase opened the menu, then drew his head back with a frown. "Print's awful small." Reluctantly, he took out his glasses case and slipped on his magnifiers. "That's better."

"I don't know why you're even bothering to look. You know you're going to order a steak," Cat chided.

"I just wanted to see what he's got. Might be something new," Chase said defensively.

"One thing that's new is his help," Trey remarked. "Looks like most of them aren't from around here."

"Well, somebody needs to tell those girls at the bar that they need a few more clothes."

Cat's comment drew a throaty chuckle from Trey. "Somehow I don't think that's the idea, Aunt Cat."

"What are you talking about?" Chase tipped his head down to peer over the top of his half-glasses. His attention instantly centered on a blonde in shorts and a low-cut knit top, balancing a tray laden with beer. "Looks like this place has come full circle."

"What do you mean?" Sloan turned curious eyes to him.

"When I was a young buck, a fella by the name of Jake Loman had this place," Chase recalled, leaning back in his chair, a reflective tilt to his head. "And there was always a string of pretty girls on hand, willing to show a fella a good time. For a price, of course. Jake always claimed they were his nieces."

"Sounds like you're talking from experience, Gramps." Trey grinned.

"It was common knowledge," was all that Chase would admit.

Jessy snuck a glance over her shoulder. "Chase you don't really think those girls are —"

Chase interrupted before she could finish her question. "The man did say he didn't want people to have a reason to drive somewhere else, didn't he?"

His dry comment brought a round of laughter. It faded to smiles when the waitress arrived to take their orders. Afterward, a fellow rancher stopped to say hello to Chase and complain about the lack of rain.

When a discussion of previous dry spells ensued, Laredo gave Jessy's shoulder a light nudge. "Care to dance?"

Her initial look of surprise quickly turned to warm pleasure. "I'd love to."

"Let's do it." Laredo stood up and moved to the back of Jessy's chair, pulling it out for her. "We're going to take a spin on the dance floor," he told the others, then addressed Trey. "Are you two going to join us?"

Trey shook his head. "I don't think so."

"Trey knows I'm not much for dancing," Sloan explained.

"That leaves more room on the dance floor for us," Laredo said as he steered Jessy away from the table.

The dance area at The Oasis was little more than some open floor in front of the jukebox that also served as a divider separating the dining area from the bar. One other couple circled its perimeter when Jessy and Laredo reached it.

With the ease of one accustomed to her partner, Jessy turned into Laredo's arms, one hand coming up to rest on his shoulder while the other fit itself to his palm. The tune was an old-fashioned Texas two-step, simple and not too lively. Feet moving in unison, they made one circuit of the floor, neither speaking.

"So, when are you going to tell me what this is all about?" Jessy asked, amused and curious. "Not that I don't enjoy dancing with you, because I do. But something tells me you asked me out here for a different reason."

"I was only trying to oblige a pretty lady," he drawled. "I figured you had more questions for me, and I thought I'd give you a chance to ask them with some privacy."

"You're right," Jessy admitted. "Because I still don't understand what all that was about with Donovan."

"I didn't like the way he was dissecting me." For all the change in his expression, Laredo could have been talking about the weather. "But more than that, I couldn't figure out why he would. Why should he care who I am or what I do?"

"He is new here," Jessy reminded him.

"But ask yourself — why would anybody buy a business in a dried-up town in the middle of nowhere and pour a bunch of money into fixing it up? It's not smart. Did Donovan strike you as being thick between the ears?"

"No."

"Which brings us right back to the same question — what's he doing in Blue Moon? Elbow room and lack of competition, that's what he said. Somebody wanting to disappear might be more like it, but he seems to be doing his damnedest to attract customers. It could be that he plans on setting up some side business."

"Like what?"

Laredo steered her around the other couple before answering, "In a way, it has the smell of drugs. That still doesn't explain why he was so interested in me. . . . Unless . . ." A possibility occurred to him. "He could have heard that Calder's daughter was married to the local sheriff, without being told that Logan was killed. It would be natural for him to assume that's who I am. No wonder he was checking me out so closely," Laredo mused, then grinned crookedly. "It's kind'a funny when you think about it — somebody mistaking me for the law."

Jessy laughed softly in response, relieved that Laredo had no real reason to be suspicious of the man. Just for a moment she had been worried that Chase's constant warnings about Rutledge might be coming true, and Donovan was Rutledge's man. But none of that seemed likely now.

At the bar, Donovan deftly poured a shot of whiskey into a glass while simultaneously adding 7-Up. Through it all, he managed to keep one eye on the couple circling the dance floor. He couldn't seem to shake the uneasy feeling he had about the sandy-haired cowboy who called himself Laredo Smith.

Some little warning bell had gone off in his head the minute he saw the man with the Calders. It wasn't so much the way the cowboy had initially stayed in the background as it was the sharp, searching way his gaze had shot through the crowd — that, and the coolness in his eyes when they had finally centered on him. At that moment, Donovan had been ready to swear the man was a bodyguard. Then he had been treated to that good ole cowboy routine, complete with an aw-shucks grin.

Yet he'd seen something in the cowboy's eyes that he recognized right away — a willingness to shoot without hesitation. Maybe the man had done just that in the past. Which made it all the more interesting to Donovan that Laredo Smith was on the Calders' payroll.

A cowboy stepped up to the bar, blocking his view of the dance floor. Hat pushed to the back of his head, exposing a shock of dark red hair that curled onto his forehead, the man said, "Hey, draw me a beer, will ya?"

"Sure thing." Donovan shoved a beer mug under the tap and pulled the handle.

A bunch of quarters clattered onto the counter. "You're the new owner, aren't you?" the cowboy asked.

"That's right," Donovan confirmed as he caught a fleeting glimpse of the couple exiting the dance floor.

"For your information, you're paying for this drink, 'cause I just hit a fifty-dollar jackpot over there on your slots."

"Glad to hear it." Donovan declared and set the mug in front of him. "I like to keep my machines loose. It brings customers back."

"I'll remember that." The cowboy took a swig of beer, then wiped away the foam on his mouth and stuck out his hand. "By the way, my name's Matt Rivers. My dad owns the old Kennesaw spread north of here."

"Mine's Donovan. Glad to have you." He stacked some dirty glasses in the under-the-counter washer. "It's going to take me a while, I guess, to get all the names and faces straight and know who's who and who's not."

"I'll bet it is," the young cowboy agreed. "Especially when you got a crowd like this."

"It's been hard." Donovan was quick to make use of the young cowboy's willingness to talk. "And in a small town, customers expect you to know who they are. Like tonight, the Calders are here having dinner. I recognized the old man from pictures I've seen of him. The same with Jessy Calder. The son and his wife were easy to spot. But there was a cowboy with them — blue eyes, sandy hair, probably older than he looks. I can't figure out where he fits in."

"Sounds like Laredo," Matt Rivers stated without hesitation. "He's been with the Calders for years."

"Is he their foreman or something?"

"Naw. He just works there."

"Really?" Donovan said with surprise. "Do the Calders usually have an ordinary ranch hand eat with them?"

"No," he admitted, and shrugged. "Laredo's different, though."

"How so?" Donovan pressed with open curiosity.

A frown of uncertainty flickered over the man's voice. "I don't know. I think old man Calder was married to his mother or his aunt — I think it was his mother."

"Then he'd be Calder's stepson."

The cowboy smiled, his own confusion clearing. "I guess he would at that. Which just goes to prove what anyone around here will tell you — the Triple C is a clannish bunch. They always favor their own over outsiders."

"So I've heard." Yet Donovan thought it a bit odd that Laredo hadn't claimed the relationship when he introduced himself. More than that, he wondered why Rutledge hadn't mentioned it to him. But the answer to that would have to wait until morning.

A vigorous hand rang the church bell, summoning worshippers to the morning service. The only customer in The Oasis was a passing truck driver, busy dividing his attention between the tall stack of pancakes in front of him and the buxom waitress bending low to refill his coffee cup.

With the lull in business promising to be a long one, Donovan unlocked the door to the back office, stepped inside, and relocked it before crossing to the desk. He

313

took a seat and dialed the number he had long ago committed to memory.

"It's Donovan," he identified himself the minute Rutledge answered. "Do you have a few minutes?"

"I do. Did the Calders show up last night?"

"They did. You never mentioned that Chase Calder has a stepson."

"It's the first I heard of it."

"That's what a rancher's son told me last night. The stepson goes by the name of Laredo Smith. When I first met him, I would have sworn he was a bodyguard. But the cowboy claimed his mother was married to the old man."

"As far as I know," Rutledge began in a thought-filled voice, "Chase Calder was only married twice. His first wife was the daughter of a neighboring rancher up there. And his second wife was a widow by the name of Hattie Ludlow. She owned a small ranch not far from mine. Chase bought it from her shortly before they married. I don't recall that she had any children, but I'll find out."

"If this Laredo is supposed to be her son, then his last name should be Ludlow, unless he had a different father. And there's always the possibility that my

314

source got it wrong," Donovan admitted. "Initially he wasn't sure if the woman was Laredo's aunt or his mother. Whoever he is, he's in damned tight with the family."

"Is that why you're so interested in him? Do you think you can turn him? Get him to feed us information?"

"Not this one." Donovan was certain of that. "No, I saw something in his eyes I didn't like. I don't know what your plans are, and I don't want to know. But a word of warning — watch out for this guy. He can be dangerous."

"The Calders have a big name. It's logical that they would have some protection around," Rutledge replied in unconcern. "I'll check out Hattie Ludlow and see what her connection was to this Laredo Smith. In the meantime, you learn what you can about him. But make sure he doesn't find out that you're asking about him."

"Don't worry. The questions won't be coming from me." Then Donovan asked, "Did that information I sent you about the Kaufman ranch arrive yet?"

"It came Friday." Without expressing an interest, or lack thereof, in the property, Rutledge moved on to other matters before bringing the conversation to a quick conclusion.

When Donovan emerged from the back office a few minutes later, he was greeted by the sound of two sets of footsteps going up the rear staircase. A ghost of a smile touched the corners of his mouth at the sight of the semi still parked outside and the empty restaurant area.

Some thirty minutes later, he rousted the rest of his girls from their beds and gathered all of them together. His instructions came with a promise of a reward and a warning not to deviate from the reason he had given them for seeking the information he wanted. All swore they wouldn't, and he was confident they knew better than to try.

Chapter Fourteen

A relentless August sun had burned off all the early morning coolness, and the air was as dry as the thick brown grass beneath the horses' hooves. Already Trey could feel a trickle of sweat running down his back, and it was barely midmorning.

Thirty-odd head of cows plodded ahead of him. Every now and then one would pause to grab a bite of the buffalo grass that was already cropped short. When a straggler lowered her head to sample some, Trey started to rein his horse toward it, but Laredo was already there, slapping a coiled rope against his leg. Reluctantly, the cow trotted forward to rejoin the rest.

Off to his right, a pair of cows crested a low rise at a harried trot. Tank Willis was right behind them, keeping up a steady pressure until they neared the slow-moving herd. Then he backed off and swung his horse in between Trey and Laredo.

"Those two are the last from that section. Johnny and Ben rode up to check the butte." His horse released a blowing snort and settled into a jigging walk. In one continuous motion, Tank took off his hat, wiped his forehead sweat on a shirtsleeve, and rocked the hat back on his head. "You know, I can't remember ever moving cattle off their summer pasture the first week in August."

"There wasn't any choice this year," said Trey. "Another month on this grass and they would have chewed it to the roots."

Tank nodded in understanding and scanned the cloudless sky. "If it don't rain soon, we'll be feeding them a lot of hay this winter. And soon, too."

"True enough." Trey rested his hands on the saddle horn, sitting easy but alert in the saddle.

"Somebody at The Oasis told me last Saturday night that they're calling for rain next week," Tank offered on a wistful note.

"God knows, we're long past due for some." Trey made his own study of the pale blue sky.

"Hey, Laredo." Tank's sudden grin had a streak of devilry in it. "You know that redhead that works at The Oasis — the one called Bambi?"

"I remember seeing a redhead there," Laredo acknowledged. "What about her?"

"It seems she's sweet on you."

Laredo eyed him with skeptical amusement. "Where did you get a fool idea like that?"

"Andy Palmer told me last Saturday."

"That she was sweet on me?" His glance questioned that claim.

"Well, actually Andy said that she was asking about you." Tank's grin widened. "She claimed she thought you were kinda cute for an old guy." He put teasing stress on the "old" part.

"Did she want to know anything else about me?" Laredo wondered, his lazy smile still in place, but with a sharpening of his glance.

"Naw, that was about it," Tank admitted, then eyed Laredo with sly, mocking humor. "Although Andy did mention that she thought you might be a foreman or something. She was probably trying to find out how much money you make. You'd best be careful the next time you go in there, or she'll be sliding all over you, trying to coax some of it out of you." Laughing, he hauled back on the reins and turned his horse away from them. "See you later."

Off he rode in the direction of the butte. Trey ran a curious glance over Laredo, watching as he hurried along a lagging cow.

"I could be wrong," Trey began in a casual tone, "but I had the feeling that you didn't like the idea that this redhead was asking questions about you."

"Maybe I'm not sure she was the one wanting the information," Laredo countered.

"You think somebody else put her up to it?"

"Could be."

There was only one logical choice for that person. "Why would Donovan be trying to get information about you?"

"Good question. Too bad I don't know the answer."

Mixed in with that note of indifference in Laredo's voice was a touch of grimness. Trey caught it right away but chose not to comment on it. It summoned up the half-forgotten whispers he'd heard as a boy, hints that Laredo had been in trouble with the law. There had even been a suggestion that Logan had uncovered his secret while he was sheriff but chose to keep quiet about it. Until now Trey had always dismissed those old rumors as another tall tale the old-timers liked to feed people, one that would turn out to be only partly fact and mostly fiction. Trey wasn't so sure about this one anymore.

"You're positive Donovan isn't someone you might have known before you came here?" Trey put it as a question and observed the way Laredo's glance sliced to him.

"Positive." He looked Trey in the eye when he answered him. "He isn't a man I'd be likely to forget. And he isn't one I would trust, either."

Laredo never suggested that Trey should distrust the man as well. That wasn't his way. But the seed was planted just the same.

"I'll talk to Tank and make sure he passes the word for everybody to watch their step in there." Saddle leather creaked as Trey shifted his weight in the seat. "We'll find out soon enough what Donovan's game is. Blue Moon's too small for anything to stay a secret for long."

"Don't count on that," Laredo advised. "That's a man who knows how to keep his mouth shut. And he plans on being here for the long haul. If we find out anything, it's something he wants us to know."

Amusement quirked Trey's mouth. "If I didn't know better, I'd think it was Granddad talking. You sound just like him, always expecting danger to be lurking in every shadow." Trey found it hard to take this kind of talk seriously.

"When you own a place as big as the Triple C, there's always going to be somebody who resents it. Whether you're responsible or not, you'll get blamed for their troubles. Cattle prices are too low — the Calders glutted the market. Their well goes dry — the Calders lowered the water table by irrigating their hayfields. Most of it won't ever be anything more than a lot of ill-natured griping." Laredo paused to make his point. "But it only takes one to decide he wants to get even. Chase knows what he's talking about. Always check those shadows."

Trey lost some of his skepticism. "That's why he's fixated on Rutledge, isn't it?"

"Can you think of a better man to fear than one with the power and wealth that Rutledge has — and with his only son dead at the hands of a Calder?" Laredo countered.

"It was self-defense." In Trey's mind, that made all the difference.

"Do you think that matters to him?"

"It should." But Trey realized that "should" didn't mean it would.

His gaze stretched beyond the dusty

backs of the plodding cattle and drifted over the sweep of gently rolling land ahead of them, mostly covered in summer-brown grass. Wherever there was a patch of bare ground, the soil had turned to powder.

Laredo could say all he wanted to about the danger Rutledge might pose, but as far as Trey was concerned, the lack of rain was the biggest threat to the Triple C right now.

Halfway up the knoll, Chase came to a halt and leaned both hands on his cane. It galled him that he could no longer climb the smallest hill without stopping to catch his breath. Growing old could be hell at times.

As his breathing began to even out, he gathered himself to make the final push to the front steps of The Homestead, where he could sit for a minute or two and pretend to be enjoying the morning air. He hadn't traveled more than two feet when he heard the front door close and saw Sloan skipping lightly down the steps. There was an exuberance about her that made him smile.

"Just getting back from your walk, I see. You must have taken a long one this morning," she remarked.

"It wasn't long, just slow," Chase corrected, then gestured with his cane at the leather case she carried. "Where are you off to?"

"On a picture-taking spree."

He frowned. "Who's getting their picture taken on a workday?"

"Oh, I'm not taking pictures of anyone in particular," Sloan hastened to explain, "just whatever I happen to see. Trey mentioned they were moving cattle to another pasture today, so I thought I might try to capture some of that on film."

After a small hesitation, Chase nodded, a little slow at recalling. "That's right. The grass at the Broken Butte range was getting short." He ran a thoughtful glance over his grandson's young bride.

"If that's where you're heading, you might want to wait and follow the cook when he takes the noon meal to the boys. He'll be pulling out in an hour or less."

She shook her head in unconcern. "This morning light is too good to waste. Cat gave me directions. I'll find them." She struck out for the ranch pickup parked a few feet away.

Chase called out after her, "You got water with you?"

"Are you kidding?" She threw a laughing

look at him as she pulled opened the driver's door. "Cat loaded me up with everything — water, sandwiches, the works. I feel like a schoolkid with a packed lunch. See you sometime this afternoon. I'll probably be late, so don't worry." Offering a farewell wave, Sloan climbed into the cab and pulled the door closed after her.

Dust billowed around the tires when she backed away from the house and pointed the truck at the ranch yard. It hung like a haze in the air, smudging his vision. Chase turned from it and resumed his climb up the steps.

With the ranch headquarters reflected in her rearview mirror and an open road before her, Sloan increased the truck's speed. Soon there was nothing but the sun-baked plains stretching out from the road, vast and empty, constant yet ever changing. The sight of them filled her with a sense of freedom. For too many weeks she had been obliged to stay close to The Homestead while the master suite went through its face-lift. The work was finally finished, and all their clothes, toiletries, and other personal items were back in place, leaving her free to explore.

The Triple C's network of inner roads didn't follow any set grid pattern, with other roads intersecting at regular intervals. With few exceptions, most had evolved from old trails once used by buckboards, supply wagons, and the occasional buggy to reach its outlying camps. As a result, the route chosen had always been one that would be the easiest for a horse team to traverse.

Any substantial rise in the undulating prairie was skirted to avoid a hard pull for the horses. Other times routes were dictated by the location of water crossings. There were stretches where the current roads ran straight and true, but they never lasted long before resuming their snaking course through the heart of the land.

It was rare for there to be the customary four-way intersection. Usually there was just another road branching in one direction or the other, with no signs to indicate where it led.

With the whole day ahead of her and no real timetable to keep, Sloan didn't mind the dirt road's many curves. The slower pace made it easy for her to look around and study the photographic possibilities.

A half dozen times she pulled off and gathered up her oversized camera case to capture some scene that caught her eye, sometimes using a zoom lens and, at others, a wide-angle. Sometimes it was just the roll of land beneath an endless sky that invited a picture. Once it was a hawk perched on a fence post that posed for her camera, then obligingly took wing. Another time, it was a small herd of pronghorn antelopes, heads turned to stare in open curiosity. At a river crossing, she spotted a cow at the water's edge and captured the sparkle of sunlight on the ripples the animal made as it drank.

After climbing onto the pickup's roof to achieve the necessary vantage point, Sloan snapped a few shots of a fence line marching across an empty expanse into forever. But the light was all wrong to achieve the effect she wanted. A check of the sun's position confirmed her suspicion that it was nearing its zenith.

Back inside the pickup, she packed her camera away for the time being, rolled up the windows, and turned the air-conditioner on full blast to rid the interior of its stifling heat. Again she pulled onto the road, but this time she kept her attention on it, watching for the turnoff she was to take.

Roughly a mile farther, she saw a road that forked to the right. Certain that Cat had instructed her to take the third one, Sloan drove on past it. She continued another five miles before she came to the third turnoff.

According to Cat's directions, there would be a pasture gate some three miles after the turn. Sloan went closer to four miles before she saw it. There were no trucks or stock trailers in sight, but Cat had warned her that she might not see any.

As she swung open the gate, Sloan noticed a rutted track, half hidden by the thick grass, that curved off into the pasture. She drove the pickup onto it, stopped to shut the gate behind her, then followed the dim trail. She soon came across the suggestion of other tracks, some branching to the left and others to the right. Uncertain which to take, she stayed on the one that seemed to show more use.

It was rough and deeply rutted in spots, forcing her to slow the truck to a fraction of its usual speed. All the while she kept scanning the land around her, watching for the flash of sunlight on a truck's windshield or a glimpse of a rider. She saw nothing.

Suddenly the tracks disappeared. On impulse, she reversed direction and headed back the way she came. When she arrived at the first dim trail that branched north, she took it. She hadn't traveled very far before it, too, vanished. Again she back-tracked and took the next one.

Just like the others, it led nowhere, but it took longer to get there. This time Sloan ignored the lack of a trail and drove on, striking out across the open country. The decision had seemed to be a sound one until she came to the bank of a ravine that was much too steep for the truck to safely navigate. Frustrated, she switched off the engine and got out of the pickup.

The land beyond the ravine was rugged and broken, with cut banks and coulees, rising into full-scale hills in places. The sight of it drew a sigh of discouragement from her.

"I guess they call this Broken Butte for a reason," she murmured to herself and sighed again. "So what now?"

Then she remembered Chase mentioning the ranch cook would be bringing out a noon meal. All she had to do was return to the pasture gate and wait for him to arrive. Buoyed by the thought, she scrambled into the truck and started up. Automatically she glanced at the dashboard clock. A frisson of shock went through her when she saw it was already a few minutes after one.

Certain that the cook hadn't passed her, Sloan could only conclude that he had arrived at the pasture before she did. Her best bet was to drive back to the gate and catch him before he returned to the Triple C headquarters. When the hunger pangs struck, she was glad Cat had insisted she take a packed lunch with her.

Well over a century old, the timbered barn cast a long shadow onto the ranch yard, shading the stock trailer parked in front of it from the glare of the late afternoon sun. One by one the saddled horses were unloaded, each rider claiming his mount as it came off.

When a sweat-caked red dun backed out of the trailer, Trey stepped forward to catch its reins. At almost the same instant, his side vision registered the familiar shape of his mother crossing the ranch yard toward him. Hot, dusty, and tired after all day in the saddle, he grudgingly led his horse to the side and waited, knowing she would want a report.

"I thought you'd be back an hour ago," Jessy said when she reached him. "What took you so long?"

"I didn't want to hurry them in this heat. They walked off enough weight as it was," Trey stated with a certain bluntness that came from fatigue.

"That was wise." She made it a statement, not a compliment.

When he noticed the way she scanned the trailer, Trey assumed she was looking for Laredo. "Laredo's in the barn putting his horse up."

She nodded absently. "Where's Sloan? Didn't she come back with you?"

Thrown by the question, Trey frowned. "What are you talking about? I haven't seen her since this morning. Isn't she at the house?"

"No." It was Jessy's turn to look confused. "She told Chase she was driving out to Broken Butte. She wanted to take pictures of the cattle being gathered and trailed to the new pasture. Are you saying she never showed up?"

"No." An uneasiness flickered through him. Almost of its own volition his gaze scanned the main road that led west, the one Sloan would have taken. Annoyance replaced the uneasiness when he thought of the camera. "Knowing Sloan, it doesn't take much to distract her when she has a camera in her hands. She's probably out there somewhere right now waiting for the sun to shift to the right angle. Hell, she could even be waiting for a sunset scene."

"Maybe," Jessy conceded. "Just the

same, I can't help thinking that she hasn't been here long enough to know her way around the ranch. One wrong turn and she could easily get lost. And if we need to search for her, I'd much rather do it while there's some daylight left."

"Let's don't throw that loop until we need to," Trey replied. "She'll be back, you'll see."

Moving off, he led his horse into the barn, unsaddled it, grained it, and gave it a good rubdown before turning it out in the corral with the other horses. But there was still no sign of Sloan, and the sun sat on the lip of the horizon, flooding the western sky with a spectacular mixture of crimson and coral. Trey knew it was just the sort of thing that would appeal to Sloan.

He started for the house, then veered sharply to the ranch pickup, his jaw clenched in anger, certain he was worrying without cause. Yet Trey also knew it wouldn't be the first time a newcomer to the Triple C had become the subject of a search party.

When he pulled away from the barn, he spotted Laredo and rolled the window down to call to him. "Let my mother know that I've gone to look for Sloan. Either she forgot to take her cell phone, or she's turned it off, but I couldn't raise her. Tell Mom not to do anything until she hears from me."

Without waiting for a reply, he drove off.

Nowhere along the road back to Broken Butte did Trey find any trace of Sloan. Along the way he'd met one pickup, but Sloan hadn't been behind the wheel of it.

As twilight settled over the land, thickening its shadows, he switched on the headlights and started to reach for his cell phone, then changed his mind, deciding to check one more stretch of road before ordering searchers out. When he arrived at the intersection with the main road, Trey turned right, acting on the assumption that Sloan had missed the turnoff.

With the headlight beams on high, he drove slowly over the next five miles, constantly scanning the ditches on either side of the road on the off chance Sloan had driven into one of them. Reluctantly, Trey took out his cell phone and flipped it open. In the next second, he spotted something just beyond the reach of his headlights.

Sloan trotted into view, frantically waving an arm to flag him down. The sight of the camera case, firmly clutched in her other arm, brought his teeth firmly together. He braked to a stop and made his phone call.

When his mother answered, he said somewhat tersely, "I found her. She's fine."

"Thank God —" Trey flipped the phone shut, breaking the connection as Sloan pulled open the passenger door, flooding the cab's interior with light.

"Trey. Am I ever glad to see you." Relief was in her voice, made a little breathless from the sprint to the truck. But it was the radiance in her expression that had him wondering if it was for him or the after-glow of a satisfying day spent with her camera. She scrambled onto the passenger seat and slumped in weariness. "I had just about decided I would have to walk all the way back."

"What happened? Where's the truck?"

"Back there." She pointed into the darkness. "The left rear tire went flat, and I couldn't find a jack to change it."

"I've got a jack with me. We'll go change it." Trey put the truck in gear and continued down the road. "Why didn't you call? Isn't your cell phone working?"

"I didn't bring it. Can you believe that?" Sloan said in disgust. "I had it laid out with all the rest of my equipment, but somehow it didn't end up in my bag." She sat up, her attention focusing on the road ahead of them. "Take a right at the next turnoff."

Trey slowed the truck to make the turn. "I thought you were on your way to Broken Butte. How did you wind up here?"

"Obviously, I turned onto the wrong road." She seemed completely untroubled by her mistake. "There's a pasture gate about three miles farther. That's where the truck is."

"Are you telling me it took you all day to figure out you were in the wrong place?" His gaze narrowed on her in disbelief.

"Not hardly," she scoffed. "I stopped a bunch of places to take some pictures, so it must have been close to noon before I got here." She turned sideways in the seat, her expression all earnest and curious. "There were all these dim trails crisscrossing the area. I must have driven over every one of them thinking I'd find you — or someone. Finally I went back to the gate. Chase had mentioned they would be bringing out a noon meal. So I thought I'd catch whoever it was when he left. It was probably after three before it sunk in that I wasn't at Broken Butte. Right after that, I discovered I had a flat tire. But I couldn't figure out why there are so many old trails that didn't seem to lead anywhere. Was that a former site of one of your outlying camps?"

"No. You were wandering around the old oil field. Those trails are what's left of the roads Dy-Corp used to service the wells." The pickup's headlights illuminated the pasture and exposed the pickup's dark shape just beyond it.

"There's oil on the Triple C?" Sloan said in surprise.

"There was." Trey pulled up to the gate. "The wells have been capped for years."

Leaving the engine running and the lights on, Trey piled out of the cab and retrieved the jack, then unlatched the gate and walked to the rear of the other truck. Sloan wasn't far behind him, but she stopped to stow her camera bag inside the disabled truck before she joined him at the back.

Trey never looked up from his task or said a single word, just went about the business of removing the flat tire and replacing it with the spare in briskly efficient fashion. Sloan was confused by his continued silence. When she thought back over the short ride, she realized he had been a bit cool and abrupt with her.

"Were you worried about me, Trey?"

He shot her a cutting glance, then went

back to tightening the wheel nuts. "What do you think?" He continued tightening the wheel nuts, grim and tight-lipped.

"I was fine," Sloan replied in easy assurance. To her that made all the difference.

With the spare tire in place, Trey removed the jack and stood up, his hard gaze connecting with hers only briefly. "I know." He brushed past her. "You're all set. I'll follow you back."

He walked to the gate, swung it open, then climbed back in his pickup and reversed it onto the road. As soon as Sloan drove through the opening, he got out and closed the gate while she waited for him.

Trey followed her taillights all the way back to The Homestead and held the front door open for her. "I can't decide what I'm looking forward to the most," Sloan declared as she walked by, "hot shower or food. I'm starving."

Trey had no opportunity to respond even if he had been so inclined. Seconds after they walked in, the entire family descended on them. Never breaking stride, Trey continued straight to the staircase, leaving Sloan to field all their questions.

The hat came off the minute he entered the master suite. He gave it a fling at the couch in their newly redecorated sitting room and walked straight into the bedroom, pushed by a nameless anger.

In short order he stripped out of his trail-stained clothes and stepped into the spacious new shower. He scrubbed away the day's caked grit and sweat with rough impatience and emerged from the shower in no better mood than when he had stepped under the spray.

With a towel wrapped around his middle and his wet hair finger-combed into a semblance of order, Trey padded into the bedroom just as Sloan entered it, still toting the camera case. His glance flicked over her.

"The shower's yours." He continued on his way to the tall bureau.

"Thanks," Sloan murmured absently and set the camera case on a chair cushion, then slipped off her cap and shook loose her hair. "Your mother just told me that she was getting ready to organize a search party to look for me. I never realized everybody was so concerned when I didn't show up at dinner time."

"We've had experience with people getting lost before."

She gave him a look of mild reproof. "I wasn't lost, Trey. I just took a wrong turn."

He turned from the underwear drawer,

eyeing her with cool challenge. "You not only didn't know where you were going, but you didn't know where you were. If that isn't lost, what do you call it?"

Stung by the sharp bite of his voice, Sloan glared at him in annoyance. "That isn't true. I knew where I was going. Cat gave me directions. And I can assure you I would have made my way back if that tire hadn't gone flat."

"That's all that matters to you, isn't it?" Temper claimed him, rooting him to the spot. "You don't give a damn about who might have been worrying about you."

"Of course I do. How can you say that?" Sloan stiffened in indignation.

"Actions speak louder than words. I noticed you managed to pack all your camera equipment." He flung a hand in the direction of the case. "Yet you forgot to take your phone."

"You make it sound deliberate. I told you it was an oversight. Why are you so angry?" she demanded in frustration, upset and confused by his attack.

"Why?" The word exploded from him, and Trey had to make a conscious effort to rein in his anger. But it lay tight in his voice. "It couldn't be because you took off — with no good idea of where you were going — and ended up in the wrong place. And what do you do? You go driving across broken country — by yourself — without a soul knowing where you are. You ended up with only a flat tire, but you could just as easily have rolled the truck and been knocked unconscious or worse. And God only knows where-all you went with that camera. You could have been snakebit or stepped in a prairie-dog hole and broken a leg. Do you have any idea how long it might have taken us to find you?"

"But it didn't. I'm fine. So stop yelling at me!" Her voice broke on the last as tears blurred her vision. Turning away, she hurriedly wiped them from her eyes, furious with herself for crying. She tilted her head back, opening her eyes wide in an attempt to keep the tears from reforming and muttered in a spate of self-pity, "Why did I ever think I wanted to have your baby?"

At first she didn't hear the almost soundless tread of his bare feet. By the time Sloan sensed his presence, Trey was already behind her, his fingers encircling her upper arm and squaring her around to face him.

"What did you just say?" His gaze bored into her, a dark, doubting scowl on his face.

Struggling to control her emotions, Sloan pushed the words out, almost with defiance. "I said I'm pregnant."

"You're . . ." He never finished it. The scowl lines were smoothed away, as a look of stunned wonder claimed his hard features. "Are you — ?" he hesitated and started again, "Are you sure?"

"Of course I'm sure. It's my body." Anger wasn't something she could let go of as easily as he had.

"A baby." A smile broke across his face, softening all its hard angles. A breath later, he let out an exultant whoop and caught Sloan under her arms, lifting her high in the air and swinging her in a half-circle.

Sloan clutched at his shoulders for balance. "Trey Calder, you put me down." But his joy was much too contagious for her to remain angry with him any longer.

He let her toes touch the floor but kept an arm firmly around her, holding her close while he cupped a hand to her face, a look of inexpressible tenderness and pride in his eyes. "You're right. I shouldn't have yelled at you. I'm sorry." His thumb wiped away the wet track of a tear on her cheek. "A baby. You and me." That grin reappeared. "How long have you known?"

"I've suspected it for close to a couple

weeks," Sloan admitted, feeling a bit smug and pleased with herself. "But I only found out for sure this morning."

"You've already been to a doctor," he said with some surprise. "When?"

"I haven't seen one yet, but . . . I went to the dispensary this morning and got one of those test kits. Liz assured me they were ninety-percent accurate."

Holding her like this, seeing her sun-streaked hair gleaming in the room's light and her lips lying softly together, Trey felt all his acute hungers revive. The look of her, the feel of her churned the depths of his emotions. The heat of something rash burned him. Trey worked to hold it in check as he nuzzled the smoothness of her cheek.

"I'll bet the whole ranch knows by now," he murmured.

"Only that I purchased a kit," Sloan reminded him. "We're the only ones who know the result. No one else."

He drew back an inch, his gaze making a caressing study of her face. "Did I mention that I love you?"

She spread her hands over his bare chest, thrilling to the feel of its muscled flesh and a little stunned that she felt so thoroughly aroused. "Didn't you just tell me a minute ago that action speaks louder?"

He went still for a split second, a glimmer of uncertainty in his eyes. "I don't want to hurt you."

With Eve's wisdom, Sloan laughed. "You won't."

Already growing hard for her, Trey needed no more encouragement. Once again he scooped her up and carried her to the bed. Working together between hungry kisses, they managed to remove her clothes and discard his towel.

As one, they stretched out on the bed, their bodies eagerly intertwining. He kissed her, moving his mouth over her lips and parting them with the hard insistence of his tongue. His hand took the weight of a full breast, shaping itself to its plumpness. He bent his head to taste its erect nipple.

Her hands pressed and urged him as her body writhed in need, eager to satisfy and be satisfied. She was warm and giving, hot and taking, all at the same time. When he finally mounted her, her nails raked his back — and a gasp of pleasure came from her throat.

"Love me, Trey," she demanded.

He shuddered, and his flesh's need became entangled with his soul's need. It was a combination that wrought grace and perfection out of something that was otherwise bestial. They were joined, two parts alternately thrusting together until the pressure left them and they lay in a tangle of contentment.

Trey moved his hand onto the flatness of her stomach where the life they had created now lived. "It's going to be a boy," he stated.

"You don't know that," Sloan chided at the certainty in his voice.

"Yes, I do. It's a Calder tradition," he informed her. "The firstborn is always a son."

Sloan released a sigh of mock regret. "I guess all that will have to change when our little girl is born."

"Why do you always have to be so contrary?" Trey eyed her with amusement.

"It's a woman's right. Hasn't anyone ever told you that?" Her smile teased him.

The remark had the ring of something his sister would say, but Trey chose not to dwell on that. "One thing's for sure, we aren't going to name the little guy after me when he's born. He's likely to get tagged with some nickname like Four-Bits or Quatro."

"I don't know. I kinda like Chase for a

girl's name." Sloan worked to keep a straight face, but the shock and dismay that leapt into Trey's expression made her laugh. "Just kidding."

"I should hope so," he murmured. "I don't think it would sit too well with Granddad to have a girl named after him."

"Girl or boy, I think the poor thing is starving. I know I am." Sloan rolled away from him to the edge of the bed, then paused and looked back at him. "It just hit me. Do you realize how ironic it is? We no more than get all the work done in here and now we have to start thinking about a nursery."

"That's easy. We'll just set up a crib right here in our bedroom," Trey replied.

"It takes a bit more than a crib, Papa." Sloan informed him, then made her way into the bathroom.

Trey remained on the bed, hands clasped behind his head while he gazed at the ceiling, smiling as that word "Papa" played around in his mind.

Chapter Fifteen

An August wind, laden with the last of summer's heat, swept across the plains, word of the new Calder bride being with child traveled almost as fast. In less than three days, the news had reached every corner of the Triple C and gone beyond its boundary fences to Blue Moon.

An hour after he confirmed the rumor, Donovan was on the telephone to his boss. "Just thought you'd want to know," he began with no preamble, "you'll soon have another Calder to deal with."

"What do you mean — another Calder?" Rutledge demanded. "Is somebody getting married? Jessy? The daughter?"

"No." Donovan smiled. "The new bride's expecting a child."

"A child." His tone changed. "Are you sure about this?"

"I got it from three different sources. The last one claimed she'd been to a doctor and — as the old saying goes — the poor rabbit died."

"And when is this new Calder due to arrive?"

"Late February, early March is what I'm hearing."

"I see. By the way, it seems likely that your Laredo Smith cowboy is a nephew. Hattie Ludlow's first husband came from a large family — nine children, I believe it was. One of his sisters married a man named Smith. Of their six children, five are boys. We haven't tracked them all down yet. I'm not sure it's necessary, since he appears to be who he says he is."

"That's up to you. I was just giving you my read on the man."

"Keep me posted. On everything. I don't care how trivial the information sounds to you," Rutledge stated and abruptly hung up. His hand remained on the receiver a moment longer as the beginnings of a smile lifted the corners of his mouth. "A baby," he murmured, a scheming light in his dark eyes.

The moment of reflection was a brief one. Briskly, he pulled his hand from the phone and hit the controls on the armrest, pivoting the wheelchair away from the desk and sending it rolling away.

"Harold!" he barked the summoning call.

Almost immediately the burly manservant and nurse appeared in the study's doorway. "I'm right here, sir."

"Get me a cigar and a glass of bourbon."

Bennett hesitated a second, surprised by the request for a cigar, but not so surprised that he didn't know the order in which Rutledge wanted the two items. He delivered the drink first, then returned with the humidor, opening the lid to allow Rutledge to select his own. Using the tool designed for its specific purpose, Bennett then snipped off the end of the cigar, waited while Rutledge dipped it in the liquor, and held the lighter the proper distance from the tip.

Taking a chance that he wasn't misreading the supremely pleased look on Rutledge's face, he indulged his own curiosity. "Something to celebrate, sir?"

"Indeed." The word rumbled from Rutledge like a lion's purr. "It appears there will be a great-grandchild in the Calder house come spring."

Startled, Bennett stared. "You mean —"

"Yes, the new bride is with child." A craftiness was in his employer's smile. "That could open up a whole new avenue."

No more was offered than that. In silence, Rutledge puffed on his cigar, losing himself in thought.

* ★ ★

Two days into fall roundup, the rain came. In some sections of the Triple C, it fell in a steady, soaking drizzle. Over the rest, it came down in sheets. Soil that had been little more than layers of dry powder quickly turned into a tawny-yellow gumbo that made treacherous footing for both man and beast.

Downpour or drizzle, no halt was called to the roundup. As long as no deadly lightning came out of the clouds, work would continue, though at a pace dictated by the inclement weather. There were no breakneck pursuits after escaping steers, no fancy rollbacks or quick cuts, not in that mud-slick terrain.

During those times when the rain fell in buckets, visibility was reduced to mere yards, forcing some areas to be worked two and three times in an attempt to ensure that no cattle were missed. And there was no slicker made that could keep a cowboy dry. Water always managed to seep inside and add its wetness to the bone-chilling damp air.

Yet the need for the life-giving rain had been so great that few grumbled about it — least of all Jessy. She was present because it was an unwritten rule on the

Triple C that no culling of the herd would take place without the ranch boss there. Riders, working in pairs, quietly walked their horses into the gathered herd and went about the business of separating the steers destined for market. Any cow deemed too old or too weak to survive the winter was also cut out of the herd. It was hard, slow work for both horse and rider.

Partnered with Laredo, Jessy pointed her horse's nose at a young steer. The wild-eyed animal snorted in alarm and swung in the opposite direction, only to be confronted by the sight of Laredo and his horse. It made an attempt to bolt past Jessy, but her horse jumped into its path, stumbled slightly, and righted itself. Laredo was there to fill the momentary void, blocking the animal's escape. In seconds they had the steer trotting to join the gather.

Jessy followed, but only partway, pulling up when she felt an unevenness in her horse's stride. She reined him toward the makeshift camp located some distance beyond the pocket of ground where the herd was gathered. Having spotted Trey sitting astride a claybank stallion at the lip of the rise, she angled in his direction. His hat was pulled low, and the collar of his slicker was turned up, but she recognized him instantly just the same.

"It feels like my horse lost a shoe," she said when she was almost to him. "I'll have to switch to another."

"Grab a cup of coffee while you're there. I'll take over." Lending action to his statement, he nudged his horse forward, moving past her toward the waiting herd.

That moment stayed with her all the way to camp. Taking Trey's advice, Jessy left her horse at the picket line where the extra horses were tied and trekked across the muddy ground to the motorized chuck wagon. A heavy tarp, supported by upright poles, offered some shelter from the falling rain. Jessy helped herself to coffee from the never empty pot and wandered over to the fifty-five-gallon drum and the small fire that blazed inside it.

Behind her came the stomping sound of someone trying to dislodge clumps of mud from his boots. Jessy looked back to see Laredo duck his head under the tarp and head for the coffeepot. A mug of steaming coffee in his gloved hand, he joined her at the barrel, his hat pushed to the back of his head.

"Horse threw a shoe, did it?" he challenged. "You could have told me. One minute you're there, and the next you're gone. I thought the rain had swallowed you up. Good thing Trey told me where I could find you or I'd have been searching the puddles."

"Right," she said in a voice dry with disbelief, but the mention of her son switched the direction of her thoughts. "Do you know I didn't have to tell Trey to take over? He told me. I don't know if it's getting married or having a baby on the way that's done it, but he seems to have matured a lot over the summer."

"You always hear, blood tells," Laredo remarked idly. "Taking the lead comes natural to him, I've noticed."

"You must have seen it more than I have."

"Only because you're stuck too much in that office." An impish gleam lit his eyes. "Just look at what you've been missing — mud up to your eyeballs, rain pouring down your neck, and your clothes soaked to the skin."

"I'll take this over choking dust and heat any day, and you know —" Distracted by a set of headlight beams slashing through the rain curtain, Jessy never finished the sentence. "Who could that be?"

Five feet from the corner upright of the

tarpaulin roof, the ranch pickup rolled to a stop and the headlights and engine were switched off. A figure in a hooded slicker emerged from the cab and hurried, head down, to the tarp's shelter at a running walk. The head came up, and a hand pushed the hood partway back to reveal Sloan's smiling face.

"Hi, Jessy, Laredo." She crossed to them and cupped her wet hands over the barrel to absorb some of the fire's warmth. "It is pouring. There's two inches in the rain gauge at The Homestead, but I'll bet more than that fell out here."

Her easy chatter eliminated Jessy's initial concern that some problem had come up at headquarters. If there was any, she sensed that Sloan was unaware of it.

"With all this rain, I know you aren't here to get your first look at a roundup." Jessy smiled. "So I'm guessing you're here to tell Trey about your doctor's appointment this morning."

Sloan's quick laugh was an admission of sorts. "I knew he'd be late coming home tonight, and I didn't want to wait. Cat said he'd probably be grabbing a cup of coffee sometime around the middle of the afternoon, so I thought I'd talk to him then."

"Now that you mention it," Laredo

began, "he's due for a break about now. I'll go get him."

"You don't have to," she rushed.

"That's all right. It's time we headed back out anyway." He downed a final drink of his coffee and dumped the remainder on the ground.

"He's right," Jessy agreed. "We've had our break."

Sloan watched them disappearing into the rain and waited in eager anticipation for that first glimpse of Trey. A good five minutes passed before she spied his familiar shape approaching the cook shack on foot.

The minute he stepped beneath the tarp's roof, his hands came up to catch hold of her upper arms while his eyes drank in the sight of her upturned face. The radiance of her smile reached out to him and gripped his throat with an aching tightness. Not for the first time, Trey was reminded of the old claim that pregnancy made a woman seem more beautiful and more desirable. And the soft drape of her raincoat's hood only seemed to enhance the Madonna-like quality she possessed.

"You crazy little idiot, what are you doing driving out here in all this rain?" His smile made it clear that he was glad she had.

"Surely you didn't think I'd get lost," Sloan chided him. "How could I, when I had my map with me?"

The hand-drawn map was her pride and joy, one that she had created herself after studying old aerial photographs and topo maps of the ranch. While not precisely to scale, it was accurate down to the last road. Locations of various camps and landmarks were all marked and identified by name. It was next to impossible now for Sloan to get lost when she ventured from the Triple C headquarters.

"Drove straight to the spot, did you," Trey guessed, taking a certain pride in the time and effort she had put into the map.

"I did," Sloan asserted with a jaunty smugness.

"That's what I thought. So what did the doctor have to say this morning? Momma and baby are doing fine, I hope?"

"We are. But I failed to mention one thing before you left this morning." Sloan attempted to assume a serious expression, but the deep blue of her eyes never lost its bright gleam.

"And what would that be?" he prompted when she failed to continue.

"I almost don't want to tell you, because I know how you're going to gloat. You see, we did an ultrasound this morning —"

"It's a boy." Water from his hat dripped onto her face as Trey dipped his head and stole a warm kiss. The love and pride of a father was in his eyes when he drew back. "I knew all along we would have a son. Like I told you, it's tradition.

"You're very pleased with yourself, aren't you," Sloan teased.

"Oh, I'm definitely glad it's a boy, but I would have loved a daughter just as much," Trey assured her.

"Well, she'll have to wait, because we aren't having twins."

The drumbeat of rain on the tightly stretched canvas tarp picked up its tempo. Runoff cascaded over the edge of its down-tipped front, creating a long, sheer curtain of water. Some distance away, cattle lowed in confusion.

Trey was oblivious to all of it, his attention centered on Sloan. "You don't mind that it isn't a girl, do you?"

"As long as the baby is healthy, I don't care if we have a son or a daughter."

"Me either."

"You say that now only because you're getting the son you wanted."

"Naturally." He grinned to let her know he wasn't serious.

"That's what I thought." Sloan paused briefly. "So . . . do you want to hear the rest of my news?"

"There's more?" An eyebrow arched in mild surprise.

"Indeed there is," she declared, excitement sparkling in her eyes. "While I was at the doctors, my agent phoned. When I returned his call, he informed me that *National Geographic* is doing a feature on Yellowstone in the winter. The arrangements have already been made for a photographer to be there in November. Unfortunately, the photographer who was scheduled for the shoot was in a car accident and ended up with several broken bones. So he can't make it. But listen to this. It seems he saw some of my photos of snowfall I took in Hawaii, and he recommended me to take his place. How exciting is that?"

"That's quite an honor," Trey agreed. "Too bad they can't postpone it until next year."

"What do you mean?" Bewilderment was in the look she gave him.

He regarded the answer as obvious. "You can't go, Sloan. You did tell them that, didn't you?"

"What do you mean I can't go?" She bristled a little. "Why not?"

"Because you're pregnant."

"That hardly makes me an invalid," Sloan retorted. "We're talking about November, Trey. I'll barely be five months along then."

"But you aren't talking about doing some photographic essay on a tropical island. Your destination is the snow, cold, and ice of Yellowstone in winter. I know you, Sloan. You aren't going to be content to snap a few pictures of Old Faithful blowing off steam. No, you'll be trekking into the backcountry, trying to capture an angle nobody's ever seen before. I swear to God, every time you even think about getting your hands on a camera, your common sense goes out the window!" He turned from her in disgust.

Sloan immediately snared his arm and angrily planted herself in front of him. "That isn't true!"

"Isn't it?" he challenged with heat. "Not two minutes ago, you claimed that all you cared about was having a healthy baby. Now you're talking about traipsing up and over snowpacked mountains."

"You're being ridiculous. I would be careful."

"Sure you would" — a muscle leaped convulsively along his jaw — "right up to the moment when you just need to move a little bit to the left to get the shot you want. What happens if the snow gives way under you, and you go tumbling? How safe is our son then?" Trey demanded, then abruptly sighed. "I don't know why we're even arguing about this. They aren't going to hire you when they find out you're pregnant. They won't want to expose themselves to that kind of liability."

"I suppose you're going to tell them." She glared in accusation.

Trey cocked his head to one side, his gaze cool and hard. "Weren't you?"

Her chin dipped slightly down, her gaze faltering under his steady regard. Then once again her chin was up and out, her eyes returning his look, stare for stare. "Of course I was. And you're right. They probably will want someone else."

He saw the bitterness of regret in the tight way her lips were pressed together. "You still want to do it, don't you? Even though you know there's a risk something could happen to our baby."

"Life is a risk." But her hands spread protectively over her stomach. "But I don't think I could ever forgive myself if something did happen. It isn't easy to pass up an opportunity like this, though. It's exactly the kind of thing I love doing. I wish you could understand that."

But he couldn't. He doubted that he ever would. Still, he gathered her loosely in his arms and pressed a kiss on her forehead. "I'm sorry," Trey apologized for his lack of understanding.

"Thanks." She managed a small but grateful smile. "There'll be other chances, though, after the baby's born."

Trey realized that Sloan thought he was sorry that it had been necessary to turn down this opportunity. Wisely, he didn't bother to correct her.

"I'd better get back out there," he told her. "We'll be loading in the dark as it is. You'll be careful driving home, won't you?"

"Just call that truck a turtle," Sloan promised.

After a parting kiss that lengthened into something more than a farewell peck, they went their separate ways, Sloan to the pickup that would take her back to The Homestead and Trey to the picket line, where a fresh horse waited for him. For both of them, the memory of their brief but heated disagreement was relegated to a back corner of their minds.

★ ★ ★

The rain continued on and off for another week, prolonging the fall roundup by an equal amount of time. By the time the sun came out, every river and creek on the Triple C was running full, and fresh hints of green could be seen in the autumn grasses.

The rain had rejuvenated more than just the land and its watercourses. With the long dry spell behind them, men walked with more spring to their step. The smell of winter was in the air, but no one minded now that the land was healthy and strong again.

For once, the road ahead looked smooth. An easy contentment was in the air. With the roundup over, autumn's last chore was underway — the trailing of the horse remuda to its winter range.

Minutes after the flanking riders succeeded in getting the herd lined out and moving in the right direction, a helicopter swooped toward the airport's landing pad, and all hell broke loose. Every man on the drive cursed the culprit by name as they raced after the spooked horses.

Not long after the helicopter landed, the front door opened and Tara swept into The Homestead, a sable coat flaring about her legs. Anticipating her arrival, Cat was already on hand to greet her.

"This is a surprise, Tara. You rarely come to Montana at this time of year. What's the occasion?" Cat wondered.

"Obviously it's a special one," Tara stated as she tugged off her gloves, one finger at a time, and regarded Cat with a glance dark with rebuke.

"Why? What have I done?" Cat said in all innocence.

"It's what you didn't do, and you know it." Gloves in hand and head held high in offended dignity, Tara sailed past her into the living room. "I probably shouldn't even be speaking to you."

With a roll of her eyes and a despairing shake of her head, Cat followed after her. "Please spare me the theatrics, Tara. I swear you get more dramatic with each passing year," she said with impatience. "Just tell me what it is that I am supposed to have done."

"It's what you didn't do," Tara corrected as she slipped off the sable, depositing it on the sofa with a graceful toss. "Honestly, Cat, you are the nearest thing I have to a little sister. But do I hear from you that Trey's bride is carrying Ty's first grandchild? No. Who knows when I would have been told if I hadn't stopped to see Laura on my way back from Europe?"

"Wonderful news, isn't it?" Cat deliberately refrained from offering any excuses for not contacting Tara.

"The best. And it's going to be a boy, too. Just imagine a little Ty Junior running around here."

"This old house is liable to become a lively place in the next few years," Cat agreed.

"Where is the little mother?" Tara's gaze made a curious circle of the living room and its exits.

"Upstairs, I think."

Tara pressed a hand near her throat and made an attractive moue of sympathy. "Morning sickness, of course. The poor thing."

"Actually, Sloan's one of the lucky ones. She hasn't had a single bout of nausea. About the only thing that makes her queasy is the smell of coffee."

"Speaking of coffee, I'd love a cup." Pausing, Tara looked toward the staircase. "But first I should go up and congratulate our mother-to-be. You go ahead and make some fresh coffee. I won't be long."

"My pleasure."

The underlying tone of sarcasm in Cat's

voice was lost on Tara as she crossed to the oak stairway and began her ascent, one hand maintaining a graceful glide over the smooth banister.

When she arrived at the master suite, she rapped lightly on the door and turned its brass knob in advance of the voice within bidding her to enter. By then, Tara was halfway into the sitting room. Her eyes were quick to locate Sloan, seated on the edge of the sofa cushion, a multitude of photographs spread across the coffee table in front of her.

Rising, Sloan greeted her with a polite smile. "Hello, Tara. I thought I heard a helicopter a few minutes ago. Obviously it was you."

"I flew in as soon as I heard the blessed news." She walked straight to Sloan and kissed the air near both cheeks, then drew back to run a critically assessing eye over Sloan's figure, finding only a small, be-traying pooch of her stomach. "Look at how slim and trim you still are," she mar-veled. "Why you barely show at all."

"Not yet, anyway," Sloan admitted.

"Losing your figure is just one of the curses that goes along with having a baby, I'm told." Tara's attention shifted point-edly to the array of photographs on the coffee table, a mix of broad vistas and artful nature vignettes. "What's this?"

"Excuse the mess. I'm in the middle of updating my portfolio."

A small laugh slipped from Tara, bell-like in its softness. "Here I thought you'd be engrossed in planning the nursery. So which of the spare rooms will you be using? You need to do a western decor. I saw the most darling mobile for the crib with cowboys on purple and green horses. It was absolutely precious and just perfect for a little boy. You can use that idea and do the entire room with variations on it."

"We aren't going to have a separate nursery, at least not until he's older," Sloan informed the older woman. "We're going to have the crib in our bedroom."

"Really." Disdain was in Tara's voice and expression.

"Yes." Sloan found that she took supreme pleasure in doing the opposite of what Tara thought she should. "There's plenty of room for a crib and a changing table once we take out those two chairs. That way I won't have to worry whether I'll hear him when he cries in the night."

"A baby monitor can accomplish that. Your bedroom should be restricted to you and your husband. It isn't a place for a child."

"Some might feel that way, but we don't."

One shoulder moved in an elegant but dismissive shrug. "It's your bed and your marriage. I should think it will make it a bit awkward for your nanny. You are going to have a nanny, aren't you?"

"Absolutely not," Sloan replied without hesitation, determined that no one else was going to raise her child.

"Then you decided to give up your career, after all. That's a wise choice," Tara declared with approval. "I was confident that once you had time to think about it, you'd see for yourself. It would just be a source of conflict for you. And, I assure you, you will be much too busy with all your other responsibilities to devote yourself to it as you would want, both as a mother and the mistress of this house."

"Sorry, but I intend to continue my work after the baby's born. After all, I wouldn't presume to usurp Cat's position."

"And you shouldn't, either," Tara agreed, to Sloan's surprise. "Cat is such an incredibly unselfish woman — and so devoted to her father. I mean, the way she has stayed here to care for him even though she would love more than anything to move to Texas to be near her only son. Yet, you never hear a word of complaint from her. It's sad, really, but Chase needs her now, and, heaven knows, none of us can be sure how much longer he'll be with us." Releasing a dramatic sigh, Tara gave a little shake of her head. "That's much too morbid a subject when we should be talking about little Tyrone."

"Tyrone?" Sloan looked at her blankly.

"You are going to name the baby after his grandfather, aren't you?"

Sloan tried to dodge the question. "We haven't decided on a name yet."

"But Tyrone is such an obvious choice. I'm surprised Trey hasn't insisted on it. What better way for him to honor his father's memory than to name his son after him."

"I certainly wouldn't object," Sloan stated, determined to make that clear. "But Trey feels that our son should have his own name."

"We'll have to change his mind, won't we?" Tara declared. "Perhaps I'll talk to Cat about it over coffee. I would ask you to join us but —"

"No thanks, I'll pass." For the first time, Sloan was glad she couldn't stand the smell of coffee. It provided the perfect excuse to decline spending any more time in this woman's company.

Some two hours later, Sloan heard the helicopter take off. It was a beautiful sound, considering it meant Tara wouldn't be joining them for lunch.

Sloan made a point to mention Tara's visit to Trey when he returned to The Homestead for the noon meal, as well as Tara's desire that their son be named after his father. Trey's reaction was instant and emphatic.

"If that woman thinks she can use emotional blackmail to force me to name our son after my father, she is very mistaken."

Cat spoke up, "You could use it for a middle name."

"Is that your idea, Aunt Cat? Or Tara's?" Trey challenged.

"It's nothing more than a suggestion."

"As suggestions go, there's nothing wrong with it — except we all know that if our baby has Tyrone anywhere in his name, Tara will be here constantly, fussing and cooing over him. I don't think any of us want that." He sat down at the table and dragged a napkin across his lap. "The next time Tara says anything about it, tell her that Laura is planning to name her first son after our father."

Chase frowned. "She is?"

"She is now." Trey grinned, then added, "I'll give Laura a call later and remind her that she owes me some favors."

But they hadn't heard the last of Tara. The second week of November a delivery truck arrived. The driver made trip after trip into The Homestead, hauling the larger boxes on a dolly and carrying the smaller ones. All were addressed to Mr. and Mrs. Trey Calder, and all identified the sender as Tara Calder.

When everything was opened, Sloan could only stare at the lavish assortment of baby items in amazement. There was everything from a new crib, baby dresser, and changing table to a complete layette, a crib bumper, and custom-made bedding based on the colorful cowboy mobile. She couldn't see a single thing a baby might need that wasn't there.

Not every item was one she would have chosen, but at the same time, she could find little fault in Tara's taste. Still, she couldn't shake that sense of disappointment at being deprived of the pleasure of shopping for these things herself.

Jessy was the first to return to The

Homestead that evening and view the munificence. A dry smile tugged at her mouth when she glanced at Sloan.

"Let me guess," she said. "This is from Tara."

"Yes." Sloan tried to look happy about it.

"You're lucky," Jessy told her. "At least you have a few practical items here. You should have seen the store-full of toys, stuffed animals, and fancy outfits she sent when the twins were born."

"I almost wish I could send some of it back," Sloan murmured.

"It wouldn't do you any good. She'd just send more. So just keep what you like and we'll give the rest away." There was a warm glint in her eyes. "That's what I did."

Just for a moment, Sloan felt as if she and her mother-in-law were co-conspirators. "So will I."

In the end there were only a few items that Sloan chose not to keep, but she felt better knowing the choice had been hers and that she still had a few things to buy.

Naturally, Trey didn't understand why she was giving away things that she'd have to go out and replace. In the end, he gave up trying to reason with her and told her to do what she wanted. Which Sloan had every intention of doing anyway.

Chapter Sixteen

Snow fell soft and steady out of a leaden sky. With no wind to scatter them, the flakes accumulated in layers, blanketing the Montana plains in a thick mantle and capping the trees' barren branches in white.

In the hush that settled over the land, the hum and click of the gasoline pump dispensing fuel into the pickup's tank seemed loud. Trey stood next to the truck, his gloved hands thrust deep in the pockets of his sheepskin-lined jacket, his shoulders hunched against December's bite and his collar turned up. His warm breath created a steamy vapor that mixed with the smell of gasoline fumes.

Idly stamping his feet to keep the blood flowing to them, he made a visual sweep of the area. Lights gleamed from the windows of the houses where the married ranch hands lived. At first glance, he seemed to be the only one out and about, but there was another pickup parked in front of the commissary, a thick dusting of snow already coating its windshield.

The pump kicked off. For a moment there was absolute silence. Trey pulled his hands from his pockets, squeezed the nozzle's lever to top off the tank, then set it back on its cradle and screwed on the gas cap.

Finished, he struck out for the commissary to sign the gas ticket. Johnny Taylor walked out the door, his down jacket unzipped, exposing his chest to the weather, ungloved hands holding a letter and the envelope it came in. Intent on reading it, Johnny was oblivious to the crunch of Trey's approaching footsteps until he was nearly upon him.

"Trey." Startled, Johnny came to a full stop. "I didn't know you were out here."

"Got a letter from Kelly, did you?" Trey guessed.

There was a touch of embarrassment in Johnny's quick smile, but it couldn't compete with the way the rest of his expression brightened. "Yeah. Looks like she can come home for the ranch Christmas party. She's been working part-time to help with costs, but she's got the weekend off. I told her if she did, I'd pick her up and drive her back."

"That will cost you some gas money. Sounds like things are getting serious."

Johnny dipped his head and pushed around some snow with the toe of his boot. "I been thinking about asking her to marry me. Not right away o' course," he added, hastily shooting a glance at Trey. "She's got her heart set on becoming a nurse, so she has her schooling to finish first. But I figure it'll be a good thing to have a nurse in the family."

"Should cut down on the medical expense."

But the teasing gibe didn't register with Johnny. "That's the way I looked at it, too." Hesitating, he turned solemn. "This marrying business — it's working out okay for you, isn't it?"

"It couldn't be better." And Trey meant every word of it.

"Sloan being a photographer, sort of a working girl, and all, that isn't causing any problems, is it?"

"She won't be doing much of that with the baby coming."

"I guess not," Johnny conceded and angled toward his truck. "See you around."

As he started to move away, Trey noticed the cassette tape that poked its head out of Johnny's jacket pocket. "What's that you got there? Don't tell me you're going to sit home on a Saturday night and watch a movie?"

"I gotta start saving my money."

"I've never known you when you didn't," Trey retorted. "You probably got the first quarter the tooth fairy gave you."

"Damn right I do." But Johnny grinned when he said it, making light of his tight-fisted ways.

Chuckling softly to himself, Trey headed into the commissary, signed the fuel ticket, came back out, and climbed into the pickup. Snow was still falling, and the windshield wipers slapped away the powdery flakes as he drove to The Homestead.

Tracks left by other feet made a path through the snow to the front steps and onto the porch. Trey followed them all the way to the wreath-clad door. Pausing on the mat, he knocked the worst of the snow from his boots, then turned the knob.

A toasty warmth engulfed him when he walked in. As he shrugged off the heavy jacket, Trey noticed Cat in the dining room adding the finishing touches to the table settings.

"Where's Sloan? In the kitchen?" he asked.

"Upstairs. She wanted to finish her

Christmas cards before supper. It's in the oven now. Be about another hour before it's done."

"Thanks." Leaving his jacket and hat on the coat rack by the door, Trey crossed the living room and climbed the stairs to the master suite.

A small, but cheery fire crackled in the sitting room's fireplace to greet him when he entered. There sat Sloan, curled up in an easy chair next to it, a mix of blank Christmas cards and addressed envelopes spread over the ottoman in front of her and an address book balanced on the chair's broad armrest. The flames' flickering light shone on her face, enhancing its natural glow.

She looked up in surprise, the pen in her hand poised in midstroke. "Is it that late, or are you home early?"

"I'm a little early," he admitted while he made his way to her chair. "You look like a contented little kitten, curled up in front of the fire."

"A very pregnant kitten." There was a definite roundness to her stomach now that not even her bulky sweater could disguise.

"A pregnant and beautiful kitten," Trey corrected and bent to exchange a warm and lingering kiss with her.

"Your lips are cold," Sloan murmured when he lifted his head.

"In case you haven't noticed, it's snowing outside."

"I did notice a few flakes drifting by the window."

"I'll have you know there's more than a few out there."

"Personally I hope it stays on the ground through the holidays. It's been years since I saw snow on Christmas day." A wistful quality was in her voice.

"You might just get your wish this year." Trey straightened up from the chair. "Speaking of Christmas, how are the cards coming along? Cat mentioned you were trying to get them done before supper."

"Only three more after this one." Sloan tapped the card with the half-finished note on her lap.

"If you just signed your name instead of writing those newsy little notes, they'd go a lot faster," he teased.

"You're trying to get a rise out of me, but it isn't going to work. Sit down here by the fire and get warm and tell me all about your day like a good husband." She started to lean forward to clear a space for him on the ottoman.

"Sit back. I'll do that." He scooped the

unused cards into a stack and set them on the table next to her chair. The sealed envelopes he pushed to one side, clearing a space on the ottoman.

Sloan waited until he sat down. "So what's new?"

"Not much, although I did run into Johnny Taylor when I stopped to get gas. He told me he's thinking about asking Kelly to marry him."

There was utter surprise in her expression. "Was he serious?"

"Johnny isn't the kind to joke about such things," Trey answered dryly.

"Do you think she'll accept?"

"Who knows? I never thought they'd ever have more than one date, but they went everywhere together this summer. Which shows how wrong I was."

In an attempt to arrange his long frame in a more comfortable position on the low seat, he stretched his legs and jostled the ottoman in the process. The stack of addressed envelopes shifted toward the edge. Sheer reflex enabled him to catch them before they slid to the floor.

"Isn't she in nursing school? She wouldn't quit, would she?"

"Johnny doesn't want her to." The envelopes were turned every which way, corners catching in the flaps of those above it. One by one, Trey straightened them until his eye was caught by the name on one of the envelopes. He felt like he'd been gut-kicked. "What's this?" He showed it to Sloan, his hard gaze dark with questioning.

"It's a card to Uncle Max. What did you think it was?" she asked with amusement.

"Max Rutledge is the man you call Uncle Max?" The statement bordered on an accusation. "Why am I just now finding this out?"

"How should I know? It was never any secret," Sloan insisted.

"Then why didn't you tell me?" Trey demanded.

"Why didn't you ask?" She hurled the question in response and angrily shoved aside the card and ballpoint pen from her lap, then struggled awkwardly out of the chair. "What difference does it make, anyway?"

"Maybe none — and maybe a lot." And that thought kept twisting inside him.

"You're not making any sense, Trey. What have you got against Uncle Max?" Temper was in her eyes, challenging him to explain.

"Personally, I have nothing. But I'm not sure Rutledge could say the same about us." Trey stood as well, every ounce of his attention trained on her, watching and waiting, and all the while wanting desperately to believe the innocence she showed him was no act.

"Stop talking in riddles, and tell me what you mean!" Sloan all but shouted the demand.

"Are you saying that you didn't know his son Boone died in a fight with my cousin Quint?"

"Quint." The shocked and dazed look on her face seemed genuine. Sloan partially turned from him. "I heard Boone had been killed in a fight, but —" There was a small, uncertain movement of her head. "Boone was such a bully and a brute, I just assumed it was some barroom brawl." She looked back at Trey, her blue eyes all dark and troubled. "I was on an assignment and couldn't get away to attend the funeral. When I did talk to Uncle Max on the phone, it didn't feel right to ask for details — the how and the who. But . . . you say it was Quint. That's hard to believe. How? Why?"

Trey found himself in a private debate, trying to decide how much he should tell. Sloan was his wife; he should feel free to confide anything and everything to her. Yet he was instinctively hesitating, and that troubled him more than finding out Max Rutledge was her former guardian.

"There was a fight. Boone came at Quint with a knife. In the struggle, Boone was killed. It was self-defense." He stated the facts, with no embellishment.

"But what were they fighting over? With Boone, I know it never took much, but there had to be something."

"Our Texas ranch shares a boundary with Rutledge's Slash R. Rutledge tried to buy it from us. When we turned down his offers, he tried to force a sale by making sure no one would work for us, arranging for our credit to be cut off, burning our hay along with some five hundred acres of pasture, and infecting our herd with anthrax. The anthrax was where he slipped up. Quint was able to prove he was behind it."

Sloan shook her head in instant denial. "Uncle Max wouldn't have done that. That kind of sneaky, evil thinking is the way Boone's mind worked."

"Boone definitely became the convenient scapegoat." Like the rest of his family, Trey was certain Boone had done nothing that Max hadn't told him to do.

Quick to pick up on the cynicism in his

voice, Sloan gave him a sharp look. "You believe Uncle Max is responsible, don't you?"

"Do you honestly think that a man like Max Rutledge wouldn't know what his own son was doing?" Trey countered.

"It's possible," she insisted, but it was purely a defensive reaction.

"Maybe it is, and maybe it isn't," Trey responded tightly. "Either way, it isn't likely that Max Rutledge has any warm feelings for the Calders. If anything, he may think he has a score to settle with us."

"Wait a minute." Sloan stiffened, hurt and anger combining in her expression. "You thought he was using me as an instrument of that revenge, didn't you?"

"No, of course I didn't —"

"You're lying." Her voice shook with emotion. "I saw the way you looked at me — like I was a stranger." Hot tears gathered in her eyes. "I'm your wife. It's our baby I'm carrying! How could you?"

When she spun away and took the first step to flee from him, Trey moved quickly to stop her, catching her by the shoulders and pulling her back against him, but making no attempt to force her to face him.

"That isn't true, Sloan." He was conscious of the stiff way she held herself, resisting his touch, and the silent, shaking sobs that trembled through her. His head bent close, his face brushing against her hair, as he tried to explain. "What you saw was the shock of finding Max Rutledge's name on that envelope. It was the last thing in the world I expected to see. Dammit, you've got to understand that."

She twisted angrily out of his hold and turned to glare at him, stormy-eyed, cheeks wet with tears. "You're wrong about Uncle Max, and you're wrong about me."

"I'm not wrong about you. I love you, Sloan. Just because Max Rutledge is your former guardian, that doesn't change the way I feel." That much was true, lending conviction to his voice. "I love you," he repeated and saw a crack in her resistance. "I know you're a little oversensitive right now, with the baby and all. A part of me wishes I'd never said anything when I noticed that card. But you need to look at it from my side. I had to ask about it. I didn't do it to hurt you."

"But you did. It was . . ." Sloan hesitated, searching for the words. ". . . like you suddenly didn't trust me."

"It might have seemed that way. Look,

I'm sorry. What more can I say?" A trace of frustration was in his voice.

"I don't know," she admitted, looking down.

"Sloan." With one finger, he tilted her chin up and tipped his head toward her. The kiss was gentle and persuasive, an attempt to heal the rift. She responded, but without much eagerness, and Trey decided not to press for more than that. Instead, he cocked his head and smiled a little wryly. "This is a rotten time to have our first misunderstanding, isn't it?"

Sloan managed a small but conciliatory smile of agreement. "I suppose it is."

"It was bound to happen some time, though. There are always bumps in every road. This is just one of them. We'll explain everything to the family at dinner tonight." Before he ever finished the sentence, her glance shot to him, a battle light in her eyes. Trey spoke quickly to defuse it. "Like you said, your relationship to Max was never a secret as far you were concerned. And there's definitely no reason to keep it from them now."

Mollified by his reasoning, Sloan agreed. "You're right."

"Still love me?" he asked, a touch of joshing humor in his look.

"Most of the time," Sloan countered, matching his tone.

"Mmmm, I'll have to work on that," he murmured and kissed her soundly. Yet neither could so easily banish the shadow of doubt that had fallen on them. A loss of trust, however momentary, was not something easily forgotten.

That evening Chase was at his customary place at the head of the table, with Jessy seated on his right and Laredo next to her. Cat was just about to take her seat opposite Chase when Trey and Sloan walked into the dining room.

"Excellent timing," Cat declared, all smiles. "We were just about to start without you."

"We would have saved you something, though," Laredo inserted with a grin.

Normally the easy family banter would have been a welcome thing, but not tonight. Not for Trey. Yet he managed a smile. "You're all heart, Laredo." He escorted Sloan to the two remaining chairs, pulled out one for her and sat down in the one to Chase's left.

"Has anyone heard the forecast?" Jessy glanced around the table. "Is it supposed to snow all night?"

"I don't know," Cat replied. "I did have the radio on in the kitchen, but obviously I didn't listen when they gave the weather."

Aware that the conversation was headed for a discussion of the snow and its effect on the next day's agenda of ranchwork, Trey spoke up. "Before we get started, there's something Sloan and I want to tell you." Discreetly he reached over and curled a hand over Sloan's. "As you all know, Sloan's parents died when she was a little girl, and her father's business partner served as her legal guardian until she came of legal age. But what you don't know is that man happens to be Max Rutledge."

The instant of silence was electric as all eyes focused on Sloan. But it was Chase's reaction that Trey watched. He knew his grandfather's conviction that Rutledge posed a potential threat to the family colored the thinking of everyone else. Chase didn't make a sound, but his eyes narrowed in a hard and close study of Sloan.

Laredo was first to break the silence, his gaze pinned on Sloan. "That's a vital piece of information to omit, don't you think?"

"If there's any fault in this, it's mine," Trey spoke before Sloan could answer. "She called him Uncle Max. I don't know how many times she mentioned him. But it never crossed my mind that they might be the same person."

Laredo sat back, one arm hooked over a corner of the chair's backrest while his other hand idly fingered the silverware. He looked all loose and indifferent, but he was alert, every sense tuned to Sloan.

"The trouble we've had in the past with Rutledge, I suppose you're claiming that you weren't aware of it." His statement bordered on a taunt.

Stung by it, Sloan reacted with a forceful denial. "I wasn't."

He released a derisive breath. "That's what I thought."

"It's true!" No longer finding any comfort in the warm clasp of Trey's hand, Sloan brought both of hers up to rest against the table edge as she leaned toward Laredo, her hands balling into determined fists. "I didn't know anything about it until Trey told me a little while ago. How could I? I was out of the country when Boone died, and he was already buried when I got back. Uncle Max didn't seem to want to talk about it, so I never asked for details."

"Being out of the country the way you were, obviously you wouldn't have seen any of the initial press coverage, but what about later, at the inquest? Miss that, too, did you?"

"I think you forgot I lived in Hawaii!" she flared.

"Back off, Laredo," Trey said in warning.

Sloan instantly turned an angry glare on him. "I can defend myself! I don't need your help."

Chase raised a hand, keeping it palm down and patting the air. "All of you, calm down," he stated in a reasonable voice, then directed his next remark to Trey. "Laredo's questions are ones that need to be asked. Since Sloan seems willing to answer them, we're willing to listen."

"Thank you," Sloan said, but with a touch of curtness that indicated resentment still simmered below the surface.

Cat reached out to her in sympathy. "I hope you can understand what a surprise this is to all of us." Yet behind the concern in her expression, there were questions and a hint of suspicion.

"That has become very obvious," Sloan replied, again in that clipped tone.

Once more Laredo picked up the questioning. "So, when was the last time you saw your dear old Uncle Max?"

For a split second she said nothing. "Understand that I have called him Uncle Max since I was old enough to talk. It's become a habit. Who knows? Maybe it was some subconscious way of pretending I actually had a family. But we were never close. I barely spent any time at all with him after his wife died. He was always busy or gone somewhere. As for the last time I saw Uncle" — Sloan caught herself and immediately rephrased it — "I saw Max, I had dinner with him — it must have been somewhere around the last of February or the first of March."

"And you're saying you haven't talked to him since?" Laredo's voice was dry with disbelief.

"I never said that at all!" Sloan snapped in answer. "You asked when I saw him last, and I told you."

"Then you have talked to him?" Laredo made it a question.

"Probably two or three times. No, it was definitely three times."

"Obviously he knows about your marriage to Trey," Laredo guessed.

"As a matter of fact, I talked to him shortly after we became engaged. He called me in Hawaii about some papers I needed to sign. While I had him on the phone I told him the good news."

"I'll bet he congratulated you, didn't he?"

"And why shouldn't he?" Sloan fired back. "He was happy for me."

"I'll bet he was," Laredo agreed, then slanted a look at Chase. "Want'a bet the prenuptial agreement was his idea?"

Sloan rushed to his defense. "He was trying to protect my interests. It's what he's always done."

"I'm curious, Sloan," Cat inserted. "Why didn't you invite him to the wedding?"

"There wasn't any point. He had already told me there was some business trip he had to make that couldn't be postponed."

"He did send us a wedding present," Trey volunteered.

"That sculpture thing," Cat remembered.

"So you talked to him twice more since he phoned you in Hawaii," Jessy said, shifting the discussion back to Sloan's contact with Rutledge.

"Yes, I called to thank him for the wedding present, and the second time was to let him know about . . . our baby." She paused a beat and her gaze raked the table, her posture defiantly stiff and proud. "Regardless of what you think, I never deliberately tried to conceal my association with . . . Max . . . from you. If I had wanted to keep it a secret, I never would have left the envelope with his name and address on it out for Trey to see. I would have hidden it."

Trey was the only one other than Sloan who knew the card had been buried in the middle of a stack. He couldn't help wondering if she had forgotten that detail.

"Let me make sure I understand this right," Laredo said. "During those phone calls you had with Rutledge, he never mentioned that he had any dealings with the Calders in the past?"

"No, he didn't. For that matter, none of you have said a single word about him until now," Sloan retorted.

"Until now, there wasn't reason to," Laredo replied smoothly.

"And there isn't one now!" Sloan insisted, the volume of her voice raising in proportion to her anger. "Trey told me that all of you think Uncle Max was behind the problems you had in Texas. But you'll never convince me that he had anything to do with it. It makes absolutely no sense at all. The man has a multibillion-dollar empire to run. He wouldn't stoop to something like that. That was Boone's style."

"I admire your loyalty, Sloan," Chase told her. "But in this case I think it's misplaced."

"Well, I don't. He's no more guilty of anything than I am." There was a betraying quiver of her chin as Sloan looked around the table, daring anyone to say differently. "You know, it's really a shame you didn't do a background check on me before I married Trey. Then you could have made sure I was a suitable mate."

"That's enough of that talk, young lady," Chase said sharply. "Here at the Triple C we don't judge people based on their past."

"Really?" Sloan looked at him in hot challenge. "And just what do you call this?"

Laredo answered for him. "It's an attempt to get at the truth. After all, you're asking us to believe an awful lot of coincidences."

"I don't particularly care what you believe! Everything I said was the truth, and I know it. That's all that matters to me. And if you don't like it, that's just too bad." Angrily, Sloan shoved her chair back from the table and stood up. "Excuse me, won't you?" she said tightly. "I seem to have lost my appetite."

Head high, she walked out of the room. Trey pushed his chair back and threw a dagger-sharp glance at Laredo. "You didn't have to be so hard on her," he muttered.

Eyebrows raised, Laredo reminded him, "There was only one hostile voice at this table, and it didn't come from any of us."

"The way all of you ganged up on her, what did you expect?" Trey challenged before going after Sloan. With long strides, he caught up with her just as she placed a hand on the stairway's newel post. The instant Sloan felt the touch of his hand she went rigid.

"Let me guess — they have more questions." Her voice wavered.

Trey guessed she was close to tears, but she refused to turn and look at him. "I wouldn't know. I just wanted to make sure you're all right."

"You mean, after being interrogated like a criminal?" This time her voice did catch on a near sob.

"In your shoes, I'd probably be as angry and upset as you are. But try to look at it from their side —"

"How can I when 'their side' makes no sense at all? Uncle Max has never done anything to them. It's ridiculous that they think he did."

Like the rest of his family, Trey knew Max Rutledge had created all the trouble at the Cee Bar; Boone had been nothing more than his puppet. But any attempt to convince Sloan of that would only lead to another argument, and she was upset enough as it was.

"You just need to give them some time, Sloan," he said, knowing himself that the family would judge his wife based on her present and future actions, not her past associations. That was the way things were done on the Triple C — that was the Calder way.

"Please, I know they are your family, but right now I just want to be alone for a while."

Trey wasn't certain that it was a wise decision for her to be alone. At the same time he was reluctant to insist that she return to the dining room.

"If that's what you want," he finally said. "How about if I bring up a tray for you later?"

"I don't care. That's fine." She moved away from him, climbing the stairs.

Watching her, Trey saw the hand she placed under her protruding stomach. Her chin was up and her back was ramrod straight, but he was struck by how alone and vulnerable she looked. It was a sight that aroused all his protective instincts. He abruptly turned from the staircase before he could give in to the urge to go up those stairs with her.

Reluctantly, he retraced his steps to the dining room. As he approached the archway, he heard the comment Cat made.

"I always wondered why Sloan never talked much about her past. Maybe now we know."

"I don't think that's a fair conclusion to draw, Aunt Cat." Calm and a little cool, Trey crossed to his chair and sat down. "When you reminisce, it's usually about the good times. Sloan had no family, no home, no roots. That doesn't exactly make for pleasant memories."

"I think we have discussed this topic enough for one evening," Chase stated. "Let's eat before the food gets any colder than it already is."

But Laredo wasn't ready to let go of the subject. "What do you think we should do about this?"

Calmly, Chase lifted a slice of roast beef onto his plate before deferring the question to his daughter-in-law. "What's your answer to that, Jessy?"

"We do nothing." Showing the same calm, Jessy reached for the meat platter's serving fork. "Sloan is family. Until she proves otherwise, that's the way she will be treated."

"We only have her word about this," Laredo reminded her.

"And the word of a family member is accepted."

Nothing was as simple as that, and Trey knew it. Their level of trust in Sloan had been changed, and only time would correct that. But he wasn't sure how Sloan would handle it, and there was little he could do other than stand beside her. The rest was up to Sloan.

Better than anyone, Trey knew how sensitive and proud Sloan was. He couldn't help being concerned that she wouldn't tolerate the situation very well.

Chapter Seventeen

A steady fall of snowflakes drifted past the windowpane, creating an ever changing pattern of white dots against the gray-black night. Staring out the window, Sloan saw none of this. All trace of her earlier tears had been scrubbed from her face, but resentment continued to simmer, as evidenced by the tightly folded arms across her front and the dig of fingers into her sweater sleeves.

Never had she been more innocent, yet made to feel guilty — and for no reason other than that Max Rutledge had once been her guardian. The entire Calder family seemed obsessed by him. She was convinced their suspicions were totally ludicrous.

But every time Sloan replayed the conversation at the table — not a conversation, she corrected herself, an interrogation — the mental tape always stopped on the question from Laredo for which she had no adequate answer. There was only one person who could supply it.

Coming to a decision, she turned briskly from the window and walked to the black telephone on the sofa's end table. She picked up the receiver and punched the area code and phone number from memory.

Her call was answered after the third ring. "Slash R Ranch."

"Is that you, Bennett?" she guessed, but never gave him a chance to confirm it. "This is Sloan. I need to talk to Uncle Max if he's there. It's important."

"One moment," was the reply.

And she was put on hold. As the seconds continued to tick away, Sloan sat on the arm of the sofa and impatiently tapped a hand on her leg.

After what seemed an interminable wait, the familiar voice of Max Rutledge came over the line. "Yes, Sloan. Bennett said you needed to talk to me. What's wrong?"

"Nothing. Everything —"

"What is it? Has something happened to the baby?"

The concern in his voice was like balm to her raw nerves. Sloan took a long, steadying breath and said, "No. The baby and I are fine. Did I tell you it's going to be a boy?"

"A son. That's wonderful. But I take it

that isn't the reason you called."

"No, it isn't." The tension came back, along with the confusion. "Why didn't you tell me that you knew the Calders? Why did you let me think you'd never had any dealings with them?"

"So they have learned of your connection to me, have they?" he said with a degree of resignation. "I suppose it was bound to come out sometime. And it's my fault for not providing you with the details of that unfortunate business with Boone. But you sounded so happy and so very much in love when you told me of your engagement to Trey that it seemed unkind to bring up that unpleasantness."

"I wish you had," Sloan declared with feeling. "Now they think I deliberately kept it from them."

"Is that what they said?" Surprise and anger crept into his voice.

"Not in so many words, but they implied it."

"Why? What reason would they have?"

"It's a long story. But you have to understand that the Calders are convinced that whatever Boone did, it was on orders from you."

"What?!" Max exploded, outraged and indignant.

Sharing the same view, Sloan released a disgusted sigh. "I know. It's ridiculous, and I told them so. Even worse, though, they actually think it's possible you want to get back at them for Boone's death."

"You can't be serious?"

"I am. Trey told me himself. At the time, I didn't really believe him. Then tonight at the dinner table, the way the family grilled me about you —"

"You?! Why? What has any of this to do with you? Wait. Let me guess. They're probably wondering whether your marriage to Trey is part of some conspiracy of mine."

The instant he said it, Sloan felt a little chill as she remembered the mocking way Laredo had asked if Rutledge had congratulated her upon hearing the news of her engagement. It was exactly what they suspected.

A short, derisive laugh came over the phone line. "Obviously the Calders don't know you very well, Sloan, or they would realize you would never consent to such a thing."

"Trey knows better." She clung to that.

"I'm relieved to hear it. For a moment I thought they were all against you, and I was about to order my plane to come get you."

"That isn't necessary," Sloan assured him. "I'm upset, and I've probably made it sound worse than it is. The Calders couldn't understand why you never told me about the trouble Boone had caused. And I couldn't give them a reason. That's why I called."

"I'm glad you did. And if they start giving you a rough time, don't you dare sit there and take it. Call me, and I'll have you out of there in a heartbeat."

"Thanks, Uncle Max."

The line of her mouth softened into a near smile when she hung up the phone. It took her a moment to realize that all of the Calders' suspicions about Max had planted a few seeds of doubt in her own mind about him. Yet his reaction when she told him about it had echoed her own. It served to solidify her convictions concerning his lack of culpability.

Snowflakes danced in front of the bright lights that focused their beams on the building sign for The Oasis. In this part of Montana, pickups, equipped with four-wheel drive, were as common as flies in summer. And on a Saturday night, snow was no deterrent for the bar's customers. If anything, it provided them with an excuse to stay longer and party harder.

Amidst the blare of music from the jukebox, the melodic ding of the slot machines, and the crowd's nonstop chatter, punctuated by hearty guffaws and giggling laughter, the bang of the cash-register drawers closing on sale after sale could nevertheless be heard, bringing a smile to Donovan's face. A handy profit was something he hadn't expected when he first opened the doors to The Oasis. But here it was, and, by agreement, it all went into his pocket.

Of course, Donovan didn't kid himself. It wasn't the booze or the two-inch-thick T-bones that pulled in this size of a crowd; it was the girls and the gambling.

Turning from the cash register, Donovan made an automatic survey of the bar, on the lookout for trouble. It was a rare Saturday night that didn't have at least one fight. The red light glowing above the door to his private office caught his eye.

"It's all yours, Sammy," he told the bartender and stepped out from behind the long counter.

Shouldering his way through the throng of half-drunk cowboys, he reached the door marked PRIVATE, slipped the key into the lock, and gave it a turn. The telephone with the private line was ringing when he walked in. The red light was something Donovan had rigged up to it so he wouldn't miss a call from Rutledge.

He took the extra seconds to close and lock the door behind him, then picked up the phone. "Donovan here."

"It took you long enough," Max growled.

"Saturday nights are busy."

"Good. I hope it's very busy. I want you to start putting a bug in as many ears as you can that Trey Calder and his young wife are having marital problems."

"They are?" Donovan frowned in surprise. Everything he had heard about them indicated just the opposite.

"Not yet. But this is the time to start some. I have a few ideas on how to go about it."

"Fire away."

The old-fashioned bed tray held a full glass of milk, a covered plate of food, and silverware wrapped in a linen napkin. It was the drink Trey watched as he slowly climbed the stairs, pausing whenever the milk sloshed dangerously close to the rim of the glass.

At the top of the steps, he turned and headed for the master bedroom. Finding the door closed, he braced one end of the tray against his stomach, freeing a hand to turn the knob. He gave the door a shove, caught hold of the tray with both hands again and walked in.

Sloan was by the fireplace, jabbing at the glowing coals with a poker. She turned when he entered, and Trey ran a quick but discreet glance over her in an attempt to assess her current mood. To his relief, her eyes no longer had that wounded and angry snap to them. She looked almost calm.

"I brought you some dinner," he announced. "I thought you might be getting hungry."

"Starving." She returned the poker to its stand and looked at him with a hint of chagrin. "I thought I was going to have to swallow my pride and slip downstairs to raid the refrigerator."

Hearing that, Trey was sorry he'd brought the tray. As far as he was concerned, the sooner Sloan was obliged to mingle with the family again, the better off they would all be. But it didn't seem wise to say that.

Instead he asked, "Should I set this on the coffee table or the ottoman?"

"The coffee table."

He waited until she sat down on the sofa, then placed the tray in front of her. "Feeling better, are you?" he observed.

"A little." The easy way Sloan answered offered its own reassurance. "A part of me still resents how suspicious your family behaved tonight — and for no good reason."

Trey could have argued that point, but the fire was out and he didn't want to fan it back to life. "Considering all the trouble in the past, it's only natural for them to be leery, especially when the memory is so fresh."

"Uncle Max had no part of that," she stated firmly as she removed the plate cover. "He told me so himself."

"What do you mean?" Trey frowned in sudden wariness.

"I talked to him," Sloan replied in unconcern.

"When? Tonight?" He stared at her in disbelief.

"Yes." The minute she looked up, all the ease left her expression, and she tilted her head in defiance. "Why? Is something wrong with that? Don't tell me I'm not supposed to talk to him anymore?"

"I never said that," Trey protested.

"You didn't have to," Sloan retorted.

"You looked at me like I just committed a cardinal sin."

"I was surprised," he said in his own defense. "It never occurred to me that you would call him."

"Well, I did. Did you think your family were the only ones who were curious why he never mentioned that there had been contact between his family and yours?"

"And what was his" — Trey started to say "excuse" but quickly changed it — "answer?"

"He explained that I sounded so happy when I told him I was engaged to you, he had been reluctant to mention the things Boone had done." Sloan paused, suddenly turning earnest. "I don't think you understand, Trey. He's such a proud man. He has to be ashamed of what his son did. I know that's why he must find it so painful to talk about."

The sympathy in her voice touched a nerve. As far as Trey was concerned, there was no man less deserving of it than one who shifted all the blame onto his dead son just to keep his own name clean.

"Are you sure we're talking about the same Max Rutledge?" he challenged tightly. "The one I met would only be ashamed that his son got caught."

"How dare you say that!" Sloan erupted in anger. "You don't know him at all!"

"And you do? I thought you said you were never that close. Yet here you are, claiming to understand how he feels. Which is the truth, Sloan?"

"I have known that man all my life." Every word was carefully and firmly enunciated, a tight anger trembling in her voice. "How many times have you met him? Once? Twice?"

Working to haul in his temper, Trey looked at her for a long second. "One of the first things I was taught as a boy was how to recognize a rattlesnake. It doesn't matter whether it's coiled and ready to strike or just slithering through the grass, it still has fangs and venom. Only a fool is blind to that."

"Uncle Max is a rattlesnake now, is he?" Sarcasm was thick in her voice.

A muscle leaped convulsively along his clenched jaw. "I think we'd better agree to disagree where Max Rutledge is concerned and just drop the subject."

"Fine," she snapped and jerked the napkin across her lap.

The solution was far from a satisfactory one, and Trey knew it. At the same time he couldn't pretend that Rutledge was innocent of any wrongdoing, not even to please Sloan. And she refused to concede the possibility of his guilt. Which left no area for compromise.

Swept by a sudden raw energy, Trey pivoted away from her and muttered, "I'll throw another log on the fire."

Before he could take the first step toward the wood box, the phone rang. Trey swung around to answer it. When he saw the way Sloan's glance ricocheted from the phone to him, suspicion reared its head.

"Was Uncle Max going to call you back, or should I answer it?" he challenged smoothly.

"You can answer it. I'm eating." She dipped a fork into the vegetable medley on her plate, all cool and stiff. "But if it is Uncle Max, I'll talk to him."

One rigid stride carried him to the telephone. He snatched the receiver from its cradle and carried it to his ear. "This is Trey," he said curtly.

A man's voice spoke above a background din of music and voices. "Is Johnny there?"

"Johnny?"

"Yeah, I was given this number and told to ask for Johnny. This is the Calder Ranch, isn't it?"

"It is, but Johnny isn't here. Who is

this?" Trey couldn't place the man's voice.

"My name's Al. I'm the bartender at The Oasis. We got one of your cowboys here who's too drunk to stand, let alone walk or drive. Sounded like he said his name was Tank, but it's probably Hank."

"No, it's Tank," Trey acknowledged.

"Well, Tank is tanked. He said this Johnny fella would come get him."

"There's bound to be other Triple C hands there who can give him a ride home."

The initial response was a partially muffled, "Yeah, yeah, I'll be right there." The promise obviously was issued to someone else. "Look, this place is packed," he said to Trey. "I haven't got time to poll the customers and find out who works where. Donovan said I should call out of courtesy since a lot of our business comes from the Triple C. But I don't really care whether the guy spends the night in the drunk tank or not."

Sighing in grim resignation, Trey glanced in Sloan's direction, but she appeared oblivious to his conversation. "Give me an hour," he told the bartender.

"That's all you got," the man replied and hung up.

Trey pushed down the disconnect

button, then released it, and punched in Johnny's phone number. Sloan continued to ignore him. Trey waited for the phone to ring. Instead, the intermittent buzz of a busy signal came over the line.

Turning, he said to Sloan, "That was the bartender at The Oasis. I guess Tank passed out. I have to run into town and get him. There and back, it'll probably take me a couple hours — maybe longer with this snow."

"Be careful." The phrase sounded more like a perfunctory statement than an expression of concern.

"I will." He was almost irritated enough to leave it at that. But Sloan was pitting her will against his. As much as he had always admired her strength and determination, this was something he couldn't allow to continue. "While I'm gone, you can think about this," he told her. "You're my wife, Sloan, even when I totally disagree with you. So get that damned chip off your shoulder."

Her eyes flashed to him in surprise, but he was already striding toward the door. Downstairs, Trey paused long enough to inform his mother where he was going and why, then headed to the door and collected his coat and hat from the rack.

Snow covered the windows of the pickup. While he let the engine warm up, Trey brushed the snow from the windshield and side mirrors, then took a few swipes at the side windows as well before he slid behind the wheel.

The ranch yard was blanketed in white, all previous tracks obliterated by the new-fallen snow. And more flakes continued to fall when he reversed away from The Homestead. On impulse, he pointed the pickup toward the Taylor house.

Johnny's mother came to the door when Trey knocked. Rather than track snow into the house, Trey waited on the porch while she went to get Johnny.

"Something wrong?" Those were the first words Johnny spoke when he came to the door.

"I got a call from the bartender at The Oasis. Tank's drunk," Trey explained. "I'm headed into town to go get him. Somebody will have to drive his pickup back. Want to ride along?"

"He's drunk?" Johnny said in surprise. "Hell, it ain't even half past nine. 'Course, he did take off right after he picked up his paycheck. It'd be just like that fool to try to drink it up in one night. Let me grab my coat and I'll be right with you."

Taking him at his word, Trey retraced his footsteps to the pickup. Johnny climbed into the truck only seconds after Trey did. The minute the door closed after him, Trey set off, aiming for the east lane that would take them to Blue Moon.

"Can't help wondering why he called you," Johnny mused. "Tank knows you've got a wife with a little one on the way."

"The bartender asked for you when he called." Snowflakes swirled in the pickup's headlight beams, and the wipers maintained a fast, steady cadence to prevent the flakes from accumulating on the windshield. "I figure Tank got the phone numbers mixed up and gave him ours instead of yours."

"More than likely," Johnny agreed. "I don't imagine your little woman was too happy about you going out on a night like this, though."

"She was fine with it."

Trey's somewhat clipped response suggested something entirely different to Johnny. He ran a considering glance over Trey's profile, noting the closed-up expression on his rawboned features, visible in the dim glow of the dashboard lights.

"Glad to hear it," Johnny replied. "I know some women can get real emotional when they're carrying and fly off the handle at the smallest thing."

"When did you become such an expert?" Trey mocked.

"I remember how touchy my mother was when my little brother came along so unexpected-like. Dad always claimed that no matter what he said, it was the wrong thing. She'd either bust into tears or blow up like a rank bull out for blood. I learned real quick to walk soft around her. 'Course, after little Joey was born, she was fine again. Kelly tells me it's a hormone thing that makes their emotions get all out of whack. So it wouldn't surprise me if your wife's a bit testy."

"She's a little more sensitive, but that's about all." Trey wished he could blame hormones for their current rift, but there was more to it than that.

"You're lucky, then," Johnny said and lapsed into silence.

Not in a mood for idle talk himself, Trey made no attempt to break the silence. Instead, he focused his attention on the snow-covered road ahead of them, its track delineated by the fence posts that ran parallel to it.

A few miles from the Triple C's east gate, Johnny remarked, "The road crews are gonna be busy tomorrow plowing off all this snow. It sure won't melt in a hurry, not as deep as it's getting."

"According to the forecast, we could get as much as a foot."

"Let's just hope that wind don't start howling," Johnny murmured.

Snowplows had already been at work on the highway, exposing the bare pavement when they reached it. With a cleared road ahead of him, Trey increased the pickup's speed. It wasn't long before he spotted the lighted canopy over the gas pumps at Fedderson's. The lights of The Oasis were a fainter glow on the opposite side of the highway.

There wasn't an empty parking space to be seen when they pulled into the lot. "This place is really jumping tonight," Johnny observed.

"We won't be that long," Trey said and parked behind another vehicle near the door.

Entering the bar was like walking into a wall of noise. The jukebox was cranked up to its full volume, blasting out a honky-tonk, beer-drinking tune. Voices and laughter were loud, as folks tried to make themselves heard above the din, while the slot machines rattled and rang in the background.

Trey paused a few steps inside and surveyed the crowded area. He spotted dozens of familiar faces, but he didn't see Tank sprawled anywhere.

"Where's Tank?" Johnny spoke near his ear.

"We'll check at the bar," Trey said and struck out for it.

Donovan was working the far end of the bar, filling drink orders for the waitresses. The second man was closer. Trey shouldered his way between two customers and leaned an arm on the counter.

"Are you Al?" he asked.

"Yeah." The man looked up from the mug he was filling with beer. "What'll you have?"

"Where's Tank? We're here to pick him up?"

"Who?" The man frowned. Then his expression cleared. "Oh, you mean the cowboy." He jerked his thumb upward. "Top of the steps, second door on the right."

Shoving himself back from the bar, Trey swung to Johnny. "Upstairs," he said in a near shout and repeated the bartender's thumb signal.

The staircase to the second floor was narrow and dimly lit. They climbed it single file, Trey going first. Bypassing the first door on the hall's right side, he proceeded to the second. He knocked twice, but with all the noise filtering from downstairs, he doubted that anyone inside could have heard him, certainly not Tank if he was as drunk as the bartender claimed.

Turning the knob, he gave the door a push and followed it when it swung noiselessly inward. The only light in the small bedroom came from a bedside lamp with a scarlet shade that cast a diffused red glow over the room. There was Tank, sprawled across a satin coverlet, his shirt unbuttoned except for the last one.

Trey stopped short when he noticed the redhead crouched on all fours next to the bed, scrubbing at a spot on the rug. As if sensing the presence of someone else, she looked back in irritation.

"This room is occupied, mister," she snapped.

"I know," he said. "We're here to take him home."

"Too bad you didn't get here before he threw up on my rug." She gathered up the rag and a can of spot cleaner, then stood up, giving the hem of her red leather miniskirt a downward tug as she turned her back to both of them.

Johnny walked to the opposite side of the bed and jiggled Tank's shoulder. "Up and at 'em, Tank."

But Tank only groaned and flung a limp arm out in protest. "You're gonna have to carry him out of here," the girl declared.

"How'd he get this drunk?" Johnny grumbled in annoyance.

"He got into a chugalug contest." A match made a raspy strike against a rough surface. A flame erupted, and the redhead held it against a candlewick on the bedside table. "Somebody bet him fifty dollars he couldn't drink two pitchers of beer. Your friend won, so we came up here to celebrate. Then all that beer hit him."

"Where's his jacket?" Trey asked.

"In the corner, on the chair," she answered without turning as a spicy and cloying fragrance drifted through the room. "His hat, too."

"Time to go home, Tank." Johnny put a knee on the bed for leverage and hoisted his friend into a sitting position, propping him up against the headboard's brass posts.

Trey retrieved the coat and jacket from the corner chair, but it took both of them to get Tank into the jacket. Johnny added the final touch, shoving Tank's hat on his head and pushing it down around his ears. Then he stepped back.

"I'll carry him," Trey said.

Johnny waved aside the offer. "I can manage. First we'd better dig those truck keys out of his pocket. I ain't about to dump him in that cold pickup and have to start searching for the keys to start the thing."

After a search of his jeans pockets failed to turn up the keys, they found them in his jacket pocket. Johnny tucked them in his own pocket, then rolled a semiconscious Tank onto his shoulder and straightened.

When Trey started to follow him out of the room, the redhead called out, "Wait."

Pausing, Trey turned back around.

"His wallet." She held it out. "He's liable to miss it come morning."

"Thanks." He walked back to take it from her and automatically glanced at the edges of some bills that poked out of it.

"Don't worry," she said with cynicism. "It's all there. I didn't take any."

"I never said you did," Trey replied evenly.

Her head lifted in a defiant toss, and she looked at him for the first time straight on. "You thought it."

Trey stared at the swollen area on her

left cheekbone. Its redness already showed signs of purpling into an ugly bruise. "What happened to your face?"

"Your friend." There was a bitter and angry curl of her lip when she spoke. Again she turned at right angles, showing him only the unblemished side of her face. "It really finishes my chances of making any money tonight."

"Are you saying Tank hit you?" Trey questioned in disbelief. "I don't buy that."

"Why? Because he's your friend?" she jeered. "You men are all the same. You take one look at someone like me and see a green light to indulge in rough stuff."

"You're wrong. In my book, no man ever has a good excuse to hit a woman. I don't care who she is." The statement was calmly worded.

She studied him for an instant, a look of wonder stealing into her eyes. "You mean that, don't you." Long, red-nailed fingers lightly touched his cheek. "I wish more guys like you visited me." Before he could guess her intentions, she rose on her toes and planted a quick kiss on his cheek, then drew back. "Thanks."

Her fingers again touched his cheek. "Sorry, I got lipstick on you."

"No problem." He pulled a handkerchief

from his back pocket and wiped his cheek, then tucked it back away. "Thanks for returning Tank's billfold." With a nod in parting, Trey headed for the door.

"Your friend didn't hit me." Her voice came after him. "He was getting undressed and grabbed me when he started to fall. We both went down, and I cracked my cheek against the foot rail."

"That, I believe," Trey replied and stepped into the hall, pulling the door closed behind him.

Johnny was just driving out of the lot in Tank's pickup when Trey emerged from The Oasis. He tooted the horn and pulled onto the highway. Trey soon followed.

On the plowed and salted highway, the going was relatively easy. Within a few miles, Trey had the red taillights of Tank's pickup in sight. The driving conditions deteriorated rapidly, though, when he turned onto the main ranch road. Blowing snow reduced the visibility to a matter of yards and created deep drifts that had to be negotiated with care. The last thirty-odd miles to the Triple C headquarters Trey covered at a crawl. It was close to midnight when he finally pulled up in front of The Homestead.

Upon entering the still and darkened

house, Trey paused to remove his heavy jacket and snow-encrusted boots. In stocking feet, he made his way to the staircase without bothering to turn on a light. Only one tread creaked under his weight, but that was all that was needed.

A door opened as he neared the top step, and his mother's slim shape, clad in a pair of tailored pajamas, filled its gap. "Is Tank all right?"

"He's fine," he assured her, then added wryly, "But he's bound to have the mother of all hangovers come morning."

"Were the roads bad?"

He nodded. "This storm is trying to turn into a blizzard."

"Let's hope not. Good night," she murmured and faded back into her bedroom.

"Good night," he echoed and crossed to the master suite.

All was dark in the sitting room, but Sloan had left on the bathroom light for him. Tired as he was, the thoughtful gesture brought a smile to the corners of his mouth. He glanced at the bed where Sloan lay on her side, the white of the pillowcase framing her dark head. The slight rise and fall of her breathing told him that she was sound asleep.

Not wanting to disturb her, Trey undressed quietly. But the instant he lifted the covers to slip into bed, she stirred, her head lifting and turning drowsily in his direction.

"You're home," she murmured thickly.

"Yes." He slid under the sheet, stretching out beside her.

She started to snuggle her head back into the pillow, but first she looked at the digital clock's lighted numbers. "It's already midnight. How come you're so late?"

"The snow started blowing, and that made it hard to see the road." It pleased him that she was concerned, considering how cool she had acted toward him when he left. Maybe everything was going to be all right between them after all, in spite of this business with Rutledge. Rolling toward her, he reached under the covers for her. But the second his hand touched her rib cage, she flinched.

"Your hands are like ice," she protested.

Trey searched but found nothing in her tone that suggested she was interested in warming him up. He withdrew his hand and leaned over instead to brush a kiss on her cheek.

"Go back to sleep," he said.

She made an agreeing sound in her throat, the sleepy kind that said she was close to doing that very thing. Yet something drifted to her, something that shouldn't have been there. She tried to identify it, but it eluded her. Sloan let it go and drifted back to sleep.

It wasn't until after breakfast the next morning when she was straightening up their bedroom that any memory of it came back to her. It happened while she checking the pockets of Trey's jeans before tossing them in the clothes hamper and found the handkerchief with its lipstick smear. The scarlet color was definitely one she had never worn. That's when she recalled the cloying fragrance of some cheap perfume that had lingered in the air when Trey returned last night.

She stared at the handkerchief and thought of The Oasis, the so-called waitresses, and the bitter words she and Trey had exchanged before he left.

Trembling with anger, Sloan shoved the handkerchief into his pocket and put his jeans back where he'd left them.

Chapter Eighteen

Along about midmorning, the snow stopped falling and the wind died to a murmur. Less then an hour later, the last of the clouds moved on, and the sun came out, creating a sharp contrast between the vivid blue of the sky and the pure white of the snow-covered ground.

The wide blades of the road graders ripped paths through the snow, digging deep enough to cast off dirt with the snow. The rattle of their tire chains and rumble of their engines competed with the roar of the tractors to shatter the winter stillness.

Activity was everywhere as water tanks were checked to make sure they were clear of ice and hay was hauled to livestock where it was needed. Shovelers were out in force, flinging snow in all directions, while children played in it, roly-poly figures squealing with glee whether hurling snowballs at each other or making angels in any blank white patch they found.

This was one Sunday on the Triple C

when nobody rested except Sloan. She had little else to do except think about that lipstick-stained hankie in Trey's jeans pocket.

A light lunch was served at noontime instead of the usual Sunday feast. Jessy had made a run to South Camp with Laredo after learning the snowfall had been much heavier there, marooning cattle in isolated areas, and Trey was off helping the ranch electrician with some downed power lines. Which left only Sloan, Cat, and Chase to eat by themselves.

"So much for decorating the Christmas tree this afternoon. It seems we'll have to put it off until one evening this week," Cat said with regret, then explained to Sloan. "Decorating the tree is something we've always done as a family."

"That's a nice tradition," Sloan murmured, unable to summon much interest in it, not when her thoughts were otherwise occupied.

"When the children were small, they absolutely loved it. Unfortunately, most of the ornaments ended up on the lower branches. Remember how quick they were to notice when we tried to move a few of them higher, Dad?"

"They didn't like it all," he recalled.

"But you were just as bad when you were little."

"Of course I was. After all, I was Daddy's little girl. All I had to do was pout and climb on your lap, and you'd see that I got anything I wanted."

Sloan paid little attention to their conversation as she dipped her spoon into the hearty homemade stew and went through the motions of eating it. But her silence didn't go unobserved by Chase.

"You're very quiet, Sloan," he remarked.

"Too busy eating, I guess. The stew's delicious," she added in support of her half-truth.

"You didn't have a lot to say at breakfast this morning, either, I noticed." His gaze traveled over her in an assessing fashion. "After last night, I imagine you feel uncomfortable with us. It's only natural that you would. But understand this — we respect your opinion about Max Rutledge. At the same time, we totally disagree with it," he stated simply. "Now you know where we stand. By the same token, we know where you stand. Marriage into this family doesn't mean that you're obliged to share all of our opinions. The Lord knows, my late wife and I disagreed on several points. It made for some heated arguments at times. Seeing how angry you got last night reminded me of that. My Maggie was full of spunk when she thought she was right."

"And was she ever right?" Sloan asked with a touch of challenge.

"Sometimes," Chase admitted, then smiled, showing her some of that old Calder charm, "And sometimes I was." When Sloan laughed softly in spite of herself, Chase nodded in approval. "That's more like it."

Sloan might have felt easier about their differences if she hadn't noticed that Cat failed to echo his comments. Instead, the older woman maintained a tight-lipped silence and kept her gaze averted.

"I'm glad you feel that way, Chase," Sloan said, still finding it difficult to refer to him as "Grandfather." "Because I certainly never meant to cause hard feelings."

"This is one time when I think all of us hope that you are right about Max Rutledge."

Sloan started to assert that she was, then chose a more conciliatory reply rather than stir up those waters again. "Thank you."

Chase noticed it and winked. "You're learning."

After lunch, Sloan helped clear the dirty

dishes from the table while Chase hobbled into the den to await the coffee Cat would bring him. With so few dishes, cleanup was quickly accomplished.

Leaving Cat to fix Chase's coffee, Sloan headed upstairs to the rooms she shared with Trey. Almost the minute she stepped inside them, she was reminded of the hankie that had yet to be explained and the angry things they'd said to each other before Trey went into Blue Moon. When the walls started to close in, Sloan rummaged through her wardrobe for her winter boots, a woolen scarf, and mittens to go with her heavy parka.

Bundled against the cold, she made her way down the steps. As she reached the landing, she heard voices coming from the den, but it was the sound of Cat's voice, edged with impatience, that prompted Sloan to pause and listen.

"I wish I could be as open-minded as you are, Dad," Cat said. "But I can't forget the way Rutledge forced Dallas to provide him with information about what was going on at the Cee Bar. For all we know, Sloan could be his plant here."

"I'm aware of that," Chase replied.

For a stunned moment, Sloan stood motionless. Then the sickening realization washed over her. All Chase's friendly talk at the table was nothing more than an attempt on his part to lull her into thinking the family no longer regarded her presence as suspect, when the opposite was true.

All her life Sloan had felt like an outsider, but the feeling had never been as strong as it was at this moment.

Abruptly, she turned and went back up the steps, angry with herself for being so foolish as to think she might have found a place where she actually belonged. It was obvious the Calders only tolerated her because she married Trey — and because of the baby she carried. But this baby was the one thing that was hers.

Sundown came in an explosion of color that tinted the snowscape with pastel shades of coral and magenta. But Sloan never noticed. She stood at the window and watched for Trey's return to The Homestead. The lavender of dusk was creeping across the land when his pickup finally pulled up to the house. Sloan moved away from the window before he climbed out of the cab.

She heard the faint slam of the pickup door, and in her mind she tracked his progress up the front steps and across the columned veranda to the door, then visualized him shedding his coat and hat in the entry hall and pausing outside the den to exchange a few words with his grandfather before continuing to the staircase. She was only a minute or two off in her estimation when he walked into the sitting room.

Those hard, angular cheekbones of his were ruddy from winter's cold temperatures. A touch of the same color shaded the end of his strong nose. His dark gaze was quick to locate her. There was something intimate in the way his glance touched her that made her throat ache with longing for those early days of the marriage when everything had seemed so right.

"You look cold," she remarked.

"Frozen is more like it," Trey corrected dryly, a betraying stiffness in the movement of his lips that lent credence to his words.

"Why don't you change out of those clothes," Sloan suggested. "I'm not sure you'll have time for a shower before dinner."

"Probably not," Trey agreed, heading for the bedroom.

Sloan waited until he passed her, then followed him into the room. Sticking to her carefully planned script, she said, "You can put on those jeans from last night. I left them on the chair for you."

As Trey scooped them up, he noticed the faint chalky line near the leg hems. "It's the dirty clothes basket for this pair. Looks like I got road salt on them."

When he turned toward the hamper, Sloan said quickly, "Better check the pockets first."

The first pocket he checked was empty. It was the second that contained the handkerchief. Sloan watched his expression, but he seemed oblivious to the red smears on it as he dipped a hand in first one hip pocket then the other.

"Is that blood on your hankie?" Sloan silently applauded herself for how un-suspecting she sounded.

Trey checked the stain and shook his head. "No, it looks like lipstick."

"It can't be mine. I never wear red."

"You know what? I'll bet it belongs to that redhead at The Oasis," Trey said with dawning recollection.

"And what's your explanation for her lipstick being on your hankie?"

Quick to note the undertone of righteous anger in her question, Trey shot her a quick look, puzzled and a little wary. "It's not what you're thinking," he said. "Tank was with her. She gave me a peck on the cheek. That's all."

"Of course." A cool skepticism coated her voice.

"You've decided that I cheated on you, haven't you?" Trey demanded, his voice low and heavy.

"You wouldn't be the first man to look for sex outside marriage." Sloan made it a flat condemnation of his gender. "It's too bad I woke up when you got home, isn't it? Otherwise I wouldn't have known how late it was."

"I told you the roads were bad —" He started to say more, then checked himself. "Johnny would tell you the same thing, but you'd probably think he was only saying it to cover for me, wouldn't you?"

"Well, wouldn't he?" Sloan countered with some defiance.

"You want to believe that, don't you? You want to believe all of it. Why?" The frown he wore was dark with confusion.

Pride lifted her head, her chin tilting at a mutinous angle. "I'm not one of those women who will turn a blind eye to her husband's philandering ways."

"You don't happen to be married to a man who goes in for that," he stated curtly. "You're going to believe what you want. But that happens to be the truth."

His words were too close to the ones she

had used when addressing his family. Which made it impossible for Sloan to dismiss them. As a consequence, she had her first doubts about the conclusions she had drawn.

"Maybe." She hesitated, still warring with her pride. "Maybe I was wrong."

He stared at her for a tick of seconds, his features all tight and hard. Then his broad chest lifted with the deep breath he inhaled. Briefly, he tipped his head down and away from her, letting the indrawn breath rush from him in a long sigh. When he looked at her again, the hardness was gone from his face.

Unhurried, Trey moved to her. "I'm told women in your condition can be highly emotional at times. In this case, I think it's your imagination that became overactive."

"Just as yours is about Uncle Max," Sloan was quick to retort.

"Now, wait a minute. Before we start another argument, let's clear up this one first." His hands settled on the rounded points of her shoulders, a gentleness in their touch. "And I'll begin by saying there's nothing and no woman out there better than what I have right here with you. I know, because I looked before I ever met you."

"But you were angry with me last night," Sloan reminded him, unable to let go of all her suspicions.

"That doesn't mean anything. You're the only woman for me, Sloan. I knew it the first time I saw you. We can have all the arguments in the world and it won't change that."

With only the slightest pressure, he drew her to him, looking down at her face when she tipped it up. There was no smile on her lips, but they were parted and waiting. When he kissed her, Trey felt again that rush of inexpressible tenderness through him. He had to know if it was the same for her. But when he lifted his head, the pull of her hands brought it back down, and he met her lips again. Somehow they never got around to arguing about Max Rutledge that night.

Feet propped on the desk, Donovan rocked back in the old office chair, ignoring its protesting squeaks. One muscled arm was raised over his head, holding the phone to his ear.

"I've gotta hand it to you, Max. The word spread like you said it would. What's it been — a little over two weeks since I planted the rumor? Already I have customers whispering to me about the marital problems Trey Calder and his wife are having. For the most part, everybody's putting the blame on the wife, either claiming that she can't stand the cold and isolation of Montana after living in Hawaii or else that she married him for the Calder money but hasn't been able to get her hands on it."

"We can't let that continue," Rutledge stated. "You'd better arrange for one of your girls to receive a very expensive piece of jewelry. And make sure it gets known that it's from someone she met on the sly — not at your place where he would be recognized. The way people's minds work, it won't take them long before they'll link one rumor to the other and conclude that Trey's got himself a mistress on the side."

"Consider it done," Donovan replied. "By the way, my anonymous phone calls are beginning to get to her. I've been careful not to call too often, just once or twice a week. The last time, though, she was really mad, demanding to know who was calling and why I didn't speak." He gloated a little. "I swear, nothing makes a woman more suspicious of her husband than to answer a phone, hear music and noises in the background, and have the caller hang up."

"Keep it up, but get to work on the other," Max ordered. "I don't want the Calder son looking like the injured party."

"You make it sound easy, but it won't be," Donovan warned him. "Trey Calder's a popular guy around here. People talk about him with the same respect they show his grandfather."

"Remind them of his father's first marriage and the affair he had with Jessy during it. People will quickly shift to thinking 'like father, like son.'" Supreme confidence was in his voice.

This piece of information was news to Donovan. "You've done some digging into the Calder family history, haven't you?"

"Damn right. Now get on it." There was a click, and the line went dead.

Icicles hung from the old barn's overhang, glinting in the waning light like so many crystal pendants. Built well over a century ago out of hand-hewn timbers, the barn towered above the rest of the ranch buildings. On this night, scores of pickup trucks were parked around its stone base, and lights gleamed from every window.

The barn was the traditional site for the

annual Christmas party thrown for the Triple C ranch hands and their families. The interior had been transformed for the occasion by lighted garlands draping its rafters. A giant Christmas tree anchored one end of its broad alley, and pine wreaths hung from every stall.

By late afternoon the children had already performed their Christmas program, and Santa Claus had already distributed presents to the youngsters. The older children were the only ones who suspected it was really Trey Calder underneath all the padding and snowy white beard. But it was a secret they whispered only to each other.

With the Santa outfit safely stashed in the tack room, Trey slipped back into the throng. His searching eyes spotted Sloan standing next to one of the serving tables, its array of food already showing signs of being well grazed. He worked his way to the food area and came up behind her, curving an arm along the back of her waist and sliding a hand familiarly against her decidedly rounded stomach. Her glance skipped briefly to him, then reverted to the happy, chaotic scene before them.

Crushed bows, torn ribbons, and scraps of brightly colored wrapping paper were strewn all over the floor. The toddlers played among it all, indifferent to their presents, while the older ones scrambled to show off their gifts to others.

"Looks like Santa made some kids very happy, don't you think?" An easy smile curved his mouth, warmed by the looks of pleasure on so many young faces.

"He always does," Sloan murmured with little feeling.

Almost on cue, Trey felt the sharp kick of the baby in her womb despite the heavy sweater she wore. "I think one little guy disagrees." The sensation of it stirred through him, reawakening all those new, tender feelings that were part pride and part awe. He smiled down at Sloan. "Just think. In a couple years, our son will be out there ripping and roaring with the rest of them."

"Let's let him be born first."

Trey caught the faint but slightly irritable note in her voice and ran an inspecting glance over her. "Tired?" he guessed.

"A little." Nothing in her expression indicated to him what Sloan was thinking or feeling. It wasn't the first time in the last few days that he'd felt shut out.

Patience had become his motto. It wasn't something that came easy to him, yet Trey had decided it was best to overlook her odd moods rather than try to find their source. Operating on that principle, he ignored her current one. "By the way," he began, hoping to improve things with a compliment, "Cat told me that you helped pick out the presents for the children — and wrap them. I'm glad you're lending a hand with some of family duties."

"I suppose you would like me to do more."

From the cool way she gave him, Trey sensed he had said something wrong. "Only if you feel up to it, of course."

"Of course," Sloan echoed the phrase, but dryly.

Clamping down on his impatience, he asked, "Are you feeling all right, honey?"

"I'm fine. Just tired. It's been a long day." Like all her other answers, the sentences were short and clipped, the kind that didn't encourage further conversation.

Still he tried. "There goes Johnny and Kelly." Trey nodded in the direction of the couple, making their way to one of the side doors. "Want to bet that he waits till Christmas to pop the question."

"Really?"

"Don't you want to know why?" he prompted.

"Why?" But her tone was indifferent to his answer.

"Knowing how tight Johnny is with a dollar, he'll figure that if he gives her a ring for Christmas, he won't have to buy her a present." But his attempt at humor fell flat, failing to draw even a ghost of a smile from Sloan. He glanced at the smiling pair exiting the barn via its side door, all bundled up against the nip of a December evening. Trey had a feeling he knew their destination. On impulse, he glanced at Sloan. "Want to slip out of here?"

Her head snapped around to him, her face aglow for the first time. "Will it be all right?"

"Sure. I'll get your coat and hat."

Within minutes, Sloan was swaddled in her heavy parka, a stocking cap on her head, and a scarf wound around her neck. Trey buttoned up his own jacket and tugged on his lined gloves.

"Better put your mittens on. It's cold outside," he warned as he escorted her to the closest door. Obediently, she dug them out of her pocket and pulled them on.

Outside most of the snow that had fallen earlier in the month had melted, but enough remained to leave a thin crust of dirty white in protected areas. Trey kept a supporting hand on Sloan's arm as they made their way across the frozen and rutted ground between the parked vehicles.

Beyond the row of trucks stood a horse team hitched to an old wagon, mounded with fresh hay. One of the heavy-coated horses shifted in place, setting the bells on its harness to jingling. Old Jobe Garvey sat in the driver's seat, his back to the couples already nestled close together in the hay. Trey was quick to spot Kelly and Johnny getting ready to climb aboard.

"When was the last time you were on a hayride?" he asked Sloan.

"When I was twelve at summer camp. Why?" she asked, then spotted the wagon and guessed the reason. "Is this why we came out? I thought we were going to the house."

"If you went on a hayride when you were twelve, it was probably with a bunch of giggling girls. This one is adults-only," he told her. "The kids got their ride this afternoon. Come on, you'll enjoy it."

When he started to guide her toward the wagon, Sloan drew back. "No, I'd — I'd just be uncomfortable."

"No you won't. Not with all that hay to cushion you."

"I'm not talking about the ride." Her

voice had a low and angry pitch to it. "It's the others. They don't want me on it." She turned to face away from the wagon as if to keep from being overheard.

Dumbfounded by her statement, Trey frowned. "What are you talking about? That's ridiculous." But, like her, he kept his voice down.

"Don't tell me you didn't notice the way everyone treated me today? Why do you think I was standing by myself while you were playing Santa?" Her voice trembled with the effort to keep all the roiling emotions inside. Truthfully, Trey hadn't thought a thing about it, but he didn't admit that. "No one was openly rude to me. It was much more subtle than that."

"You're going to have to explain what you mean," he said on a near sigh.

"It's simple — nobody would talk to me. Oh, they'd smile, say hello, wish me a Merry Christmas, but after that nothing. And when I'd walk up to any of them, they were quick to find somewhere else they needed to be, leaving me standing by myself."

Almost from the moment Sloan had stepped on the ranch, she had been warmly received by the Triple C family. Recalling how quickly everyone had taken to her,

Trey found her claim difficult to believe.

"You're imagining things, Sloan," Trey muttered in annoyance.

"No, I'm not." She bit out the words. "Even when I was with you, no one ever addressed a single remark to me. They spoke to you. For all the notice they took of me, I could have been a block of wood." Resentment laced her expression as she looked back at the barn. "I felt like a pariah in there."

Over the course of the afternoon Trey had talked to nearly everyone at the party. Trying to recall who had addressed whom — or hadn't — was impossible for him. But he hadn't paid any attention, either; there was too much going on.

"I'm sure nobody meant anything by it."

"That's not the impression I got," Sloan retorted. "I'm going to the house. You can do what you want."

Without waiting for his reply, she set out for The Homestead. Trey stared holes in her back, almost angry enough to let her make the walk by herself. Before he could start after her, Johnny wandered over, his head turned to watch Sloan.

"I thought you two were gonna come on the hayride with us," he said, nodding at Sloan's retreating back.

"Sloan didn't feel like it."

"Is she feeling okay?" The question came from Kelly as she reached Johnny's side and linked arms with him.

"She gets tired easily these days." Trey glanced Kelly's way and encountered a pair of eyes that seemed to say she knew something he didn't. "So how's nursing school going?"

"Good." Hesitating, she darted a look at Johnny, then began, "Trey —"

Johnny immediately broke in, "Sure sorry you two aren't coming with us. It'd be fun."

"Maybe next year." Trey stole a glance at Kelly, his curiosity aroused by Johnny's deliberate interruption.

Not to be denied, Kelly said quickly, "Johnny thinks I should keep my mouth shut. But the whole ranch is buzzing about your wife."

"What about Sloan?" All his defense mechanisms kicked in, smoothing all expression from his rugged features.

"Last Wednesday she brought a package to the commissary that she wanted mailed. It was addressed to Max Rutledge. I thought you should know that," Kelly stated firmly while Johnny nudged at a frozen clod of dirt with the toe of his boot.

The information came as a surprise to Trey, but it helped a few odd pieces fall into place. "I imagine she was sending him a Christmas present." He was careful to inject a casual tone.

"To Max Rutledge?" Kelly stared at him in disbelief. "After all the trouble he caused you? I've heard about the Christmas spirit, but that's carrying it a little too far, don't you think?"

"Max was her legal guardian after her parents were killed," Trey explained matter-of-factly.

"And you knew this when you married her?" Kelly looked incredulous.

"We don't always get to choose the people in our lives," Trey replied smoothly, dodging the question as best he could while he shifted in the direction of The Homestead. "I'd better go check on Sloan. Have fun on the ride."

He walked off, giving neither a chance to ask more questions. But he had no doubt that the answers he had given would circulate to every adult on the ranch before the night was out. Yet their attitude toward Sloan was unlikely to undergo much change. Because of her connection to Rutledge, they'd draw back and wait to see if she was worthy of their trust and respect

— especially the older ones with memories of Tara.

And there wasn't a single thing he could do to change that. Only Sloan could — in time.

The house had a silent and empty feel to it when he walked in, the kind that said no one was home. Stripping off his gloves, Trey caught a glimpse of Sloan halfway up the oak staircase, the rubber soles of her boots making no sound on its wooden treads. Her parka was hanging on the rack, the stocking cap and wool scarf partially stuffed in a side pocket. Trey hung his own jacket next to hers, tucked the gloves in a pocket, and balanced his hat on top of it all, then headed for the stairs.

There was nothing silent about his hard-soled boots as he climbed the steps to the second floor. The door to the master suite stood open. With all of his senses tuned toward the rooms, Trey heard the faint grunts of exertion that preceded the thunk of a boot hitting the floor.

Sloan was standing, fur-lined boots in hand, when Trey entered the sitting room. There was a becoming flush to her cheeks, either from the brisk walk on a chilly night, the physical effort required to remove her boots, or a combination of both.

"You didn't have to come." Sloan gave him a look of cool indifference. "I can take care of myself. I have for years."

Her words were like a straight-armed shove intended to push him away; they were difficult to ignore. But he managed it. "I found out something that I thought you might want to know," he began.

"And what would that be?" Showing little interest in his reply, Sloan carried her boots into the bedroom.

Trey had no choice but to follow. He stopped in the doorway and waited until she emerged from the walk-in closet, empty-handed. "It seems that this time maybe I was wrong."

"This is a red-letter day, isn't it. I've always had the impression the Calders were never wrong about anything. I think I'd better sit down for this one." Sloan perched herself on the edge of the bed, hands braced at her side, striking a slightly regal, if mocking, pose.

It took every ounce of will to keep his temper in check. "It's possible that our people were a bit standoffish with you tonight. Care to know why?" Trey challenged.

"Oh, you've found an excuse for them, have you?" There was an unmistakable taunt in her wide-eyed look of innocence and interest.

"I'm going to take an educated guess and say that you bought Max Rutledge a Christmas present."

"Naturally. I get him something every year. What of it?" She tossed the challenge right back.

"You might have mentioned it to me." Trey couldn't keep the annoyance and frustration out of his voice.

"Why? I already know your opinion of him, and it isn't one I happen to share. It would have only started another argument, and I would have sent Max something whether you liked it or not."

"But it would have been better if I was the one who took the gift down to the commissary and arranged for it to be shipped to him. When you showed up with it, word traveled like a shock wave across this ranch."

"What did? You mean that I know Max?" She tipped her head at a perplexed angle.

"You're damn right!" Trey said with force. "Good God, Sloan, everyone on this ranch knows about the trouble he caused. And here you are, sending the man a package. As far as they're concerned, it's an act of betrayal."

"That's ridiculous!" Sloan declared in outrage.

"Not to them, it isn't!" Trey paused a beat, reining in his temper. "You're right. I wouldn't have liked the idea of you sending him a present, but I wouldn't have stopped you. So why the hell did you have to mail it here? Why couldn't you have stopped at the post office in Miles City after one of your doctor's visits?"

"My God, Trey, you make it sound like I should be ashamed that I know him — that it's some dirty secret the world shouldn't know. And all because of the prejudice you and your family have for him. It's even infected the people who work for you. Do you know how revolting that sounds?" Sloan demanded in righteous anger. "And if you think that I'm going to let a bunch of small-minded people dictate to me who I have contact with, you're wrong!"

"Dammit, Sloan, I'm only thinking of you. Before this happened everybody liked you. They had accepted you. Now you'll have to win their trust all over again. Loyalty to them isn't just a word; it's a way of life. In their eyes, you've crossed the line." Trey saw the objection forming on her lips. "I'm not saying that's right or fair. It's just the way it is."

Before Sloan could respond to that, the phone on the bedside table rang, an echo of it coming from the sitting room. She started to reach for it, then pulled her hand back.

"You might as well answer it. It's for you, anyway," Sloan declared, then added caustically, "Probably that redhead from The Oasis."

His half-narrowed gaze locked on her in shock. "Why are you bringing that up? We settled that weeks ago."

The phone rang a second time. "Aren't you going to answer that?" Her chin lifted with the saccharine challenge, and the smile that followed had the same sweet coating. "That's right. I'm sitting here. It does make it awkward for you, doesn't it?"

Uttering a barely smothered imprecation, Trey crossed to the nightstand and snatched the receiver in mid-ring. "Yes," he muttered, none too pleasantly.

"Is that you, Trey?" Cat's voice came across the line, full of uncertainty and question.

Trey released a long, silent breath and cast an irritated glance at Sloan. "Yeah, it's me."

"It didn't sound like you. I —"

He never heard the rest as Sloan walked

up and jerked the phone out of his hand. "Who is this?" Hot demand was in her voice.

"Sloan!" Cat said in surprise. "I was about to ask Trey if you were all right. When Jobe Garvey told me you'd gone to the house, I got worri—"

"I'm fine. Just tired. Here's Trey." She shoved the phone back in his hand and turned away, all tense and frustrated, too much so to pay attention to whatever Trey said to his aunt.

Nerves raw, Sloan raked her fingers through her hair and sat back down on the bed as an overwhelming weariness swept through her. It only seemed to increase the helpless, lonely feeling that tied her up in knots. She never heard the rattle of the receiver settling back on its cradle.

Then Trey stood in front of her, tight-lipped and hard-eyed. "What the hell was that all about?"

"I've been getting calls lately," Sloan answered stiffly. "Nobody answers when I pick up."

"Good God, Sloan," he said in disgust. "It's probably some telemarketer."

"With laughter and music in the background? I doubt it." Her voice was thick with scorn.

"Then I don't know who the calls are from," Trey declared, "But they aren't from some woman, redhead or otherwise, wanting to talk to me. So get that idea out of your head."

Sloan was unmoved by his denial. Men lied all the time about their extramarital affairs. But she didn't have the energy to throw that reminder in his face, so she didn't offer any response.

"Look." Trey crouched in front of her, balancing himself on the balls of his feet. "You're used to being more active. Lately you've had too much time on your hands, and it's never good to sit and brood." He attempted to sound reasonable, but his voice still had a hard edge to it. "I know the weather hasn't cooperated, but it's supposed to warm up for a few days. You need to get out, walk, get some exercise. It'll be good for you and the baby."

"Yes, it would," Sloan agreed and edged farther onto the bed. "I think I'll lie down and rest for a while. Will you turn out the light?"

"Sure." He straightened when she stretched out flat on the bed and rested one arm across her forehead. "I'll be in the other room, watching some television, if you need me."

Sloan nodded in acknowledgement. Trey flipped off the light on his way out of the bedroom and pulled the door partially closed behind him. For a long time Sloan stared at the darkened ceiling. Everything boiled down to his word and her suspicions.

One of them was right. But which one? That was the question that kept drumming through her mind. That one and one other — did she really want to know the answer?

To love, she had to trust. Without trust, how long could any love last? That was a question Sloan had never asked herself. But it was at the bottom of all the others.

Chapter Nineteen

Stars glittered in the Texas sky, but their brilliance was dimmed by the city lights of Fort Worth. In the exclusive River Crest district, strategically placed lights marked a sweeping driveway that led to one of the area's many mansions.

There was just enough chill in the January air to provide the perfect excuse for the female occupants of the arriving limos to don their favorite furs. Fully aware of how dramatic she looked in ermine, Tara had chosen an ermine jacket.

One side slipped, baring a white shoulder when she moved to exit the limo's rear door, then paused to address the chauffeur. "Remember — you are to be back here promptly in one hour. I won't need to stay longer than that."

Privately she thought an hour was too long, but to leave sooner would be an insult to the Holcombes, her misguided but well-intentioned and well-heeled hosts.

Accepting the assistance of the liveried

attendant, Tara stepped from the limousine and continued straight to the front door. The murmur of many voices, intermixed with the tinkle of crystal, greeted her when she walked into its spacious foyer. But an underlying boredom was what Tara's experienced ears heard instead of the electric buzz that a successful party generated.

Aware that her arrival might be observed, Tara surrendered her wrap to the waiting maid with an unhurried grace, then made her way to the richly appointed living room where the bulk of the guests were gathered. Good manners dictated that she seek out her host and hostess first, but she used the winding journey to discreetly survey the other guests. As she expected, most were from the B list. In all honesty, Tara knew she wouldn't have attended the party herself if the charity it was to benefit hadn't been one of her pet projects. At such times sacrifices had to be made.

After chatting up her host and hostess, Tara collected a glass of champagne and went about the task of mixing and mingling. Turning from the first group, she caught a movement in her side vision and turned that way. For a split second, she went still at the sight of the wheelchair-bound Max Rutledge. He almost managed to look distinguished, with his grizzled hair and full black-tie regalia.

Hesitating only briefly, Tara approached him. "Max Rutledge, you old rogue." She bent and kissed the air near his cheek. "I don't know why I'm surprised to see you here. Lately you've been keeping a very high profile — and an open wallet. It's amazing what a little spreading of the green will do to improve one's image, isn't it?" she cooed in a voice that was all Texas honey.

But Max only smiled with a hearty broadness. "Ah, Tara, still the stunning Texas vixen. How good to see you. The Holcombes said that you planned to come, but I had my doubts." He cast a jaundiced glance at the gathering, and murmured, "I think it's been a night of disappointments for them."

Tara couldn't disagree. "Poor Margaret. I did try to warn her that at this time of year all the right people were either yachting in the Mediterranean or skiing in Switzerland. Next time she'll listen."

"I'm surprised you're in town," he remarked.

"Actually, I leave tomorrow for St.

Moritz, before going on to Monte Carlo."

"Good. That means you'll be back in time for the blessed event."

Tara released a short, amused breath. "What on earth are you talking about, Max?"

"Sloan's baby is due somewhere around the end of February. Had you forgotten?" He tipped his head back, studying her with mild interest.

The smallest frown flickered across her forehead. "You talk as if you know her."

"Perhaps it's because I do. Almost from the day she was born, as a matter of fact." Satisfaction gleamed in his eyes at the surprise Tara couldn't completely conceal. "Her late father and I were partners in a few business ventures."

Recognition dawned. "She's that Davis," Tara murmured. "You were named her guardian, weren't you?"

"I was," Max confirmed. "And, yes, the Calders are aware of it. I take it they haven't mentioned it to you."

Tara managed an elegant shrug of indifference. "Why should they? It's hardly important."

"I agree." Max nodded. "Sloan deserves her happiness. Although I was troubled to hear they're having marital problems. The first year of marriage always requires many adjustments, though."

"It's probably nothing more than that foolishness about her work," Tara guessed at once. "Once Sloan fully understands the obligations that will fall to her as Trey's wife, she'll put aside all this nonsense about a career in photography."

"Trey objects to it, does he?" His idle tone masked his keen interest in her answer.

"Really, Max. What husband would be in favor of his wife being absent from home for long periods of time?" Tara chided.

"You're right. I hadn't thought of it that way."

"Tara," A feminine voice called an instant before a slightly tipsy blonde descended on her. "What are you doing here? I thought you were supposed to be Switzerland."

"I leave tomorrow," Tara informed her.

"Excuse me, ladies." Max reached for the controls on the wheelchair's armrest.

"Now, be generous with your check, Max," Tara called after him as he rolled away. "It's for a worthy cause.

"And a worthy night," he murmured to himself.

★ ★ ★

A strong Chinook wind swept over the rough-and-tumble roll of the Montana plains. Its warmth was a welcome relief from the freezing temperatures that had gripped the land for much of February. With calving season in full swing, its arrival couldn't have been more opportune.

As he made his final tug to tighten the saddle's cinch strap, Trey let his gaze skip beyond the corral fence to the section of range beyond it. These first hours of morning were the time when the cattle were up and about, seeking water and graze. A cow heavy with calf never strayed too far from either. Armed with that knowledge, the stock tank and hay bales at the South Branch camp were both located close to the calving sheds, making a check of the herd easier for those ranch hands unlucky enough to pull calving duty.

Thanks to a flu epidemic that had sidelined a good number of the Triple C riders, Trey was among those assigned to the chore. Behind him, saddle leather creaked as Laredo swung aboard his horse.

"Are you about ready?" Laredo kept a still hand on the reins.

"Yup." Trey unhooked the stirrup from the saddle horn and scooped up the trailing rein, then swung himself onto the seat, toeing his boots into the stirrups.

First to reach the fence gate, Laredo reached down and unlatched it, then pushed it open as he maneuvered his horse through the gap.

"I noticed the thermometer was tickling the forty-degree mark this morning," Laredo held the gate for Trey. "It's going to feel downright balmy today."

"True."

The abruptness in his answer had Laredo running a speculating eye over him. But Trey's young, rugged features had that closed-up look, typical of a Calder determined to keep his thoughts to himself. For Laredo, that was telling in itself.

"As warm as it is, I thought Sloan might come along to get a look at the calving sheds." Laredo gave the gate a push, swinging it shut after Trey rode through.

"She wanted to, but I talked her out of it. Too many have the flu bug here at South Branch, and she's too close to term to risk getting sick now." Trey pointed his horse at a large, round bale some distance away where a half dozen cows were gathered, their sides ballooned by their advanced pregnancies.

"Sounds like you had to do some talking

to convince her," Laredo guessed as they approached the cows, keeping their horses at an unhurried walk, the strike of their hooves on the still-frozen ground making a dull clop.

A heavy breath spilled from Trey. "You got that right. She was upset with me anyway. She has a doctor's appointment at the end of the week. She wanted me to take her. Needless to say, she wasn't happy when I told her that I couldn't, not at calving time. I'll be damned glad when this baby's born. Maybe she'll stop being so testy then."

"Been hard to live with lately, has she?" Laredo surmised.

"Yes and no. She gets some crazy ideas in her head sometimes, and nothing I say seems to make any difference."

Trey didn't volunteer more information than that, but Laredo was certain he knew what kind of crazy notion Sloan had. "You mean like you're cheating on her."

Trey abruptly reined up, his gaze shooting to Laredo, a dark anger in its depths. "Good God, don't tell me she's spouting off to others about it."

"Not that I've heard." Laredo halted as well.

"Then how did you know?"

"I picked it up in Blue Moon when I was

there the other day. Rumor has it that you're seeing someone on the sly and it's causing problems at home."

Trey made a small, disgusted movement of his head and kneed his horse forward again. "I'd like to know when I'm supposed to be doing this. I've been home every night for months," he muttered.

"Easy." Laredo relaxed the pressure on the bit, letting his mount move alongside Trey's gelding. "An afternoon here. An afternoon there."

"You're serious," Trey realized.

"That's the talk."

A grimness settled around his mouth. "Let's hope Sloan doesn't hear it." Yet it was something Sloan was smart enough to figure out by herself.

"It does make you wonder how the rumor got started, though," Laredo remarked with seeming idleness.

Wise to his ways, Trey studied him. "Any ideas?"

"It seems the rumor started circulating not long after we learned about her connection to Rutledge. I suppose that could be another coincidence," he added dryly.

"Tongues wag all the time. It doesn't mean anything." Yet Trey couldn't totally dismiss his words.

"This time the tongues are drawing comparisons between you and your father — and the poor choice he made in his first wife." Laredo paused, then spoke with a note of caution. "There are more Taras in this world than we'd like to believe."

"You still think Sloan might be some tool of Rutledge's," Trey muttered in irritation. "And I still say you're wrong."

"Maybe I am. But something about all this doesn't smell right."

"It isn't Sloan."

"I hope to hell you're right. You two have enough troubles without throwing that into the mix."

"The only problems we have are in her mind," Trey stated flatly.

"Really? What about her career?"

Trey stiffened. "What about it?"

"Talk is that you're insisting she give it up."

"I've never said a word to her about it." That was the truth. Yet it didn't alter that vague resentment he felt nearly every time he saw her with a camera. "It hardly matters, though, considering she'll soon have a baby to look after."

"Makes me wonder where the Triple C would be if your mother thought like that. And you can't say you didn't know Sloan was a professional photographer when you married her."

Amusement was in the look Trey gave him. "You can't seem to make up your mind about Sloan. One minute you're talking against her, and in the next you're taking her side."

Laredo grinned. "Kinda sounds like I'm riding the same horse you are."

The discussion, already near its end, came to a quick close when Trey spotted a cow standing well apart from her herdmates. Her raised tail and anxious air were sure signs she was in the initial stage of labor, making her a prime candidate for the calving shed.

A few notches past its zenith, the sun was a big yellow ball of light in a freeze-dried sky. Below it, the two-lane highway stretched like a gray ribbon across a winter-brown landscape. Here and there, old snow could be seen clinging to the shady sides of its flanking ditches.

Only one vehicle sped along the road, heading north, a narrow shadow racing along the shoulder, keeping pace. Cat was behind the wheel with Sloan in the passenger seat. Music from a CD played softly over the Suburban's speakers, covering the silence. On this return trip from Sloan's doctor's appointment, all the topics of conversation had been exhausted.

For about the fifteenth time in the last fifty miles, Sloan shifted in her seat, seeking a more comfortable position. The movement didn't go unnoticed by Cat.

Concern was in her face as she said, "Are you sure you don't mind if we stop at Fedderson's before we go home? I can always run back to town and pick up the shrimp Marsha's holding for me."

"Honestly? I'd welcome the chance to stretch my legs after riding for two hours." Sloan arched her back briefly, then shifted in the seat again.

"Stiff, are you?" Cat eyed her with sympathy.

"Stiff, sore, achy — you name it, I feel it." The breath Sloan released was a grunted sigh. "These trips to the doctor just seem to get longer and longer. I wish his office was closer."

"It was a lot more convenient when we had the clinic in Blue Moon, but we all knew it was bound to close sometime," Cat agreed, then smiled in encouragement. "At least you received a glowing report from Doctor Wilson. He told me he hadn't seen two healthier patients than you and the little guy."

Sloan absently rubbed her side. "One more week," she murmured on a wistful note. "I just hope he comes on time. One of the other women there told me she went three weeks past her due date."

"Calder babies usually arrive on time," Cat assured her with a touch of pride.

The near boast was like a scrape across nerves that were already raw. For a moment, Sloan almost surrendered to the urge to tell Cat how sick to death she was of hearing how great the Calders were. If they were so perfect, why hadn't her husband taken her to the doctor instead of going off to some calving shed — assuming that was really where he was. But she said nothing and looked away when she noticed the massive stone pillar wings that marked the east entrance to the Triple C Ranch.

Again, music filled the silence that fell between them. Sloan kept her attention focused out the side window, without ever seeing the utility poles and fence posts that raced by. The seemingly never-ending discomfort soon had her changing positions again.

It was with relief that she felt the Suburban slow its headlong pace and saw the buildings of Blue Moon. When Cat braked to make the turn into the combination gas station, grocery store, and post office, Sloan made a quick check of the vehicles parked in front of The Oasis. There were only two, and neither had the Triple C insignia on its doors. Sloan couldn't decide whether she was glad or sorry, but she'd been torn like that for weeks now — full of doubts and suspicions, yet wanting desperately to believe they were unwarranted.

Reaching around her protruding stomach, Sloan unbuckled her seat belt the instant the Suburban rolled to a stop in front of Fedderson's. After riding so long in the heated vehicle, the coldness of the outside air was a bracing shock when she climbed out. She stood for a moment, breathing it in, a hand resting lightly on her back while she stretched muscles stiff and sore from the ride.

At a much slower pace, she followed Cat into the store. The proprietress, a slightly built brunette, was behind the counter, chatting with another customer. When she saw Cat walk in, she quickly excused herself and emerged from behind the counter.

"I've got your shrimp in back," she told Cat. "They aren't as big as the ones Ross usually gets. If you want to pass on them, I'll understand."

"They should be fine."

"Take a look at them first to be sure," Marsha urged.

"Okay," Cat agreed and glanced at Sloan. "I won't be long."

"Don't hurry on my account," Sloan told her and wandered over to a display of handcrafted items near the counter. She didn't have any real interest in them but used them as an excuse to keep moving and ease some of the cramping of her muscles.

Almost immediately she felt herself under the scrutiny of the customer still standing by the cash register. She was a sandy-haired woman, a year or two younger than Sloan, her dark blue parka unbuttoned to reveal the tan cable knit sweater she wore with a pair of jeans. The instant Sloan glanced her way, the woman seemed to take it as invitation to speak.

"You're Trey's wife, aren't you?" Curious hazel eyes studied her with an almost avid interest.

"Yes," Sloan confirmed.

"You probably don't remember me. I'm Annie Walters. We met last November outside church. My boyfriend Gil is the calf-roper that used to compete with Trey in jackpot events."

"Of course." Sloan pretended to remember the encounter, but it was little more than an extremely vague recollection that included no memory of faces. "How are you?"

"Just fine." As if feeling the need to keep the conversation going, the young woman volunteered, "I was just over to The Oasis, grabbing a bite of lunch, and they told me Ross had brought some shrimp back on his last trip. So, like you, I thought I'd swing by and get some — although I'm so stuffed from lunch that the thought of food doesn't have a lot of appeal. They have the best soup at The Oasis today. Beef pepperpot, I think they called it. It was delicious. You oughta try it." The words were barely out of her mouth before she got a panicked look. "Sorry. That's probably the last place you want to go. Forget I said anything."

That was an impossibility, and they both knew it. Too hurt and too angry to speak, Sloan stared at Annie, who guiltily ducked her head and picked up the sack on the counter.

"I'd better get going before this shrimp thaws. Tell Marsha I'll talk to her later." She moved quickly to the door.

Her departure from the store coincided with Cat's return to the front with the owner. Wrapped in her own little world of pain and fury, Sloan never said a word to either and never heard the words they exchanged while the sale was rung up.

On the way back to the Suburban, Sloan was careful not to look directly at Cat when she asked, "Do we have to go straight back to the ranch? I'm a little hungry. A cup of soup might tide me over until dinner. Annie was just telling me how delicious the soup was at The Oasis."

After an only momentary hesitation, Cat shrugged. "There's no big rush to get home. I think I'll forgo the soup, though, and have a slice of pie."

Only one other customer was in The Oasis when Sloan and Cat entered it, and he was an old-timer, sitting at a back table, nursing a cup of coffee and reading a newspaper. Darkly tinted windows allowed little of the sunshine to filter inside, leaving the place dimly lit in both the bar and eating areas. There was no clank and clatter from the slot machines, and the jukebox was silent.

Pausing a few feet inside the door, Cat scanned the interior and murmured to Sloan. "This used to be such a bright and cheerful place when Sally owned it. Now it's —" She checked the rest of her comment when she noticed the new owner emerging from the bar's shadows to approach them.

"Good afternoon, ladies," Donovan greeted them. "At this hour, you have your choice of tables. Would you like menus?"

"No, thanks," Sloan answered for both them.

"Have a seat then." He gestured to the tables. "Your waitress will be right with you."

Cat nodded an acknowledgement and led the way to a table situated at a midway point between the front door and kitchen. The entire time Sloan's gaze never stopped moving, searching in every dark corner. For what? She wasn't sure. But it was goaded by the high tension that screamed through her, demanding answers.

Her gaze continued its watchful dart as she sat at a table and slipped off her coat, letting it drape over the back of her chair. High heels made a sharp, clicking sound on the wooden floors. Certain it came from the bar area, Sloan looked in that direction.

A cold anger swept through her when she saw a redhead sauntering toward them, dressed in a jumpsuit of metallic blue spandex that hugged every line and curve of her body. The front of it was partially unzipped to reveal the deep cleavage created by her ample breasts. Sloan's catty side immediately dismissed them as implants.

There was an air of supreme nonchalance about the redhead when she paused at their table and divided her glance between the two of them. "What can I get you ladies?" Her pouty red lips twitched with a smile as if secretly amused by the term.

Looking at the woman, Sloan saw nothing but red — in more ways than one. Everything about the waitress screamed sex, from the tumble of titian hair and overdrawn scarlet lips to the slinky, skintight outfit and staggeringly high heels.

"Do you have any banana cream pie?" Cat asked.

"Sure." The redhead stood hip-locked, a play of amusement still in evidence.

"I'll have a slice of that and a glass of water," Cat ordered.

With an effort, Sloan managed to find her voice. "A cup of soup, please."

"Cream of broccoli or beef pepperpot?" The redhead fixed her gaze on Sloan, something smug and knowing in her expression.

"The pepperpot."

"Anything to drink?"

"Milk."

"I'll bring it right out," the redhead promised and made an unhurried turn away from the table. Hips swaying, she angled for the free-swinging kitchen door.

Chair legs scraped the floor as Cat pushed back from the table. "My hands smell like shrimp. I'll wash them before I get that pie. I won't be a minute."

Sloan responded with an absent nod, tension coiling through her nerves. Mere seconds after Cat left the table, the redhead sashayed out of the kitchen, a serving tray negligently balanced on her right palm. Again her gaze made an amused skim of Sloan when she approached the table.

Halting next to Sloan's chair, the redhead reached in front of her, first to place a glass of water, then a napkin-wrapped setup at the place Cat had occupied. Sloan kept her gaze rigidly fixed on the table area in front of her, refusing to look up. But she couldn't avoid seeing the scarlet-nailed hand that kept passing across her vision — or the gleam and glitter of the diamond bracelet that draped the redhead's wrist. Instinctively Sloan knew it wasn't a piece of costume jewelry.

Suspicion was running too thick to allow Sloan to ignore it. "That's a lovely bracelet you're wearing."

"Gorgeous, isn't it?" Keeping the hand extended in front of Sloan, the redhead turned her wrist to let the diamonds flash in the low light. "They're real diamonds, too. Not CZs. My guy gave it to me."

"How nice," Sloan murmured, tasting bile.

Regret was in the sigh the redhead expelled. "I don't get to see him as much as I'd like. He tries to make up for it with little things like this."

"I wouldn't call that so little." A cold fury tightened Sloan's jaw.

"It sure isn't." Her red lips had a feline curve to them as she set a glass of milk before Sloan. "When's the baby due?"

"Soon." The single word was all Sloan you could manage.

"I'll bet it can't be soon enough for you." The redhead slid a setup onto the table. "You must be feeling really fat and miserable."

Infuriated by the insulting comment, Sloan looked up, but the redhead was already walking off, the loud tap of her stiletto heels masking the sound of Cat's returning footsteps.

Sloan barely glanced at Cat when she sat down at the table. Instead she reached for the milk glass, wrapping both hands around it in a stranglehold, and fervently hoped that Cat wasn't in one of her chatty moods. Sloan doubted that her nerves could tolerate a round of idle conversation.

But Cat simply went about the task of unrolling her silverware and arranging the napkin on her lap with a calmness that made Sloan want to scream, especially when she was torn between wanting to throw everything within reach and getting up and walking out the door. But either action would require an explanation. One of the first lessons Sloan had learned in her life was never to let anyone know how deeply she'd been wounded.

Again the swinging door to the kitchen rocked open and the redhead emerged, this time with their food order on her tray. As Sloan watched her approach, inwardly seething, a little voice inside her head demanded to know how much more proof she wanted? Did she intend to subject herself to the humiliation of actually catching the redhead in Trey's arms?

Wise up, the voice ordered. *Why show loyalty to a man who abuses it?*

The final jab came when Sloan was reminded that she was surrounded by people who didn't trust her. She wasn't even sure why they tolerated her. Then the baby moved, and Sloan knew the reason. The only reason.

She never registered the sight of the redhead setting the cup of soup in front of her, but there it was, with a spoon nestled on its plate. Nothing had ever looked less appetizing. Still, Sloan picked up the spoon and dipped it into the soup. It was tasteless on her tongue. After two spoonfuls, she gave up the exercise and laid the spoon on the table while leaning back in her chair.

Observing the action, Cat glanced over in question. "Is something wrong with the soup?"

"It's a little too spicy," Sloan lied and pressed a hand against one of the tightly banded muscles in her back.

"Are you feeling all right?" Again, concern filled Cat's expression.

"I'm fine. My back just hurts."

"You're sure it isn't labor pains? When I had Quint, that's the way mine started."

"I don't think so," Sloan replied, then almost laughed. "But how would I know? I've never had a baby before."

All uncertainty vanished some ten minutes later when the first contraction twisted through Sloan. The Triple C's east entrance was in sight. But Cat didn't slow to make the turn.

"There's probably plenty of time," she told Sloan. "But I think we'll play it safe and drive straight to the hospital." One-handed, she fished the cell phone out of her purse and held it out to Sloan. "You'd better call Trey and let him know. I have his cell number on speed-dial. Just press four."

Rebellion formed at the prospect of speaking to him. Sloan had to force herself to take the phone from Cat and place the call. After a dozen rings with no answer, she broke the connection. An ugly bitterness wound through her as she wondered what occupied Trey so thoroughly that he couldn't be bothered to answer the phone. And she found herself wishing that she had checked to see if his truck was parked behind The Oasis, out of sight.

Afternoon sunlight pressed against the windows of the calving shed, but dust-coated panes diffused much of its brilliance. Inside, all the lights were on. Somewhere straw rustled, stirred by the hooves of a restless animal, and a cow lowed in mild distress.

In one of the shed's many maternity stalls, a two-year-old heifer rolled an anxious eye at Trey as he released his hold on the pull chains and worked to push the calf a short distance back into the birth canal. Succeeding at that, he went about the task of rotating the calf half a turn. A trickle of sweat ran along his temple despite the coolness in the air.

"Hey, Trey." Old Jobe Garvey hobbled up to the stall. "Chase is on the phone. He wants to talk to you."

Trey never glanced up. "Tell him I've got a heifer with a hip-locked calf. I'll have to call him back."

"I'll tell him." Jobe shuffled off.

After the calf was turned, Trey picked up the chains again and tried again to walk the calf out, alternately pulling on first one chain, then the other. Intent on his task, he never heard Jobe come back.

"Chase said your wife's on the way to the hospital to have your baby," Jobe announced with a touch of personal pleasure.

The news kicked through Trey, bringing a heady rush that had him expelling a short, exultant laugh. That and the grin on his face marked his only reaction. He didn't look around for someone to take his place on the pull chains. He already knew that no one else was available.

"He also said you were to swing by The Homestead and get her suitcase 'fore you head to the hospital yourself," Jobe added.

"Thanks." Trey relaxed the pressure on the chains as the calf's hips finally slipped through the young cow's narrow pelvic area. "Better roust somebody from the night crew to take my place."

Thick layers of straw cushioned the calf's fall. Trey knelt beside it and made certain its mouth and nose were clear of any mucous, then removed the obstetrical handles from the calf's forelegs. He stayed long enough to make certain the young cow was going to accept her offspring before heading for his truck.

His clothes reeked of the calving shed. He showered and changed after he reached The Homestead, then Sloan's suitcase in hand, climbed back into the truck and started for the hospital, some three hours away.

Cat was waiting in the lobby when he walked in. The smile on her face and the sparkle in her green eyes told him the news even before she spoke.

"As of" — she paused to check her watch — "eighteen minutes ago, you are now the father of a healthy eight-pound, seven-ounce boy."

He temporarily checked the rise of feeling within. "How's Sloan? Is she all right?"

"She's fine. They both are," Cat assured him. "They'll be taking her to her room shortly. You go ahead. I'll call home to let them know."

Eagerness was in his stride as Trey made his way to the hospital's maternity section and the private room that had been assigned to his wife. Within minutes Sloan was wheeled into it. He was moved by how pale she looked. The winter months had taken much of the golden tan from her skin, but this pallor, he knew, came from exhaustion.

"Hi, Momma," he murmured and covered her lips with a warm kiss that elicited only a feeble response. "I came as quick as I could."

There was something darkly resentful in the look she gave him. "I called, but you didn't answer."

"I guess I didn't hear the phone ring. It was in my coat pocket. I probably wouldn't have answered, though. I was in the middle of pulling a calf. Gramps called, and old Jobe brought the news that you were on the way here. As soon as I got the little heifer calf safely into the world, I stopped by The Homestead to get your suitcase and take a shower. I knew they'd never let me into the delivery room, as filthy as my clothes were. But you didn't wait for me to get here."

"No," Sloan admitted, finding some comfort in the knowledge that this time Trey had been where he said he would be. But it changed nothing in her mind.

"Are you doing all right?" His work-roughened fingers smoothed an odd strand of hair off her brow. "You look tired."

Sloan readily accepted the excuse he offered. "I am. Have you seen him?" The mere thought of her son evoked a powerful tenderness within her, more profound than anything she had ever known.

"Not yet," Trey replied. "The nurse said they'd be bringing him shortly."

Cat walked into the room just as the nurse transferred the blanket-wrapped infant into Trey's arms. The expression on Trey's face when he gazed at his baby son made Cat pause. He looked incredibly proud and incredibly humble both at the same time. It was a sight that tugged at her heart.

Some slight movement betrayed her presence, drawing Trey's glance to her. A father's smile broke across his face. "Come say hello to your new great-nephew, Jacob Matthew Calder."

PART THREE

*The storm has exploded
over Calder land.
Now he has no choice
But to take a hard stand.*

Chapter Twenty

Little Jacob Calder remained the center of attention as visitors streamed in and out of the room for much of the next day. Most were friends of the family, there to welcome the newest addition to the Calder family. To Sloan's relief, none seemed to notice when she contributed little to the conversations.

The rare times when she found herself alone with Trey, she had only to plead tiredness and a desire to rest, and Trey would wander off to the cafeteria for some coffee, leaving Sloan free to make phone calls and put her hastily devised plan into motion.

In the early morning hours of the third day, her attending physician came by just as Sloan had privately signed the release orders she had arranged for herself. She wasted no time changing into her street clothes and requesting that her son be brought to her so she could leave.

The nurse looked at her with a bewildered frown. "Aren't you going to wait until your husband gets here?"

Prepared for the question, Sloan replied smoothly. "He's staying at a motel here in town. I thought I'd surprise him."

"But — what about all these bouquets and stuffed toys?" the nurse protested.

"Why don't you distribute them among your other patients," Sloan suggested.

She wasn't able to persuade the nurse to ignore hospital policy that dictated she be wheeled to the door. Which meant she had to suffer through another delay while a wheelchair was located and brought to her room.

After an interminable wait, she finally climbed into the rear passenger seat of a waiting taxi, her precious son in her arms. But she didn't draw an easy breath until the driver pulled away from the hospital entrance.

Exactly twenty-five minutes past eight o'clock, Trey walked past the nurse's station, carrying an infant carrier by its handle. With his attention focused on the open door to Sloan's room, he never noticed the surprised looks he received.

As he approached the room, an aide wheeled out a cart, packed solid with floral arrangements. Trey stepped aside to let her pass.

"Can I help you?" She eyed him curiously.

"I'm here to get my wife and son." His glance skipped past her into the room, stripped of its balloons, flowers, and cuddly toys. But it was the empty bed that made him check the room number.

"What's her name?" the aide asked in an attempt to he helpful.

Trey answered automatically while he was still trying to make sense of what he was seeing. "Sloan Calder."

"Mrs. Calder?" the young girl repeated in surprise. "Why, she's already left."

Features that had initially appeared youthful and ruggedly handsome, hardened into something forbidding. "You must be mistaken."

The aide drew back. "I'm sorry, sir, but I'm not. She's gone."

The sound of approaching footsteps, whisper-soft in their tread, intruded, and the aide was released from the pinning glare of Trey's cold eyes when it sliced to the nurse moving toward them.

"Good morning, Mr. Calder." The greeting gave a touch of normalcy to a moment that was anything but. "Is there a problem with the flowers? Your wife did leave instructions that she wanted to share them with the other patients."

"Where is she?" Trey demand curtly. "Where's my son?"

Surprise left the woman momentarily speechless and a little flustered. "I believe they left right before I came on duty, probably thirty or forty minutes ago. If I'm not mistaken, Tessa — Nurse Hutchins — accompanied them to the lobby."

"Where'd they go?"

Confusion and concern came together in the woman's expression. "They didn't arrive at your motel?"

"Would I be here if they had?" Trey countered, his voice low and rough.

"I suppose not," the nurse admitted. "It's just that Tess — Nurse Hutchins — mentioned that your wife said something about wanting to surprise you. Naturally she assumed the taxi was going to take her to your —"

Trey walked off before she could complete the sentence, swift strides carrying him toward the lobby. The nurse sent an anxious glance after him.

"I wonder what happened to Mrs. Calder," the aide murmured. "Do you think we should call the police?"

After a moment's hesitation, the nurse made a small negative shake of her head. "I don't think so. At least — not yet," she added and hurried after Trey.

Even at a running walk, she didn't catch up with him until he reached the lobby. Oblivious to her calls for him to wait, he never slowed until she caught his arm. Halting, he swung around to face her, bristling with impatience.

"Maybe you should check at the other motels in town," she suggested earnestly. "It's possible she went to the wrong one."

Without even a nod of acknowledgement, he turned back and started across the lobby again, taking no notice of the heavyset man in a billed cap standing at the information desk. But the gray-haired volunteer manning the desk saw him and waved an envelope in the air.

"Yoo-hoo, Mr. Calder," she called. "Ken just brought this in for you."

One glimpse of the envelope in her hand and Trey changed course, crossing to the desk. He took the envelope from her outstretched hand and ripped open the flap.

"It's a good thing I caught you before you left," the woman declared brightly. "Oh, it would have been forwarded on to you, of course, but as slow as mail is these days, who knows how long it might have taken?"

Inside was a single sheet of plain paper, folded in half. Trey snapped it open. The message was one sentence long. *My lawyer will be in touch.* It was signed *Sloan.*

Trey's fingers curled into the paper, stopping short of wadding it into a ball. He turned the full bore of his attention on the man in the billed cap.

"Are you the one who brought this?" His voice was tight with challenge.

"Yeah." The man's shoulders moved in a small, so-what shrug.

"Who gave it to you?"

"Mrs. Calder," he replied. "She asked me to leave it here at the hospital after I dropped her off at the airport. That's my cab out there." He waved a hand in the direction of the sedan idling outside the entrance.

Clouds rolled across the Montana plains, pushed by a fast-moving cold front. Their thick layers blocked the late afternoon sunlight from the land, casting a premature darkness over the Triple C headquarters. Smoke curled from one of The Homestead's chimneys, its gray trail blending into the skyscape.

Inside the big white house, the snap and crackle of flames in the den's fireplace dominated the stillness. On this afternoon, Chase had bypassed his chair behind the desk and chosen instead to sit in a wing-backed one near the fire, angled to expand his view of the area directly outside the house.

One liver-spotted hand gripped the head of his cane, and the other patted the arm-rest in a show of impatience. With all his senses trained on the sights and sounds beyond the glass panes, Chase was quick to catch the distinctive rumble of an approaching vehicle.

Using his cane for leverage, he pushed himself out of the wing-backed chair and stumped over to the window. But the minute his sharp eyes identified Laredo as the driver, he turned from the window in disgust and clumped back to the desk.

When a search of a top drawer proved fruitless, Chase released a cranky bellow. "Cat! Get in here!"

Three sets of footsteps responded to his summons, but Cat was the first to enter the room ahead of Laredo and Jessy. "What is it? What's wrong?" The questions tumbled from Cat in an alarmed rush.

"Where'd you hide my damned cigars?" he demanded.

"Your cigars?" Cat repeated in disbelief.

"Isn't that what I just said?" he demanded, all testy.

In a huff, Cat crossed to the desk and flipped open the lid of the small wooden humidor that sat atop it. "Your cigars are right where you put them this morning. If you had bothered to look instead of carrying on like the sky was falling, you would have seen them."

Chase grunted a nonresponse and plucked a cigar from the box. "Are you going to smoke that now?" Cat frowned.

"Damn right. If I can't hold that new great-grandbaby of mine, then, by God I'll smoke a cigar to him." He turned a scowling look on Jessy. "What's taking Trey so long to get here? I thought Sloan and little Jake were supposed to leave the hospital this morning."

"That's what Trey said last night," Jessy admitted. "But there are any number of reasons why they aren't here yet. For all we know, the doctor might have been late getting to the hospital to sign her out. I'm sure they'll be arriving soon."

"They'd better be. I'm tired of waiting." Chase propped his cane against the desk to free his hands and proceeded to light his cigar, taking quick puffs to draw the flame to its tip.

Laredo wandered over to the drink cart. "How about a shot of whiskey to go with that cigar, Chase? It might make the waiting easier."

"Not unless you're having one. Drinking alone is a bad habit for a man my age to get into." With the smoldering cigar clenched between his teeth, he hobbled back to the wing-backed chair and lowered himself onto its seat.

"In that case, I'll join you." Laredo removed the stopper from the whiskey decanter and slid a questioning glance at Jessy. "How about you?"

"I think I'd rather have coffee," she said.

"That's probably wise," Laredo agreed with a teasing grin. "Grandmas shouldn't have whiskey on their breath."

"Or great-aunts, either," Cat inserted. "I'll get the coffee, Jessy."

When Cat left the den, Chase removed the cigar from his mouth and directed a look at Jessy. "How have our numbers been running in the calving sheds?"

"So far the live births are one hundred percent, although Shadow Rock Camp had one calf that's too weak to nurse, so they're bottle-feeding it. We checked the records, and that same cow lost her calf last year, so she's one we probably want to cull."

At the drink cart, Laredo listened to the run of conversation behind him while he poured whiskey into two glasses and added a splash of water and ice to his. As he put the stopper back on the decanter, his glance strayed to the window and stayed there when he saw the Suburban pull up to the house. He started to alert the others of Trey's arrival, then checked himself when he noticed the absence of any passengers.

But it was the cold set of Trey's expression when he emerged from the vehicle and the look of tightly caged energy in the way he crossed to the steps that prompted Laredo to say in warning, "I think we've got trouble."

"Trouble?" Chase reared his head back. "What kind of trouble? Where? What are you talking about?"

Laredo didn't have to answer as the slam of the front door reverberated through the house, followed by the sound of hard-striding footsteps coming straight to the den. Laredo had the advantage of knowing it was Trey before he walked in, his sheepskin-lined jacket hanging open and his dress black Stetson pulled low on his forehead.

"Trey." Chase's expression brightened like a child at Christmas, then clouded with confusion when he realized Trey was alone. "Where's Sloan and little Jake? Why aren't they with you?"

Without bothering to answer, Trey crossed to the drink cart and jerked the stopper out of the decanter. His hat brim shadowed much of his face, but Laredo was close enough to see the glitter of banked savagery in his eyes.

"Dammit, boy, you answer me," Chase thundered.

"Remember last spring, Gramps?" Trey poured three fingers of whiskey into a glass, jammed the stopper back on, and snatched up the drink, then turned to face his grandfather. "You warned us that Rutledge might want to get even. He has. An eye for an eye. My son for his."

Jessy's mouth opened in a wordless protest, and she took an instinctive step toward Trey, then sensed that physical contact was something he would reject. Chase's only reaction was to lean slowly back in his chair.

"I think you'd better tell us what happened," Chase stated calmly.

Trey tossed back a hefty swallow of whiskey, but if it burned on the way down,

Laredo observed no indication of it in Trey's expression. Instead there was a look of cold resolve in his dark eyes that Laredo had only seen in one other man, and that was Chase Calder.

"When I arrived at the hospital this morning, I was told Sloan had left with our son thirty minutes earlier. After calling in favors, twisting a few arms, and greasing some palms, I learned that she boarded one of Rutledge's private jets. According to the flight plan, its destination was Fort Worth."

His response was a clear, concise statement of the facts without embellishment or emotion. But Laredo was more impressed that Trey hadn't assumed anything; he had dug for the facts.

"I managed to get a look at the phone charges from the hospital. Sloan placed two long-distance calls to an unlisted number in Texas. The first three digits are the same as the Cee Bar's number."

"It's plain the two of them planned this together," Chase concluded, then released a troubled sigh. "I'm surprised she didn't leave you some kind of note — just to throw some salt on the wound."

"She did." Trey pulled the crumpled sheet from his jacket pocket and tossed it to him. "She had the cab driver bring it to the hospital and added a fifty-dollar tip to make sure he waited until he saw her plane take off."

Chase reached into his shirt pocket to retrieve his magnifiers, only to discover they weren't there. With no hesitation, he handed it to Jessy. "Read it aloud."

"My God," Jessy murmured when she saw what it said, and she directed a commiserating glance at her son. " 'My lawyer will be in touch.' And it's signed 'Sloan.' "

"That's cold and to the point," Chase declared on a grim note.

"Is that what you're going to do?" Laredo made a sideways study of Trey. "Wait for her lawyer to call?"

"Like hell I am!"

With navigation lights blinking in the dusk of day's end, the helicopter settled gently onto the Slash R's private helipad, strategically located near the main house. Harold Bennett stood well back from the aircraft, but not far enough to escape being buffeted by its powerful downdraft.

As the helicopter's engine was cut, slowing the rotation of its blades, a specially designed lift was rolled to the cabin door. It was a rare occurrence for Harold to observe his employer's arrival from the ground. Any other time he would have been aboard the helicopter with Rutledge. But the day's events had dictated otherwise.

In short order, Rutledge was lowered to the ground in his wheelchair, a briefcase on his lap. Harold moved to meet him when Rutledge sent his chair speeding toward him.

As always, Rutledge didn't waste time with pointless greetings. "I ordered extra security. Have they arrived?"

"Yes sir. Two are on duty at the main gate. Another one's stationed in the ranch yard. They've got three vehicles on the road and two men with dogs patrolling the house yard."

"Have there been any problems? Any phone calls?"

"None, sir," Harold replied, allowing a faint smile to show.

"Good." Rutledge nodded in approval, some of that charged tension leaving him. "What about Sloan? Is everything all right there?"

"Yes sir. She was understandably tired and stressed by the time she got here. Other than that, she and the baby are doing fine and settling in nicely."

"And you're sure they've got everything they need," Max challenged.

"If they don't, I don't know what it would be," Harold told him. "The nursery is stocked with every baby item there is, and Sloan has a whole new wardrobe. If I overlooked anything, it's a phone call away."

"Where is she now?"

"In the nursery, feeding the baby." Behind them the wheelchair hoist was rolled away from the helicopter, and the cabin door was shut and locked in preparation for liftoff.

"It's time I saw this Calder heir." Rutledge's mouth curved in anticipation, but Harold knew better than to mistake it for a smile. It wasn't the prospect of seeing the infant that put that gleam in Rutledge's eye; rather, it was the knowledge that the child was in his house.

The pilot waited until the pair was nearly to the house before he throttled up the engine. The roar of it once again filled the air, disturbing the stillness of the warm spring evening. Like a great lumbering dragonfly, the chopper rose slowly, made a slight sideways dip, and swooped upward.

With a hand at the controls, Max steered the wheelchair down the wide corridor, designed, as was every inch of the house, for easy wheelchair access. The door to the newly created nursery stood open, but Max brought the wheelchair to a stop within its frame. Sloan sat in a rocking chair, gazing adoringly at the infant in her arms, one finger stroking a soft cheek.

Max rapped twice on the door. "May I come in?"

"Uncle Max." A smile spread across her face in welcome. "Of course you can. In fact, your timing couldn't be better. Jake just finished his bottle. I was about to put him back in his crib so he could sleep."

"He weathered the flight all right, then." Max rolled his chair into the room.

"He fussed a lot on the plane," Sloan admitted. "I'm sure the changes in cabin pressure hurt his ears. But he's fine now."

"And you, are you all right, too?" Head cocked at a considering angle, he studied her with a show of gentle concern.

"I will be," she asserted.

"Spoken with the grit of a Davis," Max stated, emphasizing his approval with a single nod of his head.

"Thanks." There was something almost shy in the smile Sloan gave him, but her following comment told him it was born of uncertainty. "I just hope I've done the right thing."

"You have. We all make mistakes. The weak close their eyes to them and pretend everything will be all right in time. The strong admit them and take steps to correct them — just as you have done. I'm not saying it won't be painful," Max added. "But a swift, clean break is the best."

"That's what I keep telling myself," Sloan murmured, but a sadness stole into her expression.

Harold Bennett paused in the doorway and rapped lightly to gain their attention. "I wanted to check on our little guy and see how he's doing," he said when they looked up. He nodded at the empty baby bottle sitting on the table next to her chair. "He drank all his formula, did he? That's a good sign."

"He was hungry." Sloan looked at her son with pride and smiled. "Now he's sleepy."

While she was distracted, Max made eye contact with his personal nurse and signaled for him to get the baby. Harold nodded and advanced into the room.

"Let me put him to bed for you." Halting at her chair, he stretched out his arms to take the infant, wrapped in a blue receiving blanket.

"You're spoiling me, Harold." Sloan surrendered her son to him.

"You've had a long day, too, and you need your rest as much as this one does," Harold replied in his best professional voice.

When he turned to carry the baby to his crib, Max spoke up, "May I hold him a moment first?"

Harold managed to contain his surprise. Recovering quickly, he smiled. "Of course." He carried the infant to his employer and placed him in his arms, careful to make sure there was support for the baby's head, then stepped back to watch, certain Max wouldn't want to hold the child for long.

"My, my, look at all that hair," Max declared in a marveling voice. "Why, he's going to need a haircut in another month."

"He does have a lot of hair, doesn't he?" Sloan leaned closer, smiling with pride.

Max declined to comment on its dark color, unwilling to make any reference to the Calders, indirectly or otherwise. "It's been a long time since there was a baby in this house. I had forgotten how small they are, and how innocent. A new, young life is just what this old, tired heart of mine needed. Thank you for bringing him here, Sloan."

A quick shake of her head dismissed his thanks. "After all you've done — sending the plane and having all this waiting for us — I'm the one who needs to thank you."

"Nonsense," Max declared without looking up from the infant, then feigned a small start of surprise. "Why, I do believe he just yawned. I guess he is sleepy."

Quick to take the cue, Harold stepped forward to relieve him of the infant. "Newborns need their sleep."

"Of course they do," he agreed and looked at Sloan. "I instructed Vargas to set out some hors d'oeuvres in the living room. We'll go there and continue our talk so we won't disturb your son." As expected, he saw the beginnings of a protest in Sloan's expression and smiled in understanding. "Don't worry. Harold will keep an eye on him for you."

Showing a new mother's reluctance to be separated from her child, Sloan followed Max into the living room. Max pretended not to notice the uneasy glance she sent in the direction of the nursery before she took a seat.

He made no attempt to resume their conversation until the house servant had delivered their drinks, a lemonade for Sloan and a bourbon and water for Max. "I can't tell you how much I wish you and the baby were here under different circumstances. I had great hopes that your marriage would be a happy one."

Sloan immediately stiffened with a kind of bitter anger. "It wasn't to be — not unless I wanted to be one of those who pretended she didn't know there was another woman. But I can't and I won't."

"Well, in all honesty, I can't say I was surprised when you told me Trey was stepping out on you." His sigh had a trace of disgust in it. "Given the history of that family, I suppose it was inevitable."

"You're referring to the affair Trey's father had with Jessy," Sloan guessed at once. "I heard all about that. After meeting Tara, though, I could understand why he did it." Pausing, she made a wry grimace. "It's funny, but I feel sorry for Tara now. No one at the ranch liked her. Like me, she was never accepted into the family in anything but name."

"And like you, Tara was too strong a woman to quietly endure that kind of humiliation. That wasn't always the case in the Calder family, from what I've learned." Max deliberately didn't elaborate on that comment, confident that Sloan would take the bait.

She did. "What do you mean?"

He began with an apology. "Forgive me, Sloan, but when you first indicated there was some trouble in your marriage, I became concerned and did some checking into the Calders. After all, like most people, I only knew them by their reputation as giants in ranching. I never had reason to delve into their personal lives until this started."

"What did you learn, Uncle Max?" A glitter of anger was in her eyes, the kind that said Sloan was ready to believe anything he told her.

"I'm afraid the Calder men don't fare well as shining examples," Max warned. "For instance, are you aware that Trey's father was born out of wedlock, and it wasn't until some fifteen years after the fact, when Chase found himself in need of an heir, that he bothered to acknowledge him as his son? He married the mother merely to avoid the stigma of 'bastard' being attached to his son. And it seems that Chase's father wasn't much better. He was shot and severely wounded after being caught with another man's wife. There's even some question about the true relationship between the Triple C founder, Benteen Calder, and Lady Elaine Dunshill. The family would like you to believe she was his mother, but it seems more likely that she was his mistress."

"I didn't know any of that," Sloan admitted with a dazed and half-angry frown.

"I'm sure the family tries to keep its indiscretions hushed up. But I'm told such behavior becomes a kind of mind-set that passes from one generation to the next until it's regarded as not only acceptable but expected. It will probably be a shock to them that you objected so strongly to the idea of your husband seeing another woman. In their eyes, it's simply what men do."

"Not in mine, it isn't." All taut and indignant, Sloan pushed out of the chair and crossed to the window. She stood there, rubbing her arms in agitation.

Max allowed the silence to stretch for a bit, then pretended to muse, "As old-fashioned as the Calders are, I can't help but think that if your marriage hadn't broken up over this, the split would have come over your career. Photography is something you love, and I can't see you giving it up. I suspect it was only a matter of time before it became a source of contention between you."

"That's what Tara said," Sloan recalled, "when she wasn't lecturing me about the duties I needed to assume as the wife of a Calder."

"No doubt Tara was speaking from her own experience, wouldn't you say?" Max suggested.

Sloan turned back to him, uncertainty flickering through her expression. "I hadn't thought of it that way."

"I'm told Tara spent a good deal of time away from the ranch. I'm sure a part of her wonders if she hadn't been gone so much, maybe her husband wouldn't have become involved with Jessy. Perhaps her advice was meant as a warning not to make the same mistake she believes she made."

"Probably," Sloan agreed. "But it doesn't change anything. Any man who expects me to give up my career for him doesn't really love me, because it's part of who I am."

"Someday you'll meet a man who will see that," Max stated. "Unfortunately, the Calders are too selfish and self-centered. Everything has to be done the way they want it."

"The Calder way. My God, how many times have I heard that phrase?" Sloan muttered thickly.

"You're free of them now, so you don't have to be concerned with that anymore."

A heavy sigh broke from her, "I'd give anything if that were true. But I know it's only beginning."

He caught the blend of worry and dread in her voice. "Now that begins, doesn't it? The fear that he'll try to take the baby away from you."

"I never would have been allowed to leave the ranch with little Jake. That's why I couldn't go back there — why I had to take my son and run while I had the chance."

"You did the only thing you could do," Max assured her. "We both know that. If you're worrying that Trey will show up —"

"He doesn't know I'm here. I never said anything in the note about where I was going."

"By now he's bound to have guessed." Max had no illusions about that. "It hardly matters, though. He'll never get within five feet of this house. I've hired extra guards to patrol the grounds and every access point on the Slash R. Your son will be perfectly safe here, and so will you."

Surprised and confused, Sloan tipped her head to one side. "It almost sounds like you think Trey would try to kidnap Jake."

"I wouldn't put it past him," Max replied. "The Calders have been the law in their part of the world for a long time. They probably think they can act with impunity. That's why I insisted that you and your son come here. I knew I could protect you from anything they might try."

"They aren't taking my son from me." The battle light was in her eyes, born of the fierceness of a mother protecting her young. "I have every bit as much right to him as they do. If they think otherwise, they have a fight on their hands."

"I'm glad to hear it. This is one time when you can't afford to be tenderhearted, because they aren't going to worry about what's fair," Max warned, determined to feed her distrust of the Calders until it became an all-consuming thing. He doubted that this would be difficult to accomplish. "I have a top-notch divorce lawyer lined up for you, one of the best in the country. You're to call him in the morning. It's important that you remain the aggressor and keep the Calders reacting to your moves instead of making their own." He handed Sloan a slip of paper with the lawyer's name and telephone number on it.

"I'll contact him first thing in the morning," she promised.

Chapter Twenty-One

Morning sunlight flashed across the private jet's cockpit as the craft taxied to a stop near the FBO terminal. A member of the ground crew trotted up and set the wheel chocks in place.

Inside the aviation terminal, Quint Echohawk stood near the glass door that led to the concrete apron. High, hard cheekbones and the deep black of his hair spoke of his Sioux ancestry. The gray of his eyes was his father's gift to him, but the granite jaw and strong, straight nose came from the Calder side of his bloodline.

His sharp eyes watched as the plane's door swung open and the steps were lowered. First to descend them was the copilot, toting a dark leather carryall. Then Trey came down, a brisk impatience in his movement. With little more than a nod to the copilot, he took the bag from him and struck out for the terminal.

Quint tossed a quick glance at the silver-haired man dressed in a business suit and tie and seated at one of the tables, a closed briefcase at his side and an open laptop before him. "He's coming." Then he gave the door a push, swinging it open to admit his younger cousin.

One look at the cold set of Trey's features advised Quint that no innocence of youth remained, and the hard vitality that blazed in Trey's eyes now had a cynical twist to it.

"Is everything set?" Trey's quick question checked any words of regret Quint might have expressed.

"It is," Quint confirmed and turned sideways to include the silver-haired man, who stepped forward, the laptop once again stowed in his briefcase. "This is Wyatt Breedon. You spoke to him on the phone last night."

"Mr. Breedon." Trey briefly gripped the man's hand, the abruptness of his handshake revealing more of the restless impatience that churned behind his cool exterior.

"Make it Wyatt," the attorney replied. "That 'mister' business just makes everything sound a little too formal, and that's not the tone we want to convey when we meet with Mrs. Grunwald. Were you able to get your hands on all those documents before you left this morning?"

"They're right here." Trey patted the bag he carried.

"Good. I've got a car waiting for us."

Trey started toward the exit, then paused to glance at Quint. "Are you coming with us?"

"No. I need to get back to the Cee Bar before Rutledge's people start wondering where I went," Quint replied, then added, "I already told Wyatt, Rutledge has guards stationed all around the ranch, and more patrolling it. You can't get within an inch of his fences without somebody seeing you."

"It doesn't surprise me." There was no change in Trey's iron composure.

"It's always better to go in the front door, anyway." Quint smiled encouragement. "If you need me, you only have to call."

"Thanks." But Trey knew this was one thing Quint could have no part in.

High atop the glass and granite building of his corporate headquarters, Max Rutledge sat in the darkened boardroom and watched the computer-generated presentation of the proposed expansion of the company's oil business. He paid little attention to the droning voice that explained the numerous facts and figures that flashed on the screen. He was too busy calculating the net revenue increase that would result.

A door opened behind him, spilling light into the room and breaking his concentration. He flashed an irritated look at the brunette who attempted to tiptoe to his wheelchair.

"I thought I left instructions that I wasn't to he disturbed, Miss Bridges," he muttered.

"I'm sorry, Mr. Rutledge." She bent close to his chair, enveloping him in her expensive perfume. "But Deputy Sheriff Krause is on the phone. I told him you were in a meeting, but he insisted it was important that he speak with you at once."

Rutledge went still for an instant while he considered the possible reasons for the deputy sherriff's call. "Have there been any calls from the ranch?"

"No sir."

Her response did little to allay the new concern that needled him. "I'll take the call," he told her, then signaled to his personal secretary and chief assistant. "Continue the presentation. I shouldn't be long. Make notes on anything that you feel should be brought to my attention."

With the instructions issued, Max sent his wheelchair gliding toward the connecting door to his executive office. A remote button opened the door before he reached it, allowing him to wheel through without any pause in speed. He rolled straight to his corner desk and picked up the phone.

"This is Rutledge. What is it?"

"Yeah, it's Deputy Krause." In the background was the whining roar of a passing semi. "I know I'm not supposed to call you at the office, but I figured you needed to know this."

"Know what?" Rutledge snapped, annoyed by useless explanations.

"Anna Grunwald, the old battle-ax over in the child welfare office, called thirty or forty minutes ago and asked for a uniform to go along on a call she had to make. It sounded like a dog job, so dispatch sent the rookie Hobbs. I heard him radio in a couple minutes ago. He's on his way to your ranch."

"He didn't say who was with him?" Max questioned, quietly furious that he hadn't anticipated this move by Calder.

"No, and he didn't say why he was going there, either. I know Clyde and his wife's got some kids, but —"

"Right. You hear anything else, you let me know," Max said and hung up, then pressed the intercom button. "Get Yancy Haynes on the line, and I want him now! Then alert the pilot that I want my helicopter ready to fly."

He sat back in his chair and let his mind sort through the potential problems this could create while seeking the right countermoves for them. As far as he was concerned, this setback was purely a temporary one.

The intercom buzzed. "Mr. Haynes is on line two, sir."

Without acknowledging the message, he picked up the phone and punched the blinking line. "Yeah, Haynes, this is Rutledge —"

"How are you, Max? I phoned earlier to let you know that I spoke with Mrs. Calder, but I was told you —"

"Never mind that now," he interrupted. "My helicopter is leaving to pick you up. I just learned that someone from child welfare is on the way to the ranch. More than likely, Calder is with her, and I don't want him alone with Sloan for one minute. Do you understand? Not for one minute!"

"I'll have to cancel —"

"I don't give a damn what you have to do. Just get there." Rutledge slammed the phone onto its cradle.

★ ★ ★

Alone at the expansive dining room table, Sloan dipped a spoon into her soup and carried it to her lips. As tasteful as it was, she found little enjoyment in it. She laid the spoon down and picked up her bread knife to butter the crusty roll on her side plate.

Each soft clink of her silverware seemed loud in the room's crushing silence. Sloan realized how accustomed she had become to the ebb-and-flow conversation that marked mealtimes at The Homestead. Eating alone was another of those things she would have to relearn, just like sleeping alone.

She took a bite of the fresh roll and chewed, then picked up the spoon and tried the soup again. Restraining a sigh, she dabbed at the corners of her mouth with the napkin, then spread it over her lap again.

The ever observant Vargas moved from his post near the doorway. "If the soup is not to your liking, senora, I will be happy to bring you something else."

"It's fine," she assured him and reclaimed the soupspoon.

From another room came the muted br-r-ring of the telephone. It was the third time in the last five minutes, which was a curiosity in itself, considering the phone rarely rang at all until Max came home. A hushed voice answered it. Sloan couldn't make out what was said, but she recognized Harold Bennett's voice.

As at previous times, the conversation was short. But at the end of it, Sloan heard the soft squeak of rubber-soled shoes approaching the formal dining room. She looked up as the male nurse appeared in the archway.

"Excuse me, but I thought I should inform you that we are about to have visitors."

The note of caution in his voice produced a frisson of alarm. "Who?" Sloan asked.

"A representative from the local child protection office, accompanied by a sheriff's deputy and two other men. One of whom is your husband."

"Trey is here?" The spoon clattered from her fingers as she stood up, mindless of the napkin that fluttered to the floor near her feet. "He's here to take my son, isn't he?"

Bennett raised a calming hand. "That isn't the purpose at all. This seems to be an official visit to verify your son's location as well as his safety and well-being. Nothing more. Your attorney, Mr. Haynes, has been informed of this, and he's already en route. He should be here momentarily. So you have nothing to be worried about."

The initial wave of panic receded as Sloan took note of how ready Bennett had been with his explanation. "The phone calls that came — this is what they were about, isn't it?" she guessed.

"Security has been stalling them at the gate to give your attorney time to arrive. Unfortunately, all their delaying tactics have been exhausted and they had to let them through."

The melodic chime of the doorbell served to confirm his statement. Her heart jumped at the sound, tension skittering along her nerves.

"That's them." Sloan took a step toward the living room.

Bennett stopped her. "Vargas will answer the door. We need to gain every second we can to let your attorney get here. It's a fine line to walk — stalling without testing their patience too much."

"I understand." She glanced over her shoulder, surprised to find the soft-footed servant, Vargas, had already left the room.

"Everything will be fine," Bennett assured her. "Mr. Rutledge has made sure that everything will be handled with no problems."

Looking back, she could see Max's hand at work behind the scenes — the phone calls summoning the attorney, the stall tactics, all the while shielding her from unnecessary worry. It was a thoughtful gesture; at the same time, she would rather have known what was going on instead of learning about it at the last minute.

The faint murmur of voices came from the entryway. Stiffening, Sloan listened intently but failed to detect Trey's voice among them.

Vargas entered the dining room, carrying a small silver tray with a business card on it. He offered it to Sloan. "There is a lady at the door who wishes to speak with you, senora."

She went through the motions of examining the card, but little registered other than the official insignia for the state of Texas and the woman's name, Anna Grunwald. "Thank you, Vargas," she began, then saw the quick warning shake of Bennett's head. Sloan quickly altered what she had been about to say. "Please tell her I'll be right there."

"*Si,* senora," Vargas replied while Bennett nodded approval behind him.

When the servant passed him to retrace his steps to the entrance, Bennett murmured something to him in Spanish. Sloan had been kept ignorant of too much to allow this to pass without questioning him.

"What did you say to him?" she asked.

"I told him to walk slow, like an armadillo out for a midnight stroll." There was a hint of self-satisfaction in the smile that touched his mouth, giving Sloan the impression he was pleased that he had come up with an excuse to gain more precious seconds.

Those seconds passed with excruciating slowness. Then Vargas reappeared. "I delivered your message, senora."

"Gracias," Sloan murmured in thanks.

Again Bennett signaled that she should wait. But the strain of that was already more than she cared to tolerate. Ignoring him, she walked out of the dining room, maintaining a steady but unhurried pace.

Approaching the spacious entryway, Sloan caught her first glimpse of Trey. She thought she had steeled herself for it, but she was surprised to feel that old familiar fluttering of her pulse. And she realized that love was an emotion slow to die, regardless of how badly it had been abused.

The minute Sloan walked into the entryway, a rather benign-looking, immaculately clad woman with gray hair stepped forward to meet her. "You must be Mrs. Calder." Her grandmotherly smile matched her rosy cheeks. "I'm Anna Grunwald. I see the servant gave you my card."

Sloan had forgotten she was still holding it. "Yes, he did. How do you do, Mrs. Grunwald?" Even as she extended a hand in greeting to the woman, her glance skipped to Trey and the silver-haired man in business suit and tie standing next to him.

Trey had his head tipped down, the muscles in his jaw and cheek tautly defined. There was an almost glacial coldness about him that froze her out. She felt the chill of it despite the distance between them.

The older man with him acknowledged Sloan's glance with a courteous nod, then stepped forward. "We haven't had the pleasure of meeting, Mrs. Calder. My name's Wyatt Breedon," he declared in a drawl as thick and smooth as Texas oil. "Your husband engaged me to represent him."

Before Sloan had a chance to respond, Anna Grunwald inserted, "These two gentlemen have accompanied me strictly as observers. I am the one you will have to satisfy." The firmness in her statement carried an undertone of warning.

"What is it you wish to know, Mrs. Grunwald?" Sloan pretended she was unaware of the purpose of the woman's visit.

"I have been shown official records that indicate you recently gave birth to a child," the woman began.

"A son, yes." Sloan nodded.

"Where is your son now?"

"Asleep in his crib."

"Here in the house, I assume."

"That's correct. Why do you ask?" Sloan tipped her head, feigning curiosity.

"Merely to verify that this is the residence in which the child is now living. Now, if you will be good enough to show me where he is," the woman stated with a no-nonsense lift of her head.

"Of course. The nursery is this way. Please follow me." Her glance strayed to Trey, but his own gaze was fastened on the matronly woman in the wine-colored suit. Sloan couldn't help feeling a little stung that he had yet to look at her as she pivoted sharply to lead the way.

But Trey had no need to look at her. Never in his life had he been more aware of her presence than he was at the moment. Her perfume trailed in the air behind her, enveloping him in her scent. The warm cadence of her voice struck deep and strong to vibrate through him. And he didn't have to look to remember the taste of her lips or the feel of her body beneath his hands.

Yet, despite all the ways that she was familiar to him, she was still the stranger who had plotted with Rutledge and taken his son from him. Being this close to Sloan, it was something Trey had to constantly remind himself of; there was Sloan, and then there was his illusion of her. They had turned out to be two very separate things.

Ahead of him, Sloan turned into a room that opened off the wide corridor. He saw Anna Grunwald halt two steps inside the room. "And who are you?" he heard her challenge someone. It was a second before Trey located the man she addressed. He was at one of the small bureaus, stowing something in one of its drawers.

Sloan made the introductions. "This is Mr. Harold Bennett. He's a registered nurse, employed by Mr. Rutledge."

"Anna Grunwald." The woman thrust out a hand.

Trey stopped listening to the exchange

the instant he caught sight of a tiny fist waving in the crib. Automatically he moved toward it, his chest tightening with the knowledge that the hand belonged to his son. But Sloan was closer, reaching the baby before he could.

Halting, he watched while she bent over the crib and crooned softly. The softness in her expression and the love shining from her eyes was the same look she wore in the hospital when she'd held their son. Anger pushed through him, the kind born of pain and all that had been lost to him.

"You must be feeling proud of yourself right now." Trey kept his voice pitched low, for her hearing only.

Stormy blue eyes threw him a glare. "What do you mean?"

"Isn't it obvious?" Trey countered. "You saw to it that Max got his revenge. My son for his."

"Max had nothing to do with this." Her voice trembled with heat.

"Right," he mocked. "It was just a co-incidence that you flew straight here — and on his plane."

"He helped me, and that's all he did," Sloan insisted.

"You stick to that story. Someone will believe it," After a pause, Trey added, "I have to hand it to you, Sloan. You're a helluva an actress. You actually had me convinced you loved me."

"You are such a hypocrite." Disgust riddled her words.

"Are you talking about me or yourself? It must be you," Trey said, answering his own question. "Taking off with my son was no last-minute decision. It was something you planned."

"What other choice did I have?" Her voice grew even quieter with the anger she held in check. "We both know if I had told you I was leaving, you never would have let me take Jake."

"You're damned right. I wouldn't have liked it, probably even have argued against it. But I would have put my son's needs first. That doesn't mean I wouldn't have insisted on seeing him as often as possible. I know what it's like to grow up without a father."

"Do you think I'm so heartless that I would have refused to let you see Jake? Why do you think I left you that note saying my attorney would contact you? It was to arrange visitation rights for you. There's no reason why we can't work out some sort of joint custody."

"Did Max tell you to suggest that —

hoping I'd back off? Well, it won't work. Because I know he'll do anything and everything to make sure my son never leaves this house. Jake is his key to everything the family owns, and Max knows it."

"That is a lie!" Sloan said with force, drawing the attention of the others in the nursery.

"Don't pretend to be naive, Sloan." His words cut. "It's true, and you know it."

"Now, now." Anna Grunwald was quick to intervene, bustling to the crib area. "We will have no fighting here. I thought that was agreed, Mr. Calder. Or do I have to ask you to leave?"

"My apologies, Mrs. Grunwald." Trey dipped his head to her in a show of respect. "It was a difference of opinion that became a bit heated. I regret that, and assure you it won't happen again."

"I intend to see that it doesn't," the woman stated, then lifted her head in a listening pose. "Do you hear that?" The thickly walled house failed to completely muffle a staccato drone. "It sounds like a helicopter." She turned a questioning look on Sloan.

But it was Bennett who responded. "Mrs. Calder has a meeting scheduled with her attorney. I expect that's Mr. Haynes arriving now."

"Perhaps he'll bring a note of civility." Mrs. Grunwald divided her glance between Sloan and Trey, alert to the crackling undercurrents that ran between them. "Excuse me." She nudged Sloan out of the way, taking her place next to the crib. "Aren't you a sweet baby," she declared, all warm and grandmotherly.

To Sloan's relief, Trey moved away from the crib. Yet distance did little to relieve the apprehension she felt. It hurt to remember the way he had twisted everything, making it seem that she was the one in the wrong when nothing could be farther from the truth.

The drone of the helicopter reached its peak, then lessened for a short stretch of minutes. Again the roar of it invaded the house as it lifted off the heliport, once more taking to the air. The noise of it had yet to fade when an Armani-suited Yancy Haynes strode into the nursery.

Introductions were made all around, and the two attorneys exchanged hail-fellow greetings that spoke of past encounters. Then Yancy Haynes moved to Sloan's side, effectively dividing the room into two camps, with Anna Grunwald as the only bridge.

"I hope you have assured yourself, Mrs.

Grunwald, that the baby couldn't possibly have better care." Yancy Haynes smiled with confidence, then made a sweeping gesture with his hand. "Here we have a room designed for an infant, complete with a registered nurse, not to mention, of course, the absolute devotion of his mother."

Without acknowledging his comment, the woman turned a gentle look on Sloan. "You certainly have a very beautiful and healthy-looking baby boy."

"Thank you." Her expression softened with a mother's pride.

"Am I allowed to hold him?" There was a trace of challenge in Trey's question.

"You're his father. Of course you may," Anna Grunwald replied, then fixed a firm look on him. "But if you attempt to remove him from the premises, I will see that you are stopped."

"Don't worry," Trey assured her dryly. "I would never try."

Sloan felt anything but easy when Trey gathered up their blanket-wrapped son from the crib. She saw that fiercely tender and fiercely possessive look on his face and knew he would fight to gain custody of Jake. In his warped reasoning, he would see it as wresting control of the baby from

Max. And this attitude of his made it virtually impossible to arrive at any fair resolution.

Some twenty minutes later, Anna Grunwald brought her official visit to an end, thanking Sloan for her time and patience. Sloan wasn't sure how much of the latter she had left. She only knew that her nerves were worn thin by the time she escorted the trio to the door. Even then she didn't feel safe until she had closed the door on Trey. She leaned against it, shaking a little on the inside.

Yancy Haynes studied her with shrewd eyes. "I'm sorry I couldn't get here in time to be with you when they arrived. But you seemed to have handled yourself very well."

"Thank —" The doorbell rang, it's chime jangling nerves that were raw. Sloan turned with a start and backed away from the door, a panic rising with the thought that it was Trey on the other side. She wasn't sure she could face him again.

The attorney stepped forward and opened the door. Standing outside was a uniformed sheriff's deputy with youthful face that looked totally nonthreatening.

"I need to see Mrs. Calder, sir." The request was made with grim regret.

Curious, Sloan walked back to the door and stood next to her lawyer. "What is it?"

"You're Mrs. Sloan Calder?" he asked.

"That's right," she confirmed.

"It's my duty to serve you with this." He handed her a sealed envelope and walked off.

For a stunned second, Sloan stared at the envelope in her hand. Before she could react, Yancy Haynes relieved her of it.

"Better let me have a look at this." He turned and headed toward the living room, ripping open the envelope and removing the document within.

Sloan hurried after him. "What is it?"

"Your husband works fast," he murmured, partly to himself. "I had intended to tell you this afternoon that you should anticipate being served with this in the next few days."

"Served with what?" Sloan demanded, running out of patience with his roundabout way of avoiding an answer. She didn't need to be coddled, and she resented that he thought she did.

"A custody hearing has been set for next week in Montana," he told her. "You are ordered to appear before the judge with your son."

"Why Montana? Why can't that be done

here in Texas?" she said in protest.

"Since you haven't been a Texas resident for the last six months, federal law gives jurisdiction to Montana," he explained, then smiled. "Naturally I'll file for a postponement."

"Naturally," Sloan echoed in a murmur.

"Have a seat, Mrs. Calder, and we'll get down to this unfortunate divorce business." He gestured to one of the living room chairs and remained standing until she took a seat. He sat down on the sofa, placed his briefcase on the coffee table, and opened it. "Mr. Hensley was kind enough to provide me with a copy of your prenuptial agreement." He removed a folder and flipped it open. "I almost forgot. He asked me to give you this as well." He passed her a sheaf of papers, paper-clipped together. "It's a document that names your son as your new beneficiary. As I understand, he's already discussed this with you."

"Yes, he has," Sloan confirmed.

"If you want, you can go ahead and sign it. I'll see that Hensley gets it. I tend to agree with him. It is something that should be done as soon as possible." He supplied her with a ballpoint pen.

After a quick skim of its provisions, Sloan signed it and passed it back.

★ ★ ★

When Max returned to the ranch that evening, he was no more concerned about the new turn of events than Yancy Haynes had been. "A custody hearing is just what we want," he assured Sloan, then smiled wryly. "Next week doesn't allow us much time to prepare, I admit, but Haynes will get it postponed."

"I was so sure Trey and I could agree to come to some kind of joint arrangement. But today —" Sloan felt a chill when she remembered the accusations Trey had made.

"Did something happen today?" His head lifted with quickening interest.

"I always knew the Calders were paranoid about you, Uncle Max. I told you how they reacted when they learned about my connection to you," Sloan reminded him. "Trey said something today that made me realize the Calders are absolutely convinced this is some evil plot by you to get revenge for Boone's death. Trey even said you had taken his son as payment for your own. He thinks that ultimately, through Jake, you intend to take control of everything the Calders own."

"What nonsense," Max scoffed.

"But it's real to them," Sloan explained.

"That's what is so terrifying. You can't reason with them."

"It's that western attitude of theirs. Probably comes from the days of the old cattle barons. Shoot first and ask questions later. Violence has always been a way of life for the Calders." Reluctance was in the look he gave Sloan. "You might as well know that my son wasn't the first man to die at the hands of a Calder."

"But according to findings at the inquest, Quint was only defending himself." Sloan had the impression Max was saying something different now.

"That's what the only eyewitness testified. Of course, a few months later, she married Echohawk. So I can't say, in all honesty, that's what really happened. Knowing my son, though, I recognize it's entirely possible. Something tells me the Calders would never admit to anything similar."

"As far as they're concerned, they're always right," Sloan agreed with resentment.

"It's an arrogance they have. It allows them to justify any action they take. Quite honestly, Sloan, it's the reason I insisted that you come here. Alone, you wouldn't have been able to stop them if they walked in and took the baby. Once they had him, you would have played hell trying to even see your son, with all the judges they have in their pockets. Here, there are too many guards. You can bet your husband saw that when he came today."

"But what happens when I have to take Jake to Montana?" Fear was just below the surface, gnawing at her nerves.

"You and the baby will be safe. I'll see to it," Max promised. "I don't care if it takes a battery of lawyers or army of body-guards. When you leave that state your son will be in your arms. Believe that."

She did. "I don't know how I can thank you for everything you're doing, Uncle Max."

"For starters, you can stop worrying and leave everything to me. Deal?" He smiled.

"It's a deal." For the first time all day, Sloan didn't have to force the smile she gave him.

Chapter Twenty-Two

The first evening star winked in the night sky, keeping watch over a sickle moon. Indifferent to it, Laredo focused his attention on the plane making its final approach to the ranch's landing strip. The night breeze stiffened enough to prompt Laredo to turn his collar up to escape its cold fingers.

With barely a thud the plane touched down. The night's quiet was broken by the squeal of its brakes and slowing thrust of its engines. Laredo never budged from his watching post beside the pickup until the aircraft taxied to a stop on the apron.

Reaching inside the cab, he switched on the truck's headlights to make it easier for Trey to locate him when he deplaned. He was quick to note the slow, heavy way Trey came down the steps but careful not to read too much into it. He waited until they were face to face to make his assessment. The weary flatness in Trey's eyes showed the aftereffects of a long and stressful day.

"How was the flight?" The casual question was Laredo's way of opening his probe for information.

"Long. Both of them," Trey added dryly.

"But you didn't run into any major problems?"

"Nope." Trey circled to the passenger side and climbed into the cab, dropping the soft-sided bag on the floorboard by his feet. "Rutledge had guards all over the place. Getting past them was a hassle, but that was about all. One of them tailed me back to the airport. I imagine Rutledge wanted to make sure I left town."

"And little Jake, he was all right, too?" Laredo gave the ignition key a turn.

"He was fine." Trey's mouth curved at the mention of his son. Then a soberness returned.

"I don't imagine Sloan was too happy to see you."

A muscle flexed along his jaw. "She must think I'm really gullible."

"Why do you say that?" Laredo threw him a curious glance and steered the pickup away from the hangar area.

"Because she tried to make me believe that Rutledge had nothing to do with her taking Jake and leaving. She claimed he merely helped. Good God." Anger surfaced in his voice. "You should have seen the room Jake was in. It was no temporary setup, but a full-fledged nursery. Want to bet Rutledge had it ready and waiting long before she ever left the hospital with Jake?"

"Probably," Laredo agreed. "Did she get served with the notice for the custody hearing?"

"Yeah. Breedon, the Texas attorney Quint recommended, guaranteed that her lawyer will try to get it postponed."

"According to Chase, he'll play hell getting Judge Abrams to give more than two or three days," Laredo replied. "Which reminds me, Jessy has Walters and his men digging to see what they can learn about Sloan, on the off chance there might be something damaging."

"I'm not going to hold my breath that they'll find anything. Rutledge would have made sure of that first." Trey paused to muse, "You've got to hand it to her, though. She had me fooled completely."

"At the start, she had us all fooled."

Trey found little consolation in Laredo's reply. A part of him still had trouble believing that it had been a lie from the beginning.

Rain pelted the Maresco building as ominous dark clouds rolled across the Greater

Fort Worth area, spitting lightning and issuing rumbles of thunder. Oblivious to the spring storm raging outside, Max Rutledge tightened his grip on the telephone.

"What the hell do you mean you could only get it postponed two days?" he exploded. "I thought you said you could put it off at least two weeks."

"I thought I could, but the judge refused. Two days was all he would grant. And to get that I had to provide him with a host of affidavits. Short of an act of God or an illness of the child, the date's set in concrete."

"Get the judge excused, then," Max refused to accept that nothing could be done.

"I tried that. We're stuck with this one, at least for this first hearing. We both know there will be more."

Max seized on the one opening the attorney had offered. "But if a doctor declared the child was too —"

"Careful of going down that road, Rutledge," Yancy Haynes warned. "You'll have the social worker out to verify it — and probably seek a second opinion. Unless that baby really is ill, it would only create more problems and alienate the judge more than he already is."

"Then you'd better make damned sure Sloan leaves with that baby in her arms," Max warned and slammed the phone down.

A loud clap of thunder reverberated through the building. Its loudness finally gained Max's attention. He hurled an impatient glass at the rain-sheeted windows and punched the intercom.

"Yes, Mr. Rutledge."

"Find out how soon this storm will pass."

"Yes sir. And your three-thirty appointment is here. Shall I send them in?"

"That would be Musgrave and his cronies," Max recalled. "Go ahead and show them in, then cancel the rest of my appointments for this afternoon."

An hour later the severe storm cell moved east, but flying conditions remained marginal, leaving Max with no choice but to return to the ranch by car, more than doubling his travel time.

Chafing at the delay, twice he reached for the car phone. Each time Max checked the impulse, reminding himself that a mobile phone was not secure. And he was too close to success to take such a risk now.

Alerted by the security guards at the

gate, Harold Bennett was outside waiting for him when Max's car pulled beneath the portico. He had the wheelchair out of the trunk and ready for him by the time the chauffeur opened the rear door. Years of experience made the transfer from the car to the wheelchair a smooth, single action with never a falter along the way.

The instant he was settled in chair, Max demanded, "How did the day go?"

Bennett did not mistake it as an idle question, aware that his employer expected a full accounting of Sloan's activity in his absence, no matter how mundane. "Mrs. Calder took the baby for a short walk in his stroller this morning, then exercised in the pool for nearly an hour."

"Did she speak to anyone on her walk?"

"Only myself, sir, and that was mostly to comment on what a beautiful day it was. Of course, that was in the morning before the storm arrived. Although she did mention that she wished she had the camera equipment that she left behind. She talked about a portfolio, too. Seemed very concerned getting it back."

Max nodded. "She would be worried about that more than the rest of the things she left. I'll have the attorney see that Calder returns it. In the meantime, find out what kind of camera equipment she's talking about and see that she gets it." He rolled his chair to the ramp. "What about this afternoon?"

"She lay down for a short nap once the baby was asleep, then listened to some music and read a little. All in all, it was a quiet afternoon, unless you include all the thunder and lightning," Bennett replied.

"But no phone calls?"

"She received none and made none."

"I thought Haynes might have contacted her." Max murmured and halted his wheelchair to wait for Bennett to open the front door.

He had barely glided into the large foyer when he caught the sound of Sloan's voice coming from the living room. He whipped his chair around in that direction and spied Sloan sitting on the couch talking on the phone. He fired a piercing look at Bennett.

"No phone calls, you said," he muttered in accusation, then sent his chair speeding into the living room, rearranging his expression into something warmly benign.

Sloan acknowledged him with a distracted smile. His gaze narrowed on the pen between her fingers and the notepad on the sofa's armrest, a half dozen notations scribbled along the top half. The handwriting was too small for him to make out what it said.

"Thanks. I will. Talk to you soon. Bye," she said and hung up to give the fullness of her attention to Max. "I didn't expect you home so soon."

"My last appointment was canceled, so I took advantage of the chance to come home early," Max replied, then allowed some of his curiosity to show. "Who was that on the phone? Yancy Haynes?"

"No, I haven't heard from him today. That was my agent, Phil Westbrook. I called to tell him about Jake and give him this address and phone number so he could get in touch with me if something came up."

"He has some assignments lined up for you, does he?" With a nod, Max indicated the notes she had jotted on the pad.

"A couple of possibilities for later this summer, if I'm interested, and he passed on messages for me from —" She never finished the sentence as a faint, hiccoughing cry came over the portable monitor on the end table. "Sounds like Jake just woke up."

"In that case, you go look after your son while I go make a few business calls." With a touch of the controls, Max reversed the wheelchair. "Join me in the den later, and we'll have a drink before dinner."

"Sounds good." Pen and tablet in hand, she rose from the couch and turned in the direction of the nursery.

Sloan was halfway there before she realized the baby monitor was still on the end table. Deciding to check on Jake first and retrieve the monitor later, she continued down the hall. All was quiet when she entered the room. Moving softly, Sloan crossed to the crib. Peering over the side, she saw that Jake was asleep, his little lips moving in a sucking motion. She watched him, half-tempted to pick him up anyway, then thought better of it.

As quietly as she had entered the nursery, she left and retraced her path down the wide corridor. Within steps of the den she caught the sound of Max's voice, forceful with anger.

In a reflexive action, she glanced toward the den and noticed the door was opened a crack. She didn't mean to eavesdrop, but it was impossible not to hear him.

"I know what I said. The situation has changed. I don't care how you do it, but you've got to lure Calder into town within the next ten days." Sloan came to a dead stop when she heard the name Calder. All thought of the baby monitor fled from her mind. "After that, I don't particularly give a damn whether you plant the drugs on him or in his vehicle. I just want an arrest for drug possession on his record within ten days."

Shock splintered through her. Even though he hadn't mentioned Trey specifically, Sloan knew that was who Max was arranging to have framed for drug possession. The reason was obvious: to influence the judge against Trey at the custody hearing. She took a step toward the door, intending to stop this before it went any further. Then Max spoke again.

"I wouldn't worry about that." Scorn was in his voice. "Once he's been arrested for drug possession, it won't take much to convince people he's using. Look at how easily you convinced them he was having an affair. So what if nobody's seen him high on anything. They never saw him with a woman, either, but they believed the story just the same."

Her mind whirling with questions, Sloan stood motionless. What was he saying? That there wasn't another woman? That it was no more true than the drugs he intended to plant on Trey? But the phone calls? Had they been fake, too? But why would Max do that? He had to have known it would create problems in her marriage? Or was that part of his plan?

She suddenly had a sick feeling in the pit of her stomach that Trey had been right all along. Max had engineered everything. And, like a fool, she had believed it. Anger swept through her that she could have been so gullible.

In agitation, Sloan turned away and faltered when Bennett entered the living room from a side hallway. There was an instant sharpening of his gaze at the sight of her, as if something in her expression had caught his attention.

"Is anything wrong, Mrs. Calder?"

Thinking on her feet, she searched for an answer that wouldn't arouse his suspicion. "Yes, but I don't think you can help me. I came back here for something, and now I can't remember what it was. Of course!" she said, pretending to remember at that moment. "The baby monitor."

Acting was a skill she had never needed to practice before. With all the insecurities of an amateur, Sloan strove to project an air of normalcy while she collected the monitor from the end table and retreated again to the hallway. Her nerves screamed with the certainty that Bennett had seen through her pretense. Yet she didn't dare check his reaction.

Bennett studied her thoughtfully until she was out of sight. He resumed his original course and crossed to the den, noticed the door wasn't tightly shut, and walked in.

"Was that Sloan's voice I heard," Max demanded the instant he appeared.

"Yes."

"What was she doing out there?" Suspicion was sharp in his look.

"She left the baby monitor in the living room. She came back to get it."

"Then she wasn't listening at the door?"

"She didn't appear to be," Bennett replied.

A grunt was the only response.

Before Sloan reached the nursery, Jake started crying. This time it was no half-hearted sob, but a full-blown wail. The cause was a dirty diaper. Changing it was a mindless task that allowed Sloan time to think and satisfy the need for contact with her son.

"Does that feel better, little guy?" Sloan crooned when she lifted him off the changing table and cradled him against her shoulder, a hand lightly supporting the back of his head. Lovingly, she nuzzled the top of it, breathing in the fresh, clean baby scent that clung to his skin. "You certainly smell better," she murmured. Then fear ran its icy finger over her. "What are we going to do, Jake?"

Without an answer, Sloan wandered over to the window. Outside the rain had stopped, but water continued to drip from the eaves, falling past the glass panes. Off to the west the clouds had lightened in color as the sun worked to penetrate their thinning layers.

One of the security guards, in full rain gear and with a leashed German shepherd at his side, crossed the far side of the lawn. He was a visible reminder of the cordon of armed guards on the ranch. Ostensibly they were there to protect her, but Sloan realized they could also prevent her from leaving.

Alone, she might be able to slip past them. But she knew she'd never make it with the baby, and there was no way she'd leave without him. Sloan felt trapped.

Yet there had to be a way out, some excuse that wouldn't arouse suspicion.

It was only when she went through her options that she realized how clever Max had been, eliminating virtually any need for her to leave the ranch. Someone else did the household shopping. Anything she and Jake could ever need had already been supplied. She had a lawyer who came to the house, and Sloan didn't doubt that Max could arrange for doctor's visits as well if any illness should arise. And there wasn't a chance of faking one, not with a registered nurse in residence.

"Oh my God," she gasped softly as she suddenly realized the true danger Bennett posed. On two or three occasions over the years, Sloan had seen him removing medicine from a locked drug cabinet. She could only guess at the myriad of sedatives, painkillers, and muscle relaxers that were kept on hand for Max's use. But they could just as easily be given to her if she raised any objection to being kept there — or worse, confronted Max with what she knew.

Then Sloan remembered the document she had signed making Jake the beneficiary of her estate. Among the provisions was one that dealt with her death. If it occurred before Jake reached his majority, Sloan had designated Max Rutledge as Jake's legal guardian.

Fear was a cold hand clutching at her throat. Sloan realized that she didn't dare call Trey and warn him of Max's plan. It would be just like Trey to come charging to her rescue, and the consequences of that could be disastrous — for all of them.

Her only chance was to find a legitimate

reason to leave the ranch with Jake. It had to be something Max would easily accept, or he'd realize that she knew she and Jake were in actuality his prisoners. She had to come up with something that Max would regard as an innocent whim, easily indulged.

And she had to come up with it quickly. Sloan wasn't sure how long she could maintain this charade of ignorance.

Jake's head moved in her hand as his mouth searched to find his fist. Everything inside her softened at the sight of his baby-smooth skin and perfect little nose.

In the blink of an eye, the solution presented itself to her. The soft laugh that slipped from her lips was part relief and part jubilance.

"You and Mommy need our picture taken together, don't we," Sloan murmured. "An official portrait."

Coming up with a logical purpose for leaving the ranch was only the first hurdle. Knowing Max, he would insist someone accompany them, probably more than one person, which presented a second obstacle. If she managed to elude them, she would have to find a safe place to stay until she could get word to Trey. And it had to be a place where Max wouldn't expect her to go.

Confident that these were simple details that could be worked out, Sloan was quick to present her idea to Max when she joined him in the den before dinner. His response was exactly what she had anticipated.

"A picture of mother and child. What a wonderful idea," he declared. "Tomorrow I'll have my secretary contact a photographer and arrange to have him come here and take it."

"Dear Uncle Max." Sloan smiled in a show of amusement. "It's obvious you don't know much about photography."

"Why?" The startled look he gave her had an element of doubt. Where photography was concerned, he accepted that she knew more than he did.

"Because I'm talking about a professional portrait, the kind that's done in the controlled atmosphere of a studio. Not an impromptu setup with a few lights strategically placed." Keeping the right note of lightness in her voice was difficult, but she knew she didn't dare sound argumentative.

"I see." He paused, running a subtly assessing glance over her. "I hate to say this, Sloan, but this isn't a good time for you to be going anywhere, especially with the baby. Perhaps later —"

"But it has to be now." Her objection

was too forceful. Recognizing it, Sloan hurried to regroup. "If Mr. Haynes can't get the hearing postponed, we'll have to go to Montana next week. If anything happened there —" Seeing another opening, she broke off the sentence. "That's what you're worried about, isn't it? That Trey has someone watching the ranch."

"I would be surprised if he doesn't have the Slash R under surveillance," Max agreed.

"Couldn't two of the guards go with me? I'd be safe then, wouldn't I?"

"I would think so," he began.

Sloan never gave him a chance to say more as she crossed to his chair, careful not to gush too much. "Thank you, Uncle Max." She brushed his cheek with a kiss. "This means so much to me. I knew you'd find a way to make it happen."

His smile was a little tight, providing the only outward indication of his displeasure. "I'll have my secretary set something up for you with a photographer."

Leaving the arrangements for the session in his hands was something Sloan couldn't allow. It would be all too easy for him to manufacture reasons to postpone it.

"If you don't mind, Uncle Max, I'd rather call myself. I'm sure your secretary is very competent, but I'd want to verify the kind of film and equipment he uses, his developing process — things that wouldn't mean anything to your secretary."

"I suppose that's true," Max conceded grimly. "Before you set a firm time, check with me in case there are any difficulties getting an extra security detachment to accompany you."

On that point Sloan was forced to agree. "Of course."

By noon the following day, she had settled on the studio that best suited her needs. Setting a photo shoot for the next morning required a good bit of cajoling, but she succeeded in the end. However, she didn't pass the information on to Max until she had chatted with the head of ranch security.

Satisfied that she had all bases covered to this point, Sloan placed the call to Max. After providing him with the studio's address and phone number, she told him, "As luck would have it, he had a cancellation for tomorrow at ten. And I spoke to the man in charge of security — Grazanski, I think his name is. I mentioned what I wanted to do, and he said it would be no problem at all. I guess the company has extra guards available who can accompany me to the photo session. Isn't that good news? I know you were concerned about it. Frankly, so was I."

She held her breath, half afraid Max would come up with some objection. Instead he asked, "How long will this take?"

"He had two hours blocked off for the client who cancelled, although I don't think it should take much over an hour. I imagine it depends how cooperative Jake is."

"In that case, I'll confirm the arrangements with security so you can have that portrait taken with your son. I have a meeting to attend, so we'll talk this evening."

If anything, her tension increased when she hung up. Everything was going almost too smoothly. And that scared her. If anything went wrong this time, Sloan doubted that she would ever have another chance.

"Dressed to kill" was the phrase that kept running through her mind when Sloan studied her reflection in the mirror the next morning. Her hair was coiled in a sophisticated style atop her head, matching the tone set by a double strand of pearls around her neck. Her face felt stiff under all the makeup she wore, but the overall effect of someone smart and chic was exactly the look she had sought to achieve.

With her stomach in knots, Sloan turned from the mirror and crossed to the crib where Jake lay, dressed in his best as well. His expression was a study of concentration as he tugged at an edge of the blanket. Tucking the blanket back around him, she slid a hand beneath him and lifted him out of the crib.

"What do you think, Jake? Will we be able to do this?" Sloan said in a soft murmur. A whisper of movement warned her that she wasn't alone in the nursery. A little louder, she added, "We're going to have our picture taken, aren't we." Turning, she pretended to just notice Harold Bennett standing there. "Is the car here?"

"Yes ma'am."

"Good." She tipped the baby a little more upright to provide the nurse with a better view of him. "Doesn't he look precious?"

"Indeed he does," Bennett agreed.

"I thought so, too. Just to be safe, I packed his little white suit in case he spits up. She nodded to the bulging bag atop the dresser. "Would you carry that to the car for me? But I warn you, with all his things, plus my makeup and everything else, it weighs more than Jake does."

Part of that "everything else" included a change of shoes and clothes, as well as extra bottles of formula and diapers for Jake. But all of that was hidden beneath the expected items.

Bennett made no comment on its heaviness when he lifted it by its strap and followed her out of the nursery. With each step, her tension rose another notch.

The ride into the city was going to be a long and nerve-wracking one. But at the end of it was the moment of truth, and Sloan needed to ready herself for it on the drive.

Chapter Twenty-Three

After arriving at her destination, Sloan waited while the two security guards made a sweep of the studio to satisfy themselves that no one other than the photographer and his assistants was present. Thankfully, they raised no objections when Sloan instructed them to wait for her in the small lobby area.

The hardest part was pretending to be interested when the photographer suggested various poses that could be used. Sloan chose one that would require the most setup time, then asked to be shown to the changing room so she could freshen herself after the drive.

Along the way, she made sure that the photographer pointed out the studio's rear exit, claiming a phobia of being trapped in a burning building. She had no idea if the photographer believed her, but she didn't particularly care.

In the changing room, Jake fussed a little when she first laid him on the oversized counter, but he soon quieted. Hurriedly, Sloan emptied the overstuffed bag of her makeup, hairbrush and spray, then dug underneath the layers to pull out the change of clothes and shoes. She piled all of it on the counter near Jake.

Wasting no time, she scrubbed off the makeup and brushed out her hair, then carelessly plaited it in two scraggly braids. Changing into a pair of jeans, a loose cotton top and sneakers came next. After that she had only to wrap Jake in a different-colored receiving blanket and stuff her purse into the considerably lightened bag, and she was all set.

Shaking inside, she gathered Jake into her arms, slung the bag over her shoulder, and opened the door a crack to peer out. Noises came from the studio, but the hallway was clear. She slipped out as quietly as she could and made her way to the rear exit.

Sloan didn't fool herself into thinking she was safe, even when she stepped into the alley behind the building. At best, she had maybe five minutes before the photographer started wondering what was taking her so long. Once he discovered there was no one in the changing room, the alarm would go out.

At a swift pace, she walked down the alley and crossed the intersecting street to the opposite side, then made her way to the corner. She threw a quick glance in the direction of the studio and noticed the driver leaning against the hood of the car parked out front. Even worse, he was looking away from the studio.

Almost the same instant, Sloan saw an approaching cab with a vacancy light on. Unsure how far she might have to walk to find another, she immediately threw up a hand to hail this one. The cab veered toward her and braked close to the corner.

Heart pounding, Sloan struggled to maneuver herself, the baby, and the cumbersome bag into the backseat. Finally she pulled the door shut and cast an anxious glance over her shoulder, but she couldn't tell whether the driver had seen her get into the cab. She dug the slip of paper with the address written on it out of her jeans pocket and handed it to the driver. "Please hurry."

If he found any contradiction between her appearance and the address, he didn't comment but simply pulled back into the traffic. Jake started crying, sending Sloan on a search through the bag for his pacifier. One-handed, she stripped off the elastic bands securing her braids and finger-combed her hair loose.

A dozen times she darted looks behind her, convinced her absence had been discovered by now. But with any luck, they would check all the obvious places first.

"What the hell do you mean, they're gone?!" Max bellowed into the phone.

"She went into a dressing room in the back — to freshen up, she said. When the photographer went looking for her, he couldn't find her or the baby. Her dress, shoes, and makeup were in the dressing room, but Mrs. Calder and the baby were gone. The studio has a rear exit to the alley behind the building. We're assuming that's how she left."

"You were supposed to be guarding them. Why didn't you have a man stationed there?" Max demanded.

"It was a solid metal door, locked from the inside. No one was going to come in that way, and we had no reason to think Mrs. Calder —"

"Dammit, you screwed up. Admit it!"

"Yes sir. It was an oversight."

Furious as he was at their laxity, Max recognized that fixing blame was a pointless exercise. "What are you doing to find them?"

"We've got men on the way to the bus

and airport terminals just in case she's headed there. She mentioned she had a home in Hawaii, but is there anyone here she might —"

"She has in-laws at the Cee Bar. Get men over there to cover the approaches to the ranch. How long has she been gone?"

"Roughly ten or fifteen minutes. It couldn't be more than that. Just a minute." A hand muffled the phone, garbling the exchange on the other end of the line. "We may have something. A young woman with a baby was seen getting into a cab half a block from here."

"Track down that cab and find out where he took her. I don't care what you have to do — or how much it costs — you get that address."

"We're on it."

Pushed by a cold rage, Max slammed the phone down and pivoted his wheelchair from the desk to face the glass wall of his executive office. There was only one explanation for her actions — Sloan had overheard his phone conversation with Donovan, just as his instincts had warned him. His mistake was not trusting them.

But all wasn't lost yet. All he had to do was keep her from reaching the Calders and putting that baby in their hands.

★ ★ ★

Spring flowers abounded, brightening the exclusive River Crest district located in the hills overlooking the Trinity River. Sloan barely noticed them as the cab wound through its curving streets. The vehicle's pace was a slow one, allowing the driver to scan the street signs and estate numbers. Aware of the necessity for that, Sloan held her tongue.

Ahead of them, a set of scrolled iron gates on the right stood open, marking a driveway's entrance. The cab made the turn between them and followed a looping driveway that culminated in front of a grand Italianate mansion.

Hurriedly, Sloan pushed some bills in the driver's hand, more than enough to take care of the fare, slid out of the backseat with the baby, and pulled the bag after her. She glanced back at the lane to make sure she hadn't been followed, then crossed to the front door and rang the bell.

When the cab pulled away from the house, she briefly wondered whether she should have asked the driver to wait. Now it was too late. Then Jake started to cry. This time the pacifier didn't satisfy him. Sloan rang the bell again, feeling much too vulnerable standing out there in the open.

The door opened, and she found herself standing face to face with an older, balding gentleman, dressed in the dark formal gear of a butler.

"May I help you, ma'am?" he inquired with cool politeness.

"I need to speak to Tara right away, please. It's extremely important," Sloan rushed.

"I'm sorry, but Mrs. Calder isn't here at the moment. Perhaps if you —"

She cut him short. "How soon will she be back? I'd like to wait for her. I'm Sloan Calder."

Something that was almost a smile took the aloofness from his expression as his attention shifted to the baby in her arms. "Then this must be the late Mr. Calder's grandbaby. Mrs. Calder will be delighted to see him. She just returned from Europe. She called a few minutes ago to say she was on her way home. She should be arriving any time. My name is Brownsmith. I'm Mrs. Calder's houseman. Please come in." He took a step back to admit her, then paused as he spotted the sleek black car coming up the driveway. "What excellent timing. Mrs. Calder is just now arriving."

When Sloan turned toward the driveway, the houseman moved past her to greet his mistress, traveling with the shuffling gait of the elderly. Jake continued his cranky cry, and Sloan rocked her shoulders in a side-to-side motion to calm him as she followed the houseman out to the driveway.

Seconds after the car rolled to a quiet stop, the chauffeur exited the vehicle and trotted around to open the rear passenger door, extending a hand to its occupant.

Tara stepped out, clad in a silvery gray traveling suit and trailing a sable coat. The houseman inclined his head in a respectful greeting.

"Welcome home, Mrs. Calder," he said, then lifted a hand to draw Tara's attention to Sloan. "You have a visitor. Two of them."

Surprise flickered across Tara's flawless features as she recognized Sloan. "Sloan. What are you doing here?"

"I need your help, Tara." Sloan jiggled the baby as his cries grew increasingly demanding.

"What's wrong? Is the baby sick?"

"No, he's fine. It's Max. He's looking for me —"

"Max? Max Rutledge? What does he have to do with you being here?" Confusion drew a tiny line across Tara's forehead.

"Everything. Trey tried to warn me about him, but I wouldn't listen. I was sure he was wrong and —"

Looking around, Tara broke in, "Where is Trey? Why isn't he here?"

"I left him. It's all very complicated, and there isn't time to explain it all," Sloan began.

"You argued with him over Max." The harshness of Tara's tone made it an accusation.

"We argued over a lot of things, but it turns out that Max was behind all of it. I didn't know that, though, not until the other day —"

"Are you saying that you sided with Rutledge against your own husband?" Tara demanded in a contained fury.

"It was wrong. I admit that —"

"You fool! You have no idea how wrong you were! Don't you see, he'll never forgive you for that. Never. Good God, I should know, I made the same mistake, and it destroyed my marriage. How could you be so stupid?"

Stunned by the outrage and vehemence of Tara's attack, Sloan had to work to find her voice. "But I can explain." Although for the first time she wondered whether that would make any difference. "I just need to talk to Trey. If I could use your phone —"

"You don't really think he'll speak to you, do you?" Tara said with derision. "Even if he doesn't hang up when he hears your voice, he'll never believe anything you tell him. Not any more. You killed whatever trust he had in you when you walked out on him."

"I won't accept that. I can't," Sloan insisted while still trying to calm Jake's cries. "Not for my sake, but for our son's."

"The baby." Tara appeared to notice the infant in her arms for the first time. "Yes, that might be your one chance. But not over the phone. That will never work. Hurry." She grabbed Sloan's shoulder and gave her a push toward the open passenger door. "Get in the car."

"But you don't understand," Sloan began in protest.

"You don't realize what you've done. Just get in the car," Tara ordered, then addressed her houseman. "Call the field immediately. Tell them to have my plane fueled and ready when we get there. I'm taking Sloan to Montana."

Hearing their destination, Sloan slung the bag into the car and climbed in after it with the baby. While the houseman hurried to the front door with as much speed as he could muster, Tara turned and saw the chauffeur standing by the opened trunk, half of her luggage already sitting on the ground.

"What are you doing?" she demanded sharply. "Put those suitcases back in the trunk, and let's go."

With haste, he tossed them inside and closed the trunk, then moved swiftly to the driver's side. Within seconds the car was traveling back down the lane.

Outside the Cee Bar ranch house, Quint listened while his wife's grandfather, Empty Garner, repeated his story, almost sputtering with outrage. "I'd just pulled onto the road after fixing the fence when this young fella in shirtsleeves flags me down. When I stopped to see what he wanted, I spotted a car parked in the Rigsby's lane. Suddenly this other fella shows up, and the two of 'em started snooping around my truck like a pair of bloodhounds. Claimed they were admiring it. Called it a classic. Classic, my foot. They were looking for something. Want'a bet Rutledge put 'em up to it?" Empty challenged.

Quint ignored the question to pose his

own. "Dallas, and now you. Why? What was he hoping to find?"

"What do you mean Dallas?" The mere mention of his granddaughter shifted the focus of Empty's attention.

"She had her vehicle searched too." Convinced that something was afoot, Quint struck out for the house.

Startled by his sudden departure, Empty called after him, "Where you going?"

"To make a phone call and see if I can learn what this is about," Quint replied as he crossed the covered porch to the back door.

Upon entering the house, he went directly to the corner desk in the kitchen and picked up the phone. Empty followed him inside, spotted Dallas by the sink, and immediately bombarded her with questions, seeking details of her encounter.

"Hi, Jessy. It's Quint," he said when she came on the line. "I thought I'd check to see if anything is happening that I should know about."

"No. Why?" She sounded both surprised and puzzled.

"Because something's in the wind down here, and it has Rutledge's thumbprint on it."

"What do you mean?" Jessy asked, then

immediately added, "Wait. Trey just walked in. I'll put you on the speaker phone." An instant later, in a voice that had that hollow sound of distance, she said, "Go ahead."

"A sheriff's deputy pulled Dallas over on her way back to the ranch from the university. He told her an inmate had escaped from jail and asked to search her vehicle. She got suspicious when he started asking a lot of questions about where she'd been and why. When she told me, curiosity kicked in, and I checked. There is no escapee on the loose. Now Empty showed up with a similar story, except the two men who searched his truck weren't officers."

"And you think Rutledge is behind it?"

"It's possible."

"But what were they looking for?" Trey asked, his voice instantly recognizable to Quint.

"That's what has me puzzled. Trey, I don't know. It crossed my mind that it might have something to do with Sloan."

"I don't know how." Trey's tone seemed to dismiss the idea.

"Neither do I," Quint admitted. "But it doesn't seem likely that Rutledge did it just to harass us. There has to be more to it than that — something or someone that he doesn't want to reach us."

"Somebody who works for him, maybe?" Trey suggested.

"Could be. Maybe you'd better alert Walters. His investigators might be able to eavesdrop on some crosstalk among the guards stationed at the Slash R."

"We'll give him a call right away," Jessy told him. "In the meantime, you be careful."

"I —"

Trey interrupted before Quint could finish. "If it's someone who works for Rutledge, he wouldn't be trying to contact any of us unless it had something to do with Sloan or Jake. And it would have to be damned important for him to take that risk."

"I'm with you," Quint said and took that half-formed speculation to the next. "And if it's important, then it's time-critical."

"I can think of only one reason that time might be a factor," Trey said. "If Sloan planned to take Jake and leave the country before the custody hearing next week."

"Now you're thinking like Rutledge," Quint said in approval. "Call Walters and get his men on it right away. If that's the plan, she won't be leaving on any commercial carrier. Rutledge will fly her out of the country on one of his private jets."

"I'm on it." Trey reached over and severed the connection. Before he could ask, Jessy supplied him with the phone number for the Walters agency. Even as he punched the numbers, he muttered, "Subpoenas and court orders are nothing but pieces of paper to Rutledge. I should have realized Sloan wouldn't honor them any more than he does."

The buzz of the intercom had Rutledge reaching for the phone. He punched the blinking light and demanded, "Did you track down that cab driver?"

"Yes, sir. The description of his passengers fits Mrs. Calder and the baby," the agent confirmed.

"Where did he take her?"

"The house belongs to Tara Calder."

"Tara." Max cursed himself for not thinking of her. Then he remembered, "She was spending the winter in Europe. Is she back already?"

"Evidently, although we couldn't get any information from her butler. Her chauffeur, however, told us that he'd just taken his employer back to her plane, along with a young woman and a baby. According to him, they were flying to Tara Calder's summer home in Montana, but he couldn't give me the name of any town."

"It doesn't matter. I know where it is," Max replied and calculated his chances of reaching the private airstrip next to Tara's luxurious stone cabin.

"Do you want me —"

"I need to know how long ago her plane took off — and I need to know it now. Get on it, and quick," he ordered and hung up.

No one had to tell Rutledge that he had only a slim chance of intercepting Sloan before she made it to the Calders. But as long as he had a chance, he had to take it. With any luck, he could convince Sloan that she misunderstood the phone conversation she had obviously overheard. If not, there were other means he could employ to bring Sloan and the baby back to Texas with him.

But first he had to get there.

With the decision made, Max issued instructions to his assistant to notify the crew he was on his way to the building's rooftop helipad. After that, Edwards was to call the airfield and order his fastest jet to be waiting for him when he arrived. Any call from the security agent was to be patched through to him as soon as it came in.

The helicopter was a few feet from touchdown at the airfield when the phone call was relayed to him. The news couldn't have been better. Tara's plane had taken off roughly nine minutes earlier, after encountering some minor mechanical delays.

Sloan sat in a plushly upholstered seat across the aisle from Tara, doing her best to hush the fussing infant in her arms. Tara threw an irritated look at the pair. "What is that baby crying about now?" she said with impatience. "Don't tell me he needs his diaper changed again."

"His ears are probably hurting from the change in cabin pressure. I should have remembered that and had his bottle ready for him," Sloan answered while she rummaged through the bag on the adjoining seat.

"Good heavens, give it to him, then," Tara snapped in ill temper.

"It needs to be warmed first." Locating the bottle, Sloan removed it from the bag, sounding as cranky and harried as Tara.

Tara motioned to the attendant. "Kurt — Dan — Whatever your name is — heat that bottle for the baby," she ordered. "And bring me some aspirin."

While the bottle was being heated, the

attendant returned with the aspirin. Tara washed down three tablets with some water and leaned back in her seat. Eyes closed, she tried desperately to shut out the baby's strident cries and silently congratulated herself for never having one of those smelly, squally infants of her own. Motherhood was something Tara regarded as vastly overrated.

At long last the baby's cries diminished to an occasional whimper, bringing a semblance of quiet to the cabin. Confident that she would now no longer have to compete with the bawling child for Sloan's attention, Tara sat up.

"Tell me the whole story," she commanded. "Everything that happened. Don't leave out any details."

"All right," Sloan agreed, then paused to organize her thoughts before relating the events that had culminated in her arrival at Tara's Fort Worth mansion.

When she finished, Tara questioned her about the telephone conversation Sloan had overheard. To Tara's annoyance, Sloan focused on one aspect of it.

"I felt like such a fool when I realized Trey had been telling me the truth all along — he wasn't seeing another woman," Sloan recalled. "All those phone calls seemed so damning, but how easy they were for Max to arrange! And that redhead with the diamond bracelet — Trey never gave it to her. It was something I just assumed. Max probably set that up, too."

"Let's go back to the drugs," Tara insisted. "Max has someone who intends to plant drugs on Trey. You don't know who, do you? Max didn't mention any names."

"No. I don't even know if he was talking to a man or a woman. It could be that redhead at The Oasis — or possibly the man who owns it. I think his name is Donovan."

"Maybe I was wrong," Tara murmured absently.

"About what?" Sloan eyed her curiously.

"About calling Trey," Tara replied. "That conversation took place when? Two days ago?"

"Almost two days."

"Then that plan has already been put into motion." Reaching down, Tara unfastened her seat belt and crossed to a swivel chair anchored next to an executive-style writing table, complete with a telephone. "I think I'd better call Trey and warn him about it — before he's lured into the trap."

"Let me talk to him," Sloan said quickly.

"It will be better if I explain the situation first," Tara insisted and took her seat, then picked up the phone. After two abortive attempts to place the call, she summoned the cabin attendant. "Why isn't this phone working?"

"It's probably part of that electrical malfunction they were trying to fix before we left," he replied.

"We brought a mechanic along. Tell him to fix it. I need to make a call."

"Sorry, ma'am, but I don't think it's something he can do while we're in the air.

Annoyed, Tara dismissed him "That'll be all."

"Don't you have a cell phone?" Sloan asked when Tara returned to her aisle seat.

"I never carry one. I always found them to be more of a nuisance than a convenience," Tara stated. "We're less than two hours away. We'll wait and explain everything to him when we get there. There should be sandwiches and salads on board. Would you like anything?"

"No, thanks."

"I'm sure you're much too anxious to eat anything," Tara guessed.

Sloan neither confirmed or denied it. Instead, she stood up and stepped over to Tara's seat. "Would you hold Jake a minute? I need to use the restroom."

Taking her agreement for granted, Sloan

placed the baby in her arms. Tara opened her mouth to protest, but Sloan was already moving away. Looking down at the sleeping infant, Tara recoiled a little, half-expecting it would start shrieking any second. But the tiny thing continued to sleep. She eyed it warily, holding herself stiffly.

A little fist emerged from the blanket folds, wagged a couple times, then settled against his chest. Watching it, Tara gradually noticed the baby's fingernails, exact in every detail yet so diminutive. Tentatively, she touched one and discovered the softness of his skin.

The baby sighed in his sleep. Unconsciously, Tara smiled at the little bubble that formed between his lips. The longer she looked at him, the more fascinated she became with this miniature version of a person. Gently, so as not to disturb his sleep, she smoothed her fingers over the mass of dark, nearly black hair.

"Your granddaddy's hair was this very same color," she murmured. "I wish he was here to see what a precious little boy you are."

When Sloan returned only moments later, Tara was surprised by her own reluctance to surrender the baby into his mother's care. Her arms felt oddly empty without the infant's slight weight on them. It wasn't something Tara could explain, not even to herself. Yet she felt a trace of longing when she saw Sloan cuddling the infant close. Deliberately, she turned and stared out the cabin window at the passing clouds.

Trey walked the feed salesman to the door of the ranch office and saw him out. Yet he couldn't remember a single word they had exchanged when he turned from it. Trey couldn't shake off the image of Sloan on some private jet, bound for a foreign country, taking his son with her.

"Trey." The familiar sound of his mother's secretary, Donna Vernon, reached out to claim his attention. "I just put a call through to Jessy from Ed Walters. She wants you to join her."

"Thanks." His stride instantly lengthened to carry him to his mother's office. Laredo was lounging on a desk corner when Trey walked in. Glancing up, Jessy said, "Trey's here, Ed. Go ahead and tell us what you've learned so far."

"First off, we confirmed that Rutledge left Fort Worth on one of his jets." The male voice came from the speaker phone.

"According to the ground crew, he had no passengers with him and definitely no women. So I think you can put that concern aside for now. Unfortunately, I can't tell you much about what's going on at the Slash R. We were able to zero in on the frequency Rutledge's security guards are using. As Quint suggested, they seemed to be watching for someone, but no names were used, just code words, which is typical. Then, about twenty or thirty minutes ago, it all came to a stop, and the order was given for everybody to return to their assigned posts."

"That's it?" Trey frowned in surprise. "No explanation? Just the order?"

"There was only one remark made along those lines. Maybe it's something, and maybe it's nothing, but one of the guards was heard to ask, 'Where was she found?' "

"She." So they were looking for a woman, Trey realized. "What was he told?"

"That it was none of his damned business. All the chatter has been limited strictly to scheduled check-ins since then. We'll keep digging for more information on this," the investigator assured them. "In the meantime, we have all of Rutledge's planes under observation. I thought by now I'd be able to give you Rutledge's destination, but we haven't obtained it yet. I'll call you when we do."

"What kind of surveillance do you have in place at Rutledge's ranch?" Laredo asked.

"Just a video camera, and I'm not sure how useful that is," Ed Walters admitted. "Too many of the vehicles going in and out have tinted windows, which makes it almost impossible to see who's inside. Since there appears to be a chance your wife might take the child and leave the country, we'll have to come up with a better way to monitor who comes and who goes. Short of following every vehicle that leaves, I'm not sure what that will be yet, but I'm on it."

"Thanks, Ed," Jessy said. "Keep in touch."

"You'll be the first to know anything I do," he promised and hung up.

A heavy silence followed, weighted by all the questions that remained unanswered. Pushed by the edgy impatience swirling through him, Trey swung away from the desk and headed for the door. "I can't wait around here all day for the phone to ring."

"Stay right here at headquarters. And make sure your cell phone's on," Jessy told him.

"I will." The grudging agreement was issued as he walked out the door. Laredo stared after him a moment, then glanced at Jessy, one eyebrow lifting. "If there was ever anyone who needed to chop some wood, it's Trey."

"I know," Jessy said and sighed. The sound had the same troubled edge to it that was in her son's eyes.

Chapter Twenty-Four

The sleek executive jet streaked above a scattering of clouds, its heading set on a northerly course. Inside the gleaming chrome- and wood-adorned cabin, Max occupied his time by reviewing a raft of monthly reports, dictating correspondence, and placing a few phone calls. Yet his thoughts never strayed far from the race he was in.

Somewhere behind him stood the Colorado Rockies, and twenty-odd thousand feet below him the broken plains of Wyoming. Just ahead was Montana. With each mile, his tension grew. Defeat was something Max refused to acknowledge, even now, when time and distance were against him. His plan was too perfect; he wasn't about to abandon it until all hope of success ran out.

In front of him, the cockpit door swung open and the shirtsleeved copilot stepped through and made eye contact with Rutledge.

"Sorry to interrupt you, Mr. Rutledge." A bob of his head accompanied the apology.

Immediately sensing the man had something of importance to tell him, Max stiffened, bracing himself for bad news. "What is it?" he said brusquely.

"We copied a transmission from the aircraft with the call letters you gave us. The pilot advised Air Traffic Control that he was experiencing electrical problems and intended to land at an airstrip adjacent to an abandoned open-pit mine about a mile south of Blue Moon."

Alarm raced through Max. "They're making an emergency landing?" Images flashed through his mind of the plane crashing and bursting into flames, killing everyone on board and eliminating his chance of seizing control of the Calder empire through the child.

The copilot shook his head. "He never declared an emergency, sir. It seemed to be a precautionary measure. The pilot did say he had a registered mechanic on board. I got the impression he didn't want to risk an electrical problem escalating into a crisis. That can happen in these high-tech birds."

Max smiled at the unexpected opportunity that had just been given him. "How far ahead are they?"

"Roughly fifteen or twenty minutes."

"We'll land at the same airstrip and offer our assistance to their passengers." A smug calm settled over him.

"Yes sir."

Turning, the copilot headed back to the cockpit. Max waited until the door closed behind the man, then picked up the phone and placed a call.

After the fourth ring, Donovan's voice spoke in his ear. "What do you need?"

"You," Max replied. "A plane is about to land at Dy-Corp's old runway. Sloan's onboard with the baby —"

"Sloan?! What's she doing coming back here now?"

"That's not something you need to know," Max retorted. "Your job is to get down there and make sure she doesn't connect with Calders before I arrive."

"You're on your way here? To Montana?" Donovan repeated in a stunned voice.

"Isn't that what I just said?" Rutledge snapped in impatience. "I should be there in fifteen minutes. And don't let Sloan see you. I don't want her raising any alarm that might bring a lot of unwanted witnesses."

"I'll take care of it. Just a sec." There was a slight pause. "I think I hear a plane."

"Then get moving."

The cabin attendant was the first to come down the airplane's steps, Sloan's bag slung over his shoulder. At the bottom, he turned and offered an assisting hand to Tara. Sloan followed, carrying Jake in her arms, a corner of his blanket covering his face. A gust of wind flipped it off, exposing him to the sun's full glare.

"Hand the baby to me." Tara reached to take him when Sloan paused to cover his face.

"I can manage," Sloan assured her and descended the last few steps.

Shielding her own eyes from the sun and blowing dust, Tara looked around, making no attempt to disguise her irritation. "It was absolute nonsense to land here when we were so close to the ranch."

It was a protest she had voiced numerous times since being informed of the pilot's decision, often enough that neither the cabin attendant nor Sloan bothered to comment on her complaint. Instead the attendant gestured in the direction of an open metal hangar a short distance away.

"You can get shelter from the wind and dust over here."

"I am not about to wait around in a drafty old hangar while the repairs are being made," Tara informed him and opened her slim black handbag.

"I'm sorry, Mrs. Calder," he began with tested patience, "but as I explained, it's going to get too stuffy on the plane with all the onboard systems shut down."

"Fine. But I am not waiting in that hangar when there is a perfectly good office building over there. As I recall, when I stopped here last spring, there was still an old chair in the lobby. We'll wait there." She unzipped a small compartment inside her purse.

"It's bound to be locked, Mrs. —"

Tara held up a solid gold key. "Not a problem," she replied. "I have a master to all the Dy-Corp properties. It was one of the last things my daddy gave me. I always carry it with me. Now, go fetch my sable in case it turns cooler."

"And a cell phone, if anyone has one," Sloan added.

"I have one in my flight bag," the attendant told her and ran lightly up the steps into the cabin.

"Let's get the baby inside." Tara's hand

urged Sloan toward the single-story building with dust-caked windowpanes. "It'll be a bit dusty in there, but it's better than standing out here."

A double set of locks was on the front door. Tara had no difficulty opening either of them. The hinges creaked from disuse when she pulled the door open and held it for Sloan.

Her footsteps echoed through the building, adding to its empty feel when Sloan entered. The sun's hot rays had invaded the small lobby area and removed any lingering chill from the air.

Along one wall sat a vinyl-covered settee with a chair angled toward it, its upholstery ripped along the backrest and on the seat. The only other item of furniture was a low table with one leg partially collapsed under it, canting its surface at a drunken angle.

Completing a critical survey of the area, Tara released a dramatic sigh. "I should have told Daniel, or Kirk, whatever his name is, to bring something to dust off this furniture."

"I have something in my bag we can use," Sloan replied.

"It's a pity you weren't here when the mine was in operation," Tara declared and launched into a lengthy narrative about the tonnage it produced, the people it employed, and the many benefits it brought to Blue Moon.

Sloan barely listened as she wandered about the small space, nerves on edge with the anticipation of her coming meeting with Trey, trying to guess what he would say and what she should answer.

"What is keeping him?" Tara's forceful demand was riddled with exasperation. "How long does it take to fetch one coat and a cell phone?"

"Longer than we thought, obviously," Sloan murmured. "Or maybe it just seems long."

"It's been a good five minutes at least." Impatient, Tara crossed to the door and pushed it open, then paused, her stiff posture relaxing a little. "Here he comes now." She stayed at the door, holding it open for the young attendant loping toward the building.

With a sideways turn of his body, he slipped through the opening and halted, letting the bag strap slide off his shoulder and lowering the soft-sided tote to the floor. "Here you go." He handed the sable coat to Tara and pulled a cell phone out of his pocket. "I had to borrow the pilot's. The battery was low on mine."

"Thanks." Sloan shifted her hold on the baby, freeing a hand to take the phone from him.

"You dallied all that time just to borrow a phone?" Rebuke was in the cool look Tara gave him.

"Actually, I was waiting to make sure the mechanic could get the part he needed," he replied.

"What part? What are you talking about?" Tara demanded.

"There's a part he needs before he can get things working right again. It's okay, though. It's on its way from Miles City," he assured her.

"Someone's flying it here?" she said in surprise.

"No, it's coming by courier."

"But it's a good two-hour drive from Miles City," Tara protested.

"At least they had the part in stock," he reminded her. "Anyway, I'm supposed to hike to that gas station up the road and wait for the courier to arrive with the part. The pilot thought that would be easier than trying to explain how to get here, especially when the gate's padlocked. Would you like me to see if I can rent or borrow somebody's car and come back here for you?"

Sloan never let Tara answer. "No! Absolutely not."

"Surely you don't want to stay here for two hours, do you?" Tara looked at Sloan as if she'd taken leave of her senses.

"If that's how long it takes, then yes," Sloan answered without hesitation. Turning to the attendant, he said, "And I don't want you to tell anyone that we're here. Do you understand? Absolutely no one."

He shot a quick glance at Tara to make sure she had no problem with that. By then Tara had guessed the reason for Sloan's request. "Sloan's right. Under no circumstances admit that anyone other than crew was onboard the plane."

"Yes ma'am. I won't say a word," he promised and stepped to the door. "I'll be back as soon as the part gets here."

Alone again, Tara turned to Sloan. "That was quick thinking," she said in approval. "It had slipped my mind that Max has someone in Blue Moon working for him, and that person certainly doesn't need to know we're here."

"That's what I thought," Sloan replied, then asked, "Would you hold Jake while I call Trey?"

"Are you sure you don't want me to talk to him first?" Yet Tara was already reaching to gather the baby into her arms.

"I think it's better if I do." Sloan relinquished her son into Tara's care.

Emerging from the ranch office, Trey automatically let his glance sweep the yard and its buildings, then reach beyond it to the wide plains and its winter-brown grass. The barren look of the land suited his mood.

The honk of a horn dragged his attention to an approaching pickup. When it rolled to a stop near him, Tank's head emerged from the driver's-side window. "Thought you'd want to know we got trouble at the foaling barn. Looks like we might lose both that dun mare and her colt."

Without waiting for a response, he drove off. Trey stood there a moment, knowing he should go lend a hand if he could. The decision was taken from him when the cell phone vibrated in his pocket.

Half irritated, he answered it, certain it was one of the other hands at the foaling barn, calling to tell him of the problem there. "Yeah, what is it?"

"Trey. It's Sloan."

With an effort, Trey hardened himself against the pull of her voice. "What do you want, Sloan?" The dry demand was anything but friendly.

"You were right about Max. He's been behind everything that happened. Even now he's arranging for you to be arrested on charges of drug possession."

"Is that a fact?" he countered with disinterest. Even though she had gotten his attention, Trey was wary of believing anything she said.

"It's true. I swear it, Trey."

"I appreciate the warning — if that's what it is."

"I don't know why I bothered to tell you that." There was a note of defeat in her voice. "It isn't why I called. Look, this morning I managed to slip away from the guards that Max had watching me. I made it to Tara's with Jake."

The instant she mentioned Tara, Trey turned and headed back to the ranch office.

"We were on our way to the Triple C when something malfunctioned on the plane," Sloan continued, "and we had to land here at the old coal pit outside of Blue Moon. It's going to take another two hours before it's fixed. Please. Can you come get us?"

As she finished, Trey pushed open the

door to Jessy's private office and walked in, signaling to both her and Laredo. Caution made him ask, "Is this some kind of trap, Sloan?"

"No, it's a call for help. But don't take my word for it. Ask Tara."

The pause following Sloan's faintly annoyed statement was a small one. "Really, Trey, you need to stop being so hardheaded and listen to Sloan. Every word she said is the truth," Tara informed him most insistently.

"Where are you, Tara?" His use of her name was deliberate, intended to alert his mother and Laredo.

"In the lobby of the old Dy-Corp office at the coal pit. It's dusty and awful — and certainly no place for your son to be."

"Then you do have Jake with you?" Trey wanted that confirmed as well.

"Yes, we do. Don't we, sweetie," Tara cooed, obviously to the baby.

"Tell Sloan I'm on my way."

"What's up?" Laredo asked the instant Trey closed the cell phone.

"Sloan's in Blue Moon. She has Jake with her — and Tara." He shot a questioning glance at his mother. "Are the keys in the Suburban?"

"Under the seat," she confirmed.

"I'll ride along," Laredo said, "just in case you need somebody to watch your back."

The whine of a semi coming from the south invaded the natural stillness, but Donovan wasn't concerned about the approaching vehicle. All his attention was on the man walking along the highway. He remained motionless, his back pressed tightly against the rear wall of the coal mine's former operations office. His own vehicle was parked on the shoulder of the highway, its hood raised to indicate mechanical trouble. Any passing motorist seeing it wouldn't think twice about why it was there or where the driver was.

Donovan counted himself lucky that no one else heard the plane land. Such an occurrence was just enough of an oddity to draw the curious. With the abandoned airstrip a mile from town, the few residents of Blue Moon had evidently mistaken the sound of its engines for highway traffic. It suited Donovan that he was alone there, and he suspected that was exactly the way Rutledge wanted it.

Satisfied that man from the flight crew was far enough away that a backward glance from any of them was unlikely to detect any movement, Donovan slipped around the corner of the building and worked his way to the front. Briefly, he considered approaching the old hangar area where the plane was parked, but there was too much open ground to cross. Until Rutledge arrived, Donovan didn't intend to show himself unless it became necessary.

He made a quick scan of the sky, but there was no sign of another plane yet. Halting at the building corner, he peered around it. The door to the plane's cabin was latched open, its steps lowered, but he failed to spot any movement, either inside the plane or out.

Catching the sound of a vehicle on the highway, he crouched low, making himself less visible from the highway, and automatically slipped a hand over the gun in his pocket. But the pickup zipped on past the padlocked entrance without slowing.

Donovan relaxed, then tensed again when he thought he heard someone talking. It was nothing distinct, yet its pitch suggested the voice of a woman. He stole another look at the plane, thinking one of them might have stepped outside, but there was no one in sight.

Logic told him that the plane was too far

away for him to be picking up conversation from inside it. Same with the hangar. Which made the office building itself the most likely location.

Keeping a cautious eye on the aircraft, Donovan inched around the corner to a dusty window and peeked in. One look confirmed the presence of both women. Unwilling to risk being seen himself, he didn't chance another look. Instead he acted on the assumption they had the baby with them and backed away from the window.

As he slipped around the corner, he spotted an incoming plane low in the sky. The winds aloft carried the sound of it away from the strip. A check of the highway verified the absence of any traffic, coming or going.

The drone of throttled engines reached Donovan as the sleek aircraft neared the end of the landing strip. The wheels touched down with a short, skidding squeal. Then the craft was rolling smoothly while the engines roared in a reverse thrust.

A short distance from him, the door to the office opened. "It was a plane I heard, Sloan," a woman's voice declared. "It just landed. I'll bet they flew in that part we need." As if drawn by the sight of the aircraft, Tara Calder stepped across the threshold to watch it, a hand lifted to shade her eyes from the sun's glare. Donovan immediately walked forward. She swung to face him, all stiff and cool with challenge and said, "Who are you? What are you doing here?"

"Sorry. I didn't mean to startle you, Mrs. Calder," Donovan apologized smoothly. "The name's Donovan. We met last year. I own The Oasis, just up the road."

"I remember now." But there was no friendliness in her look.

"I heard a plane land a little while ago and got curious. What's going on? Are you planning to open the pit again?" The questions were a means to keep her focus on him, not the plane taxiing closer.

"No, I'm not."

"That's a shame. It would have been good for my business if it was up and operating again. The place doesn't look like it's suffered much from standing empty." Feigning a casual interest, he poked his head around to glance inside. "Why, Mrs. Calder! I didn't realize you were here."

Sloan looked up with an almost guilty start. That's when Donovan noticed, in addition to holding a baby, she was trying to place a phone call.

"I see you have that new baby of yours with you." Even as he spoke he was slipping past Tara into the building, moving with an easy swiftness that prevented Tara from reacting in time to block him. He walked straight to Sloan while she worked feverishly to punch in the last of the numbers. "It's a little boy, isn't it?"

Deliberately, he bumped her arm when he reached to push the blanket away from the infant's face. There was just enough force in it to knock the phone from her hand. When it clattered to the floor, he bent to pick it up.

"That was clumsy of me. I'm sorry." Donovan held the phone to his ear as if checking to make certain it still worked. "A busy signal," he lied and clicked it off before handing it back to her. "At least I didn't break it." Again he switched his attention to the infant. "He's a healthy-looking little guy. What's his name?"

It was Tara who answered. "It's Jacob," she asserted, moving to Sloan's side.

"Jake. That's a good, strong name for a boy. Is it a family name?" His questions were nothing more than a ploy to distract them from the aircraft outside. Donovan sensed that Sloan had guessed that. Yet she seemed uncertain what to do about it, except to keep darting glances behind him.

"No, it isn't." Sloan added nothing more that could invite further conversation.

Undeterred, he directed his question to Tara. "Do you often land here when you fly in?"

"No. We had a small mechanical problem. The crew is taking care of it now."

"Do you need a ride into town? I'd be happy to give you a lift.

"No, thanks," Sloan refused, "my husband's on his way to take us home. Is that what you wanted to know, Mr. Donovan?"

"I don't know what you mean, but I'm glad to hear you aren't stranded." Yet the only thought in his mind was the need to get this vital piece of information to Rutledge. And right away. "Since it seems you have everything under control, I won't bother you anymore. That's a good-looking baby you've got, Mrs. Calder," he said and backed to the door.

The muscled bulk of his torso briefly filled the doorframe, blocking the light. Then he was outside and moving away.

"There should be something you can push to call the last number dialed." Sloan hurriedly shoved the cell phone into Tara's hand, an urgency in her voice and action.

Tara stared at the foreign object she held. "Who am I trying to call?"

"Trey. Hurry," Sloan urged and started toward the door to see which way Donovan had gone, not trusting that he had actually left. "Oh my God." The words came out in a strangled murmur when she saw the familiar sight of Max in his wheelchair. At the moment he was halted in conversation with Donovan. In a burst of near panic, she turned to warn Tara. "It's Max. He's here."

"Max? You mean that was his plane?" Her expression mirrored Sloan's initial shock. "But how did he know we were here?"

"That isn't important now. Is there another way out?" Sloan looked around with a desperation that had her wrapping both arms around her son, gathering him close.

"There's a back door, but I wouldn't bother to try for it," Tara replied, turning all shrewd and cool. "Even if we did make it out, we'd never get to the plane. That Donovan character would stop us. Obviously, he's Max's man here."

"We could try for the road," Sloan reasoned, following Tara's lead in fighting down her panic. "Trey's on his way and —"

"Exactly," Tara stated. "All we need to

do is stall Max until he arrives. After all, he isn't about to drag you out of here by force. Between my flight crew and his, there are too many witnesses."

"You're right." With that realization, Sloan felt an iron calm settle through her. The only fear that remained was the kind that heightened the senses.

Chapter Twenty-Five

When Sloan caught the telltale whisper of slender wheels rolling across the gritty concrete outside, she turned to face the door. There was Donovan, walking behind Max's chair. When they reached the door's raised threshold, it was his hands that rocked the chair over it and into the building.

"Max, how on earth did you know we were here?" Tara declared in feigned amazement.

But Max never looked her way, his dark gaze fastening itself on Sloan. "Thank God, I finally caught up with you, Sloan," he declared, his wide shoulders sagging in a show of relief. "What are you doing here? Don't you realize that if the Calders find out you're here, they'll take your son from you?"

"What else could I do?" Sloan lifted her chin in defiance. "You were just using me — and Jake — to get even with the Calders."

"What nonsense is this?" Max frowned,

looking properly stunned. "I've done every-thing I know to help you keep your son. I thought that's why you came to me."

"Is that what you were doing when I overheard you talking on the phone the other night — I assume, to Mr. Donovan here?" she challenged.

"You were listening." He sighed, in re-gret. "That's unfortunate. It's better if you know nothing about such things."

"What things?" Sloan demanded, cold with anger. "The lies you had Donovan spread about Trey having an affair? Or the phone calls he obviously made to convince me it was true?"

His frown deepened in confusion. "You're the one who told me that your husband was seeing another woman. I had nothing to do with that."

"Just like you'll have nothing to do with Trey being caught with drugs, I suppose," Sloan taunted.

"Like I said earlier, it's unfortunate you overheard that," Max admitted with a con-trite look. "But I don't think you realize what an ugly thing a custody battle can be-come. The Calders already have people digging to uncover anything they can about you that might be twisted into some-thing damaging. What they can't find, they'll manufacture and find somebody who'll swear to it. What you overheard about the drugs was just my way of striking first. I admit that. But this suggestion that I had anything to do with your husband's affair is false. You must have misunderstood something I said."

"So you're saying that I made it all up?" Sloan knew better, but she stopped short of calling him a liar. Time was what she needed, and little of that could be gained through open hostility.

"It's the only logical explanation," Max replied. "Considering the strain you've been under, it's understandable. What with the anxiety of being a new mother, the loss of sleep from all the nighttime feedings, and your fears about losing custody of your son, you've been a bundle of nerves lately. Is it any wonder your mind has started playing tricks on you? There's only so much anyone can take before something snaps."

Fear shivered through her at the convincing picture he had painted of an unstable woman in need of professional care, too distraught to know what she was doing. Worse, she had established the pattern herself, fleeing first to Texas, then running again.

"I'm not your enemy, Sloan," Max continued in his calm and reasonable tone. "Haven't I looked after you all your life? And I always will. Deep down, you know that. The danger isn't from me. It comes from the Calders. But don't take my word for it. Ask Tara. She can tell you the deplorable way she was treated by them — despised by the family, cheated on by her husband. You must have heard the way they talk about her. Believe me, she has no love for them, either."

There was no mistaking the certainty in Max's voice that he had an ally in Tara. Stunned, Sloan looked at her in disbelief. "Are you in this with him?"

"Don't be ridiculous." When Tara made a reassuring move toward her, Sloan instinctively recoiled from her reaching hand. "What is the matter with you, Sloan?"

"Careful." Max raised a cautioning hand to check Tara. "No one is trying is trying to hurt you, Sloan. We're here to help."

"There is nothing wrong with me," she insisted, more forcefully than she intended. "You make it sound like I'm crazy. I'm not."

"Of course you aren't," Max soothed. "You'll be fine. We just need to get you and the baby home. My plane's right outside. Come on. Let me take you home."

As the Suburban barreled north along the highway, Trey kept his gaze fixed on the empty road ahead and a heavy foot on the accelerator. Laredo lounged in the passenger seat, a relaxed looseness about him that was at odds with the vigilance of his gaze.

A thick silence lay between the two men, as it had since Trey had filled Laredo in on the few details of Sloan's phone call. Laredo had asked only a few questions and offered no speculation on what awaited them when they reached their destination. Neither had Trey. Privately, though, Trey thought there was a fifty-fifty chance Sloan had told him the truth.

The roofs of Blue Moon jutted into the skyline. Trey reduced the Suburban's speed at the sight of them and started watching for the entrance road to the abandoned pit mine. He spotted it about the same time he noticed a vehicle parked beyond it on the shoulder, its hood raised. The longer he studied it, the heavier the certainty settled in his gut.

Braking, he made the turn onto the mine road and drove all the way to the padlocked gate. With an economy of movement, Trey climbed out of the vehicle, walked to the back, opened its rear door, and removed a rifle and box of shells from its trunk.

"It looks like it might be a trap after all," he told Laredo and nodded in the direction of the vehicle parked up the road. "That looks like the car Donovan usually drives."

"I wondered if you noticed it," Laredo drawled, "Or if you even knew what he used for wheels."

"You did warn me to check the shadows," Trey reminded him with a slightly grim smile and finished loading the rifle. "Sorry I can't supply you with a rifle, but we only keep one in the Suburban."

"No problem. I carry a friend in my boot."

"Ready?"

Laredo nodded. "Let's do it."

"Tara said they were at the old mine office. We'll make that our first stop."

Ignoring the padlocked gate, they slipped under the side fence and angled toward the office, skirting the dirt road. Halfway there, Laredo signaled with two fingers and pointed to the two planes parked some distance apart. Trey nodded in response, aware of the new questions they raised and recognizing that he had to be ready for anything.

As they neared the building, he saw that its front door stood open. Immediately he altered his course, steering clear of its field of vision to approach the building from the side. Before he reached the shelter of its wall, he caught the sound of voices coming from inside. The alert tilt of Laredo's head told Trey that he heard them as well.

"You're frightened, Sloan. Too frightened to know what you're doing."

Laredo caught his eye and mouthed the name Rutledge. Trey nodded, recognizing the man's voice. But who else was in there with him? Sloan for sure, probably Tara and Donovan. He held up four fingers, then added a thumb and shrugged his uncertainty, Laredo nodded agreement and inched closer to him.

"If this place was built to code," he said in a low murmur, "it has to have two exits. I'll slip in the back way. Give me five minutes."

Trey didn't ask how Laredo intended to deal with a door that was bound to be locked. A man resourceful enough to carry a gun in his boot wouldn't be stopped by a lock. Trey watched him slip along the outer wall, barely rustling the weeds growing up against it, then inched closer to the corner himself, trying to practice the same brand of stealth.

"I'm not getting on that plane with you, Max, and that's final." Sloan's voice rang out, sharp and determined.

But it was the force of her assertion that raced through Trey like a fire, erasing all doubt about where she stood. He was eager now for the confrontation that was to come as he realized just how much was riding on it.

"You don't seem to understand the danger you're in," Rutledge insisted with his first show of anger. "You don't think the Calders are going to welcome you back with open arms, do you? Sure, they want the baby. But not you. If you set foot on that ranch, the chances are you'll never leave it. My God, Sloan, these people have a man on their payroll who's wanted for murder. That's their answer to everything. Violence. Why else would they have him?"

"Am I supposed to believe that simply because you say so?" Sloan was too angry to care what she was saying. "I know you wish that I'd be that stupid, but I'm not."

"You think that's a lie, do you?" Rutledge jerked a set of folded papers from inside his suit jacket and thrust it to her. "Read it yourself. Among his many aliases is the name Laredo Smith."

"The hell you say." Donovan grinned broadly while Sloan stared at the papers with a sudden feeling of dread. "I knew the minute I laid eyes on him, he could be lethal."

"Take it." Max shook the papers at her. "And tell me you can still trust the Calders after you read this. Or maybe you just don't have the stomach for the truth."

It was like the jab of a spur to her pride. Reacting to it, Sloan snatched the papers from his outstretched hand and moved away, keeping Jake tightly cradled in one arm. One-handed, she shook open the folds. A quick skim of the first page confirmed everything Max had said and more.

"This is talking about something that happened over twenty years ago — before he ever came to the Triple C." It was hardly justification. Yet it was the only argument Sloan could find.

"Doesn't it make you wonder why they would harbor a fugitive all this time?" Rutledge challenged with a certain smugness.

"Not as much as it makes me wonder if this document is real, or something you made up to trick me." Sloan countered. "It would be rather simple for someone with your money. You can buy anything. Even a lie. Which is what this probably is."

"Let me see them." Curious, Tara reached to claim the papers.

Sloan immediately held them behind her back. "This piece of art is something Max gave *me.*"

"Stop it, Sloan," Tara snapped with impatience. "I know something about forgeries. Let me look at them."

Distracted by Tara's persistence, Sloan failed to notice when Donovan bent toward Rutledge and said in an undertone. "We may have company. I caught a glimpse of shadow outside."

In response, Rutledge looked directly at Sloan. "We have no more time to waste arguing about this. I'll ask you one more time — are you going to get on that plane or not?"

Sloan answered with equal sharpness. "Never!"

"So be it." Rutledge glanced sideways at Donovan and nodded.

His hand moved to the controls of his wheelchair, sending it into a pivoting turn toward the open door. At the same instant she was taking in that sight, Sloan saw Donovan coming toward her.

"I told you I'm not getting on that plane." Instinctively, she drew back from him.

"Stay here if that's what you want." His broad, muscled shoulders moved in a seemingly careless shrug. In the next instant, the shrug became a precursor of a lightning-fast movement that wrested the baby from her grasp. "But your kid's going on that plane."

"No!" With that strangled outcry, Sloan threw herself at him. But with one backhanded sweep of his arm, Donovan flung her aside. The impetus of the blow sent her sprawling to the floor. Sloan fell hard, pain shooting through her knee, hip, and shoulder. Fighting through it, she struggled to rise as a frantic Tara sank to the floor beside her, hands reaching in a helpless need to do something.

"Sloan. Are you hurt?"

Deaf to everything but the uncertain whimpers coming from her son, Sloan scrambled awkwardly to her feet, pressing a hand to her sore hip. Only vaguely was she aware of the painful tingling in her knee.

Rutledge observed the first hobbling step she took after Donovan said, "Let's go. She'll follow."

Five minutes hadn't passed yet, but time had run out. Trey couldn't wait for Laredo to get into position. He lunged into the doorway, blocking the exit, and snapped the rifle to his shoulder, cocking the hammer and sighting down the barrel at Rutledge.

"You better hold it," Trey warned. "You're not going anywhere."

In a fraction of a second, his senses registered a dozen details at once — the building's dusty and closed-up odors, the sight of Rutledge in his wheelchair, with the muscle-bound Donovan off to the side, a small fist waving from the blanket-wrapped bundle clutched in one arm, the gasping call of his name by Sloan, the feel of the cold steel in his hand, and the heavy, solid thud of his own heartbeat.

Donovan backed up a step, his glance flicking to the rifle in Trey's grip. Rutledge reversed his chair by a foot as well, then stopped, his hard gaze boring into Trey.

"You're bluffing, Calder," Rutledge mocked. "You're not going to shoot — not in such close quarters where even a slight miss could mean it's your son who might get hit."

"I don't miss a sitting target." Trey shifted the barrel, aiming at Rutledge.

"Be careful." Tara's plaintive voice came from his left. "Don't hurt the baby."

His side vision gave Trey a glimpse of Tara pushing Sloan farther from Donovan and Rutledge. He could feel Sloan's eyes on him, but he didn't allow himself to look at her. A sudden sharp wail came from his infant son.

"You're scaring your boy, Calder." Donovan smiled and lightly jiggled the bundle in his arm. The action served to screen the movement of his other hand producing a short-barreled pistol from his pocket. "I guess this could be called a Mexican standoff, except I've got your kid."

"Put the rifle down," Rutledge ordered.

Briefly, Trey tightened his grip on the weapon and silently debated his chances. But the risk was too great; too many things could go wrong. As much as he wanted to see Rutledge dead, he wanted his son alive more.

"You win." He uncocked the hammer and lowered the rifle from his shoulder.

"Lay it on the floor. Carefully." Donovan gave a warning emphasis to the last word. The barrel of his pistol tracked along when Trey crouched and slowly set the rifle on the floor. "Now slide it to the side." Trey did as he was told, then straightened again.

"Step inside. Over there." A twitch of the pistol ordered Trey to the right.

"Sorry." Trey never moved, straining to catch some sound that might tell him Laredo had made it inside. "You'll have to go through me."

"You, a half-crazed husband who shows up to take his son at gunpoint? That's not a problem." Still smiling coldly, Donovan extended his arm out straight from his body and used Trey's chest as a target.

When he saw Donovan's finger slide onto the trigger, Trey glanced at Sloan one last time.

Suddenly there was Tara, her face contorted in a strange mask of fury and fear, rushing at Donovan, arms outstretched. Donovan saw her at the last second. He fired just as she struck his arm. Rutledge lurched to the side, but no bullet ripped into Trey. He took a step into the building, intending to charge Donovan, as Tara pulled the baby out of Donovan's arm, leaving him clutching an empty blanket. Screaming at Sloan to take the baby, Tara held him out to her.

At almost the same instant, Trey saw Donovan bringing his gun around again. There was too much space between them. Trey dived sideways after his rifle.

"Sloan!" Laredo shouted from the opening to the rear hall.

Trey had a glimpse of Sloan running, the baby in her arms, and Tara right behind her. Laredo's yell had drawn Donovan's attention. He whipped around and snapped off two quick shots. There was a short cry of pain, and Trey knew somebody had been hit.

Not Sloan! he thought even as he rolled onto his back, pointed the rifle barrel up, and squeezed the trigger, firing at Donovan just as Donovan shot at him. A bullet plowed into the wall an inch from Trey's head, and Donovan crumpled to the floor, the pistol falling from loose fingers. Trey's own muscles went limp for a moment.

The silence that followed was eerily loud. It didn't last, as Laredo plunged into the lobby, gun in hand and quickly kicked Donovan's gun away from his body, then bent to feel for a pulse.

"Sloan?" Trey asked and forced his limbs to push himself back onto his feet.

"She and the little one are fine. We're going to need an ambulance for Tara, though. She's been hit bad. These two won't need one."

Laredo's oblique reference to Rutledge had Trey's glance snapping to the wheelchair and man slumped sideways in it. He felt not an ounce of regret at the man's death.

Leaving the rifle on the floor, Trey pulled out the cell phone and placed an emergency call as he headed into the hall. He found Sloan, sitting on the floor, holding the baby and cradling Tara's head on her lap. Blood streaked the front of her top, and an unnatural pallor was in her face. Then Sloan lifted those midnight blue eyes to him, gazing at him with an inexpressible hunger for all the good things they had shared.

Gripped by the same feeling, Trey went down on one knee and kissed her with rough need until a tiny fist punched his chest. Drawing back, he caught hold of the little hand and looked with relief at his son.

Only then did Trey resort to words. "You're both okay?"

"Yes." Her gaze clung to his face an instant before, dropping to the ghostly pale, dark-haired woman lying motionless on the floor. "It's Tara."

"An ambulance is on the way." That was the only hope Trey could offer.

Laredo reappeared with a couple of diapers from Sloan's bag. "Let's try to put some pressure on the wound with these."

Kneeling, he rolled Tara toward him, exposing her bloodied left side. When he applied the absorbent pads, pressing hard, she groaned.

Long, black lashes fluttered. She mumbled something that was unintelligible to Trey, but Sloan seemed to understand.

"Jake's right here, Tara. He's fine. You saved him," Sloan said, an emotional catch in her voice.

Tara's red lips curved in something close to a weak smile, and she mumbled again, ". . . such a beautiful bab . . ." The rest was lost in a thready sigh.

Laredo immediately felt for a pulse. "I think we just lost her."

Sloan looked at Trey in silent anguish. But there was no time to mourn, as the thudding sound of running feet, more than one set, reached them. "It's probably the crew," Trey guessed. "They must have heard the gunshots. Better get the hell out of here, Laredo. The same way you came in."

Laredo grinned at him. "You're right. I was never here."

He slipped down the hall at a silent run while Trey helped Sloan to her feet. "Come on. Let's get Jake a blanket and cover him up."

They walked into the lobby just as Tara's

copilot and two of the crew from Rutledge's plane barged into the building and stopped short at the sight of the two bodies. One took a step toward Rutledge.

Trey stopped him. "I don't think the police will want you touching anything."

"What the hell happened here?" Tara's copilot demanded and glanced at the second body. "Who's that guy?"

"His name's Donovan," Sloan answered.

Trey could tell by her expression that she was preparing to launch into a recounting of all that happened. He never gave her a chance to start.

"He moved to Blue Moon last summer and bought the bar up the road. I don't know much about him except he's an ex-Marine. He must have had a flashback or something. We'll probably never know why," Trey stated, then suggested, "It'll be best if you wait outside. I know the police will need a statement from all of you."

"We didn't see anything," one of them protested. "We just heard what sounded like gunshots."

"I guess that's what you tell the police when they get here," Trey replied.

With one more glance at the bodies, the three men walked out and drifted toward their respective aircrafts. Trey watched them a moment, then turned to Sloan.

Glancing at him, she shook out an extra receiving blanket that had been stowed in her bag. "Why did you tell them that?"

"Sometimes the truth is too complicated. The story I gave them is much easier to believe," Trey answered. "As it is, there's going to be plenty of headlines, with both Tara and Rutledge dead, but the story will be short-lived. Agreed?"

Sloan didn't have to think about it. "I do. Stories of vengeance, broken marriages, and lies belong in novels, not the eleven o'clock news."

"That's what I thought." Understanding flowed between them, a warm and uniting kind.

Sirens wailed in the distance, a reminder that this wasn't over yet. Still, Sloan smiled when she spread the blanket on the settee and lay Jake on it. She was fully aware that there was much more they needed to say to each other, but all those words could wait until they were alone.

Then she remembered something that couldn't wait.

"Oh my God. Where are they?" She cast a frantic look around the room.

"What are you talking about?" Trey frowned.

By then Sloan had already spotted them, lying on the floor a few feet away. Leaving Jake lying on the blanket, she darted over and scooped up the folded sheets.

"That's the information about Laredo that Rutledge gave you," Trey guessed immediately.

Sloan nodded and hurriedly began folding the papers into a small square. "The police don't need to find them," she said and tucked them inside Jake's little suit pants before wrapping him in the blanket and gathering him into her arms. Finished, she turned to Trey. "We can burn them after we get home."

He moved to her and cupped a hand to her cheek, gratitude, love, and approval shining in his dark eyes. "You know what we call that out here?"

"What?" Sloan was conscious of the quick hammer of her pulse at his nearness.

"Riding for the brand," he said, referring to the oldest term for the pledge of loyalty in the West.

Shouts came from outside, accompanied by the clump of more feet. Turning, Trey curved an arm around her shoulders, drawing her protectively to his side. "It's all going to be fine."

"I know," she said.

Epilogue

Afternoon sunlight slanted through the Suburban's windshield, heating the interior. Trey was behind the wheel, driving one-handed, with Sloan nestled close against his side, his arm around her shoulders. The east entrance was behind them, and the rugged, rolling land of the Triple C stretched on either side. With the warm feel of her against him, there was a rightness to his world again.

Trey stole a glance over his shoulder, the corners of his mouth lifting at the sight of his baby son in the carrier, safely strapped in the backseat. It was the same carrier he had angrily tossed in the Suburban after leaving the hospital without his wife and son. But Trey chose not to remember that.

"He's still sound asleep," he told Sloan.

"It'll be just about time for his next bottle when we get home." It was an idle remark, indicative of the way a new mother marked time.

"It's going to feel like a home again with

you in it." When he looked at her, Trey didn't see the drying bloodstains on her top, only the strong beauty of her profile and the sheen of her dark hair. "It was nothing but a big, empty house when you were gone."

"You don't know how much I regret that." A thread of unease ran through Sloan's voice. "I only hope your family understands, although I wouldn't blame them if they didn't — not after all the trouble I caused."

"That was Rutledge's doing, not yours." Trey was definite about that.

"But I believed his lies," Sloan reminded him.

"And I should have seen his hand in what was happening. There's plenty of blame to go around in this," he told her. "But it's over now. We've weathered our first storm."

"There will be others, though." Sloan saw the potential of another one coming. She decided to face it now. "Trey, I have to know. Do you object to me having a career of my own?"

He hesitated and her heart sank. Then he said, "I know how much you love photography, Sloan."

"That isn't what I asked." She kept her

gaze fixed on the road ahead, pain squeezing her heart.

"Look, I don't expect you to give it up." There was an impatient edge to his voice, a little hard and angry. "But I don't deny that sometimes I resent it."

Stunned, she turned a demanding look at him, ready to fight. "Why?"

"I know it's wrong to feel that way," Trey began in his own defense. "But, dammit, Sloan, when you have a camera in your hands, you shut everything else out — including me. It's like you're in another world, and I'm not part of it at all."

Relief washed through her, eliciting a soft, amused laugh. "You don't know how wrong you are, Trey," she told him. "You're there in every picture I take."

"Right," he replied in a voice dry with doubt.

"It's true." It suddenly became very important that she convince him of it. "Before Jake was born, I was updating my portfolio. That's when I saw it. Before I met you, all my photographs have a cold and lonely quality to them, full of shadows. The ones I took afterward are filled with light and warmth. They aren't empty landscapes, but places with people in them.

They're rich with life now — the way I am with you."

Trey looked at her with new eyes, slightly humbled. "I didn't know."

"You do now." Then it was her turn to hesitate. "Just the same, I do realize that my work may cause some problems in the future."

"Why?" Trey frowned.

"Well, your aunt isn't going to be there forever, running the household and entertaining all your guests. At some point —"

Trey broke in. "Good God, Sloan." His smile was wide with amusement. "We can hire somebody to cook and clean, and if it becomes necessary, we'll find a social secretary to handle the rest."

"You don't mind?" Sloan couldn't keep the amazement out of her voice.

"I'll mind that you're off somewhere taking pictures instead of being with me, but I'll survive, knowing that you'll come back home when you're done."

"And I always will come back," Sloan promised.

"You'd better." There was that crooked smile again that raised such havoc with her pulse. "Or I'll come after you."

She smiled and snuggled a little closer to him. Ahead of them, rising tall against the horizon, was The Homestead in all its pillared bigness. Home. Contentment eased through Sloan with the realization that she finally had one. And a family to go with it.

All were on hand to greet them when they pulled up to the house. There was a lot of touching and hugging, along with expressions of relief that they were unharmed.

Once inside, little Jake became the center of attention. Chase wasted no time clumping to a wing-backed chair in the den and lowering himself into it. He propped his cane against the armrest and held out his arms.

"Come on. I've waited long enough to hold my great-grandbaby. Hand him over," he ordered.

More than happy to oblige him, Sloan placed her son in his arms and stood back to watch. Wide-eyed, Jake frowned at this craggy-faced man holding him, but Sloan was warmed by the incredible gentleness and love in Chase's eyes.

Beside her, Jessy laughed softly in amusement. "Doesn't it look like he's trying to figure out who this strange man is?"

"I'm a Calder, just like you," Chase stated. "And I've got a heap of stories to tell you — like those horns above the fireplace mantel. They belonged to an old brindle steer named Captain."

Listening to him, Trey was reminded of all the times he'd been told the story of that first cattle drive to Montana. Now his son would hear all the legends and lore of the Calders. The sense of continuity was a good feeling.

Laredo drifted over to him, feigning an interest in the sight of the youngest and oldest Calder together. In an overtone he asked, "Everything go all right after I left?"

"It went fine." Curiosity made Trey ask, "How long have you been back?"

"About an hour. Jessy had Jobe Garvey come get me." Refusing to be diverted, Laredo returned to his primary concern. "So the law bought the story that Donovan went on a rampage?"

"Why not? That's what happened." Just for a moment, Trey met the other man's gaze — calm, cool, and sure in his lie.

"Right." Laredo smiled to himself.

Cat bustled into the den, clutching a bottle of infant formula in her hand. "I warmed the bottle for Jake," she rushed, then paused, half disappointed to see him lying content in Chase's arms. "I thought he'd be hungry by now."

"What d'ya say, little guy?" Chase asked.

"Are you ready for a drink?" The response was a forceful coo and a waving of a fist that drew chuckles all around. "I think that was a 'yes,' " Chase declared.

With some reluctance Cat surrendered the bottle to him, then gathered herself. "You two must be hungry, too. I'll go make you a quick lunch."

As she started to leave, the phone rang. Cat automatically turned to answer it, saying, "I'll get it," but Laredo waved her off and stepped to the desk, picking up the phone. "Calder ranch."

"May I speak to Mr. Calder, please?" A male voice requested.

"Who's calling?" Laredo was instantly wary.

"My name's Allen Forrester, a reporter with —"

"Sorry," Laredo cut him off. "The family isn't taking any calls. A formal statement will be released later."

"Could you confirm just one thing for me?" the reporter inserted quickly.

"What's that?" Laredo waited.

"I understand a member of the Calder family was at the Dy-Corp coal mine today when Mrs. Tara Calder and Maxwell Rutledge were killed by an ex-Marine. Would you verify his name?"

Pausing, Laredo glanced at Trey, standing tall next to his grandfather's chair, and mentally compared the strong, rugged lines of their features. The similarities went deeper than a mere physical resemblance — it went to the heart and will.

"His name is Calder," Laredo told the reporter. "Chase Benteen Calder."

*The sun is shining,
bringing fair weather.
Once again the Calders
are all together.*